KINGDOM COME

A TIME TRAVEL NOVEL

BY KATHRYN LE VEQUE

D1714741

Copyright © 2010 by Kathryn Le Veque
Print Edition

All rights reserved. No part of this book may be used or reproduced in any manner whatsoever without written permission, except in the case of brief quotations embodied in critical articles or reviews.

Printed by Dragonblade Publishing in the United States of America

Text copyright 2010 by Kathryn Le Veque
Cover copyright 2010 by Kathryn Le Veque

Kathryn Le Veque Novels

Medieval Romance:

The de Russe Legacy:
The White Lord of Wellesbourne
The Dark One: Dark Knight
Beast
Lord of War: Black Angel
The Iron Knight

The de Lohr Dynasty:
While Angels Slept (Lords of East Anglia)
Rise of the Defender
Steelheart
Spectre of the Sword
Archangel
Unending Love
Shadowmoor
Silversword

Great Lords of le Bec:
Great Protector
To the Lady Born (House of de Royans)
Lord of Winter (Lords of de Royans)

Lords of Eire:
The Darkland (Master Knights of Connaught)
Black Sword
Echoes of Ancient Dreams (time travel)

De Wolfe Pack Series:
The Wolfe
Serpent
Scorpion (Saxon Lords of Hage – Also related to The Questing)
The Lion of the North
Walls of Babylon
Dark Destroyer
Nighthawk
Warwolfe
ShadowWolfe

Ancient Kings of Anglecynn:
The Whispering Night
Netherworld

Battle Lords of de Velt:
The Dark Lord
Devil's Dominion

Reign of the House of de Winter:
Lespada
Swords and Shields (also related to The Questing, While Angels Slept)

De Reyne Domination:
Guardian of Darkness
The Fallen One (part of Dragonblade Series)
With Dreams Only of You

Unrelated characters or family groups:
The Gorgon (Also related to Lords of Thunder)
The Warrior Poet (St. John and de Gare)
Tender is the Knight (House of d'Vant)
Lord of Light
The Questing (related to The Dark Lord, Scorpion)
The Legend (House of Summerlin)

The Dragonblade Series: (Great Marcher Lords of de Lara)
Dragonblade
Island of Glass (House of St. Hever)
The Savage Curtain (Lords of Pembury)

The Fallen One (De Reyne Domination)
Fragments of Grace (House of St. Hever)
Lord of the Shadows
Queen of Lost Stars (House of St. Hever)

Lords of Thunder: The de Shera Brotherhood Trilogy
The Thunder Lord
The Thunder Warrior
The Thunder Knight

Highland Warriors of Munro:
The Red Lion
Deep Into Darkness

The House of Ashbourne:
Upon a Midnight Dream

The House of D'Aurilliac:
Valiant Chaos

The House of De Nerra:
The Falls of Erith
Vestiges of Valor

The House of De Dere:
Of Love and Legend

Time Travel Romance: (Saxon Lords of Hage)
The Crusader
Kingdom Come

Contemporary Romance:

Kathlyn Trent/Marcus Burton Series:
Valley of the Shadow
The Eden Factor
Canyon of the Sphinx

The American Heroes Series:
The Lucius Robe
Fires of Autumn
Evenshade
Sea of Dreams
Purgatory

Other Contemporary Romance:
Lady of Heaven
Darkling, I Listen
In the Dreaming Hour

Multi-author Collections/Anthologies:
Sirens of the Northern Seas (Viking romance)

Note: All Kathryn's novels are designed to be read as stand-alones, although many have cross-over characters or cross-over family groups. Novels that are grouped together have related characters or family groups.

Series are clearly marked. All series contain the same characters or family groups except the American Heroes Series, which is an anthology with unrelated characters.

There is NO particular chronological order for any of the novels because they can all be read as stand-alones, even the series.

For more information, find it in **A Reader's Guide to the Medieval World of Le Veque**.

Table of Contents

PROLOGUE

Present Day
Nahariya, Israel
Excerpt from the prequel, "The Crusader"

FOR THE ARCHAEOLOGIST and her resurrected knight, it was coming to an end.

It was difficult to see the road in the dead of night. The headlights of the jeep pierced the veil of darkness as Rory and Kieran sped south, away from the pursuing Land Rovers. To make matters worse, more clouds were gathering and the wind had picked up. Having spent more than a year in Nahariya, Rory knew a storm was approaching.

Kieran sat in the passenger seat, his left hand over his bandaged wound, taking a pounding as the vehicle lurched over the rough road. Rory knew the area well and knew that she was putting more distance between Kieran and the small hospital in the city, torn between the need to seek medical attention and the panic to be free of Corbin.

Her first instinct was to head back into Nahariya for the hospital. But Kieran wouldn't hear of it, directing her quite firmly to return to Tel Aviv where they could catch a flight back to England. He would be fine, he insisted, once he was allowed to rest. But Rory didn't believe him and tears stung her eyes as she struggled to steer in the darkness. To come so far and then risk losing him to an eight hundred-year-old wound was almost more than she could bear.

Her apprehension was made worse as Corbin's fleet closed in on their old Jeep with newer cars. Rory was doing an admirable job of driving over the bumpy road that wound its way around Nahariya and eventually ended up along the coast, but the pack of jackals was closing in and she knew she couldn't go much faster.

If she was bordering on panic, she never let on. In fact, she almost found herself wishing Corbin would catch up. At least then Kieran might agree to medical attention before the police locked them both up and threw away the key.

Twisting their way among the dusty, shadowed hills, they emerged onto a flat stretch of land and the weak glitter of the ocean could be seen in the distance. The clouds were thickening the smell of rain was pervasive. Amidst her other troubles, Rory knew the wipers of the Jeep didn't work. In the arid land of Israel, she had never given the broken blades much thought. But she was certainly thinking of them now. Lurching over a particularly bad bump, she gripped the old steering wheel too tightly and came away with a nasty blister.

The road sloped downward, heading for the Mediterranean. Corbin's cars were coming closer, like dogs nipping at her heels, and Rory spent a good deal of time watching the rearview mirror as the bright lights advanced. She was so involved with the approaching high beams that Kieran's warm, damp hand on her thigh startled her.

"Sweetheart," he murmured. "Mayhap you should stop the car. I do not believe it wise to run any longer."

She turned to him, noting how terribly pale he was. In fact, he looked very much as he had when she had first seen him in the grave; pallid and pasty. Refusing to fight her terror down any longer, she couldn't help the anguish in her voice.

"Oh, Kieran," she moaned. "We've got to find you a doctor. To hell with Corbin and his henchmen!"

He shook his head feebly, his bloodstained hand on her leg. "Libby, I've been running from Simon for eight hundred years. Mayhap, I was not meant to elude him. Mayhap I should simply succumb to the inevitable."

Simon. The man who had been both enemy and friend to Kieran eight hundred years ago, the beast responsible for the horrific wound slowly draining Kieran's life away. Simon, reborn as the man Rory knew as Corbin and who, even now, continued to chase Kieran. Redundant history, never ending animosity. Like a reincarnated guard dog, Simon would never stop.

"No!" Rory sobbed, the tears coming. "I won't let you. We've come too far for it to end like this."

He smiled, touching her cheek and leaving a crimson streak. "It will never end between us. You and I are a part of one another, in this time or any other. We have accomplished our task and now we are finished. Mayhap it is time to allow history to fulfill its destiny."

She ran cold. "What does that mean?"

He sighed, the oozing wound draining his energy. "It means that eight hundred years ago, I defied death with the magic of an alchemist's potion. I cheated the natural course of life so that I could finish my sworn task. Now that I have returned to the land where the Crusades converged, mayhap death is attempting to claim me as it should have those centuries ago. The closer my enemy looms, the more my wound bleeds. I cannot believe it to be coincidence. The man was meant to kill me."

Rory wept softly, shaking her head. "You're not going to die," she whispered. "I won't let you. I'll get you far away from Corbin and we'll find a doctor who can heal you."

"There is no one who can heal me."

"Don't say that!" She slammed her hands against the steering wheel, almost losing control when it leapt over a series of harsh bumps. Gripping the steering column tightly, she wrestled for control in more ways than one. "Kieran, you're a part of me. We're incomplete without each other. If you die, I will, too."

He touched her face again, his expression serious. Thick fingers wiped at the tears as she struggled to concentrate on her driving.

"Oh, sweetheart," he murmured. "Time could not keep us apart. Certainly death cannot either. I shall be waiting for you when you cross the threshold of Paradise, have no doubt. We shall spend eternity together, you and I."

She sobbed openly, losing focus of the road. "No, Kieran," she sputtered. "I don't want you to die. I want you to live. I want us to get married and have children and grow old together. I don't want you to leave me."

He leaned over, grunting with pain and exertion, and lay his head on her shoulder. "I will never leave you. I love you with all that I am, all that I will ever be. Know this to be true, for all time."

She tried to touch him but the road was too rough and she couldn't risk letting go of the steering wheel. They were nearing the beach now, far away from the city proper of Nahariya.

The mob of Land Rovers wasn't far behind. Their headlights cast flickering light on the sloping landscape of the sea. Sobbing as Kieran weakly comforted her, Rory took a turn too sharply and the Jeep nearly went over. Overcorrecting, she heard something snap and grind and the car suddenly came to a halt.

"Damn!" she screamed, beating at the steering wheel as if it would correct the problem. "Kieran, the car's busted. We can't…."

He smiled at her, so weakly, his gem-clear brown eyes filled with emotion. "I know we cannot run any longer. I am not meant to run any longer." When she started to weep again, he simply collected her hand, their meager possessions, and opened the door. "Come along. I would show you something."

She let him pull her from the car. The Land Rovers were just coming over the rise in the near distance as Kieran staggered across the sandy soil, heading for the ocean. His wound was bleeding profusely, trailing down his right leg and staining his boots. Rory sputtered and wept, following him, having no idea where they were going. But Kieran knew.

The clouds overhead were beginning to rumble and a light rain fell as they neared the crashing, rocky shore. Behind them, the Land Rovers came to a halt and soldiers in fatigues spilled forth, followed by two men in suits. Kieran and Rory ignored them, heading for an outcropping of rock overlooking the turbulent swells.

His voice was soft as he spoke, the clear brown gaze moving across the dark waters. "Eight hundred years ago, I came ashore on a beach not dissimilar to this one," he grunted with strain as he mounted the rocks. "Thousands of men and horses bound for the Holy Land, intending to rid God's country of the Muslim insurgents. I was one of those men and I wore the banner of England proudly."

Rory held on to him tightly as they moved to the top of the outcropping, falling into his embrace as he sank to his knees. She was weeping so heavily she could hardly hear him, and he stroked her tenderly. His heart was aching for what he knew had to be.

"It was an awesome sight," he murmured, his cheek against the top of her head. As he focused on the rolling sea, he said, "I came on the quest because I believed in my king, in my country, and I was determined to make both proud. By accepting the mission that would eventually end my life, I knew there was nothing more worthwhile I could ever do with my mortal existence. At least, that is what I believed until I met you. You and I are incredibly similar, Libby. Each wrought with determination, each aching deeply to find fulfillment, and each willing to jeopardize our destiny for what we believe in."

Rory wept into his shirt as the rain grew heavier and the army of men drew closer. She could see their features now as they crossed the sand, singling out Corbin immediately. She watched as he held out his hand to the group, silently ordering them to wait as he continued forward. A bolt of lightning lit up the sky, illuminating his evil face, and Rory raised her head from Kieran's shoulder in fury.

"Go away!" she shouted. "Go away and leave us alone!"

Corbin came to a halt several yards away. "I've come a very, very long way for you, Dr. Osgrove. I won't leave without you. You're in very big trouble for grave robbing, among other things."

She simply shook her head. "I'm staying with him."

Corbin shoved his hands into his pockets as the weather worsened. "You're both coming with me, I'm afraid. You've got a good deal of explaining to do."

Kieran heard him, the familiar voice of a man who had trailed him for centuries. But he ignored the man for the moment, focused on the delicious warmth of Rory in his arms. Warmth, he suspected, he would not be experiencing much longer.

"The night I sought the alchemist, there was a storm very much like this one," he said softly, feeling Rory's grip on him tighten. "An angry storm, cursing the fact that I intended to defy death. It is not strange that a storm has gathered here tonight to witness what I evaded those centuries ago."

Rory tore her gaze away from Corbin, focusing on the ashen features of her beloved knight. Tears were still pouring but the sobs had faded. In fact, she seemed to be calming in spite of everything and she forced a smile, kissing him with a painful sweetness.

"If you go, I go with you," she said in a tone he dare not contradict. "If death is going to take you, then it is going to take me, too. You said yourself that God brought us together and I just can't believe that He would allow us to be separated after everything we've been through."

Kieran's normally even expression laced with emotion. "My sweet Rory," he murmured. "I do not want to leave you now, not even for a moment. But I cannot deny the wound steadily draining my life. I suspect my true destiny is at hand. Now that the Christ's Crown of Thorns has been found, there is no longer any reason for me to live. But there is every reason for you to live. *You* must live. You must pay tribute to this love and duty that we have shared."

She shook her head, her composure making a weak return. "I will pay tribute by being at your side, for always. Don't deny me this, Kieran. I am nothing without you."

He didn't have the energy to argue. The rain was coming down in sheets and lightning filled the sky. He began to kiss her, tenderly at first, but with a growing passion as if knowing this would be the last he tasted of her in this world.

Corbin and his men watched, so involved with the scene before them that they failed to notice a rickety old Jeep cresting the distant rise. One headlight was out, but the wipers were working as it bounced over the rough road. The vehicle loomed closer, eventually coming to a halt behind the cluster of Land Rovers.

"Don't go any closer, Corbin!"

Rory's colleague, Dr. Bud Dietrich, was out of the car before it came to a complete stop. He and another colleague, Dr. David Peck, raced across the wet sand, struggling to gain traction. Corbin heard the shout, turning to the source of the voice and muttering a silent curse. Bud continued to move towards him, aided by David when the man threw a punch at an intrusive Marine and sent the soldier sprawling.

"Do you hear me?" Bud shouted above the wind and rain. "Leave her alone. Leave them both alone!"

"Dr. Dietrich," Corbin said slowly. "I am not surprised to find you here. But you must know you cannot help her any longer. I've come for your young associate and I demand to know what has become of the corpse she stole. What secret did it possess that she insisted on breaking the law to obtain it?"

Bud paused several feet before him, the rain lashing his face. After a moment, he gestured to the huddled pair on the rocks.

"You want to know what secret it possessed?" His voice was steady. "Take a good look at that man in Rory's arms. There's your secret, Corbin. The living corpse of Sir Kieran Hage, a real honest-to-goodness knight from King Richard's Crusade. We excavated him out of that grave in Nahariya, but he wasn't dead. He was in some kind of suspended animation brought on by an alchemist's potion. The guy was trying to save his life after he was wounded but the alchemist ended up putting him into some kind of stasis instead. Don't you get it? *That man is Sir Kieran Hage.*"

Corbin cocked an eyebrow, water dripping from his eyelashes. "Bloody Hell, Dietrich. Do you take me for a fool? Surely, you don't think I'd be stupid enough to believe such an idiotic story."

Bud shrugged. "Idiotic or not, it's the truth. Rory didn't steal the corpse or rob the grave because Kieran Hage isn't dead."

Corbin continued shaking his head, holding up a sharp hand. "Ridiculous, Dietrich. I will not listen to any more of this."

"Would you listen to me, then?"

A soft voice floated up beside him. Corbin glanced over to see Darlow looking rather stunned. After a moment, the representative from the British Embassy, who had come to claim the excavated crusader, fixed Corbin in the eye. "I told you I saw the corpse," he said quietly. "And that man on the rocks resembles the knight I saw most definitely. It's… it's truly amazing."

Corbin stared at Darlow, noting the sincerity in his voice. Sincere or not, however, it didn't erase the fact that two grown men were trying to convince him to believe in the tale of a resurrected knight from the Third Crusade. His jaw ticked with irritation as he returned his attention to Bud.

"I will not listen to this any longer," he growled. "Dr. Osgrove is coming with me and her monstrous bodyguard will be placed in the custody of the Marines."

On the rocks, Rory and Kieran were listening to the exchange. Kieran was failing, his grip on Rory loosening as she embraced him tightly. On her knees with Kieran's head clasped to her breast, her anguished gaze locked on to Bud as another bolt of lightning streaked across the sky.

"Bud," she called. "Kieran's dying. We need to get him to a doctor immediately."

Bud's brow furrowed as he took a couple of steps towards the rain-slicked rocks. "What happened to him?"

Rory started to cry again, the tears falling so easily. "His wound," she sobbed. "The wound we thought originally killed him, the one the alchemist sealed up. He reopened it somehow."

Bud leapt onto the rocks, almost slipping but managing to keep his footing. He was suddenly beside the two lovers, separating them gently. Bud groaned softly when he saw Kieran's blood-soaked shirt.

"Oh… Christ," he muttered. "He's bleeding all over the damned place, Rory. You were a Pre-Med student; what do we do?"

She shook her head. "Other than try to stop the blood flow, there's nothing we can do. He needs a surgeon."

"That'll take time." Bud's eyes flicked nervously to Darlow and the Marines. "We've got to get him out of here."

She sniffled in response as Bud suddenly noticed the bloodstained box between them. Kieran was holding it tightly and Bud couldn't take his eyes off it.

"Hey," he nodded his head at the small, wooden case. "Dave told me about the crown. Is… is that it?"

She gazed sadly at the box. "Yes." She blinked, tears splattering with the rain. "Christ's Crown of Thorns, the object we were searching for when we found Kieran's grave. It wasn't buried with him like we'd hoped, but he remembered where he had hidden it so we dug it up. But I swear I'd give it back if it would make Kieran well again. It's just not worth the heartache it's caused."

"There was a man who thought differently, once." Kieran's voice was faint. "He believed it worth dying for."

"Well, I don't," Rory snapped. "It's not worth your life. God, I wish you'd never found the damned thing."

Bud put his hand on her shoulder in a gesture of comfort and also to prevent her from spiraling out of control. Now was not the time for hysterics with Kieran bleeding to death. Tearing his gaze away from the holy treasure he had spent over a year of his life searching for, Bud's ice-blue eyes focused on the dying man.

"How ya doin', pal?" he asked, a ridiculous question considering. "Looks like we've got to get you to a hospital."

The knight shook his head weakly. "'Tis of no use. Now that my task is complete, I am to die as I should have eight centuries ago."

Bud fixed Kieran in the eye, a man he should hate for stealing Rory away from him, but a man he found he could not hate. When they had excavated Kieran from his grave those weeks ago, there was no way of knowing how Rory and the knight would have been drawn together, both in death and in life. There was something in the man's nature that earned Bud's respect in spite of everything. A determination and a sense of duty that Bud himself would have liked to have possessed.

"A doctor can help you, but we've got to go now," he said, feeling his desperation when Kieran once again shook his head. He didn't have time to argue with the man. "Look, Kieran. Rory means a great deal to me. If you die… she'll never be the same. No matter what we've been through, our differences and all, in the end all that matters is that the woman we both love is happy. Right?"

Kieran raised an eyebrow slowly, rain coating his ashen face. "Another selfless gesture, my lord. Pity I am unworthy of such respect for the misery I have caused you both."

"That's not true," Bud disagreed, casting the man an exaggeratedly selfish glance. "Besides, I haven't finished pumping you for information. I haven't found out a damned thing about the world you come from. I'd be the first archaeologist in history to get that kind of information firsthand."

"Then ask quickly," Kieran murmured, licking his wet lips. "There is not much time left."

Bud looked at Rory, seeing the desperation in her eyes. "We've got to get him to a hospital," he said to her, wondering if it wasn't already too late. "Let me talk to Corbin and see what I can do."

He turned away from the drenched pair, sliding down the rocks until he reached the soaking sand. Shuffling across the grit, he focused on Corbin's haughty glare.

"Look," he said firmly. "Kieran is very sick. He's probably dying. We've got to get him to a hospital immediately."

Corbin drew in a deep breath. "Fine. I shall take them both in my custody now and will be more than happy to have the bodyguard escorted to a hospital."

As he spoke, his right hand emerged from his pocket gripping a Beretta 9mm handgun. Bud's eyes widened.

"What in the hell are you doing?" he hissed. "Put that damned thing away."

Corbin aimed the gun directly at Bud's heart. "Not a chance, Dr. Dietrich. You and your associates have taken me on a wild ride from Nahariya to England and back again. I represent the descendants of the knight's family and they want him back, wherever you have hidden him. I'm not letting any of you out of my sight." He turned to the men behind him, keeping the gun aimed at Bud. "Take them. The bodyguard goes to the nearest hospital and the woman goes with me."

"No!" Rory shrieked, clutching Kieran tightly. "I have to stay with him. I won't let you separate us."

Corbin turned his attention to Rory, preparing to reply. Just as he did so, Bud saw his chance and lunged for the gun, receiving a butt in the face for his efforts. As he landed heavily in the sand, a Marine trained his rifle on David before the man could move. With Bud wallowing just above unconsciousness and David effectively stopped, there was no one left between Corbin and Rory except Kieran.

He knew he was dying. He had nothing left to lose by protecting the woman he loved. Somehow finding the strength to disengage himself from her tight embrace, he rose to one knee and faced the man who had plagued him like an evil curse for centuries, the one man who was responsible for all of his misery. The man who had been jealous of Kieran and the holy relic he possessed. The face Kieran remembered from eight hundred years ago, now reincarnated and standing in front of him. Even now, he was still trying to kill him.

"You will not separate us, Simon," he said weakly, feeling Rory's hands on his shoulders. "The lady will come with me."

Corbin stared at him, the odd sense of déjà vu plaguing him. It happened every time he looked at the man, a sensation he was struggling to ignore.

"Don't be a hero," he snarled. "From the look of you, you couldn't take a bullet wound."

Kieran cocked an eyebrow, holding out his arms as if to embrace the world. "Is that what you wish? To kill me as you once attempted eight hundred years ago?" He shrugged his massive shoulders. "Then complete your task. Complete what you started. But know this; I have what I came for. I have the holy relic and my lady will see that it is returned to England, as I vowed. There is nothing more you can do to me to cause me any greater pain, Simon. But you can cause the lady great pain and I will not permit it. If I am to go to this hospital, then she will go with me and you cannot stop her."

Corbin aimed the gun at Kieran's head. "You have interfered for the last time," he said with malice. "I don't know who you are and I've no idea why you insist on calling me Simon. But if killing you is what it takes to accomplish my goal, then I shall. Now, I will ask this only once. Will you go peaceably?"

"With the lady at my side?"

"No."

"Then you have your answer."

Corbin cocked an eyebrow. "Very well, hero. Have it your way."

A gun went off. Rory screamed and screamed, her voice echoing violently off the rocks. But even as she continued screaming, she realized that Kieran had not been shot. He was still on one knee, his arms outstretched, watching Corbin fall face-first into the sand. Bud, David, Kieran and Rory all stared in astonishment as Darlow, the meek little British embassy man who was standing just behind Corbin, lowered the small caliber revolver in his left hand.

Darlow felt the stunned gazes as he continued to look upon the man he had just killed. He was rather stunned himself. Where he had once been allied with Corbin, now, clearly, he was not. This crazy adventure that had all started when he had received a call at the embassy in Istanbul stating that an English knight from the Third Crusade had been discovered by an American archaeologist had been the wildest ride he had ever taken. Wild and oddly supernatural. He looked up from the body in the sand, his attention directed at Rory.

"A man like Corbin only understands violence. I've known enough Corbins in my lifetime to know that. And I simply couldn't let him kill your knight in cold blood." His gaze found Kieran. Weakly, he shook his head. "I don't know why I believe you are who they say you are. But I do. How did you come back to life?"

Kieran wavered dangerously, falling on his rump as Rory dropped to his side, supporting him. The disbelief, the disorientation glazing his expression, was blatant.

"Through the miracle of love," he murmured, barely heard above the driving rain. "My… my lady and I will not be separated. I thank you for your assistance."

Darlow simply nodded. The gun dropped in the sand beside Corbin as if Darlow no longer possessed the strength to hold it. Being a law-abiding man, he couldn't understand what had provoked him into murder, only that he feared for Kieran's and Rory's lives, for all their lives. He knew that the evil filling Corbin would never stop until someone stopped it. Until someone stopped *him*.

"You killed him." Dr. Peck's voice was filled with awe and, perhaps, a bit of jealously. "By damn, Darlow, you *killed* him."

Darlow turned to him. "I realize that and I don't particularly care. I was protecting the knight from Corbin's crazed assault and I am confident any jury will find that I did it to protect us all." He glanced over his shoulder at the lady and her knight, once again in a tight embrace as rain and lightning exploded around them. "He's a madman, you know. I just couldn't stand by and allow him to commit cold-blooded murder. And he would have, too. Can't you see that the lady and her knight cannot be separated?"

Bud simply stared at the man who had been willing to kill for the power of love. It was odd how Sir Kieran Hage seemed to provoke the strongest of emotions wherever he went. Glancing to the sand where Corbin lay, he realized that it was finally over with the man. But the fact remained that Kieran was very ill and the need to get him to a hospital took precedence over all other thoughts at the moment.

"Come on." He motioned to Darlow and to the soldiers who had thus far stood silent and basically unmoving. Even the Marine who had been aiming his weapon at David had lowered it. "We've got to get him to a doctor. There's a small hospital not too far from here, about an hour up..."

Bud never finished his sentence. A huge burst of lightning suddenly lit up the sky, a jagged bolt crashing down on the outcropping of rocks where Kieran and Rory were huddled. Chunks of rock went flying and even as Bud screamed Rory's name, trying to protect himself from the white-hot projectiles, he knew his cries were in vain. He knew, before the smoke even settled, that she never heard him.

If you go, I go with you.

She had.

CHAPTER ONE

January, Year of our Lord 1192

"LIBBY," CAME THE soft voice. "Wake up, sweetheart. Open your eyes and look at me."

Libby. The name Kieran had given her because he thought her given name wasn't suitable enough for her "comeliness", as he had put it. Rory was somewhere between the fog of lucidity and the black depths of unconsciousness, hearing him call to her in the darkness. She could hear a familiar voice calling to her and, at some point, realized there were gentle taps against her cheek. Then someone had her by the shoulders and carefully shook her.

The buzz in her head lessened and she became more aware of her surroundings. But her brain was swimming, her heart pounding. When she tried to open her eyes, everything was spinning.

"Oh… God," she gasped, trying to steady her breathing. "What… what happened?"

There was a brief silence. "I do not know."

After a moment, Rory opened her eyes as the world started righting itself. The most brilliant night sky she had ever seen was staring down at her and she blinked, struggling to orient herself. A big face, handsome and granite-jawed with gem-like brown eyes, suddenly loomed in her vision.

"Are you well?" Kieran asked gently. "Do you hurt anywhere?"

Rory gazed up at him, his head backdropped by the blazing night. She reached up, touching his stubbled cheek as she struggled to orient herself.

"Kieran?" She labored to sit up, looking around as she did so.

"What in the hell happened?"

He helped her to sit up, his clear brown eyes scanning their surroundings. "I can only surmise," he said softly. "The last I recall, we were on the beach and a storm was upon us."

"The *beach,*" Rory suddenly gasped, turning to him and trying to gain a look at his torso. "Oh, my God, you're bleeding to death. Let me see…."

She fumbled around as he straightened up so that she could see his shirt. But he had already inspected his abdomen for the wound that had been draining his life away only minutes ago; it didn't exist any longer. It was gone, he was whole, and he had awoken with a pounding head to the sound of surf. His sense of confusion was only matched by his sense of shock.

"Kieran, your wound." Rory continued to hunt. She finally unbuttoned his shirt, revealing his magnificent chest and muscular form. Running her fingers along his taut stomach, she shook her head in shock and awe. "There's nothing there. What happened to your wound?"

"I do not know."

"What do you mean you do not know? We didn't imagine it – you were bleeding to death just a few moments ago." She looked back to his belly, frustrated and in disbelief. "But … where in the hell did it go?"

Kieran could only shake his head, his eyes still scanning their surroundings. He had the oddest sense of déjà vu and could not explain why. Rory, still clutching the open ends of his shirt, began to look around, too.

"Where is everybody?" she asked. "Where are Bud and David? And Darlow? Where did they go?"

Kieran rose from a seated position into a crouch. He could see a village in the distance, flames from fires and burning torches casting heavy smoke into the air. His heart began to pound, this time from excitement and apprehension. It occurred to him that he recognized the distant village. He recognized the watch towers rising out of the sand bluffs. He never thought he would see those sights again. It was almost too much to believe.

He turned to Rory. “What do you remember last?”

She blinked her brilliant hazel eyes, a color between green and golden-brown that both captivated and captured. A thick fringe of lashes and tilted ends gave her a very feminine and sexy expression. At the moment, however, those miraculous eyes were very muddled.

“What do you mean?” she asked.

“Precisely that; what do you remember last?”

She rubbed her forehead, irritated, sick. “I don’t know… probably the same thing you do. The beach, the storm, blood all over the damned place, and then… then….” She sighed heavily, fear joining the other sensations she was experiencing. “Everybody seems to have vanished. Why did they just leave us here alone? And what in the hell happened to your wound?”

Kieran would not let her lose focus. “Think hard, Libby. Is that all you remember? Simply being on the beach outside of Nahariya?”

She nodded, not entirely sure what he was driving at. Then, her eyes flew open wide. “Wait a minute. There was a storm and a lightning strike. It was so close to us that I could feel the heat. I remember… I remember screaming because I thought we were going to get fried. But you blocked out the heat and then… wow, then I remember darkness.” She looked up at him imploringly. “What do you remember?”

He met her gaze, studying her beautiful face in the starlight. “I remember the same,” he said. “I tried to protect you from the lightning. I could feel the heat searing my back and I, too, thought we were dead. Then it was dark… and I awoke to a blanket of stars across the clear night sky.”

Instinctively, they both looked upward, studying the dense dusting of stars across the blackness. Rory still rubbed her aching head, struggling against the pain and disorientation.

“My God,” she whispered, again looking to their surroundings. “Do… do you think that we are dead? I mean, do you think that lightning killed us and this is some kind of afterlife?"

He looked back over his shoulder to the village in the distance. "From what I believe, there is no pain or suffering in the afterlife. And my head aches something fierce."

"Mine, too," she agreed, noticing what he was looking at. "I always thought Heaven was a place of angels and pearly gates. That doesn't look like Heaven over there."

He lifted an ironic eyebrow. "Nay, it does not."

She suddenly grabbed him fearfully. "Kieran, what if we didn't go to Heaven. What if that… that's Hell over there?"

The last words were hissed as if she had just uncovered the most hideous truth. She fell back onto the rock, her hands over her face as Kieran tried to keep her from smashing her skull against the stone. She wasn't feeling well or thinking clearly; that much was certain. He was feeling moderately better and believed he had all of his faculties, which made the conclusion he was swiftly reaching that much more amazing.

"Calm yourself, Lib," he said steadily. "I do not believe that is Hell. In fact, I do believe I recognize it."

Her hands came away from her face. "*Recognize* it?"

"Aye."

She sat back up again, weaving unsteadily even in a seated position. Her gaze fell on the village in the distance. "How in the hell would you recognize that?"

He wasn't quite sure how to tell her. "Because that is Nahariya."

"No, it's not."

"It is. I know this to be true."

Rory looked at him as if he had just lost his mind. "That's *not* Nahariya."

He nodded slowly. "It is the Nahariya I remember." He turned to look at her, noting how pale her lovely face was. A weak smile creased his lips. "It is the Nahariya I know, not the city you are familiar with."

She just stared at him, unsure how to reply. Something akin to panic was welling in her chest, magnified by her pounding head and lurching stomach. She was ill, disoriented and now frightened. She pushed away from him and struggled to stand up.

"I've got to get to a phone," she muttered. "I need to call Bud to come and get us. I just don't understand why he would leave us out here like this."

Kieran could see the flicker of terror in her eyes. He grabbed on to her arms, holding her fast.

"Lib," he said firmly, gently. "I do not believe you will find a phone."

She yanked an arm out of his grasp. "I'm going to kick Bud's ass for leaving us out here like this. What in the hell was he thinking?"

Kieran grabbed her free arm and held tightly as her struggles increase. "Rory, listen to me." It was rare that he called her by her given name, but he needed to get her attention. "I believe something miraculous has happened and I need your calm head. Be still and listen to me, sweetheart. Please."

She was beginning to cry. "No," she struggled furiously to break free. "I want to go back to camp. I need to get my stuff and we need to get the crown back to England." She suddenly froze. "The crown; do you still have it?"

Kieran didn't even know. He looked around them, spying the familiar box just a foot or so away. It was upended on its side, as if it had been haphazardly thrown there. But it was intact.

He sighed with relief. "It is here."

Rory saw it, too. "Thank God," she mumbled. "With everything we went through for that thing, thank God we still have it."

Kieran still had a good grip on her, but now his enormous hands were caressing rather than restraining. He fixed her in the eye, studying her expression, her senses for as much as he could determine them. He knew she wasn't feeling well but he needed her to focus. She had always been the more sensible between the two of them. He was depending on that sensibility to help determine what had really happened to them.

"Lib," he said softly. "I need your level head. I need for you to help reason out what has occurred. Can you do this?"

She sighed heavily, her panic waning. As long as Kieran was with her, whole and sound, she reckoned she could deal with anything. Or at least try to. It wasn't as if she had a lot of choice at the moment.

"I think so."

He was pleased to see that she was at least willing to try, no matter how upset she was. "Do you remember telling me that a miracle happened when I was brought back to life in your time?"

"I remember."

"And do you remember when I awoke in the morgue how upset you were?"

She lifted a well-shaped eyebrow. "I think upset is putting it mildly. I was completely freaked out. Here you were, a corpse I had excavated from a grave in Israel, and suddenly you came alive before my very eyes."

He smiled at her animated response. It told him she wasn't completely out of her mind with fear. "But you came to accept that I wasn't a walking corpse and that I had been in some kind of suspended state as a result of an alchemist's potion."

She nodded vaguely. "You were wounded by assassins and you went to the guy thinking he was a physic. But he wasn't."

"Nay, he was not."

"He gave you a potion that put you into suspended animation so that your body could heal itself."

He nodded faintly. "Something like that," he murmured, his gaze moving to the distant city once again. "Would you like to know what I think?"

She emitted a blustery sigh. "Probably not, but go ahead anyway."

"I believe we have another miracle on our hands."

She closed her eyes briefly, tightly, as if to ward off his words. "Oh, God, Kieran...," she moaned. Then she steeled herself. "Look, don't get me wrong. For the fact that you haven't bled to death in front of me, I am more thankful than you can possibly know. I almost don't even care what happened to your wound as long as you are all right. But I just want to know where we are and what happened to us. Did the lightning somehow knock us out or do something to our memories? I just don't get it. What's happened?"

He pulled her into his massive embrace. It was like being swallowed by a mound of warm, firm, deliciously masculine flesh. There was nothing on earth more comforting. At six and a half feet and somewhere around two hundred fifty pounds, Kieran was an enormous man of enormous depth with a perfectly sculptured body of flesh, bone and powerful muscles.

"You, of all people, should understand that things happen that you simply cannot explain," he murmured against the top of her head. "You and I were born eight hundred years apart, yet we are together in the flesh. God knows we belong together 'else he would not have allowed such an anomaly. You and I were destined for one another, no matter what the time."

She burrowed into him, inhaling his distinctive musk that was so desperately attractive and comforting. "I know," she whispered, her face in his chest. "But that still does not explain what has happened."

He sighed faintly, holding her tightly and stroking her arms. He had a sense of being calm and centered at the moment, far more than she did. He recognized everything about where they were; the smell, the feeling, the smoke of the torches in the distance. He was in his comfort zone, the sights and scents of his time. He didn't know how he knew everything so clearly, but he did.

"Do you believe in miracles, Lib?"

She sighed against him. "You know I do. You're a living miracle."

"Then understand well what I am about to tell you. I believe I know what has happened."

She pulled her face out of his chest, gazing up at him. "What?"

He drew in a long breath, collecting his thoughts as his gaze continued to move over the distant town. "We have already discussed the happenstance of Fate," he began. "When you uncovered my suspended corpse and awoke me from my eternal sleep, it was something that had been preordained since the beginning of Time. I was meant to be wounded by assassins and put in stasis by an alchemist so that you could dig my body up at the appropriate time and awaken me. It was simply meant to be."

She was watching him as he spoke. "I know that. But it still does not explain why…"

He put his finger over her lush lips so that he could continue. "You were searching for something when you uncovered me."

"Right. I was searching for the Crown of Thorns that Christ wore on the cross, the artifact right over there in that box."

"Correct. It was in my possession. You had manuscripts written by a fifteenth century monk that described where the crown was buried. But instead of the crown, you found me."

She nodded patiently. "But you knew where the crown was. The journal I dug up with you alluded to it."

"Alluded to, but did not describe the exact spot. To know the exact spot, you had to ask me."

"And so I did when I kissed your corpse and awoke you from a drug-induced, catatonic state."

He smiled at her. "The alchemist who tried to save my life after assassins had wounded me told me that only the strongest human emotion would rouse me from the potion he forced me to ingest. It suspended all of my bodily functions so that I would not bleed to death, allowing my body to heal itself with the gift of time."

"I know."

"Only a kiss of true love was powerful enough to awaken me."

She reached up, touching his cheek where deep dimples carved canyons from his cheekbones to his jaw. He had an incredibly handsome face. She kissed him softly on his chin.

"So it was," she said. "And then you came awake in my time."

He returned her soft kisses. "Came awake, aye; but without my crown. And I had started a mission eight hundred years before that I was required to finish. So we returned for the crown."

She pursed her lips ironically. "Not without a series of adventures that nearly killed us."

He snorted loudly. "Indeed." He sobered. "But the fact remains that I collected my crown. And I still must finish my mission."

"I know that," she said patiently. "That was where we were going when Corbin and his goons came after us."

Kieran was silent a moment, listening to the waves crash, shifting his body and trying to protect Rory from the cold sea breeze. "Corbin was my former friend, Simon, reincarnated. He tried to kill me for the crown in my time. He was still trying to kill me in yours."

"But he didn't, not in either time. Whatever he threw at you, you managed to survive."

Kieran paused pensively. "Perhaps… perhaps all of that happened for a reason."

"Corbin tried to kill you for some greater reason?"

He shook his head. "I did not mean that. What I meant was that, perhaps, we were prevented from returning to England with the crown in your time for a reason. My mission had nothing to do with your time, Lib. It has everything to do with my time and the armies who are dependent upon me. Perhaps, we were corralled to the beach for that very reason; because I was not meant to return the crown to England in your time. I am meant to return it in mine."

She was staring up at him, somewhat perplexed. "Are you saying that, somehow, some way, we're back where you started?"

He nodded slowly. "God has had a very strange hand in our lives. He has brought us together, to help and to love one another, but He has made it clear that I must not return the crown to England in your time. So many things prevented us from doing so. Do you not see all of the obstacles that were in our way?"

She thought back on the cops, the chases, and the trail of bad luck that seemed to follow them everywhere they went. From the moment Kieran had awoken in that cold morgue in London, everything had been against them. Every possible obstacle had been thrown at them. A light of understanding suddenly went on in her head.

"What if…," she began, gaining steam as she went. "What if you are supposed to return the crown in your time? What if this is a second chance to change the course of the Crusade and, consequently, the course of history? Kieran, no one gets a second chance like this. How many people hope and pray for such a thing and it never happens? You didn't even ask for a second chance. You just wanted to finish what you started. What if this is a second chance to do that?"

He nodded, seeing that she understood what he was driving at.

"Exactly," he said softly. "That bolt of lightning did something to us, Lib. We're on the same beach, with the crown, but Bud and David and Corbin and Darlow are gone. And in the distance is a village I recognize. Somehow, in some way, I have been given a second chance to complete what I was entrusted with. I have been given a second chance to bring peace to millions and end this siege."

Rory couldn't believe it was possible but, in a way, nothing could have made more sense. A miracle had already happened once when Kieran had come to life in the twenty-first century. Now, perhaps lightning had, indeed, struck twice. She had come back to his time.

"If that's true," she said, "then why am I here? I don't have a mission to complete. This is your deal, not mine."

He smiled at her. "For a brilliant woman, there are times when you are most dense. This crown is as much yours as it is mine. This is something we were meant to do together, Lib. I had the crown; you went searching for it and found me instead. Then we recovered it together. It belongs to us as surely as we belong to each other. And perhaps… perhaps the reason you have returned with me is to ensure my success. The first time, I nearly perished in my quest. With my second attempt, the difference shall be you."

She smiled timidly at him, eyeing the village in the distance. "Are you sure about all of this?"

He followed her gaze, the gem-clear brown eyes lingering on the smoking bonfires and thatched huts. "There is one way to find out."

"But how do we know that your old friend, Simon, isn't out there, waiting to stab you again? How do we know when, exactly, this is? Is it the day before you were wounded? A week before?"

"I think I will be able to deduce that in little time."

"How?"

"By returning to Hut's hostel. In theory, if it is somewhat close to the time I was wounded, all of my possessions will be there, including my armor and weapons."

"I have to tell you that I'm really scared."

"Just as I was when I awoke in your time."

"But you're braver than I am."

He lifted an eyebrow at her, letting her know just how ridiculous he thought her statement was. He picked up the box that contained the crown.

"Not hardly."

CHAPTER TWO

THE FIRST THING Rory noticed was the smell. It was as if a hundred portable outhouses had been dumped in the street along with animal carcasses, trash, and just about anything else imaginable. As a Biblical Archaeologist with an emphasis in the First through Third Crusades, she was well aware of Medieval societal conditions. She'd studied it, wrote about it, inspected it, but nothing had prepared her for the reality of it. It was beyond belief. She held Kieran's hand tightly as they entered the outskirts of the village, heading into the bowels of the berg.

The shacks that comprised people's homes or businesses weren't anything like she was used to. They were made of mud and straw, seated on foundations that were nothing like modern building foundations. And they were small; very tiny, like doll houses. Walls leaned, roofs pitched at odd angles, and she could hear voices and other noises as they walked along the dirty street. But it wasn't English they spoke; it was something else, something harsh and crude. It was, literally, like being in another world. She was in ancient times and still struggling to grasp it. It was terrifying, disorienting and thrilling at the same time.

So she was in Nahariya in 1192 A.D., at least if what Kieran believed was true. Other than the fact that she was walking in animal dung on urine-slicked roads, there was another concern on her mind. She was still dressed in her khaki jeans and tee shirt, looking as out of place as one could possibly get in a twelfth century village. She need more appropriate attire in order to blend in, especially with her fair skin. But she was horrified at the thought of wearing clothing of this time. Vermin and lice were commonplace and she wanted no part of bug-crawling clothing. Still, she had little choice.

"Kieran," she whispered as they tread quickly and quietly down a darkened avenue. "I need some appropriate clothing. People are going to have a heart attack when they see me in these clothes."

He was in a mode that Rory had never seen before. His eyes were darting about, surveying all, missing nothing. It was the look of a hunter or the hunted. Still, he managed to understand what she was telling him, even passing a glance at her attire.

He grunted. "I have become so accustomed to seeing you dressed as such that it did not occur to me." He paused, pulling her back into the shadows with him. "Hut has a wife. Perhaps she can give you something to wear until I can purchase clothing for you."

She wrinkled her nose. "God, I hope it's clean, whatever it is."

"Beggars cannot be choosers. You will take it and be thankful for it until I can purchase something better."

"I'm not a beggar," she insisted, somewhat angrily. "And I won't wear it if it's crawling with bugs or any other little creatures."

"You will wear it."

"No bugs, Kieran."

"Wear it or you will not like my response."

She stuck her tongue out at him in the darkness. He caught it out of the corner of his eye.

"Do that again and I shall take it as an invitation."

She leaned forward into his line of sight and stuck her tongue out at him blatantly, adding a sassy sound along with it. He looked at her sternly before breaking down into soft snorts.

"I accept your invitation. But later."

She giggled as he pulled her out of the shadows and they continued down the avenue. Somewhere in the mud and filth, she managed to step in a huge pile of human feces and she groaned, trying to wipe her boot off as they continued to move down the street. Just as she managed to wipe most of it off in the dirt, Kieran suddenly veered into a large structure.

It was bigger than the small, leaning houses they had just passed. From what she could see, the building was two stories with a row of narrow, gaping windows on the second floor. The door wasn't properly fitted and both light and sound poured through the gaps. When Kieran finally yanked the door open, she was hit in the face by the warmth and the smell.

The room was full of bodies, of people that Rory had only seen at Medieval fairs or in movies. They were dirty, scruffy, dressed in clothing that made her mouth hang open at the sight of it. Kieran pulled her across the hard-packed dirt floor towards the far end of the room, but it didn't prevent her from staring at the collection of rabble.

Men who looked as if they had never bathed in their lives sat hunched over earthenware cups. There were a few women about, though it was a general term regarding the sex of the individual and not a compliment. They were, by far, the most dirty, disgusting creatures Rory had ever seen. They wore little more than layers of rags on their bodies; dark, swarthy women who turned their attention to her as she crossed the room in her indecent clothing.

In the corner, one of the women was up on the tabletop, her skirts thrown up and a man going to work between her legs. The woman laughed, the man thrust into her, and his friends crowed uproariously. They were all making great sport out of it while one of their friends near the window peed against the wall.

Mouth still agape, Rory smashed into the back of Kieran when he suddenly came to a halt. Peering around him, she noticed he had engaged in conversation with a large, flabby man who wore little more than a burlap tunic and ratty leggings. She stared at the clothing, the uneven weave and rough material. It was both fascinating and shocking, like wearing steel wool. She listened to the conversation although she still hadn't gotten over her shock of the state of the tavern room. She was slipping back into disorientation again; this was real, dirty and as guttural as it got. She was beginning to feel nauseous.

"Are my possessions still in the room I rented from you?" Kieran demanded quietly.

The fat innkeeper nodded nervously, speaking a dialect of English that was barely understandable. It was obvious that it was not his native language. "I've not touched yer possessions, my lord. They are just where ye left them this morning."

A strange gleam came to Kieran's eye. "How long have I been here?"

The fat man looked confused. "How long...?"

"How long?" Kieran snapped, more loudly.

"Ye came only this morning, my lord," the man stammered fearfully. "I've not touched yer possessions...."

It was all Kieran needed to hear. He pulled Rory up the rickety stairs to the left, heading down a short, uneven hallway until he reached the last door on the left. He threw open the door, checked to make sure no one was in the room, quickly ushered Rory inside and closed the door behind them.

Rory stood near the closed door, feeling increasingly ill and disoriented as Kieran went straight for the small bed and began to pull things out from underneath it. He knew exactly where to go and what to do. An enormous satchel, saddlebags, and the magnificent sword that they had unearthed along with him were tossed upon the mattress. She continued to stand there in bewildered silence as he rummaged through everything as if checking to make sure nothing was missing.

"You realize that you're in odd clothing, too, right?" she asked quietly.

He nodded, pulling wads of material out of his satchel. "Something I intend to remedy immediately." He looked over and studied her closely for the first time since they had entered the town. She looked inordinately pale and he realized he had been rushing through all of this, focused on resuming a sense of normalcy. But his normalcy and Rory's normalcy were not the same. He hadn't been sensitive to her needs or feelings in the least. Setting his clothing down, he went over to her.

"Are you feeling well?" he asked gently. "Perhaps you would like something to eat."

She waved him off. "Good lord, no. I don't want to touch anything."

"You are going to have to eat sooner or later."

"Make it later."

He didn't push her. "Very well." He kissed her forehead. "You will tell me if you change your mind."

She nodded unsteadily and he touched her cheek, wishing he could comfort her more. But he knew from experience that this kind of disorientation would take time to heal. When he had awoken in a London morgue after eight hundred years of inactivity, his disorientation had been a miserable experience. She would not overcome this in a mere few moments although he wished he could spare her the time. But time, at the moment, was of the essence. He returned to his unpacking.

"If what Hut says is correct, then tonight the assassins will come for me," he said. "We must be well out of this place in a hurry."

"Was that fat guy Hut?"

"Aye."

"The same one who buried you in the old Roman temple?"

"The same."

Rory fell silent, digesting the information, taking the time to look around the room and trying to be very clinical about everything. It seemed to help her disorientation not to become swept up in the emotion of the moment. This time period was her specialty, her area of focus, and she should have been very detached and scholarly about the whole adventure. But she found that she could not be completely unemotional about it. Spying a stool near the sooty hearth that was really more like a hole in the wall than an actual fireplace, she went to it and sat wearily.

Kieran was digging through a massive leather bag, removing clothing that she couldn't readily identify. But the longer she stared at the bag, the more she recognized it. It was enough to get her off the stool and over to the bed.

"Your satchel," she said as she fingered the thick leather. "I remember when we found this on you. It was so brittle that we were afraid to touch it. But looking at it now, it's new and supple. Amazing."

Kieran ripped off the shirt he had bought at Fortnum and Mason, tossing it onto the bed and replacing it with a padded, linen tunic. He ran his hands over it, acquainting himself with something familiar. It was a satisfying feeling.

Rory was distracted from her fear and disorientation as she watched him transform from a twenty-first century man to a knight of the Third Crusade. In fact, it was a rather awesome experience. The only time she had ever seen him dressed in attire appropriate to his profession was when they had first uncovered his grave. She'd never even seen him in chain mail or armor. Now, he was becoming what he was born to be; a knight of Richard the Lionheart. The realization was blooming.

Rory ran her fingers over the rough linen tunic, inspecting the textile as Kieran tried to dress around her. He pulled off his jeans and pulled on a pair of leather breeches, trying to retrieve a pair of boots from his satchels as Rory studied the leather. He finally gave up trying to pull the boots on as she inspected the seams of the breeches, the stitching on the tunic, clinically analyzing what he was wearing. When she finally glanced up at him during the course of her inspection, he was smiling at her.

"What?" she asked. "Why are you grinning?"

He shook his head, kissing the hand that was on his shoulder. "Because you inspect me as one would a prized stallion," he said, finally going to his knees and, once again, rummaging under the bed.

He began to pull forth a bucket-shaped helm, some kind of padded, leather vest and a huge pile of mail. Rory stepped out of his way as he brought the heavy mess onto the bed. Then she stood there with mounting awe as he began to dress himself in his battle armor.

"Oh… my God," she breathed. "Your chain mail."

He looked at her, unsure why she seemed so amazed. "Indeed. Why do you look that way?"

As she watched him pull the hauberk over his head, tears filled her eyes and it was clear she was very emotional. She put her hands to her lips, folded, as if praying, watching every move he made. She was suddenly seeing him through new eyes, a Knight of the Realm as he was always meant to be. It was her Kieran, now in his element.

"Because," she struggled to speak through the lump in her throat. "Of course I always knew you were a knight but I never… it's just really dawning on me, that's all. When we dug you up, you weren't wearing your armor. Seeing you like this… my God, it's just too fantastic to believe. It's unreal."

He eased his rushing motions yet again and cupped her face in his enormous hands, focusing on her. As difficult as it had been for him when he had awakened in her time, he knew well what she was feeling. Her shock of ending up in his time was probably much worse and it was only going to grow more brutal. She was educated and smart, but she truly had no idea what she was in for. All of the education in the world would not prepare her for the reality.

He gently kissed her forehead. "I am sorry, sweetheart," he murmured. "I know this must be difficult for you and you are showing extreme resilience. I am very proud of your strength."

She shook her head. "I'm fine," she murmured, her gaze moving over the mail hood resting on his shoulders. "Don't worry about me. It's just that this is a truly amazing experience for me, Kieran. To see you as you really are, as you were meant to be… I never thought I would see that, not ever. But I am and it's overwhelming."

He wasn't sure what to say to that so he kissed her forehead again and dropped his hands, returning to the mail and pieces of armor that he had placed carefully on the bed. She came up behind him, inspecting the helm closely.

"I remember this thing," she said slowly, running her fingers over the bucket-shaped helm. "It was buried with you."

"Hut was most thorough in burying my possessions."

"In about a hundred years, knights are going to be wearing entire suits of plate armor just like this helm."

He lifted an eyebrow as he slipped on the heavy, leather vest that covered his chest like a bulletproof Kevlar vest. "Why?"

"Better protection."

He grunted in disbelief as he fastened the straps on the vest. "I am not sure I would wear a suit of metal. It would be difficult to move, I would think. Heavy, too."

She shrugged, watching him finish with the leather vest and move for the massive coat of chain mail on the bed.

"Some of them were ridiculously heavy," she agreed. "But this coat of chain mail is heavy. It's got to weigh fifty pounds."

He pursed his lips as he took the mail coat from the bed and began to put it on as one would put on a heavy sweater; arms first.

"It is not cumbersome or heavy," he informed her flatly. Then he ran his hands over it to smooth it down, his expression turning wistful. "I have missed it."

As unsettled as she was with the apparent time shift, he was equally as comfortable. Now that he was back in his element and his strength, his sense of urgency was gaining power. It was as if he had never left as an odd change seemed to overtake him. The mannerisms rooted to this time in history were seeping back into him, turning him from a twenty-first century transplant back to a twelfth century original. The knight, the trained killer and protector, was rapidly returning.

Rory stood back, watching him as he positioned the mail coat. It hung to mid-thigh and covered both arms beyond the wrists. He pulled another tunic over the top of it. She was so involved in watching the lines of the chain mail and the way it fit his body that it took her a moment to realize he had pulled on a scarlet tunic with three rows of yellow, royal lions on it. It was well-used but unmistakable. Her hazel eyes widened.

"Oh, my God," she breathed. "It… it…"

He fussed with the tunic, oblivious to the shock in her tone. "What is wrong?"

She didn't reply. When the wait became excessive, he turned to look at her only to find her standing there with tears spilling down her cheeks. He immediately stopped what he was doing and went to her.

"What's the matter, sweetheart," he crooned softly as he wiped at the tears on her face. "Why do you weep?"

She sobbed, pointing at him; it sounded like a squeak. "Richard," she managed to spit out. "You're wearing Richard's tunic."

He wasn't quite sure why she was crying about it. "Aye, I am." His brow furrowed. "Why? What is wrong with it?"

She shook her head, still sobbing. Kieran wasn't exactly sure how to comfort her, not knowing why she was pointing at him and weeping, when she sniffled loudly and struggled to compose herself.

"The history I am witnessing is beyond comprehension." She tried to put her amazement into words he could understand. "It would be like… like when you were presented with Christ's Crown of Thorns. The sheer value of the object, of you holding and touching the object, is something so deep and intensely personal. Do you remember how you felt when you saw it for the first time? The reverence and spiritual power? As you stand there, you are a knight under the command of King Richard of England. In my time, he was perhaps the most legendary king England has ever had with rare exception. His legend has reached almost mythological proportions and now I'm actually seeing the reality of it. It's living, breathing history, Kieran. I'm not sure if you can understand how powerful that is to me, as a student of history."

"An archaeologist."

"A Biblical Archaeologist with an emphasis in the First through Third Crusades." She winked at him when he gave her a half-grin as he continued to busy himself with dressing. She watched him a moment, cocking her head in thought. "Tell me something. Who is the military commander, other than the king, that you admire most?"

He looked up from fastening a leather strap on his torso. "Anyone?"

"Anyone."

He wriggled his eyebrows thoughtfully and returned to the uncooperative strap. "I fostered with an old and wise knight who was fond of military history," he said. "He told me the story once of the Spartans, of King Leonidas and how he held his Spartan army against ten thousand Persians. I always admired a man who would face a battle with such overwhelming odds against him."

"Then you can understand that King Richard to me is like Leonidas to you. It's a pretty overwhelming prospect."

He, indeed, understood what she was telling him and he kissed her gently on the forehead, then on her salty lips. "I look forward to introducing you to our king," he said. "He will like you a great deal."

Her mouth flew open in shock. "My God!" She grew animated again. "I never… oh, my God, I never thought I would meet him. It never even occurred to me."

"Of course you will meet him."

She waved her hands excitedly, like she was flapping wings. The tears were rapidly forgotten. "Oh my God, oh my God," she jumped up and down a couple of times. "Seriously? I can't believe it!"

"Try not to burst into tears when you are introduced."

She stopped jumping and scowled. "Oh, shut up."

"He might think you an emotional idiot and it would reflect badly on me."

"Screw you, buddy."

He laughed loudly. He had spent enough time in her era to know what she meant. He turned back to the possessions he had spread out on the bed, finishing smoothing out his tunic before reaching for his gauntlets. Rory wiped away the last of the tears off her cheeks, her interest in his attire gaining strength as she walked up behind him to inspect the tunic. Kieran could feel her behind him, running her hands over him, and he stood in place patiently long after his gloves were secured.

"Are you finished inspecting me?" he asked politely.

She nodded, though she was intrigued by the thick-threaded weave of the tunic and the uneven scarlet dye job. The yellow lions were woven in with yellow thread in a surprisingly accurate design. It was a durable, lovely piece.

"It's like a football jersey," she muttered thoughtfully.

"Football?"

"Yes, you know," she made motions with her hands like she was throwing a pass. "American football. Things like jerseys and uniforms for sports teams got their start with tunics like this."

He shook his head. "I do not remember witnessing any American football. But I do remember the rug… rugly players we met up with once. Barbarians, as I recall."

She smiled. "It's called rugby," she corrected gently. "They wear uniforms when they play, too."

She followed him around, picking at the tunic as he reached for his magnificent sword. He almost slapped her with the big, leather fastens as he secured the scabbard about his waist and right thigh. Kieran was caught up in the moment of being back in his own time, comfortable for the first time in eight hundred years with where and who he was. But he wasn't so caught up that he couldn't spare time to grin at Rory's fascination. She was quite humorous now that her shock at the situation was settling somewhat. He tried to work around her as she clinically examined him. He ended up just bumping into her. Finally, he sighed.

"Sweetheart, I realize you are consumed with all of this," he said with restrained impatience. "But it is extremely important that we leave this place. I have much to do and as much as I would like to spare you the time to examine every inch of what I am wearing, we simply cannot delay. I need for you to stay out of the way while I get organized."

Rory nodded, her eyes still on his tunic, but she did as she was told. Silently, she stood back as he gathered all of his things and shoved them back into the satchel, including the modern jeans, shirt and the highly prized work boots he admired so much. When he had all of his possessions together and was fully dressed in his mail and armor, he turned to face Rory.

She was standing quietly and was rather pale as she gazed back at him. He looked at her a moment, studying her lovely face, seeing that she was calming. But she still didn't look particularly well. Truth be told, he could still hardly believe what had happened. But he was exceedingly grateful for whatever Fates controlled their destiny. He was ready and willing to resume where he had left off. He went to her and put his enormous hands on her shoulders.

"I am going to find you something suitable to wear," he said quietly. "You will stay here and not leave this room. Is that clear?"

She nodded. "I know," she replied. "It's not safe for me to wander around alone."

He grunted and dropped his hands, kissing her as he fussed with his gloves. "Safe, indeed," he muttered, heading for the door. "Remember that this is not your time. There is no law as you know it and the characters you will come across have no morals and even less restraint. You must be cautious more than you have ever been in your life."

"I survived going to school in South Central Los Angeles for eight years."

"This is not Los Angeles. This is beyond your imagination."

She shrugged in agreement, moving for the bed as if to sit. But she peered closely at it, realizing there were vermin on the coverlet, and wrinkled her nose in disgust.

"I'm not going anywhere." Rory moved to the center of the room, away from the crawling bed. She waved her hands at him. "Go. I'll be fine."

"Throw the bolt on this door when I leave. Open it for no one."

She nodded, once more, in silence. Kieran blew her a kiss with his fingers and quietly quit the room. He was filled with a sense of purpose and seemed preoccupied, too preoccupied to coddle his lady. But she didn't blame him and she truly didn't give his manner much thought; she was more concerned with throwing the poorly made bolt. It took her a few tries to secure the old, iron rod, mostly because she was inspecting how it was made before she actually secured it. She pinched her finger on it, hissing in pain as she shook out the pinch.

It was oddly still now that Kieran was gone. Rory stood next to the door, looking around the cold and cramped room, a huge sense of shock sweeping her. She moved away from the door with her hands on her mouth.

"Oh, my God," she hissed, eyeing the details of the shabby, poorly made walls before her gaze came to rest on the bed again. "This is crazy. I just can't believe it."

She was staring at the bed with its very crude fabric cover. She suspected it was some kind of linen but she wasn't going to touch it to find out. His leather satchel was on the bed and she put it on the floor, away from the crawling bugs. There was a small, crudely built window covered by some kind of ratty cloth and she peered from the opening, feeling the cool sea breeze on her face and smelling the salt. It was a familiar scent and helped her disorientation. The sea, all over the world or in any time, always smelled the same.

She struggled to push the disorientation aside completely and focus on the here and now. It was important that she come to grips with whatever had happened. She touched the window frame, feeling the crudeness, seeing the lack of craftsmanship. Fat iron nails held the wood together. Then she smelled it; it smelled like raw, untreated wood. Whatever she was feeling, the truth was real in her fingers and her nostrils. Everything was real.

With a sigh, she turned away from the window and wandered back over to his satchel on the floor. She sat down beside it, careful not to drag her butt on the rough-hewn floor planks; all she needed was a massive splinter to get infected. To keep busy and, perhaps, reacquaint herself with Kieran's possessions that she had only seen after they had been buried for eight hundred years, she began to carefully rummage through his bag.

The first thing she came across was a dirk. It was finely crafted and extremely sharp. She took it out and inspected it, not remembering the weapon from the inventory list she and her colleagues had made of the possessions Kieran had been buried with. She suspected that Hut may have kept some nicer pieces before burying Kieran and her interest grew as she rummaged deeper into the bag. She wondered what else Hut had kept.

There was a silk purse with a good deal of money in it. She removed the coins carefully, one by one, inspecting each individual coin with awe. That was the archaeologist in her. She laid them all out on the floor, in a line, inspecting the size and shape and trying to determine the monetary value by the weight. She was in the process of studying two smaller coins when the door suddenly rattled violently.

Rory jumped, frightened. The door suddenly shook again, crazily, before the old bolt gave way and the panel flew open. Splinters sprayed into the room and Rory screamed, covering her face to protect it. A body was rushing into the room and she scrambled to leap up from the floor. But her gaze fell on the glittering dagger, lying next to the satchel, and she grabbed it as she bolted up. It was an instinctive reaction. She'd never wielded a knife in her life. She didn't even know how to really use it.

But she knew she was about to learn.

CHAPTER THREE

THERE WERE TWO men.

One of them rushed for Rory and the second went straight for the satchel on the floor. Rory was hooting and yelling, holding the dirk as the man made a grab for her. She ducked his reach, remembering about the weapon on the man's second pass and making a swipe at his hand. She made contact, cutting his fingers as the man hissed a curse.

Rory was on the run. She leapt off the opposite end of the bed but the man's long reach got her by the hair. He pulled hard and she screamed loudly as he pulled her up against his cold, mail-covered body. He stank like a thousand breweries filled with a thousand drunk, stinky bodies. The stench was beyond horrible.

"Let me go, you asshole," she tried to swing the dirk at him but she wasn't very good with the weapon and he easily slapped it away. "Let me go!"

The man had his mouth by her ear. She could hear him inhale deeply. "Ye smell sweet, little chit," he hissed in his horrible, foul breath. He licked her ear and she yelped. "Ye taste sweet, too."

Rory was terrified and furious. She began to struggle wildly, trying to kick and punch him. He was trying to get a good grip on her while his companion robbed Kieran's satchel, but she was moving around so much that he couldn't get a good hold of her. She was twisting and cussing at him in odd words he did not understand. Something about a mother's shucker, he thought. The girl spoke strangely but she was fine and delicious. It was his last coherent thought before a massive body suddenly appeared in the doorway and an enormous blade plowed through his midsection. He hit the ground dead.

Rory was pulled to the floor when the man fell, his hand still wrapped up in her hair. By this time, the dead man's companion had drawn his weapon and charged Kieran from across the room. As Rory wrapped her arms over her head and tried not to get kicked or, worse, stabbed, a massive swordfight with thirty pound broadswords commenced over her head. She was petrified.

But Kieran was cool as he charged the man who had come at him. His enormous broadsword sang through the air with deadly accuracy as he both defended himself and Rory, who was still struggling on the ground. He thought of nothing else at the moment but dispatching the man. To think of anything else, including Rory, would divert his focus and quite possibly cost him his life. So, at the moment, he concentrated on the kill.

The enemy soldier ended up kicking Rory in the back as he went after Kieran, a sharp kick from a sharp boot that caused her to grunt in pain. She managed to unwind the dead man's hand from her hair and crawl away from the fighting, getting kicked in the mouth as she went. She could taste blood as she threw herself against the wall, trying to stay clear of the blades singing over her head. She was too scared to even watch; she tucked her face into her knees and covered her head.

Although it seemed like hours, the fight only lasted a matter of seconds. Kieran had his kill within eight strokes. He managed to cut low and slice the sharp edge of his blade across the man's knee, causing him to double over. When the man folded in half, Kieran brought the sword up and nearly decapitated him. Before the man even hit the ground, Kieran was at Rory's side.

"Lib," he said, his voice was full of fear. "Are you injured?"

Rory's head came up, blood trickling from her split lip. One look at Kieran's anxious face and she threw her arms around his neck, weeping hysterically.

"Oh, my God," she sobbed. "I want to go home. I want to get out of here."

He picked her up and held her tightly, allowing himself to feel his terror. "Are you well?" his voice was shaking. "Answer me, sweetheart.

Did they hurt you?"

She shook her head unsteadily and he sighed heavily with relief. "'Tis all right," his deep, bass voice was soft and soothing. "Everything is all right now. You are safe."

"It's not all right," she wept, now angry as well as frightened. "Those guys busted in here and… and one of them grabbed me while the other guy … oh, hell, I don't know but I think he was robbing you. I couldn't really see."

He soothed her gently, rocking her gently as held her. "'Tis all right now. It is over."

"I want to go home," she repeated, begging.

He sighed faintly as he continued to rock her. He didn't know what to say; she couldn't go home. She was home.

"Your lip is bleeding," he ventured gently, trying to get her mind on something other than the panicked need to go home. "Are you sure you are all right?"

"I'm fine." She pulled her face from the crook of his neck, wiping the trickle of blood from the corner of her lip. "For the most part, anyway."

He set her carefully to her feet and tipped her chin up so he could inspect her split lip. "Did they strike you?"

Her tears were fading and she sniffled, wiping at her lip again. "No," she replied. "I got kicked while you guys were fighting."

He sighed again. "I am sorry." He kissed her cheek gently and helped her stand. "But you are otherwise unharmed?"

She wiped away the tears from her face. "Yes." The tears were gone but the panic was still there. "But I really, really want to go home."

He grunted, fixing her in the eye. "How?"

Some of her agitation returned. "Go back to the beach, I guess. Sit there and wait for another storm."

He lifted an eyebrow, attempting to force her to think about what she was saying. "Is this so? You will go sit on the beach for the rest of your life hoping another storm will come and send you back to your time?"

She was about to nod forcefully but stopped short when she saw the look on his face. Then she tried to pull away from him, shaking her head.

"I don't want to stay here anymore," she said, fighting off tears once again. "I can't. I want to go back to where I came from, where I belong."

"If you go back to where you came from, I must stay here. I cannot go with you."

Her gaze snapped to him as if the thought hadn't occurred to her. The hazel eyes widened for a moment as she realized what she had been asking, and what his response was. She was moderately irrational and coming to realize it. Fear was doing strange things to her thought processes. She suddenly didn't feel like pulling away from him any longer.

"I'll never leave you," she murmured. "If that's my choice, I'll choose staying with you hands down."

"Are you sure?"

"I'm sure."

He smiled at her and turned back to the carnage of the room. It was then that Rory realized there were two dead men on the floor of the room and, having never seen a dead body in her life, she suddenly gasped and turned away. Too much blood and gore made her physically ill. The nausea she had been experiencing since awakening on the beach suddenly returned full force.

Kieran heard her gasp and turned to her just in time to see her shove her face into the wall.

"What is wrong?" he asked, concerned.

She couldn't speak. All she could do was point to the bloodied mess on the floor. As Kieran realized her delicate senses were not dealing well with something he hardly raised an eyebrow at, a swarthy, old woman with a caved-in mouth appeared at the door. She was little and dirty. Hut was right behind her and, together, they stared wide-eyed at the destroyed room.

"We heard the commotion, my lord," Hut said. "Are ye well?"

Kieran glanced at Rory with her face still pressed into the wall. "Well enough." He motioned at the old woman. "What is this?"

The old woman held the wad of material aloft as Hut spoke. "The garments ye requested for yer lady," he said. "It is all I could find."

"Where did you get it?"

"From one of the serving wenches. She is about the size of yer lady."

Kieran nodded. "Do you have another room where she can dress?" He glanced back at the carnage in the room. "This chamber is… unacceptable."

Hut nodded, motioning eagerly to Kieran. "Across the hall, m'lord. 'Tis a small room where the serving wenches sleep but it should serve well enough."

Kieran reached out and gently pulled Rory away from the wall. She came away stiffly, almost tripping over her feet because she was afraid to open her eyes and see all of the blood and guts again. He put his big arm around her shoulders, putting his lips against her ear as he guided her from the room.

"They have located you some suitable clothing," he said softly. "You will go with this woman and allow her to assist you."

Rory had opened her eyes by now and held an odd, wide-eyed look. "Oh, God," she hissed. "What if it's crawling with bugs?"

"You will have to endure."

She shook her head and began to drag her feet but he pulled her along insistently.

"I won't wear it if it's crawling with bugs," she insisted as he pulled her through the door. "I told you that, Kieran. No bugs."

"You will wear it," he said, more firmly. "Tomorrow, I will buy new clothing for you that will be to your liking. But for tonight, you have no choice."

"But, Kieran…"

"Go." It was a command in a tone she'd never heard from him before. "Enough complaining. I know you are upset and I know you are fearful, but the time has come for you to put this foolishness aside and accept the situation for what it is. Are you truly a weak-souled complainer or are you the strong woman I believe you are?"

Her back stiffened indignantly. "Don't you dare accuse me of being weak."

"Then stop behaving like it. Time is wasting and there is no more tolerance for your idiocy, Rory. Do what you are told and do it immediately."

She was out of his embrace, looking at him as he gazed impassively at her. *Rory.* He rarely, if ever, called her by her given name because he felt it didn't suit her. He called her Libby, a nickname for her middle name, Elizabeth, because he liked it better. But he used her given name now and it sounded harsh from his lips. For the first time since she'd known the man, he was giving her a stern command. His knightly instincts were taking control and he was becoming what he had been trained for; hard, calculating, cold. He had become the warrior.

The fact that she'd been through a harrowing experience over the past hour had her emotions surging like a roller coaster. She didn't like his tone or the expression on his face. It was hard, ungiving and completely unlike the man she loved.

Furious, sick, she snatched the clothing out of the old woman's arms and charged into the room that Hut was indicating. She slammed the door in the old woman's face when the little woman tried to follow her. Kieran heard her throw the bolt.

Kieran sighed as Hut and the old woman looked at him questioningly. He simply waved them away. After a moment's pause lingering on the locked door, he went back into his chamber and collected his satchel and scattered possessions. There were dead men bleeding all over the floor but he stepped over them, not giving the carnage a second thought. Such was the norm of his world. One of the dead men still had the stolen coinage and Kieran collected his money from the man's pockets. Securing his satchel, he went back out into the hall and set everything against the wall, waiting for Rory to emerge from the room.

He leaned against the wall, staring at his feet thoughtfully. He shouldn't have been so harsh with her but she seemed to be lacking focus at what he was attempting to accomplish. Simon and his men were coming for him; that much he knew. Perhaps they were already on their way. He simply couldn't gauge the time well enough and that worried him. He was trying to get clear of the inn and Rory wasn't helping the situation. He knew she was disoriented and frightened. God only knew that he realized that more than she probably did. But she needed to understand that he was trying to save both of their lives right now. He was in survival mode. He needed her cooperation and if he had to take a firm stance in order to achieve that, then so be it.

On the other side of the wall, Rory was in tears again as she laid out the garments she was given. Her biggest fear was that they were crawling with vermin; she was obsessed with it. But much to her relief, she couldn't see any visible bugs in the rough linen surcoat. When she got over the fact that it was bug-less, she noticed that it was a lovely, pale yellow shade. Surprisingly, it wasn't a rag. There was a shift also, of a finer linen and unexpectedly soft.

Nothing was hemmed; the garments looked like they were simply basted together. She wondered if the stitching would hold. Throwing whatever reserve she had remaining to the wind, she pulled off her shirt and khaki jeans and pulled on the linen shift, acquainting herself with the feel of unprocessed material. It was raw and primitive, but it wasn't too bad. She left her bra and panties on so she didn't feel quite so exposed to the unfamiliar fabric. The surcoat went over her head and she was surprised at how well it fit. The sleeves were long and without much shape, but the neckline was a deep "V" and emphasized her full bosom beautifully. On the sides of the garment were strips of material and she tied them into small bows, which only further accentuated her shapely figure by tightening her waistline. All in all, she wasn't too displeased with the fit or the look.

But that was until she noticed her feet. The surcoat was far too long.

All she had was her boots, looking rather stupid with the rough yet surprisingly lovely surcoat. Yet it was all she had. She hoped she didn't trip on the long garment and break her neck.

As she fussed with the ties on her waist, she looked around the room and realized that she was in a chamber that belonged to a woman. There were two small beds and a very rough, unsteady table with a thick-toothed comb on it and what looked to be shoelaces scattered about. Closer examination showed that they were strips of cloth cut finely, like ribbons. Borrowing the comb, but not before she inspected it thoroughly for vermin, she divided her long hair into two long braids and tied them off with two strips of the material. She tied them into big bows, having no idea how very sweet and lovely she looked. On a peg near the door was a large, unbleached linen cloak that was relatively clean except for the dark dirt stains around the bottom. She peered at it closely, not seeing any vermin on it. She suspected it was something she might need, considering she had absolutely nothing. As she unbolted the door, she swiped it.

When she emerged into the hall, Kieran was leaning up against the wall staring at his feet. His head came up and his first look of her, in clothes he was familiar with, had him giddy with pleasure. Even in simple peasant wear, she was the most beautiful woman he had ever seen. Her long chestnut-colored hair was braided and her sweet oval face had regained some of its color. Her luminous hazel eyes gazed steadily at him under their fringes of thick lashes. When he reached out to take her hand, however, she deliberately pulled away and swung the cloak over her shoulders.

"You wanted to leave, so let's leave."

She turned away from him and headed towards the rickety stairs that led to the common room below. Kieran eyed her as she moved to the stairs, collecting his satchel and following. He caught up to her by the time she had taken the top two steps and he reached out, grasping her by the arm.

"Nay, lady," he rumbled, eyeing the room full of rabble below. "You will stay with me for your own safety."

Rory kept her mouth shut as he preceded her down the stairs. Hand still on her arm, he took her out the rear of the inn. It was a dusty, smelly yard that stood between them and a structure that apparently served as the stable. It looked like a condemned building. He started to guide her across the yard, towards the livery, but she pulled free of his grip.

"We're out of the inn." She fussed with the ties on the cloak. "You don't have to hold me with a death grip."

Kieran's temper was doing a slow build. Foremost, he wanted to get them the hell away from the inn, and then he would deal with her insolent attitude – she was an aggressive, willful woman under normal circumstances but he wasn't about to let her get out of hand. Still, he didn't like it when she was upset with him. They rarely fought and when they had, he couldn't seem to focus on anything else. As they reached the stable, he sent the boy for his charger and turned to her.

"Lib, I am sorry if you are upset with me," he said in a low voice. "But you must understand that there are priorities greater than you at the moment. I have no idea when Simon and his men are going to come for me and we must get clear of this place before they do. Every time you drag your feet or argue with me, you are jeopardizing both of us. Is that what you want? My death?"

As she gazed up at him, she lost some of her taut expression. After a moment, she lowered her gaze and shook her head. He watched her lovely face as she struggled. But she kept her mouth shut.

"Is that it?" he asked softly. "Do you have nothing to say to me?"

She lifted her slender shoulders. "What do you want me to say?"

"That you love me and will obey me without argument from now on."

She turned her head so she was looking away from him completely. He heard her sigh heavily.

"I don't like it when you order me around," she said quietly. "I know you're used to ordering people around, but I'm not one of them.

You don't have to be so mean about it. Everything about this is new and weird and scary, so you're just going to have to be patient with me. I'm doing the best I can under the circumstances."

He grunted, perhaps in resignation, and moved closer to her. He knew he was about to fold completely. Bending over, he put his lips on her cheek and suckled gently.

"I know you are," he whispered. "But so am I. As I listened to your advice in your time, you must listen to me in mine. Everything I do, I do to keep you safe. There are dangers awaiting us right now that you can't possibly comprehend. Do you understand that?"

She nodded, closing her eyes when he kissed her ear. "Yes."

"The next time I tell you to do something, will you do it without question or hesitation?"

"Maybe."

The way she said it was fairly dramatic and he knew that she was folding, too. He grinned, kissing her ear again, then her neck. He could feel her shiver beneath him.

"I love you, Lib."

That was about all she could take. Rory threw her arms around his neck and hugged him tightly.

"I'm sorry," she murmured against his ear. "I'm not trying to be a pain. I'm just so freaked out by all of this."

"I know."

"And those guys that broke into the room; God, Kieran, I've never even been around a fight much less something like that. You *killed* those guys."

"I had to."

"I know that." She pulled away and looked into his strong, handsome face. "But I've never seen anything like that in my life. Blood and… and that guy's head was… ugh…"

She made a face and trailed off. Kieran kissed her cheek, remaining silent on the subject; he knew she was a very strong woman. He had seen it. But he knew she would need all of that strength and more to endure what they were going to be facing. Now that the shock had worn off about returning to his time, he was beginning to feel some trepidation about what was to come.

The stable boy brought out Kieran's charger. The animal was big and beefy, a bright red color with a thick white blaze and cream-colored tuffs around its hooves. It was the biggest horse Rory had ever seen. Kieran went to the animal and greeted it as one would an old friend. But when Rory tried to pet it, the horse snapped at her.

Kieran was loading his satchel and saddlebags onto the back of the beast, grinning when the animal tried to bite her. Rory jumped back and threw her arms up as if someone had just pointed a gun at her and demanded money.

"This is Liberator," he introduced her to the animal. "He is a crossbreed of a destrier stallion and a Spanish Jennet mare. I bred him myself, in fact, and have raised him since foalhood. He is strong, intelligent and has a nasty temper. You must be very careful around him."

She put her arms down and made sure to stay a safe distance from the horse. "No kidding," she said ironically, watching the charger as it sniffed at Kieran's familiar scent. "He's huge."

Kieran finished securing the bags and made sure the saddle was tight before mounting. The smooth, effortless motion was not lost on Rory. She could see, in that movement, that the man had mounted many a horse. Once again, she was awed by the sight of Kieran in his natural state. As she observed both knight and charger with some amazement, Kieran held out his right hand to her.

"Come along," he urged her. "We must go."

She went to him and he pulled her up effortlessly, seating her on the back of the horse. Rory threw her leg over the animal so she was positioned astride and wrapped her arms tightly around Kieran's waist. It took him a moment to realize she wasn't sitting primly sidesaddle against him and he grunted.

"You will not ride like this," he said in a low voice. "Put your legs together and sit as a proper lady would."

She knew what he meant. "Kieran, I'm not trying to argue with you, but I'm not really comfortable on a horse and if I sit that way, I'll fall off. I don't ride every day like you do."

"I understand. But in this day, only whores ride as you do. 'Tis not proper for a finely bred lady."

"It's dark. No one will see. I'll practice riding sidesaddle another time. But for now, we'd better get out of here."

He growled but didn't push it. Spurring his animal forward, they took off at a canter. It was the equivalent of peeling out in a car. Rory had to hold on for dear life as he directed the charger down a dark alleyway that paralleled the main road, holding tightly as the horse jumped obstacles in the dark. They threaded their way through the town. She finally closed her eyes and buried her face in the tunic that she had been so fascinated with; everything about this situation was out of her control and she was going to have to trust the man. Kieran was brilliant and knew better than anyone what needed to be done and how to keep them both safe. Still, as the horse tramped through the darkness, her anxiety grew.

She didn't say a word for quite some time. At some point, she pulled her face from the rough tunic and opened her eyes, gazing up at the brilliant sky overhead. She'd never seen anything so sharp and bright; there was something very primordial and pure about the sky this night. Gradually, she began to realize they had ventured out of the city and onto a deserted road. The city was in the distance to her left and sand dunes and desert to her right. It was eerily quiet, too; no sounds of cars or music or airplanes overhead. Just a dully, deadly silence like nothing she had experienced before. Her head came up from its resting position against his back.

"Where are we going?" she asked softly.

"Richard's encampment is about four miles southeast of the city," he replied quietly. "We are heading for the camp."

"Is it safe there?"

He nodded. “Aye,” he replied. “Once I tell the king of Simon’s treachery, ’twill be Simon who will find the camp unsafe upon his return.”

Rory fell into contemplative silence. “Did you ever stop to think that you don’t have any proof of his treachery?” she asked after a moment. “He hasn’t done anything yet. He hasn’t made the attempt against your life and won’t now because you left the inn. You can’t prove he was trying to kill you.”

Kieran sighed. “He has been pursuing me for days with the intention of killing me. That is proof enough.”

She was silent a moment. “Has he made other attempts to kill you?”

“Aye,” he replied. “There were two other times.”

“You never mentioned that.”

“They were weak attempts not worth discussing.”

They plodded along in thoughtful silence. Simon de Corlet. Kieran’s blood ran cold as he thought of the man who used to be like a brother to him. They had grown up together and had come on this quest together. But something had happened to Simon during the time they had spent on the hot sands of The Levant; he had become materialistic and brutal.

It was a mission to secure a truce to end the siege of Acre. Of all of Richard the Lionheart’s knights, this mission had fallen to Kieran. A Muslim commander named El-Hajidd had sent word to the Christian armies to propose a secret meeting. He was an envoy representing several Muslim generals under Saladin’s command. Without Saladin’s knowledge, El-Hajidd arranged a secret meeting with Kieran and several other Christian knights to propose a truce, extending what was reputed to be Jesus Christ’s Crown of Thorns as a proposal of good faith. Kieran had accepted the crown and gave El-Hajidd his word that Richard would do everything in his power to end the siege peacefully.

But Kieran never had a chance to prove his honor. Several of his fellow knights, led by Simon, turned against him. They didn’t want peace, only the satisfaction and spoils of complete victory over Saladin.

Even as Kieran carried the Muslim offering to Richard, his men were plotting against him. Kieran, sensing the danger, eventually fled the group and they had followed, finally tracking him to Nahariya. Assassins had caught up with Kieran at an inn, mortally wounding him.

The proprietor of the inn, a fat man named Hut, had sent Kieran to a man believed to be a physic but the man was, in fact, an alchemist. Experimenting on the English knight with the nasty gut wound, the old alchemist had fed him a concoction of potions that had put Kieran in suspended animation. He hadn't been dead, yet not exactly living. He had been frozen in time, buried by Hut and forgotten by the world. The wound, through the centuries, had healed over. That was when Rory, a Biblical Archaeologist, had dug him up. Her inadvertent kiss had awoken the sleeping knight.

And their story continued even now, but they were in Kieran's time, not the modern world that Rory had been born in to. But they were together and that was all that mattered.

"I've been thinking," she murmured, gazing up at the astoundingly vibrant stars.

"What about?" he asked, still lingering on thoughts of Simon and betrayal.

"About the fact that you've been given a second chance to complete your mission," she said almost wistfully. "Kieran, how many people throughout the ages have begged God for the chance to live their life over or undo something they have done? And why is it you've been given that opportunity and me right along with you? I just can't help but think that you're meant for something really great, something that will change the course of history. Maybe the history I knew in my time won't be the same in eight hundred years. Somehow, you'll change it. You'll be the catalyst to greater things."

He patted the arms around his waist with a big, gloved hand. "Your faith in me is appreciated."

She squeezed him gently. "It's more than faith," she murmured. "Remember that I read your journal that had been buried with you. I know how remarkable you are. You are one of the greatest men I have ever read about much less known. I just know I'm going to witness something really amazing, something you will accomplish. Did you ever stop to think of the reason why I'm here, too? Maybe... maybe that's why; to witness it and maybe to write about it. Maybe I'll be in the history books as your chronicler."

He smiled, listening to her awesome take on the situation. "You are here because I need you," he said simply.

She hugged him again, laying her head against his back, thinking on her purpose for being here with him in his time. It was a little less scary when she realized that she must have some purpose. There was a reason why she was here. Gazing out over the distant city, her thoughts began to wander to their destination.

"So what are you going to tell Richard about me?" she asked. "He's going to want to know who in the heck I am."

Kieran grunted. "I have been trying to think of a plausible explanation," he said. "Although Richard is an accepting man, I doubt I can tell him the truth. At least, not right away. I suppose I shall tell him that you are an American heiress and we are to be married."

She made a face. "American heiress? He won't even know what America is."

He tried to turn and look at her, made difficult by the restrictive helm and hauberk. "I do not even know what American is," he informed her flatly. "In fact, I am doubtful that it even exists."

She snorted. "It's not Ameri*can*, it's America," she told him. "And yes, it exists."

"I think you have made it up."

She giggled. "I did not make it up."

"You did."

She continued to giggle, laying her cheek back against his tunic. "That brings about another issue," she said. "If I know my history about this era, and I do, if a woman traveled with a man and was not his wife, then she was considered a whore. What are we going to do about that?"

"I told you," he said evenly. "You are to be my wife."

She fought off a smile. "Not until you properly ask for my hand."

He pursed his lips. "I cannot properly ask for your hand, as I do not know your father. That means that the decision is up to another male relative."

"I don't have any."

"You have an uncle, do you not? Is he not part of the university you are indebted to?"

"I'm not indebted to the university. I work for it," she informed him with what he already knew, although his mindset was still late-twelfth century and a working woman was completely foreign to him. "And yes, he's the Dean of the Archaeology and Anthropology Department. But you don't need to ask him. You need to ask *me*."

He shook his head. "Your culture is, indeed, bizarre," he snorted. "So I assume I must propose marriage to you directly, then."

"What if I refuse?"

"Then I will sell you to a passing caravan as a slave and they can deal with your insolence."

"Seriously? Those are my choices?"

"Make your decision. If you do not want to marry me, then there are a host of other women who will gladly accept the honor."

"Other women?" She grabbed him by both arms and shook him playfully, although she wasn't able to do much considering how big he was. "What other women?"

Now he was the one fighting off a grin. "Many, many others," he said vaguely. "Too many to count. What is your decision?"

"I've decided to punch you right in the nose, buster."

His laughter broke through and he slapped his visor down. "You cannot reach it," he said. "Will you not at least consider my proposal?"

"Is that the best you can do? Really, Kieran? Your best effort at proposing to the woman you love?"

"Considering you come with no property, wealth or titles, you should feel fortunate that I have proposed at all."

"You conceited ape," she snorted, slapping him lightly on the shoulder. But then she wrapped her arms around his waist again and squeezed. "But I love you anyway."

He laughed low and raised his visor. He lifted one of her hands and kissed it. "Then you have decided to marry me?"

"I have."

He kissed her hand again and put it back around his waist. "I am glad."

He had slowed the horse to a trot by this time, feeling comfortable enough to ease their pace. They were out of the city and heading southeast to Richard's massive encampment and his mind began to whirl with what was to come. Richard would undoubtedly believe him when he told him of Simon's treachery; of that he was positive. More than that, he had within his possession the Muslim offering of peace; the Crown of Thorns that Jesus Christ wore when he was crucified. In spite of Simon's attempts to murder him, and one attempt that very nearly succeeded, he had it with him and was preparing to deliver it to the king. The mission, as he saw it, was near completion and the thought was somewhat overwhelming.

Rory's thoughts were also somewhat overwhelming and had been since she had awakened on the beach. Only now, she was growing accustomed to the miracle she found herself a part of. Off in the distance, dogs howled and Rory gazed off towards the dark and lonely desert as if to see the night creatures. There wasn't any Department of Land Management out here to keep the wolves at bay. They were wild and they were deadly. She would be glad when they reached the English encampment.

She lay her cheek against his back again, her mind wandering as the big, mean horse trotted along the road. It was a rather rolling trot, not uncomfortable in the least, and eventually she drifted off to sleep.

Kieran felt her go limp against him and held her hands together at his waist, firmly, so she wouldn't slide off. There was something inherently fulfilling having her sleeping against him. In fact, her quiet, warm presence centered and strengthened him. He took a deep breath, smelling the air, reacquainting himself with the smell and feel of his time. He'd gotten used to the exhaust fumes and chaos of Rory's time. Now, he was back.

And he had a job to do.

CHAPTER FOUR

KIERAN'S FIRST SIGN of trouble was when a projectile sailed past his head, very nearly clipping him on the helm. Startled, he yanked the charger to a halt as he tried to determine where the arrow came from. It would do no good to tear off in a panic and run right into the enemy. It was a very dark night and it took him some time to see a dark tide of figures cresting a sandy plateau in the distance. They didn't emit a sound as they rode in his direction; the only sound in the air was that of more arrows sailing towards him through the still desert air.

They were coming from the southwest, spreading out as they reached the base of the plateau. Kieran spurred his charger east, thundering out into the desolate land at top speed. He was at a distinct disadvantage. Rory was behind him and he was terrified that she would catch a stray arrow in the back. But he could not spare the time to stop the horse and remount her in front of him. His only hope was to maintain distance between him and the onslaught until he could lose them. He was familiar with the surrounding territory and he knew he was heading into increasingly open desert.

Behind him, Rory awoke with a start as the horse sped off at a gallop. She yelped, almost losing her seat but for Kieran still gripping her hands around his waist. He held her fast.

"What's wrong?" she cried. "What are you…?"

Another arrow sailed past them. This time, Rory heard it and she yelped again, burying her head against Kieran's back.

"Oh, my God," she squealed. "What's going on? Who's attacking us?"

Kieran didn't answer; he just kept running. There were a few settlements to the southeast, further out into the oases that dotted the deserts of this land, and he knew that Danun Castle about a morning's ride from Nahariya. At the moment, Danun Castle was occupied by Christian forces as it perched like a lioness on a rocky hill overlooking the arid countryside. Kieran had even spent some time there when he had first arrived in The Levant, another name for the Holy Land. He knew the castle well and he knew it would provide ample protection if they could only reach it. He pushed the horse faster.

More arrows sailed past, one of them glancing off of the armor on Kieran's right arm. Terrified, Rory tucked herself into a ball and huddled against Kieran's back, praying they would live through this. She just couldn't imagine that God, or whatever deity existed, had allowed them both to return to Kieran's time only to be murdered by bandits. The wind was whistling past her and the horse's fast gallop had her teeth rattling, but she held on tight and continued to pray. Panic or a lot of frenzied questions would not help Kieran get them out of this bind.

They flew across the rocky, sandy terrain. The wind whistled around them, whipping Rory's braids into a frenzy. The land was relatively flat but there were small, rocky outcroppings jutting intermittently out of the ground, like little hills. Kieran directed the horse around these outcroppings, creating some measure of barrier between them and their pursuers. The silver moon was a sliver against the night sky but it was enough light for Kieran to see where he was going and navigate in the direction of Danun Castle. He still didn't see any familiar landmarks as he concentrated on heading in the right direction, making sure Rory didn't slide off behind him, and ensuring that the bandits trying to catch them didn't get the chance. He was cool, collected and professional. He'd dealt with ambushes before and was relatively confident he could elude them.

But his calm demeanor shattered when Liberator suddenly went down. The horse stepped in a hole in the darkened desert landscape and went head over heels, pitching Kieran and Rory off. Kieran did nothing more than hit heavily in all of his weighty armor, which protected him from the fall, but Rory sailed through the air and landed on her head and right shoulder. Knocked unconscious, she lay lifeless as Kieran rolled to his feet.

Liberator was unharmed except for a big scrape on the side of his neck. He remained next to Kieran as the knight bolted into a standing position. He raced to Rory, lying motionless on the sand, and gathered her into his arms.

"Sweetheart," he murmured urgently. "Can you hear me? Wake up, Lib. Wake up and look at me."

Rory remained still. Her right ear and the side of her face were scraped from having come into contact with the rocky soil. Kieran tried to get a look at her ear, which he thought was trickling blood, also. Sickened at the sight to the point of being almost physically ill, he nonetheless retained sense enough to make his way back to the horse.

His panicked gaze surveyed the landscape, seeing a couple of phantom riders in the distance against the black night but little else. He had time to continue on, now with the added terror of Rory's injury. Just as he reached Liberator, an elaborate dagger with a curved, beveled blade sailed through the air and landed between him and the horse. Although startled by the weapon, Kieran appeared outwardly calm as several Saracen riders emerged like vengeful wraiths from behind a rocky outcropping.

Kieran sized up the situation in an instant. He was at an extreme disadvantage with Rory in his arms and his broadsword on his saddle. He further knew that they were in a good deal of trouble; he was an experienced warrior. He knew that all the posturing in the world would not get him out of this situation. Had it only been him, he would not have known any fear. But with Rory injured and vulnerable, he fought down the panic that threatened. Eyes on the enemy, he spoke to the horse.

"*Courir à la maison*," he hissed. "*Hâte*!"

Liberator snorted, reared up, and bolted off. Even if he and Rory were about to be captured, he didn't want the horse or the contents of his saddlebags, to fall into enemy hands. Liberator was smart; he knew the way back to Richard's camp. It was only a few miles away. Kieran could only pray that Richard found the horse and grew nosy enough to dig into the saddlebags. He didn't even care if the man sent out a search party. All he wanted was for the king to find the Muslim gift of peace that was waiting for him buried in the weathered leather.

"I do not have a weapon," Kieran announced in a steady, booming voice. "My lady is injured. I ask for your mercy."

One man broke off from the rest and pursued Liberator as the horse raced off into the night. The other riders, eight in all, lingered in the darkness in a semi-circle around Kieran and Rory, like vultures waiting for the kill. Kieran stood there, clutching Rory against his chest, waiting for someone to make a move. Knowing the Saracens as he did, he knew that if they were going to kill him, they would have done it right away and was puzzled with the apparent hesitance. It put him more on his guard. Beneath his heavy armor, he was beginning to sweat. Having Rory in his arms changed everything dramatically.

A horse finally separated from the group and moved towards him. Kieran had daggers on his body but he couldn't get to them with Rory in his arms. And he couldn't move her behind him to protect her, so he stood his ground with Rory clutched against his chest like a shield. He showed no outward fear as the horse and rider came upon him, but sweat was running in rivers down his neck.

The man braced a hand against his thigh and leaned down. His face was wrapped in a scarf of many colors that formed a turban around his head and neck. He was dressed in fairly luxurious robes made from linen more than likely imported from Egypt, as that was a major fabric port, and the fantastic scimitar sword hung off his saddle. It was a deadly, arched weapon that had been the scourge of the Christian armies. The only things visible on the man's face were his dark eyes, glittering back at Kieran in the weak moonlight.

"*Que faites-vous hors ici*, Hage?" the man asked with quiet irony.

Kieran was startled by not only the question, but by the man apparently knowing his name. He struggled to keep his calm.

"Do I know you?" he asked steadily.

The man paused, just long enough to feed Kieran's unrest, before unwinding the scarf, partially exposing his rugged features.

"Do you know this face, my friend?" he asked quietly.

Kieran's eyes widened. "Yusef?"

Yusef Ibn Ahmed Ibn ad-Din smiled, shaking his head as he did so. "You did not answer my question. What are you doing so far from Richard's camp?"

Kieran puffed out his cheeks, feeling an indistinct measure of relief roll through his body. "I was returning to camp when you and your men found me," he explained. "Why did you chase me?"

Yusef shrugged. "Because you are a Christian knight, alone. That is reason enough," he said. "You know better than to travel alone out in this land. But I did not know it was you until we drew close."

"So what do you intend to do now that you know it is me?" Kieran looked down at Rory in his arms and the tendrils of panic he had been struggling to stave off began to grab at him. "My… my wife was badly hurt when my charger fell. I must return her to camp immediately."

Yusef swung himself off his elaborately decorated horse, peering closely at Rory. Kieran wasn't a physic. He had no real knowledge of healing other than battlefield wounds. That wasn't really healing, anyway; it was either stemming a blood flow, cramming intestines back into a sliced belly, or tying off a severed limb. When Yusef lifted Rory's eyelids and inspected the blood flowing out of her right ear, Kieran let him. Yusef was one of the very few Saracens he trusted.

The man was one of Salah-ad Din's cousins, a servant of the great Saracen general El-Hajidd, one of the men who wanted peace between the Muslims and Christians. He had been at the head of the peace delegation from El-Hajidd that had presented Kieran and the other English knights with the Crown of Thorns reputed to have belonged to Jesus Christ, an offering demonstrating their willingness to cease fighting. So Kieran and Yusef knew and trusted each other, as much as enemies could.

After a careful examination, Yusef looked up at Kieran. "This is your wife?"

Kieran's gaze was steady. "Aye."

"You brought her with you from England?"

Kieran wasn't sure how to answer him. "My lady and I will not be separated." It was the truth.

Yusef grunted, looking at Rory one last time, noting the chestnut hair and exquisite features. She was quite lovely. "It was foolish, Hage."

"I had no choice."

Yusef thought on that a moment before finally waving his hand at Kieran. "Your camp is too far away," he said. "She needs help immediately. Come, let us return to Nahariya. I know a man there who can help."

Kieran watched him as he mounted his fine-featured Arabian horse. "But my charger is more than likely halfway back to Richard's camp by now," he said. "I do not have a mount."

Yusef shouted over his shoulder, speaking quickly in Arabic. One of his men dismounted and brought his horse over to Kieran. Yusef gestured to the animal.

"Ride," Yusef told him. "We return to Nahariya."

Kieran wasn't thrilled with returning to the city he was trying so hard to escape. "That may not be wise," he said, not wanting to appear ungrateful. "A man is trying to kill me and will make an attempt tonight in Nahariya. I was attempting to get clear of the city."

Yusef shook his head, barking orders to his men in Arabic. The men suddenly began to flee, heading northwest at breakneck speed.

"Mount the horse," he ordered again. "We will protect you from assassins."

Kieran wanted to protest but he didn't have much of a choice. It was more important to get Rory to a physic. Even as he mounted the horse, he reminded himself repeatedly that Fate had returned them to his time for a reason. It was, however, increasingly unclear what that reason was. As they raced across the starlit desert towards the distant glowing town of Nahariya, he prayed very hard for two things: that Simon would not find him and be given a second chance to murder him, and that Rory would be all right.

But the situation was already changed. This time, as he entered the outskirts of the town, he had bodyguards, something he'd not had the first time Simon had tried to kill him. Even as he found himself entering the heart of the city, he realized that he was not particularly fearful. Even if Simon and his cutthroats saw him, they wouldn't dare make a move with the host of Saracen soldiers surrounding him.

Turning a corner on a dusty, deserted alley, they ended up in front of a ramshackle and leaning structure. Kieran dismounted with Rory in his arms, still unconscious. He kissed her forehead, more concern than he had ever known consuming him as he approached the shack that Yusef was indicating. He didn't notice the door of the hut until they were upon it and a carving of a flaming candle came into view. As realization dawned, it was as if an unseen fist slammed into his chest. Kieran suddenly couldn't breathe. He must have swayed because Yusef reached out to steady him, encouraging him to move forward. But, for a moment, Kieran couldn't seem to move.

There before him was the door of the alchemist who had put him into stasis after Simon's murder attempt, a stasis that froze his bodily functions until Rory, eight hundred years later, dug him up and awoke him with a kiss. It was the very same man and the fact that he found himself back at the man's door was more than odd. It was frighteningly coincidental and he resisted the urge to run. There was a sickening sense of déjà vu.

History was repeating itself in a slightly different fashion.

CHAPTER FIVE

"KALEEF," KIERAN BREATHED.

Yusef looked at Kieran curiously as he pounded on the door. "You know this man?"

Kieran nodded. Then he shook his head. Truth was, he wasn't quite sure how to respond. The door opened before he could speak and Yusef was diverted when a tiny old man with skin as brown as leather suddenly yanked open the door.

"*Sharif,*" Yusef gave the man the traditional Muslim greeting. His hand touched his forehead and lips in a flourished gesture. "My English friend has an injured wife. Will you tend her?"

Kaleef waved the lot of them off irritably. "I am not a surgeon," he snapped, trying to shove his ill-fitting door closed. "Take her elsewhere."

Before Yusef could negotiate, Kieran stepped forward and lashed out a massive boot, shoving the door open. The old man nearly toppled.

"I know you are an alchemist," he growled, ducking his head low as he bowed in through the doorway. "But I also know you have the power to sustain life. You will help my wife."

Kaleef almost tripped on himself attempting to move out of the big knight's way. He scooted after Kieran as the man entered his small, cluttered hut and looked for someplace to lay Rory down.

"I told you I am not a physic." He waved his arms around like a bird attempting to take flight. "Get out!"

Yusef came in behind Kieran, trying to be more diplomatic. Yusef was a handsome man, young with fine features and a neatly-clipped beard. His manner was very calming. "She is injured," he explained again. "Will you at least look at her before determining if you cannot help her?"

"Nay!"

"There is much gold if you will help her."

That seemed to calm the old man down somewhat. Truth was, he was frightened and agitated. A host of Saracens and one enormous English knight were invading his hut and he was verging on panic. Kaleef lived a rather hermit-like life; he did not get on with other people well. He eyed Yusef as the man produced a large gold coin, took the old man's hand, and planted it squarely in his palm. The tangible evidence of money seemed to change the old man's mind.

"Do not place her there!" he squawked as Kieran moved to put Rory on something that resembled a bed. He swept his arm across the table in the middle of the room, knocking off bowls, cups and a variety of other items. "Put her here!"

Kieran did as he was told and lay Rory down on a rough-hewn table. She groaned the moment she hit the table surface and Kieran's heart lurched.

"Lib?" he whispered urgently. "Libby, can you hear me?"

She sighed painfully, her hand flying to her head. "Kieran?" she asked weakly.

He kissed her hand several times, his enormous palm on her forehead. "I am here, sweetheart."

She groaned again, both hands on her head now. "My God," she breathed as her eyes struggled open. "What happened?"

"My horse fell." His mouth was on her hands, his big body hovering over her. "You were pitched off and hit your head. How do you feel?"

She was breathing rapidly, shallowly. Before she could answer Kieran, Kaleef came up on the other side of her with a potion in his hand. Rory's half-open eyes caught motion out of the corner of her eye and she started as the old man appeared.

"Drink this," he commanded gruffly.

"Oh, my God," she said as she shrank away, pressing herself against Kieran and away from the extremely wrinkled old man. "Who in the hell are you?"

Kieran tried to comfort her. "This man is a healer."

"I am not a healer," the little old man flared, smacking his toothless mouth as he shoved the wooden cup at Rory again. "Drink."

Rory was becoming more lucid even though her head was swimming and her stomach lurched. She felt as if she were listening to everything through a tube; her ears seemed to be plugged. Her face hurt, her shoulders and back hurt, and she simply wanted to lay down and sleep. This crazy old man with the crazy-looking cap on his head wasn't helping her state.

"I'm not drinking anything," she said flatly, looking up at Kieran and squinting her eyes as if there were too much light in the room. "Where are we?"

"Back in Nahariya," Kieran said steadily.

Her muddled eyes widened. "Back in…?" she suddenly struggled to sit up. "We need to get out of here. Why in the world did you bring us back here?"

Yusef suddenly appeared next to Kieran, smiling pleasantly and greeting her with the traditional Muslim salute; fingers to forehead to lips. "Lady Hage," he spoke with an accent so thick that Rory could barely understand him. "You were injured. We brought you to the healer."

"I am not a healer!" Kaleef spat, grabbing Rory by the shoulder and shoving her back onto the table. "Drink this or I'll not lift another finger to help you!"

Rory was nauseous, in pain, and didn't like the old man in the least. He was rude and smelled to high heaven of feces. She lashed out a fist and shoved him back by the chest, spilling the contents of the cup.

"I'm not drinking anything!" She struggled to get off the table but Kieran held her firm. "Leave me alone. I'm getting out of here."

Kieran was trying to keep her calm and be gentle with her but she was struggling a great deal. "I would feel better if he could examine you to ensure that you are well enough to travel." He had her by the upper arms. "Please, Lib. Will you please do this for me?"

She was half-off the table, feeling woozy. Frightened and disoriented, the tears started coming. "I don't want to drink anything," she whispered pleadingly. "Please, Kieran. I don't want to eat or drink anything."

He held her face between his two enormous hands. "He is not going to poison you, I swear it." He looked at the old man who was standing on the other side of the table muttering angrily to himself. "Tell her what is in your potion so she will not fear it."

The old man made a face, shaking the spilt potion from his hands. "Marigold, white willow and crushed arnica petals, you silly girl."

Kieran looked down at Rory's pale face. Tears were streaming onto his gloves and she was struggling not to sob. He kissed her forehead, the tip of her nose. "Do you trust me?" he whispered.

She could only nod and he continued. "Then trust me now. I will not let any harm befall you, I swear it. I am trying to help you."

Rory gazed up into his clear brown eyes, knowing he was right. He would never intentionally or knowingly let any harm befall her. But she was injured and disoriented and the thought of drinking a Medieval potion did not sit well. She just needed a couple of naproxen and sleep and she would feel much better. But that wasn't available. She struggled to clear her muddled mind and remember what she knew about Medieval medicine and the properties of those ingredients from her Pre-Med days. Think, girl, she told herself. This is your time. You know about this period!

"If I recall, marigold was used for stomach ailments," she muttered, taking a deep breath to relax her jangled nerves. "Willow is aspirin, basically. And arnica is an anti-inflammatory."

Kieran watched her reason her way through the potion. "Will you drink it?"

Rory regarded him for a moment before turning to Kaleef. It was then she began to notice their surroundings. The hut was small, smoky, and rats skittered along the base of the walls; she could hear them. It was also hugely cluttered, like a hoarder, with things she couldn't even begin to identify. Bowls of stuff littered the three tables that were scattered throughout the hut and there were shelves of more bowls, plates, sacks and vials. It was a crazy place, like a mad scientist's lab from a cartoon. It stank of feces and other things she didn't recognize. In spite of her throbbing head and rolling stomach, she found a great deal of interest in the wild and foreign room.

"You said you're not a healer," she said to the tiny old man. "What are you?"

The old man peered strangely at her. "What are your words?"

She cocked her head. "Can't you understand me?"

"I understand you. But you speak strangely."

Kieran spoke before she could respond. "My wife asked you a question," he said in his firm, deep voice. "You will answer her."

Rory cast him an odd look. "Wife?" she mouthed.

He lifted an eyebrow at her and she shrugged, turning back to the little brown man. She was startled to realize that he had moved close to her, eyeing her most strangely. Although Rory wasn't tall, about five feet four inches, she felt like a giant next to the old man who was now standing very close and inspecting her carefully. He didn't seem as agitated or angry as he had earlier. In fact, he seemed genuinely curious.

"You have a wound on your face," he observed.

Rory's hand flew to her face, feeling the scrape on her right cheek. "Oh, my God," she gasped with horror, looking at Kieran with panic. "Is it bad?"

He shook his head. "Nay," he murmured. "You are as beautiful as ever."

But Rory was distressed. "I'd give my eye teeth for a mirror right now," she muttered, fingers still fluttering over the scrape as she looked to the old man. "Do… do you have something that can heal this?"

The old man's black eyes twinkled. "Tell me from whence you come. You are not English."

It was clear that he was more interested in her personally than in her physical state. She lifted an eyebrow at him. "I'll tell you where I'm from if you tell me why you said that you're not a healer," she replied.

"I am an alchemist."

"Alchemists don't use things like marigold and willow."

"My knowledge is not limited. I have what I have and I use what I use."

He had a slight smile on his face, as if waiting for her great secret. She couldn't help but smile at the nosy old man; she suddenly didn't feel so hostile or upset any more. The old man had transformed from something odd and scary to something odd and strangely interesting.

"I'm from a country you have never heard of, very far away. I'm not English, or German, or French. It's called America."

"Where is this place?"

She lifted an arm, pointing towards the door although she had no idea which direction she was really pointing in.

"Across the sea," she told him. "Very far away."

At this point, Kieran intervened. His Saracen comrades were listening and they tended to be superstitious and suspicious. He didn't want them thinking she was a product of black magic, or worse. Rory spoke with an odd enough accent without that additional worry.

"Will you give her your potion now?" he said rather authoritatively.

The old man's gaze lingered on Rory a moment longer before he turned away and went back to his mysterious medicaments. Rory, to Kieran's surprise, followed. As the old man began to mix things in a rough wooden cup, she stood next to him and inspected the oddities of the table.

"What's this?" she asked, pointing to a dusty bag with white powder seeping from it.

He didn't look at her as he continued to mix. "Sulphur."

She lifted an eyebrow at it for one final inspection and moved on to a bowl with dark liquid in it. "And this?"

"Ram's blood."

She made a face and moved on, smelling and touching. Surprisingly, Kaleef let her; he never uttered a word while she rummaged through his possessions. But Rory was starting to come alive, deeply interested in everything in front of her. Archaeological digs were one thing, touching items that were hundreds and thousands of years old, inspecting and studying them. She'd spent years of her life studying how others interpreted history. But to see Medieval items in their original state as they were meant to be was absolutely fascinating. Her archaeologist's mind was kicking in.

"If I recall," she said, peering into another bowl of something smelly and coagulated. "Alchemists use sulphur because they believe it emulates the sun. What do you use it for?"

Kaleef remained silent as he stirred the contents of the cup. Then he turned to her and extended it. "It is the sun," he told her flatly. "Drink this."

Rory's first reaction was to resist. She pursed her lips to retort but caught a glimpse of Kieran from the corner of her eye. His expression was pleading, calming. He had asked her to cooperate and since they had arrived in this distant place and time, she hadn't done a very good job. She was bucking and resisting at every turn and she realized that she didn't want to do that any longer; for Kieran's sake, she would behave. The man had enough stress on his hands at the moment.

Reluctantly, she took the cup and took a sip; it was bitter. Taking a deep breath, she drank it quickly like a shot of tequila. Handing the cup back to Kaleef, she looked over at Kieran and he smiled his approval. She smiled weakly in return, coming to notice the host of Saracens standing around and behind him. Now that her wits were returning, she was beginning to grow curious and fearful of their presence. She fixed on the man standing next to Kieran with the fine features and neatly-trimmed beard.

"Kieran?" she spoke to him even though she was looking at the good-looking man. "Aren't you going to introduce me to your, uh, friend?"

Before Kieran could reply, Kaleef walked up next to her, grabbed her chin, and began smearing something gooey on her scraped cheek. Rory danced around like a kid who just had a cut sprayed with antiseptic, but she didn't pull away. She let him smear.

"Hey," she protested. "What in the heck is that?"

Kaleef gave her face one last stroke with the salve. "Calendula and boiled cow's urine," he told her. "It will heal your face and prevent poison."

She let out a strangled yelp, holding her hands up but stopping short of putting them on her face. She knew that boiled cow's urine had certain medicinal qualities to prevent infection. "Oh, God," she gasped. "Cow's urine on my face. I think I'm going to hurl."

Kieran fought off a grin, bent over and kissed her on the opposite cheek. "You smell strangely," he rubbed it in.

She scowled. "You're not funny."

"Aye, I am." He took her by the arm, presenting her to the man standing next to him. "This is my friend, Yusef ad-Din. He is the one who brought us here for help."

Rory smiled faintly at the richly brown Saracen, still puzzled as to how and why the man was here. She noted the heavy, dusty robes, layers of them, in faded reds and yellows that were elaborately tasseled. He had a neatly wrapped turban around his head and neck.

"Thank you for your help," she said after a moment. "It's very nice to meet you."

Yusef's dark eyes glittered. "The pleasure is mine, Lady Hage. Are you feeling better?"

"A little," she admitted.

Yusef looked between Kieran and his absolutely gorgeous, though strangely speaking, wife. "Praise to Allah," he said. "It was our fault that you were injured. I hope that you will forgive."

Rory wasn't sure what to say. She looked at Kieran uncertainly and he put his massive arm around her shoulders.

"It 'twas Yusef and his warriors pursuing us," he explained. "They did not know it was me and, consequently, are very sorry to have caused your injury. That is why they brought us here."

Rory lifted an eyebrow, half-shrugging as her gaze returned to Yusef and his frightening warriors. She could see them lingering in the shadows, tattooed and swarthy, with assortments of daggers about their bodies. The realization that she was gazing upon true Saracen warriors did not escape her. As she had done with Kieran when the man had first donned his mail and armor, she began to visually inspect Yusef and his men closely.

"May I ask you a few questions?" she asked Yusef.

He bowed gallantly. "I am at your service, Lady Hage."

She took a step towards him, the hazel eyes glittering. "The writing you have on your bodies," she indicated the men behind Yusef. "Is it true that they are passages from the Koran? Is it put on specific places on your body to represent specific wishes or blessings?"

Yusef's expression took on an odd look. He looked at Kieran with some surprise as the big knight suddenly put his hands on Rory's shoulders and pulled her back against him. His lips went to her good ear.

"Watch what you ask, Lib," he hissed. "Men of this time do not appreciate nor respect bold women. You must learn to keep your mouth shut. If you have specific questions, you will ask me. Is that clear?"

She nodded, looking at Yusef with a wide-eyed expression. "I'm sorry," she said to Yusef. "I didn't mean to offend you. It's just that the writing is so beautiful and I was curious."

Yusef scratched beneath his turban in an indecisive gesture, eyeing Kieran again before breaking down into snorts.

"You did not offend me, lady," he replied. "You are not native to this land. You do not understand our ways."

"No, I don't," she insisted strongly, putting up her hands as if to beg an apology. "I am truly sorry. I didn't mean any harm."

"Or course you did not."

Kieran let that be the end of it, pulling Rory away from Yusef and turning her back towards Kaleef. The old man now had a rag in his hand and was carrying a bowl with an unidentifiable liquid in it. He set it down on the rickety old table, grabbed Rory by the chin again, and began cleaning out her bloodied ear.

She shrieked as he put the rag to her ear, terrified that it was filthy and unsanitary. But she said nothing as he cleaned the blood away and peered in her ear. Seemingly satisfied, he took both of her arms and pushed the sleeves back, inspecting the limbs. When he seemed content with his inspection, he turned back to his bowl and rag, carrying them back over to an uneven table against the wall of the hut where his medicaments were stored.

"She will heal," he said. "The injuries are not severe."

Kieran nodded with relief. "Then we may travel?"

"You may." Kaleef turned to cast the lady a long glance. "Her head will ache and her pains will be stronger tomorrow, but they should fade with time. It would be good for the lady to rest tomorrow if she can."

"Excellent," Kieran replied as he looked at Rory. "We shall continue on to the king's encampment tonight and you may rest tomorrow."

Rory simply nodded, casting one final glance around the strange and mysterious place. Kaleef was still looking at her and she met his gaze. It was an appreciative moment that passed between them.

"I think you really are a healer," she said, the corner of her mouth twitching. "I wouldn't be surprised if you were a very good one."

Kaleef lifted his shoulders and turned back to wiping out his bowl, but not before she caught a glimpse of an old smile. She was about to say something else to the old man when the door to his hut rattled. Someone was knocking loudly.

Someone was screaming as well. Kaleef didn't move but Kieran did. He went to the door as the Saracen warriors around him drew their elaborate scimitar swords. A few drew great bejeweled daggers but, for the most part, every man was armed with something very deadly and very beautiful. Startled, Rory ended up standing next to Kaleef as Kieran yanked the stodgy, old door open.

A very old woman stood outside, her eyes full of tears and her toothless mouth leaking mucus and saliva. She was weeping hysterically.

"What is your trouble, woman?" Kieran asked in a cold, booming voice that Rory had never heard from him before. "What do you want?"

The woman tried to speak but ended up faltering. Kieran caught her before she could go down and she clung to him hysterically.

"He… he's killed him!" she stammered. "Kaleef! Where is Kaleef?"

Kieran pushed the woman back to her feet, realizing it was the old woman from Hut's hostel. He wasn't sure why, but an alarm suddenly went off in his head. He yanked the old woman inside and slammed the door. Rory, seeing that he was being very brutal with the old woman, moved forward to assist; her assistance constituted pushing Kieran's hands off the hysterical female. She didn't yet recognize the old woman as the same one who had provided her with the clothing she currently wore.

Kieran didn't particularly notice that Rory had removed his hands; he was more concerned with the reason for the old woman's presence and focused on her intently. He was increasingly on edge.

"Who has been killed?" he demanded harshly. "Make sense, woman. Who do you speak of?"

Kaleef came up behind Rory, his old face showing some concern as he recognized the old woman. "It is Teeta," he said to no one in particular. "She is Hut's wife."

Kieran's head snapped to Kaleef as the old man confirmed his observation. His trepidation bloomed. Before he could press the woman further, she exploded with grief.

"He killed Hut!" she cried. "He came for the English but he was not there. So he killed Hut!"

A black, dreadful sense of foreboding filled Kieran. He grabbed the old woman by the arms and forced her to look at him. "Who killed Hut?"

The woman gasped and drooled. "The… the knight. The English!"

Kieran shook her and the woman's head snapped back. "Look at me," he growled. "Look at me and tell me. Who was this English knight?"

The woman's eyes widened at him as if suddenly recognizing him. She began to squeal. "He wanted you," she exclaimed.

"How do know he wanted me?"

The woman was nearly beyond the ability to comprehend what she was being asked. "You," she sobbed loudly. "He asked if Hut had seen a big Englishman taller than the sky. Hut told him that you had left and the man killed him!"

Kaleef grasped at the old woman. "Are you sure Hut is dead?"

Teeta abu-Syamm clutched at the old alchemist. "You must come," she wept deeply. "I know you can save his life. You have done this before. You can make him sleep the sleep of the dead and your potions will heal him."

Kaleef pulled the woman with him, away from the ears that were hearing of his deep, dark secrets. He did not want anyone else to know that his occupation as a healer had led to the desire to find immortality, among other things. Kaleef was a brilliant and curious man. A few knew of his miraculous potions, but not many. What he did bordered on black magic and he did not want the word to get out.

Rory let the woman go, watching her move with Kaleef and hearing nothing more than whispers between them. Kieran came to stand next to her, watching the pitiful scene right along with her.

"Kaleef is the alchemist who put me into stasis," he murmured.

It took a moment for his softly uttered words to sink in. Then Rory's head jerked to him, her eyes wide as she gazed up into his handsome face. "*That's* the guy?" she hissed. "My God, why didn't you tell me before?"

"There was no opportunity."

She was astonished; her mouth hung open as she stared up at him. "I don't believe it," she muttered. "Seriously? That's the same alchemist?"

"Aye."

He seemed rather calm about it but she was working herself up into a state. "Kieran, that guy has discovered something so fantastic that it's never been duplicated, ever." She couldn't understand why he wasn't more excited about it. "Why didn't you…?"

Kieran shushed her under the guise of a kiss. Then he kissed her again just because he wanted to. He put his big arms around her, pulling her into a protective, private cocoon where their conversation could not be heard.

"Not another word, Lib," he whispered. "I do not want Yusef or his men to hear. We have returned to the same man who gave me his potions that put me to sleep for eight hundred years, only to be awoken by your kiss. That is how I knew he could help you. He helped me to live and I knew he would do the same for you. And Hut's wife; she knows it as well because it was Hut who sent me to Kaleef after I was wounded by Simon's assassins."

The information was overwhelming. Rory struggled to digest everything he was telling her, her sharp mind working through the situation and coming to a horrifying, rapid conclusion.

"Then… then the man who just killed Hut must have been Simon, looking for you," she whispered. "Why did he kill Hut instead?"

Kieran shrugged. "I can only surmise that it was because he was angry that I had left," he muttered, glancing over his shoulder at Yusef and his men. He suddenly emitted a pent-up sigh, scratching his forehead as he did so. "So now I find myself back in Nahariya, back with the alchemist who put me to sleep in order to save my life. But this time, Hut has been killed by Simon instead of me."

Rory was truly bewildered as she, too, realized that history was taking a slightly different twist this time. "Oh, God," she breathed. "What does it all mean?"

"I do not know."

She suddenly looked stricken. "What if… what if Simon followed Hut's wife here? What if he followed her when she ran?"

Kieran shook his head. “He would have no reason to unless…”

He trailed off and Rory finished for him. “Unless he thought she was running to warn you.”

Kieran suddenly pushed Rory into the heart of Hut’s small cottage, shoving her at the old man. When she looked at him with a mixture of fear and indignation, he pointed a gloved finger at her.

“Stay here with Kaleef,” he commanded. “Do not leave this place.”

“No, Kieran.” She grabbed on to him and dug her heels in. “You’re not going anywhere. You can’t leave me.”

“You will not argue.”

“You don’t even have a weapon,” she pointed out hotly. “What in the hell are you thinking?”

Kieran was close to losing his temper with her; he hadn’t time to argue. He looked at the somewhat startled Kaleef.

“Do you have a sword?” he demanded.

Kaleef nodded, pointing to the far corner of his cottage. As Rory continued her protests, Kieran plowed his way through the clutter to the back of the hut, looking for what Kaleef considered to be a weapon of some kind. Yusef was right behind him.

“What is wrong?” he demanded softly.

Kieran spotted the sword. It was an old scimitar, dark with age and somewhat worn. But it was the only thing available and Kieran collected it swiftly, kicking aside the clutter that was on top of it.

“Those assassins I told you of,” he muttered, his eyes moving from Yusef to the weeping Teeta. “I fear that old woman may have led them straight to us.”

Yusef didn’t ask any more questions. He acted swiftly, barking orders to his men in the fluid, foreign syllables of Arabic and putting the group on alert. No sooner had the orders left his lips than the door to Kaleef’s hut rattled again, this time violently. When it suddenly exploded in a shower of splinters, Kieran, Yusef and the Saracen warriors rushed the door with weapons drawn.

Rory couldn’t even see who they were fighting. It was suddenly one big giant melee and she was rightly terrified. In the rush, someone kicked over an oil lamp and the toppled flame lit one of the old tables on fire. Kaleef grabbed Rory and began shoving her back towards the alcove where Kieran had found the old sword.

"Go," he yelped. "Get out of here before everything explodes."

Rory didn't want to leave Kieran and she protested vehemently. "No," she shouted. "I'm not leaving without Kieran. Kieran!"

Kieran was on the opposite side of the hut, battling two men he recognized from Simon's arsenal. Yet, oddly enough, he had not seen Simon yet. With all of the noise going on around him, swords meeting and men yelling, he didn't hear Rory's frantic cry. He had no idea that Kaleef had shoved her out through a small back entrance as the fire in the hut grew. In fact, he didn't even notice the fire until Yusef happened to mention it in between sword thrusts. Suddenly, Kieran realized there was a very big fire between him and Rory, and his focus began to shift.

"Libby!" he bellowed, trying not to get his head cut off as he continued to battle. "*Rory*!"

He couldn't see the main part of the hut through the smoke and fire and, terrified, he kicked his opponent away and charged through the flame, catching his tunic on fire and beating out the flames as he called Rory's name again. The smoke was growing heavy and, coughing, he noticed the small, open doorway in the alcove off to his left. He charged through it as the flames began to consume the walls of the hut.

He was barely into the open air when Rory was suddenly throwing herself at him, her arms around his neck. Off guard, he lost his balance momentarily as she tackled him. But his arms went swiftly around her, relieved beyond words that she was all right. It took him a moment to realize she was weeping hysterically. He held her tightly.

"All is well, sweetheart," he murmured into her hair, kissing her head. "Calm yourself; all is well now. But we must get out of here."

She held him a moment longer, utterly terrified and relieved, before letting go and sliding to the ground. "Are you all right?" she sniffled, wiping the tears from her face. "Are you hurt?"

He shook his head, grasping her by the elbow and leading her swiftly down the dark and spooky alley. “Where is Kaleef?”

She ran alongside him as they made their way through the shadowed streets, putting distance between them and the burning hut. “He and the old woman ran off,” she said. “He tried to get me to go with him but I wouldn’t.”

Kieran held her fast as they continued to run. “We must make haste to put distance between us and Simon’s men.”

“Did you see Simon?”

“Nay. But I am sure he was there, somewhere.”

Horses were suddenly thundering behind them. Kieran yanked Rory into an alcove in between houses, holding her tightly as the horses drew near. He knew they could never outrun the horses so it was best to hide. He could hear the men calling to each other in English and his heart sank. If there was ever any doubt that Simon had found him, it was gone. Simon was upon them.

CHAPTER SIX

HE WAS A big man with big hands and a crown of light blond hair. His eyes were brown, his face sharp and hawk-like. Sir Simon de Corlet came from an extremely old family, one that had come to England's shores with William the Conqueror, and he held the mannerisms and sense of entitlement that breeding like that produced. He was cruel, arrogant, loud and privileged.

Simon had known Kieran Hage since they had been pages at Kenilworth Castle. He both deeply loved and deeply resented Kieran. As the years passed, the men grew closer but Kieran, as always, was the favored one. He was bigger, strong, more benevolent, wiser, and the better warrior. Simon adored Kieran but mostly stayed close to him hoping to glean something from Kieran's glory.

When the secret meeting between the Muslims and the Christians took place, Kieran was at the head of the delegation and Simon only saw greater glory for Kieran than he had ever known. Simon would have none of it; at that moment his resentment for Kieran grew greater than his love. He tried to kill Kieran and take the crown. But when that didn't work and Kieran evaded him, Simon did the only thing he could. He sent word to the king that he had caught Kieran Hage in a traitorous act against the Christian armies. It was a preemptive strike that he hoped would discredit Kieran in the eyes of the king so that Simon could capture or kill Kieran and say he had done it in the name of the king.

But it was more than that. Before Simon left for The Levant, he had been given a directive from his father, a man extremely loyal to Henry II and, consequently, Prince John. Simon had been given specific instructions from his father to watch Richard and to do what was necessary to preserve the cause of Henry II and Prince John. He'd stopped short of asking his son to assassinate the king, but the message had been obvious. Simon was too fearful to outright assassinate a monarch, instead hoping that prolonged battle would accomplish the task naturally. If Kieran delivered the Muslim peace offering, then the opportunity for extended battle, and Richard's death as a result, would be ended.

But Kieran was as wise and strong as Simon knew him to be. He had, thus far, evaded Simon's attempts to kill him. But that was soon to end. Having tracked Kieran to a hostel in Nahariya, Simon and his men descended upon the place only to be told by the innkeeper that Kieran had fled.

In a rage, Simon had killed the innkeeper but the man's wife had run off screaming. It was only a hunch to follow the howling woman, a hunch that had paid off. They had found Kieran near the outskirts of Nahariya with a group of Saracens. The savages fought fiercely on Kieran's behalf and Simon began to wonder if the lie he fed to the king wasn't in some part true. Perhaps Kieran was a traitor after all. He could not account for the savages willing to defend him.

He'd caught a glimpse of Kieran as the fighting started. Then the hut that Kieran had been hiding in had caught fire and the man had disappeared into the smoke. Simon eventually recognized one of the Saracens. The man had been at the secret meeting when the Crown of Thorns had been presented to the Christian delegation. As the fighting worsened and Kieran seemed to have disappeared completely, Simon sent four of his men to see if Kieran had managed to escape from the burning structure. He ordered the men that remained with him to back off of the fight.

The hut was in flames, disintegrating before his eyes. There were several Saracen warriors inside and Simon backed off as the flames grew.

"*Sauvages!*" he bellowed. "*J'offre vous cesse*!"

The fighting continued in spite of the order to cease. Simon screamed to his own men, ordering them to halt, and they backed off even as the Saracens continued the hostilities. Simon dismounted his horse, shoving aside battling men and making his way towards Yusef.

"Ad-Din," he shouted. "*Arrêter la lutte*!"

Yusef's sword was arched high over his head, preparing to come down on one of Simon's men but he stopped mid-stroke, watching Simon walk towards him. He recognized the English knight, a colleague of Hage's. Confusion filled his face.

"You?" he spoke in a baffled whisper. "*You* are the assassin?"

Simon's brown eyes glittered. "Sir Kieran is a traitor."

Yusef's puzzlement grew. "What madness is this?"

Simon motioned to the rest of his men, silently ordering them to sheathe their weapons and mount their horses. He backed up towards his horse, keeping his weapon leveled.

"He met with savages in a secret to plot planning the downfall of the Christian armies," Simon replied evenly. "I have told the king that Kieran is a traitor. Of course, I am in fear for my life from Kieran for the man knows that I am aware of his treachery. If Kieran returns to Richard's camp, he will be arrested. Since you apparently have contact with Kieran, you will tell him this."

Yusef stared at the man, wondering at the chaos of the situation. Although he recognized Simon, he did not know the man as he knew Kieran. Kieran had been the knight with the fair reputation, close to the English king, two factors that caused the Saracens to consider Kieran a man to trust for their message of peace. De Corlet had come with Kieran as a trusted associate. But now, that was apparently not so. Simon had turned against Kieran for reasons Yusef could not even begin to guess. But there was a strong sense of resentment along with his confusion.

"Why would you tell your king that Kieran is a traitor?" He shook his head, baffled. "You were at the secret meeting also. You know this is not true."

Some of Simon's smugness fled. "I will not explain myself to a savage," he snarled, leaping onto the back of his charger. "You will tell Kieran that if he tries to returns to Richard's camp, he will be killed before he can reach it."

With that, he reined his horse brutally, digging his long, golden spurs into the side of the beast and charging off into the darkness. His men charged after him, leaving a massive cloud of dust in their wake. Yusef stood there with his warriors, watching the Christian knights disappear into the shadows as Kaleef's hut went up in flames behind them. By this time, some of the neighbors had been aroused and several threw buckets of sand on the blaze, trying to keep it from spreading to their homes. As the blaze roared, Yusef and his men simply walked away.

"What do we do?" one of Yusef's men hissed at him.

Yusef kept walking as his men grouped around him, heading for the horses that were tethered by the small livery at the end of the block. Beyond his confusion now, he was simply feeling anger and, if he were to admit it, a little fear. Something strange was happening and he began to fear for his own life, wondering if there were Muslims that felt the same way as the Christians did. Nothing was clear any longer. Goodwill and benevolence were vanished.

"Find Kieran," he snapped, watching his men run off and collect their mounts. "He cannot have gotten far. Find him before that Christian devil does."

☙

HORSES WERE RUSHING past their hiding place and Kieran held Rory tightly, his massive arms wrapped around her protectively as the clear brown eyes watched the passing horses like a hawk. There were at least four of them and he thought he could hear more in the distance. The original peace delegation that had met with El-Hajidd and his generals had been comprised of twelve knights. Out of that group, six had sided with Simon and the four that had sided with Kieran had been killed. There were still three more knights out there that wanted to see Kieran dead and he wasn't too inclined to move from his hiding place at the moment.

So he stayed put. In his arms, Rory trembled against him and he stroked her on occasion, reassuring her that all would be well. As the night progressed, she fell asleep against him and he held her fast, tucked tight into the nook that had protected them against the murderers. But at some point, he knew they would have to move and he gently shook her awake, giving her a few moments to become lucid. Whatever Kaleef had given her was making her very drowsy and he promised her they would find a more permanent rest very soon. In truth, she seemed to be taking the turmoil very well. Like Kieran, she was in survival mode and all of the complaining in the world wouldn't change the fact. She seemed oddly resigned. Making sure the alley was clear, Kieran took Rory quietly into the night.

They began to head back in the direction of Kaleef's hut. The smell of smoke was heavy in the air and they realized it was because Kaleef's burning home had set several others ablaze. Kieran kept out of sight as much as he could as they made their way down the dark and shadowed avenue when two figures suddenly emerged from another darkened alleyway. Kieran and Rory were preparing to run when Kieran suddenly recognized one of the wraiths.

"Yusef!" he hissed.

Yusef's dark eyes found Kieran in the dim light. He ran to Kieran, followed by one of his warriors. They were quiet and stealthy as they moved. Before Kieran could speak, Yusef cut him off.

"There is trouble, my friend." He grabbed Kieran and practically shoved him back into the shadows. "The Englishmen who came for you told of a tremendous tale. You cannot return to your king."

Kieran's brow furrowed. "What do you mean?"

Yusef looked nervous. The warrior beside him kept vigilant watch as Yusef continued on.

"De Corlet was with the group that attacked Kaleef," he said in a low voice. "Did you see him?"

Kieran shook his head. "I did not. Where was he?"

"He was on horseback. He stayed back as his men tried to gain entry, as we bought you time to escape," Yusef's dark eyes grew intense. "De Corlet told us that he told your king that you are a traitor."

Kieran just stared at him, hardly believing what he was hearing. "That's madness," he hissed. "I am not a traitor."

"Nay, you are not." Yusef shook his head slowly. "But you did not tell me that it was de Corlet who tried to assassinate you."

Yusef knew Simon as part of the Christian peace delegation. Simon had stood supportively next to Kieran as the man had accepted the Crown of Thorns from El-Hajidd. It was a sickening realization to both Kieran and Yusef that the Christians had turned against each other.

"Aye, it is him," Kieran confirmed quietly.

"Why is he trying to murder you?"

"I do not know," Kieran replied honestly. "Perhaps because he would rather see the Muslims a conquered people than see an armistice that would prevent more deaths on either side. Perhaps he does not want to see the siege of Acre end; perhaps he wants to see Saladin completely destroyed."

By this time, Yusef's expression was tight. "So he is trying to kill you because you have the Crown of Thorns, the offering of peace extended by El-Hajidd."

Kieran nodded angrily. "Aye," he replied. "He killed the four men who sided with me. I am the last of the peace delegation who actually wants to see this conflict end. I am the last one who can deliver the Crown of Thorns to Richard as El-Hajidd's offering of truce. So he is trying to kill me."

Yusef understood a great deal. His tight expression turned somewhat sick. "I have fellow warriors who would also like to see this battle continue until the Christians are crushed," he said quietly. "But I am not one of them."

"I know."

"Why would de Corlet tell your king that you are a traitor, then?"

Kieran shrugged. "I suppose to discredit me when I return to camp bearing the peace offering. If he cannot kill me, then he would have the king believe I am a liar and a traitor. More than likely, the remainder of the peace delegation will side with him and confirm that they saw me meet with Muslims in secret. They were there also, of course, but they will not tell the king that. It will make me look as if I was doing something subversive. It will be my word against theirs."

"But you are the king's friend, are you not? He will not believe them."

Kieran sighed faintly. "The only way he would believe me wholeheartedly is if you were to come with me to confirm El-Hajidd's peace offering. But Simon would kill you before you could reach the king. He would kill us both."

Yusef was distressed. After several long moments of pondering a situation with good intentions that had gone horribly wrong, he finally shook his head.

"Then the only answer is for you to return home and take the crown with you," he said. "You cannot stay here. No matter what you do, you are in danger and so is your wife. You cannot remain."

That was becoming increasingly clear to Kieran. He looked at Rory, who was gazing up at him with big, frightened eyes. He gave her much credit for having remained strong and silent thus far. His focus returned to Yusef.

"I cannot return home branded a traitor," he said quietly.

"You are not a traitor," Yusef insisted. "I will have a scribe take my testimony to the fact and you may take it with you. Perhaps it will clear you of these preposterous accusations when these conflicts are over."

"Perhaps," Kieran said, feeling despondent and empty. He'd spent three years in this place only to flee home like a criminal; it just wasn't fair. He had been attempting to end the conflict, to save lives, but it was apparently not to be. He couldn't get close to Richard without being killed because the king apparently believed Simon's lies. It was disheartening and sickening.

"God's Blood," he hissed, suddenly deflated and weary. "Is it possible? Is this really happening?"

"It seems to be. You must go home unless you want to die here."

Kieran shrugged his shoulders weakly. "But what of my army? I brought eight hundred Southwell men with me. I cannot simply leave them."

"You have no choice. Leave them or die."

Kieran stared at him, finally emitting a heavy sigh. "There is another problem," he said in a tone that suggested he was giving up. "I chased my charger off when you and your men attacked me. The horse is probably already to Richard's camp by now. The crown, and everything I own, was on that horse."

Yusef turned into the darkness and let out a soft whistle. From the narrow alleyway across the street where Yusef had been lying in wait, another man appeared leading a snorting charger. It took Kieran a moment to realize that it was Liberator.

"We caught your horse," Yusef smiled at Kieran's astonished expression. "Do you recall the man I sent after him? An Arabian was faster than a Warmblood, Christian. We have better horses than you do."

Kieran let out a sigh of amazement and gratitude as he took Liberator in hand. The horse snapped at the unfamiliar Saracen holding him but happily nuzzled Kieran when he recognized the man's scent. It was like watching a parent and child reunited.

"You may have better horses, but I have a smarter one," he muttered, listening to Yusef's low laughter. "Thank you for retrieving him."

Rory had remained largely silent throughout the exchange. Truth was, she was overwhelmed by all of it. She simply couldn't understand why things were turning so poorly against Kieran; all the man had wanted to do was achieve peace. But everything was against him, including his fellow knights. All he had was her, the crown, his horse and a Muslim ally. He was being crushed right before her eyes… or was he?

"Kieran," she moved forward, whispering in the dark. "You don't have to leave. We can get to Richard and explain everything. He knows you and trusts you. He will trust you when you tell him that Simon is the real traitor."

Kieran drew in a long, slow breath, still stroking the horse. "If I could speak with him and present him with the crown, I am confident that he would believe me." He turned to look at her in the darkness. "But Yusef is correct; Simon and the others will try to kill me at every turn. Moreover, I have you to worry about and I cannot allow you to come to harm."

She gazed up at him, her hazel eyes glimmering in the weak moonlight. "And if I weren't here? If I didn't even fit into this equation, what would you do?"

He thought briefly. "Do everything in my power to return to the king. This peace offering is too important not to do everything I can to see it through."

"Then why stop trying just because of me?" she insisted passionately. "I can't be the reason you didn't even try. You would grow to resent me and I can't let that happen."

"If I were to go to the king, I cannot take you with me. Do you understand that?"

"Of course I do. Who says I can't stay here, maybe with Kaleef? Or maybe Yusef can take me somewhere safe to wait this out." She suddenly put her hands on his face, pulling him down to her level. She kissed him tenderly. "Kieran, we've been returned to finish what you started eight hundred years ago. I know there have been a lot of obstacles thrown up, but you can't let that stop you. You have to finish this; you know you do. That's the entire reason why we're here."

He kissed her in return, sweetly, tasting her. "I will not leave you behind. I will not be separated from you."

She wrapped her arms around his neck. "Kieran, listen to me," she whispered. "I will be safe. I'll stay here in Nahariya and wait for you to come back. You don't have to worry about me. But you absolutely need to go to the king and straighten all of this out."

"Do not listen to her, my friend." Yusef grabbed Kieran by the arm, partially dislodging Rory from his embrace. "She speaks as a woman does, with soft thoughts and feelings. You must think like a warrior; you know that it is best for you to return home. Let time and separation heal this rift and let your innocence be proven in the years to come. The peace quest upon these sands has come to an end. If you stay here, you will die."

Kieran gazed steadily at Yusef, watching the man nod as if to reaffirm his statement. After a moment, Kieran nodded shortly and returned his attention to Rory. There was something painful and sad in his expression.

"He is correct," he murmured. "I cannot continue this quest, as much as I would like to and clear my name. Too much is working against me at the moment. I believe that I have no choice."

Rory gazed up at him, feeling hollow and defeated. She also felt some anger and frustration and she pulled away, her gaze moving between Kieran and Yusef. They seemed so resigned to accept the quick end but she understood why. She didn't want Kieran to die, either. Maybe they knew best and she should simply accept it. She jabbed a finger at the Saracen.

"You did this to him," she hissed. "Your people called that secret meeting and handed over the crown. Didn't you stop to think what would happen if things went wrong? Why didn't you just do it in the open and present it to Richard in person? Why all of the secrecy?"

Yusef wasn't particularly fond of any woman who did not know her place in the world. But out of respect to Kieran, he kept his head. That and the fact that Kieran was twice his size. He kept a civil tongue as he replied.

"Lady Hage," he began. "We contacted your husband because out of all of the Christian knights we had heard tale of, he was the one with the most honest reputation. He was not here for glory or riches. He was here because his king asked it of him and because he was a fair and virtuous man. Had we known Sir Kieran would be branded a traitor for attempting to gain peace, we would not have made the effort to contact him."

Rory was feeling ill now more than anger or frustration; all she could see was Kieran, defeated and branded a traitor. It just wasn't fair. "Look what you did to him." She was verging on tears. "Now his friends want to kill him."

"I can only apologize."

"You can do that and then you can help us get out of here."

"I will, I swear it. I will not let you or your husband die if I can help it."

She gazed at him a moment before replying in a deliberate tone. "He's not my husband," she said softly. "He told that lie to make it easier for me. We're not married but we want to be. You can help us with that, too."

Yusef looked at Kieran for a moment, holding back his initial shock, and then back to Rory. He smiled, his white teeth evident in the moonlight.

"That," he said, "would be my pleasure."

The next evening

YUSEF FOUND OLD Kaleef cowering in an alley near his burned-out home, terrified, where he had been hiding since the fire. Unable to simply walk away and leave the old man destitute, Yusef intended to return with him to El-Hajidd's encampment, a massive warrior city with thousands of Saracen warriors, reinforcements for those who were defending the massive fortified city of Acre. It was his intention to return to camp and confer with his general now that their peace offering had gone terribly wrong. They were back to the beginning.

Yusef and his men were just outside of the city under the quarter moon. Yusef was looking forward to a good meal and a warm bed and

Kaleef was looking forward to a meal and shelter. He was still rather disoriented, a very old man who had just lost everything, and Yusef was trying to do something good by assisting him. Allah was merciful with the compassionate. Since Yusef and Kieran were the reason Kaleef lost his home, the young Saracen warrior was eager to make amends.

The sky was clear and cloudless this night as the group made their way out of the edge of the city. As they neared a dry wash that was the barrier between the city limits and the desert beyond, they were suddenly cut off by a large patrol of Christian knights.

Yusef immediately drew his sword, as did the others. They were not afraid of battle. In these times, when Acre was under siege, Saracen and Christian alike roamed these lands and engagement was common. Yusef and his men were prepared. Swords gleamed wickedly beneath the quarter moon as the ancient combatants prepared for a fight.

Before the fight could start, however, one of the Christian knights held up a gloved hand with a shout.

"*Se tenir en bas vos armes*!" he cried. "*Nous ne sommes pas ici de combattre*!"

Yusef didn't lower his sword; he kept it level and replied to them in French. "What do you want?"

The knight with his hand raised moved forward slightly; Yusef did not recognize the armor, as so many Christians were identified by the style and type of armor they wore. This one was English but, beyond that, he did not know the man. It was intimidating, potent armor that all Christians wore, hiding their face and bodies from the swords and sands of The Levant. Yusef was busy inspecting the man and his weapons when the knight spoke.

"We are looking for Sir Kieran Hage," the man said. "We are told that he is being held by the Saracens."

Yusef didn't reply for a moment. "Kieran Hage is not our guest."

"Where is he?"

"Why do you want to know?"

"Because I bring him a message."

"From whom?"

"The king."

Yusef kept the sword up still. He did not trust the English knights, especially after what had happened two days ago. For all he knew, this knight was part of de Corlet's assassin contingent.

"I do not know where he is," he replied.

The man seemed increasingly exasperated. "Have you at least seen him? It is very important I relay this message to him."

"Why?" Yusef did not appreciate the games these men were playing. "So that you can kill him?"

"Nay," the man flipped up his visor, revealing brilliant blue eyes and little else. "Richard wants to warn him."

"About what?"

The man's frustration grew and he moved forward a few steps, his brilliant eyes glittering under the weak moonlight.

"If you will give him this message, then I will tell you."

"I will give it to him."

"Then tell him that one of de Corlet's men broke and confessed all to the king," the man said. "Richard knows that Sir Kieran is not a traitor. He knows that Simon de Corlet was trying to kill him and the king further knows about the treasure that Sir Kieran has in his possessions. It is the king's wish that Sir Kieran return to him immediately for all due honor and blessings."

Yusef stared at the man a long time before speaking. "Why should I believe you?" he asked. "How do I know you are not trying to find Sir Kieran so that you can kill him?"

The knight shook his head. "My name is Sir Rhys du Bois," the knight replied. "I am an ally of Sir Kieran. Under his absence, I have taken charge of his army so they will not fall into questionable hands. I assure you, with God as my witness, that everything I have said is true. The king knows of Sir Simon's treachery and of Kieran's innocence."

"Then if I am to believe you, de Corlet's life is now the one that is forfeit. Is this not the case?"

The knight shook his head. "Simon was informed of the king's fury and fled before he could be arrested. It is believed he is heading back home to England."

Yusef couldn't help it; at that point, he knew he turned pale. His jaw went slack and his eyes widened.

"Dear Allah," he breathed. "Is it true?'

"We believe so. Why? Where is Sir Kieran?"

"Heading home to England as well."

CHAPTER SEVEN

Three weeks later
Off the coast of Marseille, France

RORY HAD A text book idea of what it meant to travel by sea during Medieval times. Since her undergraduate degree was in Medieval History with a Ph.D. in Biblical Archaeology, she really thought she knew everything there was to know about Medieval culture, including travel. And she did. But the reality of it was something different altogether. It was like hell; that was the only way she could think to describe it. On the port side railing as she gazed at the distant coast of France on a cool and clear January morning, her mind was wandering over the journey of the past few weeks.

Before departing the port at Tyre, Yusef had located a Muslim cleric that agreed to marry her and Kieran. Being devoutly Catholic, Kieran wasn't too keen on the idea of a Muslim cleric but he figured that a Muslim ceremony was better than no ceremony at all so he agreed, sitting stoically beside Rory as the old cleric intoned the Muslim marriage rite yet saying a rosary throughout the entire ceremony. He paid the cleric handsomely and with that, Rory was his wife, at least in the eyes of Allah. But Kieran told Rory in no uncertain terms that he planned to have a wedding mass said the moment they reached France.

Yusef also followed through on another promise; when the ceremony was over, he had the very same cleric scribe a missive testifying to the fact that Kieran was not a traitor but an emissary of peace and that the true traitor, one Simon de Corlet, had confessed to deceit and disharmony. It took some time because the cleric was used to hieratic and had to translate everything into the English language. He was an educated man and knew several languages. But with that final and very precious gift, Yusef and his warriors escorted Kieran and Rory to the port of Tyre, about ten miles north of Nahariya.

The day they arrived, the weather had been remarkable and clear for January, with a balmy sea breeze blowing off of the Mediterranean. Rory was fascinated by the city, its people, streets and buildings, finding something vastly interesting in everything she saw. Since Tyre was a major port, many Christian knights were coming off of the boats that also brought animals and goods from all points west. It was raw, busy and exciting.

Given that it was a major import-export port, there were more goods and merchandise than in most cities. Kieran took Rory into several merchant stalls so she could find material for clothing, but when she informed him that she had no idea how to sew, he went in search of a seamstress. It wasn't difficult to locate one and he promised to pay the woman well if she would sew garments for Rory by the morning. Their boat left at sunrise and the woman agreed.

So they spent the afternoon before their departure shopping for fabric. Kieran wanted her to find something lovely but all she wanted to do was inspect the textiles like a scientist. He had to repeatedly remind her to find something she liked and to stop investigating every piece of string she came across, to which Rory responded with the traditional display of a sassy tongue. Kieran would just shake his head at her. But she managed to find several different kinds of fabric that she loved and Kieran even managed to find her a wedding ring at some point. She liked silver so he purchased a wide-band, silver filigree ring that was studded with precious stones. It was a gorgeous ring and Rory wept happy tears when he slid it on her finger.

When the next morning came, as promised, the swarthy seamstress, who was oddly missing most of the fingers on her left hand, had finished nine stunning garments for Rory. The woman had evidently been up all night sewing, assisted by her daughter and sister, and Rory was thrilled with the very pretty surcoats. Dressing in a gorgeous jade-colored linen, she told Kieran she felt like she was going to the prom but he had no idea what she meant. With her new surcoats, shifts and all manner of accessories and new trunks to put them in, she was ready to travel. She was looking forward to examining all of her new possessions on the trip to France. Since there would be no computers, videos or floor shows like a cruise ship, she was planning on how to keep herself occupied.

He had paid for passage on a ship that, when Rory saw it, looked more like a sailboat than a safe, sturdy ship that was going to take them across the Mediterranean. She knew the type of ship that sailed during the day but nothing prepared her for the reality of it. Called a cog, these ships had a high bow, low stern, and a giant mast in the center. This one happened to have a rudder, although most didn't. This was a newer ship, about eighty feet long, and it had a deck built on to it so there was an enclosed space below. Their "cabin" was really just a section of the second deck that was divided off from the rest of the ship by crudely fashioned curtains. When the ship swayed, the curtains opened and there was really no privacy at all.

So she, Kieran and Liberator boarded the ship that set sail just after sunrise on the fourth day since their appearance on that rocky beach. The weather was fine the first day out but a storm arose the next day that ruined everything. Rory had never really been on a boat and this had been a very rude introduction. She very quickly discovered that she was prone to seasickness.

The trip had been miserable from the start. The storm had lasted six of the longest, most miserable days of Rory's life. Even when the storm died down and the sun came out, Rory was still woozy. She never stopped being woozy and she hardly ate a bite. So by the end of the three weeks, she was down several pounds and her new dresses were a bit roomy. But she didn't care; she just wanted the heck off that stupid boat.

On the twentieth day of their journey, land was sighted and the captain told them that they would be making landfall by mid-afternoon in Marseille. Rory was so happy that it drove her to tears. As the boat skirted the green coast in the distance, she watched from her perch against the railing which had been her spot for the past three weeks. She didn't want to stray too far from the edge in case she had to vomit again. But these days, nothing was coming up; she'd thrown up everything in her system and then some.

Kieran, who had been below securing their possessions, found her leaning over the rail, watching the land in the distance. Her long hair was pulled back into a single braid and soft tendrils blew in the sea breeze. Her face, without makeup now for several weeks, was rosy from the sun and wind in spite of her constant seasickness, and he had never seen her so beautiful. She was a gorgeous woman as it was but, now, she was positively radiant. He couldn't explain it any other way.

He inspected her figure as he approached; the gentle curve of her backside and the narrowness of her waist now that she had been sick for three weeks straight. He approached from behind, bracing his arms on either side of her and leaning on the rail just as she was. He kissed her on the neck.

"Greetings, Wife," he kissed her again.

She turned to him with a smile on her lips before returning her focus to the land in the distance. Kieran settled in behind her, his chin on the top of her head as they watched the view together. Beyond the boat, the waves kicked up and the breeze blew strongly.

"The captain said we'll be docking by sunset," she said. "I can't tell you how glad I will be to get off this boat. I never knew I could be so sick and so scared at the same time."

He kissed the side of her head. "This will be a memory soon enough."

She made a face. "Not soon enough," she said frankly, her hazel eyes watching the coastline. "Swear to me that we will never, ever travel by boat again."

"I cannot. We must travel by boat one last time, between Calais and Dover."

She groaned. "Oh, God," she breathed. "How long will that trip take?"

He shrugged thoughtfully. "Perhaps a few hours if the weather is good."

There wasn't much she could do about that so she quieted for a moment, turning in his arms so that she was facing him. He pulled her against him, nuzzling her, as she wound her arms around his neck.

"We haven't really talked about much over the past few weeks because I've felt so horrible, but what's going to happen now?" she wanted to know. "Where do we go from here?"

He sighed, thinking on the chronology of what was to come. "After we dock, we shall spend the night along the waterfront," he said. "After that, I will make arrangements to travel to Paris and from Paris, we shall return to Southwell."

She wriggled her eyebrows. "Ah, yes, Southwell," she repeated. "I've never really asked you about your home. What's it like? Tell me everything so I know what to expect."

It was his turn to wriggle his eyebrows. He snuggled against her, thinking of the home he hadn't seen in three years and the family that lived there. It all seemed like a distant dream.

"I am afraid to tell you everything," he teased, straight-faced. "You may not want to go there."

She snorted. "Why? Is it a crazy place?"

"It can be."

"Tell me anyway so I'm prepared, at least."

He nodded as if reluctant. "Very well," he started. "Southwell Castle was built before the time of the Normans. I am not Norman, you know."

"I figured that out. Hage is not a Norman name."

He nodded. "That is correct; it is Saxon." He continued. "My ancestors were rulers over the lands we still hold. We were one of the few Anglo-Saxon families who continued to hold their lands even after the invasion. My ancestors apparently found a way to work with the

Normans and were rewarded for their cooperation. Southwell is located near Nottingham which, in ancient times, was known as North Mercia. The castle is called Southwell because it used to be the southernmost water source in North Mercia."

Rory listened to him, shaking her head in amazement. "How would you know all of this? People didn't keep written records of that time. Who told you all of this?"

"My father, Jeffrey Hage, Earl of Newark and Sherwood," he replied. "He told me so that I may pass it down to our children, who in turn will pass it to theirs. Our family history is very important."

"No doubt," she smiled faintly. "And you? You have titles as well."

He nodded. "The titles I inherited, Viscount of Dykemoor and Sewall, are hereditary titles to the first born son of the Earl of Newark and Sherwood. Our son will inherit this title once my father has passed away and I become the new earl."

She thought on that a moment. "But you have brothers," she said. "Will they inherit anything?"

Kieran thought of his beloved brothers, men he hadn't seen in what seemed like forever. As he thought of them, he realized how much he'd missed them. "I have three younger brothers; Sean, Christian and Andrew," he said. "They have their own titles and lands, but the majority of the Hage fortune goes to me."

"Tell me about your brothers. Did they go to the Holy Land with you?"

He shook his head. "Nay," he responded. "Sean is a servant for Richard and has been helping protect the throne in the king's absence. Christian and Andrew serve my father as captains of his armies. Southwell has the largest army in the province with over one thousand men."

"You were the only brother that went on Richard's quest?"

He nodded, his eyes dimming as he thought of that turbulent time. "My father thought Richard's quest was foolish," he replied softly. "He did not want any of us to go. It was quite the battle when I made the choice to accompany the king. My father strongly disagreed."

"Is he a supporter of Prince John?"

Kieran shook his head. "Not at all," he replied. "He is an old man. He did not want to lose any of his sons, and especially not his heir, on what he felt was an idiotic quest. But in the end, he understood my decision to go."

Rory fell silent a moment. "What are you going to tell him about your return? You should probably tell him the truth in case he hears it from someone else."

Kieran nodded, feeling the familiar disappointment at the way things turned out. "I will tell him," he replied. "My father is old, gruff and hard of hearing, but he is not unfair. He will believe me and so will my brothers."

"I hope so."

Kieran simply nodded, pulling her close and watching the coastline in the distance draw nearer. Rory fell silent, basking in his warmth and power as they watched land grow larger and larger. She knew he was melancholy about the whole thing, uncertain about his future once he reached England. All she could do was support him in whatever he chose to do; this was his life and he needed to make the decisions. She had decided during those days of misery upon the open sea that she was simply along for the ride; this wasn't her time or her world. She had left hers behind. But this was Kieran's time and anything he did or said could, and would, change the course of history, including his return to England.

The sea was incredibly blue, bluer than any water she had ever seen, and as they drew close to the port, the water became very clear and she could see to the bottom. She could see the city in the distance, clinging to the coastline with tight streets and whitewashed buildings. Marseille glistened like a jewel along the Mediterranean and she was fascinated by the sight; it was unlike anything she had ever seen and the historic significance wasn't lost on her.

"I've been thinking something," she said.

Kieran was fairly well wrapped around her, his head against hers. He felt so much peace and contentment when she was in his arms. "What about?" he asked.

"Me," she said. "It probably wouldn't be a good idea for you to tell your father I'm an American heiress. First of all, he'll want to know want kind of dowry I've brought to this marriage and we both know I have absolutely nothing. Secondly, America won't mean anything to him. I could be from the moon for all he'll know about America."

Kieran inhaled thoughtfully, letting out a slow, long breath. "Very well," he agreed. "What would you suggest we tell him?"

She pursed her lips in thought. "My family name is Celtic," she said. "Osgrove means 'victorious'. Why don't we tell him I'm Irish? My mother's great-grandmother came from Castlebar in County Connaught. I have a strange enough accent that he'll probably believe I'm Irish."

"You have a strange enough accent that he would, in fact, believe that you were from the moon."

She turned to cast him a threatening glare. He kissed the tip of her nose and she broke down into a grin. "Don't tell him I'm nobility, either, because I'm not. We could never prove it."

"Ah, but you must be nobility in order to marry into the Hage family," he told her firmly. "If not, my father may seek an annulment."

"Fine." She flattened her lips irritably. "Tell him I'm from a very, very minor noble family."

"Do you have lands? A title?"

"No. And tell him that my parents are dead and I'm an orphan."

"How did I meet you, then?"

She cocked her head in thought. "My brother was on the Quest with you. He was a good friend and made you promise on his deathbed that you would marry his poor, orphaned sister so that I would be taken care of. Unwilling to disappoint a dying man, you agreed."

Kieran fought off a grin at her wild imagination. "And does this dead brother have a name?"

Rory's gaze grew distant. "Bud."

Kieran lost his humor, thinking on Rory's colleague who had risked everything so that they could be together. Bud Dietrich had been madly in love with Rory but had loved her enough to sacrifice himself so that she could be happy. They owed Bud everything so it was a fitting tribute to a man who had not yet even been born.

"Of course," he murmured. "Bud was, indeed, a good friend. It would not be a lie."

For some reason, tears came to Rory's eyes as she thought on Dr. Bud Dietrich. She hadn't thought of him since the moment they discovered they had returned to Kieran's time. He had been her boss as well as her friend. Thinking of the man made her weep silently. He had loved her so much. It had been a sad thing for both of them that she could not return those feelings; her love had been reserved for Kieran.

Kieran must have sensed her mood because he kissed her a couple of times on the cheek before letting her go. He left her at the amidships' railing as he went to order their possessions brought on deck and to check on Liberator one last time. The horse had grown fat and restless in the past three weeks, doing nothing more than eat the entire time. He was as ready to disembark the ship as Rory was.

As the ship came into port at Marseille, Rory forgot her seasickness and took in the sights. The cog came to rest at the far end of a long row of ships, all docked several feet from the shore. There were no such things as piers or actual docks; ships simply got as close as they could to the shore without running aground and dropped anchor. When the ship hands threw the anchor over the side, which was actually a very large stone tethered to a rope, the ship finally came to rest in the gently rolling inlet.

Several of the hands jumped over the side into the cold, thigh-deep water. Immediately, they began offloading their cargo and there was a host of people on the shore that waded out to assist. Rory watched everything with great interest, noting firsthand how cargo ships were offloaded in a Medieval port; it was purely by manpower alone, at least at this port. No forklift or wenches as she knew them. As she observed, Kieran suddenly jumped off the side of the boat, followed by Liberator.

The huge splash came up and Rory barely missed getting soaked. The horse splashed around excitedly in the water as Kieran tried to coax him up onto the shore. But Liberator was like a child. He didn't want to go on shore; he simply wanted to splash about in the water. Eventually, Kieran gave up and let go of the horse's lead. Liberator ran out into deeper water and began to swim around in the inlet. Grinning, Rory ran to the opposite side of the ship to watch the big, silver head moving around in the blue, blue water. Even though it was January, the day was balmy and the water was inviting. Rory envied that big, silver horse.

Kieran stood with his hands on his hips, watching his horse swim around, when he suddenly heard a splash on the opposite side of the ship. He wasn't particularly concerned until he glanced at the deck and realized that he didn't see Rory anywhere. In a panic, he climbed back onto the ship, demanding his wife, when the deck hands began pointing over the side of the boat. Kieran raced to the starboard rail to see Rory swimming around below, stroking her way out towards Liberator. Kieran couldn't help but grin, watching the two of them frolic in the deep blue waters below.

"Are you not cold?" he called out to her.

She turned on her back, backstroking as she smiled up at him. "A little," she admitted. "But it feels wonderful to be off that damned boat."

He leaned forward on the rail, watching her with adoration in his eyes. She looked like a water nymph, her pale skin against the blue water. "You'd better swim to the shore before you catch chill," he told her.

She began to move around the boat, heading for the rocky shore. Kieran moved to the other side of the boat again and leapt into the water, waiting for Rory to come around the bow. Around him, men were offloading their possessions and carrying them onto the shore. As he snapped a reprimand to one of the men who was being careless with one of his wife's trunks, Rory came around the bow and into water shallow enough to stand. As she began to walk on the rocky ground, Liberator suddenly appeared behind her.

Kieran saw the horse charging up behind Rory but he was too far away to prevent the horse from trampling her; he could suddenly see disaster before his eyes. He opened his mouth to shout at the horse just as the animal rushed upon Rory, but before he could get the words out of his mouth, Liberator shoved Rory with his big head and she fell over as he charged past her. It was like watching a naughty kid push a rival out of the way. Rory whooped as she fell back into the water.

The horse was having a good time. As Kieran moved to help his wife up, the horse suddenly circled around and shoved her down again just about the time she reached her feet. Kieran prevented the horse from doing it a third time, shoving him away when he came near again. But Liberator would not be deterred and when he swung around for one more pass, Rory splashed water violently in the horse's face. Insulted, Liberator had enough and he splashed up onto the shore.

Kieran picked up his wife and carried her up to the shore, keeping her away from the horse that seemed to want to push her down. He set her to her feet.

"There's a cloak in one of those trunks." Rory was dripping wet and wringing out her hair. "Would you please find it for me?"

He lifted an eyebrow at her. "Cold?"

"Freezing."

"I warned you."

She gave him an impatient *"yes, I know you did"* expression. "Please, just find it," she asked again. "And just so you know, I'd do it again if given the choice."

He snorted as he turned for the pile of trunks and other items still being assembled on the shore. There were several deck hands piling them up and he grabbed one of the men and paid him a gold coin to stand guard over everything. The man was big and burly, and happily agreed. Meanwhile, Kieran secured Liberator to a great iron weight lodged on the shore so the horse wouldn't get into mischief before going in search of the magical trunk that held Rory's cloaks.

Fortunately, he found it on the first try and brought forth a heavy, linen cloak with a soft lining. Rory thanked him gratefully and wrapped up against the balmy breeze blowing off the sea. Eventually, all of their possessions were brought off the ship and Kieran paid a few men who worked along the ports to transport them to the nearest tavern. Because she'd been cooped up on the ship so long, Rory wanted to walk, so Kieran took Liberator in one hand and Rory in the other and followed the wagon as it moved down the waterfront.

The first thing Rory noticed was that she couldn't seem to walk a straight line. She felt like she was still on the ship and the nausea she had been experiencing for weeks returned. By the time they made it off the beach and onto the uneven, pitted road beyond, she was feeling pretty horrible. But she kept her mouth shut. She'd done nothing but complain for the past three weeks and she was sure, at some point, Kieran was going to lose patience with her. So she staggered next to him as they made their way down the waterfront, trying to distract herself by studying the Medieval scenery. It was truly something to behold.

It was a big city. There were neatly laid out streets with stone buildings and the land elevation increased as it moved further from the sea. Up on a hill overlooking the city was a church; she could see the steeple and a portion of the building. As she gripped Kieran's arm with her left hand, she pointed up to the church on the hill.

"Look there," she said, awe in her voice. "The Abbey of St. Victor."

Kieran's dark eyes moved to the church on the hill. "A perfect place to receive the wedding sacrament."

She looked at him. "What do you mean?"

"Our marriage is not recognized by the Christian faith."

Her gaze moved to the church in the distance once again. "So you want to get married there?"

"I do."

"The Abbey of St. Victor is one of the oldest around. Do you think they'll do it?"

"For a donation, the priests will do most anything."

He said it with some irony but she let it go; she knew that it was generally known that Medieval priests could be corrupt. There were loads of records and testimonies from the time period attesting to it. It was nothing new. She continued to gaze up at the abbey.

"Did you know it was built by the Romans?" she asked.

He nodded. "I do," he answered. "I traveled here, once, when I was a squire. My master was an old and wise knight, very pious, and we traveled France for two years to visit all of the prestigious churches so that he could pray. He felt that it would ensure the forgiveness of the men he had killed during his life and ensure his entry into heaven."

She continued to study the church. "If I recall correctly, St. Victor's was destroyed about three hundred years ago and has only been rebuilt in the last hundred years. Didn't the Saracens destroy it?"

He shrugged. "I do not know."

"I think they did." She was trying to recall her knowledge of the place. But her attention was soon diverted when they passed a building that had a series of paintings on a panel facing the street.

The paintings were crude but unmistakable; they were sexual positions and beneath each position was some kind of writing she couldn't make out. Rory came to a halt, peering at the panel, then the building it was on, and back to the panel again. Kieran saw what she was looking at and gently pulled her along.

"Oh, my God," she gasped, her mouth hanging open as he forced her to walk. "It's a menu for sex."

He didn't say anything as they continued, but Rory was clearly fascinated by it. "It's like a fast food menu," she pointed at it. "A la carte or in a combo. You can just order off the menu."

He continued walking stoically. "Come along, Wife."

She dug her heels in. "Wait a minute," she argued as she started pulling him back. "I want to see what it says."

He shook his head and continued walking, dragging her along.

"Well-bred women do not give notice to such things."

"But archaeologists do," she insisted. "Please? I just want to see what it says."

He came to a stop, so abruptly that she smacked into the back of him. His clear brown eyes were critical.

"I will again say nay," he told her in a low voice. "It is unseemly. You must understand that there is no room for your scientific mind in these times. If you go back and read that, no matter how innocent your heart and mind are, it will attract unwanted and shameful attention. Is that clear?"

The amazed and somewhat amused expression disappeared off her face and she averted her gaze, looking at her feet. Kieran sighed faintly, kissed her on the forehead, and continued walking.

"I apologize if I was harsh, sweetheart," his voice turned low and tender. "But you must understand that this is not your time. The situation is markedly different and I do not want you to do anything that would put you in harm's way."

She was pouting, looking at the ground as he gently led her along. But contrary to their usual exchange, she didn't argue with him. He felt bad, like he had crushed her spirit, but he didn't apologize further. She had to understand.

They weren't in her time any longer. And it was only going to grow worse.

CHAPTER EIGHT

Kieran held Rory's hand, kissing it as they made their way down the muddy, urine-smelling avenue.

It was a temperate day along the Mediterranean coast, a gentle breeze blowing off the sea and seagulls crying overhead. There were virtually no clouds, creating a bright and lovely atmosphere. After being scolded about taking interest in the brothels, Rory lifted her head at some point to look around again, seeing more houses of ill repute and quickly looking away when she realized what they were. When they passed by the main part of the waterfront, they came to an area tucked back from the ports, full of merchants. The inn that the boat captain had recommended was nestled among the merchants and they caught up to the wagon with all of their possessions, now being offloaded into the two-story inn.

There was a stable tucked to the side of the structure and, after leaving Liberator with a groom, Kieran took Rory inside. It was a fairly large structure, built of stone with great, wooden beams against the wooden ceiling and at least four main rooms on the first floor that were packed with people.

Rory followed Kieran, wide-eyed, into the main room, noting that other than the fact that the people had lighter skin, it looked much like the hostels in Nahariya. It smelled to high heaven of smoke and body odor. The room itself was odd-shaped with an uneven floor. Barrels served as tables and people sat on the floor, stools, a few chairs and each other. A minstrel sat in the corner and played on a crude mandolin.

It looked like something out of the movies with the variety of characters that were strewn across the room. A massive hearth burned brightly against one wall, spitting smoke and sparks into the air.

Although Rory was holding tightly to Kieran as he navigated his way through the room, a very drunken man made a swipe at her and she yelped, smacking the guy in the forehead with an open palm. He toppled over backwards and his friends laughed uproariously, but Kieran swung around with his fists balled. Rory put her hands on his gigantic fists to still them.

"No, no, no," she murmured softly, quickly, trying to turn him around. "He was just drunk. No harm done."

He gently but firmly pushed her aside, moving towards the man whose friends were now helping him off the floor.

"He shall be dealt with," he said in a tone that suggested she needed to stay out of it.

But Rory put herself in between Kieran and the drunk. "Kieran, *no*," she hissed. "There's no need for you to upend this room. I don't feel good and I want to go lie down. I don't want to deal with a battle the first time we're on land in three weeks. So would you please think of me for once in this situation and not your manly honor?"

She was verging on angry tears by the time she finished the sentence and he folded immediately, but not before casting the drunk and his friends a threatening glare. Putting his arm around her shoulders, he took her over to the wide, wooden stairs where men with their possessions waited. A tall, thin man in a tunic, some kind of vest, dirty pants and dirty shoes awaited them. He bowed to Kieran nervously.

"*Votre plaisir, mon seigneur*?" he asked.

Kieran flicked a wrist at him, glancing back at the room as if to make sure he wasn't about to be attacked from behind.

"*La meilleure pièce pour ma femme et I*," he said in perfect French. "*No us avons besoin de la nourriture et un bain aussi.*"

Rory watched the thin man shout to a couple of women while simultaneously directing the porters up the stairs. He ran ahead of them, babbling in a language that Rory didn't understand. She gathered her wet skirts as Kieran led her carefully up the stairs that didn't seem too steady.

"I never learned French," she told him. "Where I come from in California, it was essential to learn Spanish."

He pulled the hem of her cloak aside when she almost stepped on it. "If we go to Spain, your knowledge shall be invaluable."

She smiled weakly as they reached the top of the steps and continued down a narrow, uneven corridor. The tall innkeeper had opened a door near the end, ushering the porters in and babbling crazily in French. Rory entered the room just as the porters were exiting and the innkeeper screamed at them to vacate. As Rory looked around the small but surprisingly clean room, Kieran muttered a few orders to the man and shut the door in his face.

Kieran stood there a moment, watching Rory wearily remove her cloak. Their trunks and bags were stacked against one wall, filling nearly half the room, while a bed was pushed up against the other wall. Rory noticed the bed, larger than a twin but smaller than a double. As Kieran watched, she walked up to it and peered closely at it. After a moment, she sighed heavily and sank to the floor in a new round of tears.

"It's got bugs," she sobbed. "I'm sorry, Kieran, I really am. I'm trying to be brave and not complain and accept everything the way it is, but I'm just not doing a very good job. I'm so tired I could just die and all I want to do is lay down, but I'm not lying on a bed with bugs. I'm sorry, but I'm just not."

Weeping, she lay right down on the floor. Kieran went straight to the bed and ripped everything off it; throwing open the door, he tossed everything into the hall. He happened to catch the eye of a startled serving wench who was bringing them food. He took a few steps down the hall, grabbed the tray and pitcher from her, and pointed to the bundle of crawling linen in the hall.

"My wife wants clean linen," he ordered. "You will find fresh straw and boiled linen, clean and without dirt or vermin, or I shall tear this place apart. Is that clear?"

The girl looked at him with complete, utter fear and fled. Kieran went back into the room and set the food on the table. He went to Rory, still lying on the floor, and put his great hand on her head.

"I shall find clean linen for you, I swear it," he was on his knees, kissing her cheek. "I know you are exhausted. I have asked for a bath to be brought to our room. Let us eat something now; it will make you feel better."

She lay there and cried, completely spent and ill. "I don't want to eat," she sobbed.

He gently pulled her into his arms. "Aye, you do," he murmured, kissing her head and holding her close. "Please, sweetheart. Eat something and feel better."

"No!" she squeaked.

He picked her up and carried her over to the table. She was still damp and trembling with chill. He set her down in the only chair in the room and poured her a cup of wine.

"Drink," he commanded. "It will make you feel better."

She was sobbing pitifully. "I don't want to."

She was actually rather comical with her dramatic misery but he fought of the grin that threatened, knowing it would not be well met. He kissed her forehead again and went over to the trunks piled against the wall.

"Drink some wine, sweetheart," he urged, pulling a large satchel off the stack of three trunks and putting it aside. "I shall find you dry clothing."

She shook her head, unhappy, eyeing him as he opened the top trunk and began rummaging around. He eventually came across a feather-soft lamb's wool sleeping shift that he had purchased for her back in Tyre. As he shook it out, Rory calmed down sufficiently to where she took a sip of the tart and sweet wine. He brought the shift over to her.

"Here," he held it out. "You must change out of those wet clothes."

She shook her head. "I want to take a bath before I change," she said, sniffling and wiping her nose. "I've got sand all over me and the salt water is drying out my skin. Where are those skin oils we bought in Tyre?"

He set the shift aside, turning back to the trunks. "They are in here, somewhere."

"Can you find them, please?"

"I am looking."

"And you may as well get out all of the other toiletries we bought. I forget what I have. I didn't even touch it on the boat."

"I will."

"And the mirror we bought. Please get that, too."

He nodded wearily, as a man usually does with a bossy wife. But the truth was that, in spite of everything, he was happier than he had ever been in his life. As long as Rory was with him, nothing else mattered. He could move mountains.

"Did you find them?" she asked a couple of seconds later.

He was still rummaging around, nodding impatiently. "I am looking," he assured her with irritation. "Give me a moment, if you would."

Rory turned back to the wine as Kieran finally came across the phials of oils and salts that they had purchased. There were three bars of soap in leather pouches that he pulled forth along with an earthenware jug that contained what Rory had understood to be shampoo. There were also four phials of oils in different fragrances; jasmine, sandalwood, myrrh and lily along with mineral salts that she was told came all the way from the salt sea in Judah, which she assumed to mean the Dead Sea. Additionally, there were all sorts of other things that he pulled out, mysterious cosmetics he had purchased for her because she liked the smell or color, including a very precious mirror made from Venetian glass. It was little but the reflection was true. In truth, he'd invested a small fortune in the items but it was a small price to pay to keep Rory happy. He enjoyed it.

He set everything on the table so she could look through her assortment. Then he pulled the cloth off the tray to inspect what manner of food had been provided, hoping the food would entice her and perk up her mood. There was a large hunk of beef, well cooked and juicy, as well as a half a loaf of brown bread and boiled carrots. There was also some butter and a big knife. He pulled a piece of beef off the bone and tasted it; it was quite good. He pulled another piece off, making sure it was free of gristle, before extending it to Rory.

She waved him off. "God, no," she turned away. "I don't want any."

He sighed heavily. "Lib, you hardly ate on the boat. You have lost enough weight that your bones are sticking through. I know you are unused to the food of this time, but I assure you, this beef is well cooked and delicious. I believe you will like it and you need to eat something. I do not want to see you waste away from starvation."

She looked at him, realizing he was probably right. She hadn't eaten much since the day they had arrived over three weeks ago. But she was absolutely terrified to touch food that hadn't known any regulations or inspection process. She looked at the meat and how well it was cooked, figuring that the cooking process would have killed any worms or bacteria that might have existed. And the wine was okay; the alcohol would kill any germs. Taking a deep breath, she took the beef from his fingers and forced it into her mouth, chewing slowly.

She quickly realized it was good meat and quite delicious. Kieran saw that she ate it quickly so he cut more off the bone and gave it to her. The more he would cut, the more she would eat. She went after the carrots and ate all of them; they were boiled in brine and very salty, but good nonetheless and she was starving. When the carrots were gone, she went back to the beef. Kieran stood back and let her eat everything she had a mind to. He was just glad to see that her appetite had returned. When she moved for the bread, however, she slowed down considerably and picked off a piece, inspecting it. He knew just by her expression that she didn't want to eat it.

"What's wrong?" he asked.

She looked at him guiltily. "Well," she began reluctantly, setting the bread down. "It's brown bread. It's full of grit and dirt, and God knows what else."

"Do you want me to find suitable bread?"

She slumped in the chair, refusing to look at him. "No," she said. "I've already been too much of a pain. You haven't even eaten; you need to sit down and finish this up."

He suddenly quit the room. Rory jumped up and ran to the open door, watching him stalk down the hall and disappear down the stairs. Calls to him went unanswered. Uncertain where he was going but unwilling to follow, she went back into the room and shut the door. Going back to the table, she slowly sat, wondering what she had said to make him run from the room. She felt ill again, too; the food was making her sleepy and upsetting her stomach at the same time. So she sat, uncomfortable and exhausted, until Kieran appeared a short time later.

He was carrying another tray in his big hands. Behind him, two men were carrying a massive copper pot and following the pot were a few serving women with crude wooden buckets of steaming water. The men set the pot down at Kieran's direction and the women began to pour the water in. Kieran went to the table and set the tray down in front of Rory.

"There you are, m'lady," he smiled, his gem-clear brown eyes glimmering at her. "I scavenged the kitchens for everything they had. When their supplies were not sufficient, I went next door to the baker and scavenged his goods as well."

Rory gazed up at him, smiling gratefully. The man was trying so hard to take good care of her. She reached up, patting his cheek. "Thank you," she whispered. "You are so sweet. I love you."

He winked at her, kissing her hand and turning to face those who were in their room filling up the tub. There were many possessions and he didn't want an unscrupulous servant to abscond with something when his back was turned.

As Kieran watched the servants like a hawk, Rory investigated the contents of the tray; there were two golden buns that, when pulled apart, revealed creamy white bread inside. It wasn't like modern white bread; it was denser and heavier. There was also another loaf of bread that was white but for bits of currants in it. She picked a piece of it off and popped it in her mouth; it was sweet with what she assumed to be honey.

But there was more. A small cup covered with a cloth contained something green and briny. Upon further inspection, she realized it was cucumber and quite delicious. There were also pickled lemons, which were crazy-sour, and some kind of pancake-like thing. She could see the oats in it and smelled what she thought was cinnamon. After a little taste of everything, she ate most of the tray. Even the lemons that made her glands hurt and her eyes water.

By the time the tub was full, Rory was wallowing in gluttonous misery. Kieran shut the door when the last servant left, turning to see his wife ill with too much food. He put his hands on his slender hips, lifting an eyebrow at her.

"You refuse to eat for weeks," he pointed out. "Then when you do it, you stuff yourself ill."

She looked at him, made a face, and groaned. "I was so hungry," she said. "God, I'm so full now I'm going to explode."

He grunted, grinning, as he went to the table. There wasn't much left. "May I have your scraps, madam?"

"Knock yourself out."

"I am not sure why I would want to."

"I meant go ahead."

As Rory rose from the chair to prepare for her bath, he sat down and proceeded to devour what was left on the table. There was still plenty of food left for him, mostly the meat and brown bread, and he finished it off. Rory, meanwhile, was peeling the damp surcoat off her body and laid it across the bed frame to dry. The shift was next and as Kieran chewed on the bread, he noticed that she was still wearing her bra and panties. She clung to the twenty-first century clothing, unwilling to relinquish everything she knew and was comfortable with. He swallowed the bread in his mouth.

"Lib," he began gently, casually. "We purchased suitable undergarments for you in Tyre. Is there a reason why you do not wear them but continue wearing your old undergarments?"

She looked down at her white bra and boy-short panties that looked fantastic on her round buttocks. "I'm just more comfortable with these," she insisted, reaching around to unhook the bra. "I need to wash them before we go. They're so disgusting right now that I can't even begin to describe it."

He wasn't really sure what she meant but he let it go. It wasn't his business, anyway. Besides, he loved to watch her half-naked body parade around in the peculiar undergarments. She looked magnificent. When she unhooked the bra and let her beautiful breasts go free, he could feel himself growing hard. When she slipped the strange, white panties off and climbed into the tub, he felt himself growing hot all over. The woman had that effect on him.

But he knew any advance would not be well met so he continued to sit and drink the tart, sweet wine, his lust building as more alcohol filled his veins. He watched Rory bathe, soaping her luscious body with the white soap that smelled of jasmine, filling the air of the small room with its sweet fragrance. She washed her hair at least three times, rinsing it over and over in the water.

"Baby?" she called to him as she was washing her feet.

He was extremely relaxed, half-lidded, watching her bathe. "Aye?"

"Do you have a razor?"

He nodded, rising to weary feet and digging through his enormous saddlebags. He eventually pulled forth a leather sheath, about a foot long. Inside the sheath was a steel razor he used for shaving his face. He went over to her, handing her the butt end of the razor.

"What are you going to shave?" he asked. "Your beard does not look as if it is growing in."

She giggled at him, her lovely face rosy and pinched from the warm water. "It isn't," she rubbed at her chin with one hand, took the razor with the other. "I want to shave my legs. In fact, do you think you can buy me a razor? I hate to use yours."

He shrugged, watching her lather up her legs and carefully drag the razor over her flesh. "If that is your wish." He watched her make careful rows in the suds. "Do not cut yourself; the razor is very sharp."

"I know," she said steadily, biting her tongue as she proceeded to shave her right shin without a snag. She moved to the left one. "So what's going to happen tomorrow? Are we leaving first thing in the morning?"

He just stood there, watching her hard nipples just beneath the water line and thinking very carnal thoughts. "When you are ready," he said. "You and I and Liberator will travel to Paris and from Paris, we will go to Calais and take a boat to England. If all goes as planned, we should reach Paris in a little more than a week."

"A week?" she looked at him, shocked. "It's going to be that long?"

He nodded. "There are no airplanes or trains here. Only Liberator."

She made a face, knowing he was correct. "I know, but a whole week?" she shook her head. "I've never really ridden a horse. My butt is going to be killing me after a week on a horse."

The corner of his mouth twitched. "It will be more like eight or nine days, depending on how fast we move."

She closed her eyes. "Oh, my God," she hung her head a moment before lifting it. "Is there any way we can get a wagon? Something I can sit in? I'm not sure if I can ride on the back of that horse for nine days."

He scratched his head. "I suppose we could find a cart," he said thoughtfully. "Can you drive a wagon?"

"I can drive a car."

"That is different. I would hate to see you run amok in a donkey cart."

She snorted, her mood lightening. "Oh, don't worry about it," she offered as she splashed in the tub. "I'll live."

He grinned, moving back to the table and drinking the last of the wine as she finished shaving her armpits. He kept glancing back at her, watching her wet, supple body. The sun was starting to set outside and he went to the small, battered, bronze furnace in the corner of the room near the window. It was basically an open bucket that, when filled with coal or other substance, gave off a significant amount of heat. Since there was no hearth in the room, it was a way to produce heat. There was a small bucket of charcoal next to it mixed with chunks of peat. Kieran positioned the peat and coal, then lit it with a flint that was mixed up in the coal. As Rory finished her bath, a warm fire began to burn.

Rory continued to sit in the bath even when the water went from very hot to moderately warm. It simply felt wonderful to be warm and clean again. She knew that Medieval people didn't bathe often but that was one cultural condition she refused to succumb to. She planned to bathe every day if she could. But eventually, the water grew too cool for her taste and she knew it was time to get out. Besides, her fingers and toes were all wrinkled.

"Baby?" she called sweetly.

He was draining the pitcher of wine. "Aye?" he smacked his lips.

She leaned over the side of the tub, smiling brightly. "Can you please bring me my towel?"

He put down the pitcher and dutifully went over to the pile of trunks again, rummaging around in the top trunk until he pulled out a big, folded piece of white linen. Rory had purchased it when she had bought the oils, after she realized that anywhere they stayed would not be like the hotels she knew and would therefore not provide towels or bathrooms, for that matter. Kieran approached her as he unfolded the linen, holding it up to her as she stood up in the tub. She stepped into the linen and he wrapped her in it, picking her up in his arms and giving her a good squeeze. She squealed as he bear-hugged her, nuzzling her wet neck.

"Kieran, I'm all wet," she protested weakly. "Put me down so I can dry off."

He was feeling his alcohol, hot and lustful. "Shall I put you down near the fire?"

She looked over at the wide-open bucket that was now glowing with flame. "We'll be lucky if we don't die of carbon monoxide poisoning," she muttered. "Make sure you put that thing near the window where the fumes can escape."

"Aye, madam," he murmured into her skin.

He took her over to the furnace and gently set her down. Rory teetered when he put her on her feet because the floor was cold, so she danced around as she dried off. The linen wasn't particularly absorbent so it took some time, but she was able to dry off sufficiently. Then she hopped over to the table where her oils were.

"I think I want to use the one that smells like jasmine." She hunted around, smelling, until she came to it. "Ooo, here it is."

She popped open the stopper, which was a lovely glass cork. It wasn't perfectly made, like it would have been in her time with modern machinery, but it was gorgeously crafted with a tint of yellow to it. She poured some of the precious oil onto her palm and began rubbing it on her legs. Kieran watched her intently.

"What is in that potion?" he asked.

She rubbed it into her thighs, dropping the towel completely to rub it into her torso. "The merchant said he bought it from an old woman who pressed the flowers and poured sesame oil over them. Then she would let it all sit and steep for a while." She held up the phial and shook it, watching the liquid swirl. "You can see bits of flower petals in it."

Kieran smelled her shoulder where she was rubbing the oil in; it was too much. Having a naked woman standing in front of him overwhelmed him and, with a growl, he wrapped his big arms around her and bit softly into her neck. Rory gasped.

"Kieran," she protested weakly.

"No more talk," he ordered gently. "You have been flaunting yourself in front of me all day and I have reached my limit. I can no longer stand not having my fill of you."

She giggled as he suckled her neck, the giggles quickly turning into soft grunts of pleasure. One big hand found a breast, fondling her from behind as she purred like a kitten. As he was preparing to delve further into his tender assault, there was a knock on the door.

Rory moved away from him quickly, running to collect the linen towel on the floor. When she was properly and completely covered up by it, Kieran answered the door. The tall tavern keeper and two serving wenches stood there, their arms laden with huge bundles of material. Kieran lifted an eyebrow.

"What is this?" he demanded in French, his voice cold.

The innkeeper pointed his chin at the bundle in his arms. "I was told you wanted a clean bed, m'lord."

Kieran nodded, standing back so they could come into the room. Rory stood over by the open furnace, watching them lay what looked like a large sack on the bed. The serving wenches deposited the material in their arms and then went back into the hall, reentering the room towing great bushels of hay. There was hay all over the floor, floating in the air, but it told Rory that the hay was dry and, more than likely, relatively clean. She moved closer to the group as they worked to stuff the sack on the bed, which was quickly assuming the shape of a mattress.

She peered closely at the sack they were filling with straw. A cursory examination showed no bugs that she could see but that wasn't good enough.

"Ask them where they got this from and how they cleaned it," she told Kieran.

He proceeded to relay her request in French. The innkeeper replied that it had just been boiled because a man had been murdered on it and they needed to clean off the blood. Kieran didn't tell her that last part, however, only that it had just been boiled. Satisfied, Rory stood back as they finished her new mattress. Kieran came to stand next to her, his massive fists resting on his slender hips as he supervised the work.

"You are fortunate, madam," he told her. "Beds such as this are not commonplace."

Her brow furrowed as she looked up at him. "What do you mean?"

"I have slept on rope beds or on the ground for most of my life."

She understood what he meant. "This is a mattress," she pointed at the straw-stuffed sack. "Or at least the beginning of one. You may as well know that I intend to sleep on beds like this for the rest of my life."

He grunted. "I assumed as much," he muttered. "Do you mean to tell me you did not like the hammock of the boat?"

She made a face, putting her hand on her belly. "Don't remind me," she groaned. "That was the worst experience of my life."

He grinned. "I suspect it is just the beginning of many such experiences you will have in the future."

She slapped at him playfully and he laughed low in his throat, putting his arms around her as the tavern keeper and the two wenches finished stuffing the big bag with straw. It was enormous and lumpy. The tavern keeper then tossed the two coverlets they brought with them onto the bed, bowing swiftly as they quit the chamber. Kieran went to the door and bolted it when they were finished. By the time he turned around, Rory was changing into the soft lamb's wool sleeping shift. He watched her as she sighed contentedly and ran her hands over the garment, the first really clean clothes she'd had on her body in weeks.

"I feel so much better now," she sighed, moving to the bed and picking up the mound of coverlets left behind. She sniffed at them and looked surprised. "They smell like they've just been washed. They're kind of stiff, too. Did they boil these also?"

Kieran looked at the linens, wondering if those were the same that the man was murdered on as well. When Rory shook them out over the mattress, there was a massive faded reddish-orange stain in the middle. She let the coverlet fall on the bed, peering at the stain in the middle.

"Hmm," she smoothed her hand over the stain curiously. "What's that?"

Kieran didn't want to tell her what he knew so he tried to sound very casual about it. "It looks like rust," he said.

Rory bought it. There was no reason for her not to. She smoothed the coverlet down onto the lumpy mattress and put the other one on top of it.

"Hey," she looked at him thoughtfully. "Do you think they'll let us take this mattress with us?"

"Why?"

"Because it's washed and I know the only bodies sleeping on it will be ours."

He lifted his eyebrows. "I suppose so."

That seemed to satisfy her. "Help me smooth out the lumps in this thing," she told him, jumping on the bed. "The hay is lumpy."

Kieran watched her roll around on the bed, trying to roll out the lumps of hay. He didn't move to help her; he did, however, begin to remove his clothing. He'd long since packed away Richard's three lion tunic and now wore his father's tunic; the Hage colors of blue, black and white with the bird of prey emblem. The tunic came off, followed by the chain coat, the hauberk hood, the leather undervest and finally the heavily-padded, linen tunic. He stood there in all of his muscular glory, an amazingly built man with massively wide shoulders. He was positively enormous.

Rory continued to roll around, pounding out the lumps, as he went over to the chair and sat, removing his massive boots. The breeches were next. Now totally nude, he went over to the bed where Rory was squirming about and fell right on top of her.

She yelped as his weight came down on top of her, giggling uncontrollably as he wrapped her up in his big arms and nuzzled her neck. She was sweet, soft and clean smelling, and her damp hair licked at him as his nuzzling turned to gentle kisses. Rory wanted to get the bed made but his heated body and manly musk overwhelmed her. So she gave up trying to smooth out the bed and wrapped her legs around his narrow hips. Arms around his neck, she met his passionate kisses with passion of her own.

Kieran usually took his time with her but, at the moment, his want for her was consuming him. He slid his hands underneath the lamb's wool shift, his hands finding her soft breasts and kneading them tenderly. Rory pulled the shift over her head and met his lustful kisses once more, opening her mouth to his probing tongue, suckling on it and driving him wild. When he could stand it no longer, he took hold of her hips and wedged himself in between her legs. Firmly, but with great care, he drove his rock-hard shaft into her wet and swollen folds.

Rory groaned as he buried himself deep inside her body. It had been a long time since they had tasted one another and she felt every thrust, every movement, with the greatest of pleasure. She wrapped her legs around his buttocks, pulling him in deeper and deeper, feeling his massive member hit her G-spot again and again. In no time, she was climaxing, biting off her cries against his mouth as he continued to thrust.

Soon enough, he erupted deep inside her body, groaning as he murmured his love for her against her lips. Their passion cooled, satisfied, but only for the moment; Kieran took her twice more on the lumpy straw mattress as the night outside deepened.

Rory fell into an exhausted sleep, buried beneath Kieran's warm and enormous body. They slept, wrapped up in each other, until sunrise the next morning. Kieran awoke as the sky began to lighten; it was habit. Birds were chirping and he could hear the water lapping in the inlet. But Rory was still sleeping the sleep of the dead and he carefully disengaged himself from her, rising slowly so he would not disturb her. The fire had gone out in the furnace so he put her lamb's wool shift over her beautiful, naked body, plus the second coverlet, and went to light the fire for her.

The seagulls were already screaming outside as the morning began to dawn. Kieran could see bright blue sky beyond the window as he pulled on his breeches and boots. He then proceeded to put on the rest of his clothing, adding a couple of well-concealed daggers for protection. With Rory still sleeping heavily, he quit the room to go about some necessary business.

Rory slept well into the morning. When she finally awoke, it was because a seagull had perched on the windowsill and squawked loudly. Somewhat startled out of a deep sleep, Rory lay in bed a moment, staring at the uneven ceiling and trying to remember where she was. It took her a moment to remember she was in Marseille with Kieran and she stretched and yawned, smiling faintly as she thought about the night before. She lifted her hands, smelling Kieran on her flesh. It was a manly, musky scent, exclusive to him. It was the most wonderful scent in the world.

She sat up in the lumpy bed, immediately feeling nauseous. An upset stomach had been her constant companion since waking up on that rocky beach almost a month ago so she didn't give it much notice. Everything about this time and place in history upset her stomach. She looked around for a chamber pot but didn't see one. Thoughts of an outhouse or privy disgusted her but she had to go to the bathroom so she hurried up and got dressed.

She washed her bra and panties in the cold bathwater, scrubbing them out and putting them near the furnace to dry in the warmth. Meanwhile, she had pulled on the soft, lamb's wool sleeping shift and the only pair of socks she had, the ones she had been wearing the day they appeared on the beach, and she padded around in the room getting her clothes and toiletries together.

The oil from the previous night had made her skin luscious and soft, and she smoothed more on, loving the scent of it. She even rubbed a little on her face. As her undergarments dried out, she pulled out the cosmetics she had purchased – a color palette that had been imported all the way from Egypt that contained ocher rouge and lip color that was applied with a little paintbrush, beautiful bluish-green eye shadow that was made from crushed seashells and copper ore, and black-as-night kohl that was also applied with a tiny brush. There were also a few other colors on the palette, one a pale skin color and another that was kind of brownish. She wasn't sure what it was made of but she liked the shade. There was also a big pot of a lip ointment made of mint and very fine, strained tallow that made it very creamy.

Rory had to shake her head at the raw and rough Medieval cosmetics. She could only imagine what they might do to her skin and hoped she wasn't allergic to any of the ingredients. She also knew that the only women who wore color on their faces were whores, so she would have to be careful about how much color she applied. Taking her precious little mirror, she mixed the ocher lip color in the lip balm until it was a very faint peach shade and applied it to her luscious lips. Then she rubbed a slight amount of the rouge on her cheeks so it was barely visible. Her eyes were more of a challenge; they were big and hazel, and she didn't want it to look like she had put obvious eye makeup on, so she rubbed a little of the brown color on her lids and outlined her top lashes with an extremely thin line of the black kohl. Using her index finger, she rubbed it into the kohl and stroked it onto her lashes to see if it would stick like mascara. Once dry, it made her lashes look long and dark but not thick like mascara would. Still, she liked the results a great deal. Standing back to take a look at herself, she thought she looked rather good. A modern-day girl trying to work with Medieval cosmetics. Estee Lauder would be proud.

Her long chestnut-colored hair was a little unruly this morning; she'd slept on it wet and it was sticking up in places. Looking at herself, she had terrible bed-head. Her hair was generally straight and fairly thick but here she was with no flat iron, curling iron or blow dryer and she had no idea how she was going to handle her hair.

After a moment's indecision, her gaze fell on the warm furnace, burning hunks of peat, and an idea occurred to her. Using the cold bathwater, she wet her hair, pulled out the horsehair brush that she had purchased with the rest of the toiletries, and went over to the furnace. Then she began the laborious process of holding her head next to the furnace and brushing her hair, over and over, drying it out and hopefully drying it marginally straight.

Whatever she did worked; her hair dried straight and extremely soft. No chemicals in the water did wonders for her hair even if it was a bit fly-away. She ran her fingers through her hair, thinking it very strange not to have any modern-day products on it. Pleased with the results nonetheless, she pulled the front of her hair back off her face, tying it behind her head with one of the ribbons she had borrowed at Hut's hostel.

Testing her underwear, it was dry but semi-stiff, so she removed the lamb's wool shift and put her bra and panties on. Then she pulled the shift back on. The trunk on top of the stack of trunks was open and she began pulling stuff out, coming across all of the garments that were made for her before they sailed from Tyre. Being sick the entire time on the boat hadn't given her any time to inspect her new acquisitions, so she began laying them out on the bed.

By the time she pulled out the fourth surcoat, she decided that was the one she would wear; it was an iridescent orange color with hints of yellow and red in the fabric. The seamstress had even stitched gold thread around the plunging neckline that looked like a rick-rack accent. It had long, belled sleeves and the hem was too long. But she put it on anyway, pulling it over the shift and was truly pleased with the results. She tied off the tassel belt and went in search of her boots.

Then came the all-powerful question of finding the privy. She had to go badly but was torn. Kieran had warned her against straying from the room without him, especially in a public place. Still, she just couldn't sit around and wait for him. She had to find the privy or a chamber pot.

Bending over to pull the long hem of her dress from underneath her boot, she happened to catch sight of the chamber pot shoved far underneath the bed. Getting down on her knees, she pulled out what was quite possibly the most disgusting thing she had ever seen in her life. With a groan, she looked around for anything resembling toilet paper but there was nothing available except for the cloth that had covered their food tray from the night before. She took it, relieved herself quickly, cleaned up and threw the cloth back into the chamber pot and shoved it all back under the bed. The whole process had been revolting, but she felt a thousand times better.

Kieran returned to the room mid-morning to find Rory packed, dressed and ready to leave. He entered the chamber, removing his leather gloves and surveying the scene like the lord and master. His gaze was especially warm on his wife, who was absolutely the most beautiful woman he had ever seen. She looked rested, refreshed and radiant in the gorgeous, orange surcoat. He was a man in love all over again.

"Greetings, Wife," he smiled at her. "You look lovely this morning."

She smiled brightly in return, dipping into a rather unpracticed curtsy. She ended up tipping over and laughing at her lack of coordination.

"I'm going to have to get better at that," she chuckled.

He laughed heartily at her, moving to take her in his arms. She threw her arms around his neck and hugged him tightly. Kieran held her against him, picking her up off the ground. There was a fourteen-inch difference in their heights and her feet dangled off the floor as he cradled her.

"You are so beautiful," he murmured into the side of her head. "I am an extremely fortunate man."

She squeezed him. "I bet you don't think that when I'm sick and complaining."

"Untrue. I think it all of the time." He kissed her cheek, pulling back to look at her. "You look as if you feel better this morning."

She nodded and he set her gently to her feet. "Much better," she said. "It did me good to sleep about ten hours last night."

He wriggled his eyebrows in agreement. "No doubt." He looked at the packed and secured trunks. "I see that you are ready to leave. Did you do all this yourself?"

"Of course," she replied, somewhat incensed that he didn't think she could pack all by herself. "I didn't know when you'd be back so I just packed everything up. Are we leaving?"

He nodded. "In time. Are you hungry?"

"Starving."

He smiled at her. "Come along. I have a surprise for you."

She took his offered hand and, together, they left the chamber. At this hour of the morning, the tavern was fairly quiet but Kieran had the tavern keeper send a wench upstairs to stand outside the door and guard their possessions. Kieran then took Rory outside into the clear and balmy day, escorting her next door. It was a little shack of a shop but the most wonderful smells were coming forth. When they entered the leaning structure, Rory was hit in the face by the smell and warmth of baking bread. It was wonderful.

"Come." Kieran took her over near a hearth with a small but warm fire blazing. There were a table and two chairs, and he called for the shopkeeper as he sat her down. After a few exchanged words, the man and his wife scrambled around, bringing forth trays of food. Soon, Rory had a feast set in front of her and she was both thrilled and awed.

"Wow," she breathed as tray after tray crowded the little table. "What is all of this?"

Kieran asked the man in French what kind of food had been presented. The man answered and Kieran translated.

"Scrambled eggs with cream and cheese, three different types of breads with spices and honey, eggs boiled in wine and fried pig's skin."

She immediately spied the pig's skin; in any century, it looked the same – big, crispy, dark pieces of crackling skin. She picked one up, inspecting it.

"This is the first time I've ever heard of pork rinds being eaten in Medieval Europe," she commented, smelling them. Then she took a timid, crunchy bite and chewed. "It's really good. It tastes like they've soaked it in brine or something really salty. Can you ask him?"

Kieran lifted an eyebrow at her as he asked the man how he prepared the rinds. The man spoke eagerly in answer, smiling at Rory as he did so. Kieran sighed with annoyance as he translated.

"They are soaked in sea water to soften them and then boiled in fat," he said. "May I eat now?"

She smiled happily. "Of course. Thank you, baby."

Kieran grunted in response, plowing into the eggs and Rory knew she would have to eat quickly in order to stay ahead of him; the man had an enormous appetite. She went for the eggs with cream and cheese, and they were wonderful. But she quickly discovered that they weren't like modern eggs; they had a stronger flavor and a heavier texture. The cheese was very tart and strong but delicious. She had about a quarter of the plate before Kieran finished them off, but she beat him to the bread. She tore off a big hunk of the bread with cinnamon in it. With her bread in one hand and a pork rind in the other, she ate until she was stuffed.

Kieran had apparently told the shopkeeper that they were traveling so the man packed them an enormous amount of food, mostly breads and those wonderfully salty pork rinds all wrapped up in some kind of sea grass. Rory wasn't sure what it was but she kept smelling it, finally licking it to see what it tasted like. It was very salty. Kieran paid the man and with wrapped food in both hands, Rory quit the bread shop with Kieran behind her. The day outside was mild and sunny, and she inhaled deeply. She felt good and for the first time since arriving in this place in time, she was actually eager and excited to be here.

"So now what?" she asked as she turned to him. "Are we leaving?"

He nodded, taking the wrapped food from her because it took both of her arms to hold it. With the food in one enormous arm, he took her with his other hand.

"Come with me," he said softly.

She held on to him as they crossed behind the bakery to the livery that was part of the inn's complex. When they entered the structure that smelled very strongly of animal dung and hay, Liberator saw Kieran and nickered. Kieran clucked to the horse but when Rory walked near the beast, he began bobbing his head up and down wildly, finally sticking his big, thick neck out and pushing her with his nose. Rory teetered off balance but caught herself. Scowling, she let go of Kieran and faced the horse with her hands on her hips.

"All right, buddy," she scolded. "You and I are going to come to an agreement or there's going to be bloodshed and it isn't going to be mine. I want you to stop pushing me around. Got it?"

She was wagging a finger at the horse by the time she was finished. Liberator responded by barring his teeth and bobbing his head up and down. He tried to stick his neck out and push her again, but she moved back, thumping him on his big, soft nose when he tried. The horse didn't take kindly to that and began to snort and shake his head again.

"Stop it," Rory demanded, "or there will be more where that came from."

Kieran was standing next to her, watching the exchange. "He does not want to stop," he said as if she were fighting a losing game. "He apparently finds it great fun to push you about."

She turned her nose up at the horse and at Kieran. "Then he's going to get shoved back."

"At least he is not attempting to bite you."

"He's trying to stomp me."

Kieran laughed, taking her arm again and pulling her away from her nemesis. He took her back into a corner of the stable. When they neared the last stall, two good-sized ponies suddenly came into view. They were tethered to the wall, munching on hay, and their big, black eyes blinked at the humans who intruded into their space. Kieran pointed at them.

"Here," he said, suddenly moving away from her as he spoke. "You said that you would be more comfortable if you were not on the back of a horse, so I purchased these for you."

She was about to ask what when he suddenly lifted a cart out of the stall opposite the ponies. It was a fairly large cart but with Kieran's size and strength, it looked like he was handling a child's toy. He set the cart down and Rory gasped with both surprise and pleasure. The cart had a bench seat that would fit two women or one larger man, and a flatbed in the back for baggage. It was made out of some kind of dark wood, although Rory wasn't sure what kind, and the wheels were of sturdy iron and wood. With the two ponies to drive, it would make a delightful little ride. She was thrilled.

"It's wonderful!" she exclaimed, inspecting it closely. "You bought this for me?"

He smiled, pleased with her excitement. "Do you like it?"

She nodded eagerly. "I love it!" She moved back to the two ponies; a big, white one and a big, orange one. She scratched their heads as they ate like pigs. "They're adorable. I love them."

"I am glad you are pleased."

She suddenly whirled around and threw her arms around his neck, nearly knocking him off balance. "You're so wonderful." She kissed him. "You're the best husband in the world and I love you madly."

He returned her kisses and set her to her feet. "Which reminds me," he said. "We have an appointment to keep."

"Appointment?" She looked puzzled as he took her hand and began to lead her out of the livery. "What appointment?

"Come along," he said steadily.

She looked back at her ponies and the cart. "But what about my pony cart? Don't I get to drive it?"

"In good time. Come along."

"But I want to drive it."

"You sound like a petulant child. You can drive it later."

"I don't want to drive it later; I want to drive it now."

"Shut up."

She pinched him.

ᴗß

MARRIAGE IN THE Abbey of St. Victor was all Rory imagined it would be. The place was massive, smelling of ghosts, with a vast sanctuary and no pews. It was like a giant auditorium with uneven dirt floors and one could hear whispers from every corner. It acted like a giant megaphone, magnifying sounds. She was awed from the moment she walked in until the dirty priest appeared.

It was her first good look at a Medieval Catholic priest and she wasn't surprised to see just how raw and dirty the man was. There were stains all over his robes, which were not the beautiful ritual gowns she had grown accustomed to but plain brown wool, layers upon layers of it. He had sores on his face and hands. He looked like a leper and she looked at Kieran with disgust when the man appeared to perform their mass. Kieran stoically pulled her to her knees and crossed himself as the priest began the ceremony.

It was performed in Latin, as Rory knew it would be. She was very familiar with Latin on paper and was able to understand most of what was being said. The priest was helped during the mass by three very young boys, basically dressed in rags. Rory found herself watching the boys more than listening to the mass, noticing that two of them had pretty serious bruises on what flesh she could see.

One little boy, no more than five years old, had a black eye. In fact, that particular child had welts on his lower legs and a few bloodied toes. He looked as if he had been severely thrashed. More than that, he was terribly skinny. She watched the child throughout the mass, growing increasingly concerned. When the priest finished the ceremony, Kieran chastely kissed Rory on the forehead and smiled at her.

"Lady Hage," his brown eyes twinkled. "Now we are official in the eyes of God."

She smiled back at him, watching as he negotiated the mass donation with the priest and paid the man. Meanwhile, her attention was back on the boys, the smallest one in particular with the black eye. He was an adorable child with brown hair and big, blue eyes. She watched him carefully collect the items that the priest used during the mass, only to receive a sharp shove by the older altar boy, causing him to drop a cup. The priest turned around and cuffed the kid on the side of the head. He teetered but didn't fall down. Rory was livid.

"Did you see that?" She turned to Kieran angrily. "The priest hit that little boy for no reason."

Kieran was pulling his big, leather gloves on. He glanced around, trying to see what she was so outraged about. "I did not see," he said, rather carelessly. "Come along, sweetheart. We should be along our way."

She couldn't believe he was so cold. On the other hand, abused children during this time period were not unusual. Still, she couldn't stand by while a child was obviously abused. She knew she couldn't save every child. But she just couldn't seem to walk away from this one.

"Not yet," she told him, more calmly, knowing it would do no good to go crazy about it. "I want you to do something for me."

His mind was already on their travels ahead and he was preoccupied. "What is that?"

"I want you to go and get that little altar boy and bring him with us."

He stopped fiddling with his gloves and looked at her. "What?" his brow flickered with confusion. "What are you saying?"

She was firm and controlled. "Look," she lowered her voice. "That little boy is obviously abused. I know that's no big deal in this time, but in my time it's a huge deal. We don't allow children to be abused and I just can't walk away from that little boy without trying to help him. I want to take him out of this place. He's all covered with bruises."

Kieran just stared at her, processing what she was staying. It was obvious that he was fighting down his irritation as he put his enormous hands on her shoulders. "Sweetheart," he tried to stay patient. "What happens to that child is not our business. He belongs to the Church."

She pulled away from him. "That doesn't give them the right to abuse him," she said, increasingly hot. "Do you approve of beating a child?"

He hissed, looking for an answer that wouldn't throw her over the edge. "I would not beat my own child if that is what you mean."

"It's not what I mean," she said, exasperated. "Look, Kieran. I listened to you when you told me never to stray from you for my own safety. I listened to you when you wouldn't let me take a closer look at the brothels along the waterfront. I've been listening to you since we arrived. But this time, I really want you to listen to me for once. Abuse is not right, on any level, and I just can't walk away from that poor little kid who's so obviously beat up."

He stared at her before exhaling sharply like a man who knows when he has already lost the battle. "What do you want me to do?" he asked irritably.

She pointed in the direction that the priest and the boys had just disappeared. "I want you to go and see if that boy is an orphan. If he is, I want you to bring him with us."

His eyebrows flew up in outrage at her ridiculous statement. "What did you say?"

"You heard me. If he doesn't have any family, then he's coming with us."

He was trying to keep his mouth from hanging open in shock. "And if he is not an orphan?"

"Then there's not much we can do other than to tell the priest to stop hitting him. Threaten to punch the priest if he hits the boy again."

"I am not threatening a priest."

She knew he wouldn't but she was passionate about her feelings. "Whatever," she waved her hand at him as if to erase the threat request. "But if he has no parents, I want him."

Kieran regarded her. "For what purpose?"

She threw up her arms. "So we can take him out of this abusive environment. He can be a little servant for us or something. Anything to get him out of here. I just can't leave that child behind knowing that they're beating him. Can't you understand?"

Kieran's gaze lingered on her a moment longer before he walked away, disappearing into the shadows of St. Victor's. Rory waited for him patiently, finding interest in her surroundings as she waited. There was a massive supporting pillar a few feet away and she went to it, inspecting it, running her fingers along the stone. All the while, however, her mind was with Kieran wherever he was. She was extremely fortunate and she knew it. The man would do anything for her. But, then again, she would do anything for him as well. The more time she spent with him, the luckier and more blessed she felt.

It was some time before Kieran reappeared. Rory was leaning against the pillar when he entered the church again and she immediately straightened at the sight of him. As he emerged from the shadows, a small boy emerged with him. It was the beaten little boy.

Rory smiled when she saw the little figure, her smile fading when she saw tears all over his face. She looked at Kieran.

"What's wrong?" she asked. "Why is he crying?"

Kieran lifted an eyebrow at her. "Because this is his home and he does not want to leave his brother. But you wanted him to come with us so here he is. Satisfied?"

He said it so coldly. Rory's heart sank as she gazed up at him. He obviously didn't see what she was trying to do. She was trying to help a child. Kieran thought she was just being demanding and unreasonable. He could have done less damage had he struck her, so harsh was his expression. He just didn't understand her motives and she probably couldn't make him. There was so much about each other that they still didn't understand. Her smile vanished and the tears began to come.

"No," she whispered hoarsely. "I'm sorry if he's unhappy. I thought I was helping him by taking him out of a place where he was beaten and starved. But I guess I was wrong. I'm sorry I put you through all the trouble, Kieran, I really am. Take him back to his brother and let's get out of here."

She turned on her heel and marched off towards the door. Kieran caught up to her within a few steps and grabbed her but she resisted violently.

"Let me go." She didn't want to raise her voice in the church, struggling to yank herself from his grip. "Just… let me go and take him back where he belongs. I'm sorry I'm such an embarrassment to you. I'm sorry all I do is make unreasonable demands. I'm sorry I…!"

Kieran had heard enough. He threw his arms around her and pulled her face against his chest, effectively muffling her. She continued to fight him and he continued to hold tight.

"Calm yourself, Lib," he said in that sweet, low voice that was so effective at soothing her nerves. "You are not an embarrassment and you are not unreasonable. But I do not understand you at times and I apologize if my confusion shows."

She would not be soothed and the tears were going full force. She began to pound on his chest, trying to separate herself from him.

"Let me go," she demanded, weeping. "I don't want you to hold me right now. I want you to let me go."

After a moment's hesitation, he did. She pulled away from him, her hair mussed and her hands on her face. She walked a few feet away, pressed herself against another stone pillar, and wept. Kieran stood there and watched her, his arms aching to hold her and his heart saddened by her tears.

"I hate it here," she sobbed. "I hate this place. I hate everything about it except you. I don't get it. I thought I did, but I really don't. I have a Doctorate in Archaeology but I still don't get anything about this time and you just don't understand me."

He continued to stand there patiently, watching her vent. He felt sorry for her; he really did. He knew very well what it was to be misplaced in time, the disorientation and frustration. She was doing her best but, still, it was a struggle. He wished he could do more to help her adjust but it was something only time could heal.

As he watched her weep, he caught movement out of the corner of his eye. The little orphan boy was approaching timidly, moving to the other side of the pillar that Rory was weeping against and pressing himself against it as if hiding from her. His big blue eyes were wide as he began to creep around the side of the pillar until he came within a foot or so of Rory. As Kieran watched curiously, the little boy reached up and tugged on her sleeve.

"*La dame*?" the little boy whispered. "*Pourquoi pleurez-vous*?"

Rory looked down at the child, tears streaming down her face. But the sobbing stopped when she realized the kid was talking to her.

"What did he say?" she asked Kieran, sniffling.

"He wants to know why you weep," he replied softly.

She looked at the boy, amazed that so young a child could show such an adult emotion as concern. She knelt down in front of him, gazing up at his very handsome little face, and wiped the tears from her cheeks. She smiled.

"Tell him that I cry because I am concerned for him," she said. "I don't like it when others hurt him."

Kieran relayed the message in his beautiful, fluent French. The little boy looked at Kieran as if uncomprehending the words. He didn't know what to say. Kieran broke from his stance a few feet away and went to Rory and the child, taking a knee beside them. He put his big hand on Rory's back comfortingly.

"Your words have no meaning to him," he said. "I suspect that he has never had anyone show concern for him. He does not know what to make of it."

Rory gazed down at the little face and took the child's hands in hers. They were dirty little appendages but warm and soft.

"Please tell him that I only wanted to help him by taking him away from people that would hurt him," she said. "I didn't mean to make him unhappy or take him away from his brother. I just didn't want him to be beaten anymore."

Kieran relayed the words and the child stared at him. It was apparent that the boy had no clue what he meant. Kieran kissed Rory on the temple and stood up, towering over Rory and the child. He assumed there was nothing more to say and found himself increasingly eager to be on their way. But he wouldn't let Rory know that; she was trying to do something compassionate and kind. In spite of what she said, he did understand that.

As he stood there and tightened up his leather gloves, the child looked up at him again.

"*Mon frère peut-il venir aussi*?" he asked in his sweet, little voice.

Kieran looked at the child with a blank expression as Rory stood up and looked at him curiously.

"What did he say?" she asked.

It would have been easy to lie to her. But he just couldn't bring himself to do it. "He wants to know if his brother can come with us," he said.

Rory looked at the little boy before returning her focus to Kieran. When he looked at her, he could see the joy return to her eyes and, like an idiot, he knew his life was about to change forever. There was no way he could deny her.

"Can his brother come?" she asked Kieran.

Kieran grunted, pursing his lips with resignation. Then he nodded. "If that is your wish," he grumbled. "As if I have any say in the matter, but thank you for pretending to give me some semblance of control."

She threw her arms around his neck, squeezing him tightly. "Thank you," she whispered sincerely, kissing his cheeks. "You're such a sweet man. Thank you for your compassion and generosity."

He held her tightly, allowing her to demonstrate her thanks with her soft lips on his face. "Aye, I am compassionate and generous," he muttered. "But you are making me daft."

She gazed up at him, glowing and smiling. "Admit it. Your life would be boring without me."

"Boring, unhappy and lonely. But at least I would retain my sanity."

She giggled and kissed him. He returned her kisses, tasting her sweetness, happy that things were well between them again. They usually were when she got her way in all things, he thought. But he didn't care in the least.

Setting her to her feet, he disappeared with the little boy for a time and returned with the child plus an older boy, about seven years of age. He had also been one of the altar boys, dirty and bruised. This child was blond but with the same big blue eyes, extremely skinny and dressed in rags. He also had a small sack with him. Kieran indicated the two young lads.

"This is Little Mouse and his older brother, John," Kieran introduced the boys to Rory. "According to the priest, they have been with

St. Victor's since they were infants. They do not know who their parents are but suspect the mother works in one of the brothel's in town. The woman who brought the boys claimed she was not their mother but said the boys' fathers are Christian knights who fight with Richard."

Rory held Kieran's elbow as she gazed down at the skinny, dirty boys. "They're adorable," she said softly. "But I don't like their names. We're going to call them Bud and David."

Kieran looked at her, sharply, before breaking down into snorts. "Of course," he slapped his thigh ironically. "After Dr. Dietrich and Dr. Peck. You would name them after your colleagues?"

"They were our friends."

His smile faded and he patted her hand affectionately, leaning over to kiss the top of her head. "I know, sweetheart," he murmured, not wanting her to sink into depression reflecting upon those she left behind. Then he looked back at the boys and spoke to them in French. "*Entendez-vous cela? Votre nom est Bud et votre plus vieux nom du frère est David. Vous répondrez à ces noms à partir de.*"

Rory could guess what he said by the way the boys looked at him and each other. She shook her head. "*Deseo que hablara francés,*" she said to Kieran.

He looked at her strangely. "What language is that?"

"Spanish. Well, Mexican Spanish. It's native to the Mexicans where I'm from."

He lifted an eyebrow at her, smiling with some approval. "What did you say?"

"That I wish I spoke French."

He lifted his eyebrows at her. "I believe I like this Mexican Spanish," he said. "It sounds rather seductive. You will speak more to me when we are in private."

She chuckled, refusing to give in to his sexual innuendos in front of the boys. She shook her head at him and focused on the children.

"*Operor vos agnosco illa lacuna*?" she asked.

The boys' eyes widened and they nodded their head. Smiling, Rory looked up at Kieran. "Well, at least I can communicate with them somewhat," she said. "I took five years of Latin in college as it related to my major. It was necessary for translating Medieval documents. I'm not very good at speaking it but I can read it pretty well."

He was still smiling at her from his earlier comment regarding her Spanish. He reached out and pulled her against him. "I find your ability to converse in Spanish and Latin extremely alluring," he murmured. "Say more words."

She giggled, pushing against him until he let her go. "Stop it," she commanded weakly, a smile on her lips. "Not in front of the children."

He fought off a smirk. Rory gazed down at the confused, somewhat tired little faces and her smile began to fade as well. She reached up and took Kieran's fingers within her own.

"Ask them if they really want to come," she said quietly.

He looked at her as if she were mad. "What?" he cried. "After all this, now you think to ask them?"

"Please?"

He was back to being irritated and asked the boys, somewhat impatiently, if they really wanted to come. The boys nodded without hesitation. Then the little one took the older one's hand, holding it tightly. Rory was touched by the gesture. It was just the two of them. Perhaps, they supposed that anything was better than what they had, fearful or not. She couldn't tell if they were afraid, curious or both.

"All right," she tugged on Kieran's massive hand. "Let's go."

He nodded wearily. "Are you sure?"

"Yes."

"Do you want to rescue more boys perhaps? Or even the priest? Perhaps we have it all wrong and the boys are beating the priest and each other. Perhaps we need to save them from themselves."

She slapped him on the arm. "Oh, shut up."

He laughed heartily as they walked from the church.

CHAPTER NINE

RORY LEARNED RIGHT away that driving the amazing pony cart was not as easy as she thought. Kieran gave her and the boys a lesson, although Bud, the older boy, apparently already knew how to drive a rig. In fact, he got in the cart and took it in a circle around the stable yard neatly, much to the cheers of Rory and his brother. Little David seemed much more willing to smile and laugh than his older brother did. Bud was a very serious and guarded child.

A couple of stable hands helped load up Rory's trunks on the cart, securing them on the flat bed and taking up all of the space. Kieran saddled Liberator himself. The horse was too snappish to let anyone else near him. He loaded up his saddlebags and possessions, alternately focused on what he was doing and on Rory and the two boys as they practiced on the cart. He had to stop and grin as Rory tried to drive the cart in a circle as Bud had; she had the ponies going in opposite directions. Bud swooped in to save the day and got the ponies going in the right direction again.

Even though they didn't exactly speak the same language, Rory and the boys were doing an awful lot of communicating. It was mostly through hand gestures and a few Latin words, but the point was getting across. And Kieran was growing increasingly enamored with his wife, watching her communicate most animatedly with two orphaned boys.

He was already madly in love with her, but watching her interact with the two starving children was a sight to behold. She was patient, kind and helpful. She praised Bud repeatedly for his skill in driving the little cart, to which Bud seemed unsure how to react. It was quite clear early on that neither boy was used to anyone being kind to them. But that prospect had abruptly changed. She was happy and friendly with the boys, who seemed a bit overwhelmed with everything.

Kieran turned back to securing his possessions on his saddle, listening to Rory communicate with the two young boys. Then she climbed onto the wagon and took the reins herself. He wasn't paying attention to what she was doing when he suddenly heard a yelp. Turning sharply to identify the source, he saw Rory sitting on the ground in the middle of the stable yard laughing her head off. Bud had hold of the pony cart so it wouldn't get away but it was obvious what had happened. Kieran stopped what he was doing and made his way over to her.

Little David was helping her stand up. Rory was still laughing as Kieran got to her.

"I assume you are uninjured." Kieran's lips were twitching with a smile.

She shook her head, brushing off her bum. "I'm fine," she said. "It's not as easy as it looks."

Kieran nodded. "Bud seems to be much better at it. You had better let him drive until you become more practiced."

She nodded, rubbing her backside. "I agree."

Kieran watched the boys corral the ponies and straighten up the cart. He put his arm around her shoulders. "Are you ready to leave?"

She nodded. "Whenever you are."

He kissed her and let her go, moving to the boys and telling them to bring the cart around so Lady Hage could climb on board. They did so and Kieran helped his wife onto the seat next to Bud. David jumped on the back, his legs hanging over the edge of the cart. He seemed quite happy and even smiled at Kieran. Kieran winked back.

With the pony cart heading out to the road, Kieran mounted Liberator and, as the morning deepened in the sleepy coastal town of Marseille, they were well on the way to Paris.

*

NINE DAYS ON the road to Paris had been better than the three weeks on the boat, but not by much. The travel by land had been an extremely harsh introduction into the Medieval world. All of the books and education in the world couldn't prepare Rory for the reality of it. It had been beyond belief and not nearly as interesting as she had hoped. It was, for the most part, hellish. She tried not to hate every moment of it.

On the ninth night since leaving Marseille, they were still two days short of Paris. Traveling on the open road for days on end had seen them stop every night at a small town and finding some kind of inn or tavern. Rory had stories upon stories of bugs, vomit in rooms, sleeping in a dormitory, constant rain and other things she considered horrendous. Kieran had done his best to make sure she was always comfortable and happy but it had been a struggle.

Traveling during this time was nothing as she knew it. She had to keep reminding herself of the fact and simply accept it. No rest stops, restaurants along the road, trains, planes or automobiles. After the third night of travel when they had stayed in a very small town with no inn, spending the night in a musty stable, Rory made a silent vow to never again whine about the conditions. There was no use in complaining because Kieran was doing the very best he could. The man had a great deal of wealth with him and she knew that he would beg, buy or steal whatever he had to in order to obtain the best for her. If staying in a musty stable was the best, then she would trust him.

But the one thing she was rather adamant about was a hot bath. Kieran did his very best to ensure she had one available every night. The last four days had been particularly miserable, as they had been subjected to nonstop rain and it had been very, very cold.

They'd had to stop in a small town three nights before to purchase warmer garments for the boys, which had been something of a process. There were no stores in this time period where one could simply go and purchase anything they needed, so Kieran had tracked down a merchant with several children and bought most of the children's ready-made clothing. Bud and David came away with new tunics and hose, plus a variety of heavier outerwear that was put to good use. The boys had been amazed; they'd never had anything other than rags to wear. They told Kieran that they felt like kings.

Bud and David, in fact, had been a joyful addition to the group. After the first few days of moderate standoffishness, little David, in particular, seemed to warm to Rory. When both boys figured out that neither the knight nor his lady were planning on abusing them, the warmth came quickly. Bud seemed to relate better to Kieran and followed him around, essentially becoming something of a page, which Rory thought was very sweet. Kieran showed extreme patience and kindness with the boy which made her love the man that much more. Plus, it was very good practice for what was to come.

Rory began to suspect it once they left Marseille. She just wasn't feeling right and the nausea she had experienced on the boat never went away. In fact, it was fairly constant. Not enough to vomit but just enough to feel lousy. She attributed it to the food, the travel and the shock of the situation, but when her monthly cycle didn't come, she began to suspect something so troubling that she could barely contain herself. Certainly, pregnancy was something she knew would eventually happen, but she just wasn't prepared to think about it or acknowledge it at the moment. In fact, it horrified her.

So she ignored the thought on the entire trip. But as each day passed and her cycle didn't come, she grew increasingly frightened. She began to count the weeks since the first time she and Kieran made love, remembering back to the time when they had been running from Corbin shortly after Kieran had been brought back from the dead. She had succumbed to her feelings for the man and they'd had passionate sex for most of the night. By her calculations, that had been almost seven weeks ago. It was plenty of time for a pregnancy to gain root and announce itself.

With that knowledge, her mood darkened. The rain was miserable, the travel was miserable, she felt horrible and she was absolutely terrified to give birth without the aid of modern medicine. No prenatal care, no hospitals, no ultrasounds… just midwives, surgeons and, if she was feeling particularly angry about it, alchemists and witchdoctors. As a modern woman and a former Pre-Med student, the possibilities were horrifying. Her anxiety was building.

Two days out of Paris, they were staying in a fairly nice inn compared to what they had known up until that point. Closer to the city meant better accommodations. Kieran had sought out the most expensive, nicest inn he could find and procured two rooms, one for him and Rory and one for the boys. He wouldn't have gotten the second room for the boys but Rory had insisted. Kieran thought the boys could just as easily have slept in the stable but she wouldn't hear of it.

It was pouring rain outside as Kieran had the innkeeper and a couple of burly men bring in a tub. This one was actually a big, copper bath tub rather than a pot or a wash tub. It was meant for baths. After it was filled with steaming water, Rory pulled off her wet clothing and climbed in. Kieran sat next to the tub, eating their meal and stripping off his own wet clothing in between gulps of wine and big bites of beef. He kept up a running chatter about what would happen when they reached Paris but Rory silently lathered up her body, seemingly lost in thought. He noticed but thought she was simply tired. When he asked her a question and she didn't respond, he tapped the side of the tub with a big, greasy finger.

"Did you hear me?" he asked.

She had been picking at her wet toes, thinking she needed a pedicure. "What?" her head came up and she focused on him, realizing he was talking to her. "I'm sorry, I didn't hear you. What did you say?"

He smiled faintly at her. "I know you did not hear me." He sat forward in the chair, his elbows resting on his knees and his hands hanging. "In fact, you have not heard a word I have said the entire time. What is troubling you, sweetheart?"

She shook her head. Then she burst into tears. Kieran wiped his greasy hands off on his breeches and put a massive hand on her back.

"I know this has been difficult for you," he said soothingly. "You have shown remarkable resilience throughout this journey and I am very proud of you."

She wept painfully. Then she reached up, wrapping her arms around his neck and pressing her clean, wet body against him. Kieran rocked her gently.

"What is wrong, sweet?" he whispered into the side of her wet head. "Why do you weep so? Am I such a horrible husband?"

"No."

"The boys; have they done something awful and you are afraid to tell me?"

"No!"

She struggled not to get hysterical, but these tears had been building up for several days. "I'm so scared," she finally murmured. "I've never been so scared in my entire life."

"What about?"

"I'm going to die," she wept deeply. "I don't want to die, I really don't, but I know I am."

He fought off a smile at her dramatics. "You look healthy enough. Just how is Death going to take you away from me?"

"In childbirth," she wept. "Do you know what the mortality rate for childbirth was during this era? About fourteen deaths for every one hundred children born. That's almost twenty percent."

He chuckled softly; he couldn't help it. "I would not worry overly," he said. "There are many fine midwives and physics. You needn't worry about this right now."

She gazed up at him with her wide hazel eyes. Tears trickled from the corners. "Yes, I do," she replied, "because we're going to have a baby in about seven months and I'm scared to death."

He didn't react at first but there was a long delay before he replied. "Are you sure?"

She sniffled, wiping at her cheeks. "Uh huh," she replied sadly. "I think that's why I've been feeling so horrible the past few weeks, although that damned boat didn't help anything. Plus, my boobs are sore and my period is about a week late. That just never happens with me, ever. It's not like you and I have ever used any birth control so I'm pretty sure I'm pregnant."

Kieran's gaze held steady for a moment, but that was as much self-control as he had. As Rory watched, his jaw went slack and his eyes took on the strangest glimmer. She could feel his grip tightening around her and then, suddenly, he was off the chair and on his knees. He pulled her against him fiercely and buried his face in her bare bosom. Startled, Rory forgot her tears for the moment as Kieran practically crumbled in front of her.

"Kieran?" her hands were on his head, trying to lift it from her chest. "Baby, what's wrong?"

He refused to let her go or allow her to lift his head. He just held her, tightly, and she stopped trying to force him to look at her, unsure what was going on with him. Suddenly, she wasn't so scared anymore. She was more concerned about Kieran at the moment so she simply put her arms around his head and held him against her breasts. She wasn't sure what else to do.

The fire crackled in the hearth, the only sound in the room. After what seemed like a small eternity, Kieran finally lifted his head. She looked at his expression, trying to read what he was thinking, and was shocked to see that his eyes were moist with tears. Before she could ask him why he was so upset, he put his massive hands on her cheeks and looked her in the eye.

"I am the most fortunate man in the entire world," he whispered hoarsely, his eyes glittering with jubilation. "To be so blessed is something I hoped for but did not expect. I did not want to be disappointed. But you… you have made me the happiest man to ever walk this earth. I cannot explain it more than that."

His unadulterated joy touched her deeply. It eased her fear a great deal and she began to feel some of his joy.

"Really?" she grinned timidly.

He nodded, kissing her so sweetly that her entire body tingled with delight. "Really," he whispered against her lips.

The tears came again as she felt his adoration, his sheer delight. She was exhausted and hormonal, giving in to the gentle kisses he was raining over her face.

"I want the best midwife and surgeon in the country," she sniffled.

"I promise you shall have it," he murmured, dragging his lips across her jaw. "You and my son shall have the very best of everything, I swear it."

"It could be a girl, you know," she reminded him.

He reached a hand over and picked up the big, linen sheet she used to dry off, picking her up and wrapping her up tightly in it.

"My mother had four boys," he said. "My father also had two brothers and his father had three. Male children run heavily in my family."

"Would you be disappointed if it was a girl?"

He gave her a look that suggested she was mad. "Of course not," he said. "Would you?"

She shook her head. "No," she said, drying off. "But I'm still really scared."

He smiled at her. "No need, sweetheart. I promise I will not let anything happen to you. Do you believe me?"

She couldn't tell him no. Smiling weakly, she nodded. "I believe you."

His smile broadened and he kissed her again. "Good," he said, putting her to her feet. "Now, I am going to procure some food. Will you be all right while I am gone?"

She could see that her news had changed everything; she could just read it in his face. He was going to treat her like she was made of the most fragile, breakable glass for the next seven months and she nodded patiently. "I'll be fine," she assured him. "I'd really like white bread, butter and honey if they have it."

"Of course." He was heading for the door, lighter of mood than she had ever seen him; he was usually fairly serious and calm. He looked like a giddy teenager. "Anything else?"

She looked at him, laughing. "You look silly."

"Silly?"

She nodded, grinning. "Like you're bouncing around all over the place."

He suddenly moved back to her, cupping her face in his enormous hands and kissing her deeply. "I am," he murmured, kissing her swiftly one last time and moving back to the door. "I shall return."

"Okay." She turned away, looking for her clothes. "Bring Bud and David when you come back. They're hungry, too."

"As you say, madam."

Kieran shut the door, leaving Rory hunting for her clothing. He moved down the short hallway to the sturdy, stone staircase that led into the main room downstairs. His head was still spinning with the news, thrilled beyond measure. A son, he thought to himself, someone to carry on the Hage name, a proud reflection of his proud parents. The next Viscount of Dykemoor and Sewall, heir to the baronetcies left to him by his mother. He was full of big plans for his son already as he hit the bottom of the stairs and headed towards the kitchen. As he entered the smoky, dark area of the inn where there were a few tables for eating, he was met by the tall and rather debonair innkeeper.

The man had short, dark hair and an elegant air about him. He greeted Kieran with a swift bow.

"My lord Viscount," he said. "Someone came here a short time ago asking if I knew of an English knight by the name of Kieran Hage. I told him no and sent him away."

Kieran's expression didn't change although he felt some trepidation. "Did he say what he wanted?"

The innkeeper shook his head. "Nay, my lord," he replied. "But he was very dark. A Moor."

"A Moor?" Kieran's trepidation deepened. "Did he give his name?"

"Nay, my lord."

"Did you watch him leave? Which direction did he go?"

The innkeeper motioned for Kieran to follow him and they moved through the main part of the inn where several people were sitting, drinking. The innkeeper opened the large and surprisingly well-fitting front door, pointing down the avenue.

"Down there, somewhere," he pointed. "Perhaps he has gone to ask other innkeepers if they know you."

Kieran's dark eyes studied the street; the sun had set and the cobbled streets were muddy and shadowed. The only light was from the windows of various homes and establishments along the avenue and Kieran continued to study the area, looking for any tiny measure of movement. He saw nothing. Stepping back inside the tavern, he pulled the innkeeper with him and shut the door.

He dug into the purse he kept inside his leather vest and slipped the man a couple of coins. "Take your finest meal up to my wife," he told the man. "If she wants to know where I am, you know nothing. Is that clear?"

The innkeeper nodded. "You shall be obeyed, my lord."

"And she wants white bread with butter and honey. Make all effort to obtain it and you shall be well paid."

"It will be my pleasure, my lord."

"Good. Now, go."

The innkeeper swiftly moved away and Kieran opened the front door, slipping out into the dark and cool night. Although he was without his armor, he still had two dirks shoved into his boots and would be able to defend himself if necessary. More than anxiety, he was deeply curious as to who would be looking for him. It was possible that assassins had followed them from the Holy Land, but based on the description of the man from the innkeeper, he wasn't entirely sure why a Moor would be looking for him. He didn't know any Moors. His curiosity grew.

There were two other taverns on this road, lesser establishments than the one he was staying in. He slinked up to one of them, staying close to the wall as he peered into a window. Whiffs of stanky air met his nose as he watched the people inside, looking for a dark and swarthy man. His eyes studied the room. Not seeing anyone that fit the description, he moved on.

The next tavern was further down the road, almost to the edge of town. He made his way to the structure but the windows were over his head and difficult to look in to. He tried several times to prop himself up to take a look. Unable to achieve this, he made the decision to go inside.

He was tense as he entered the crowded establishment, smelling of smoke and roasted meat. There were a few oil lamps throughout the room but most of the light came from the blazing hearth that was spitting a good deal of smoke into the room. Kieran moved into the room, his brown eyes moving about the room, studying faces and body language, looking for the Moor that had been searching for him. All he saw were pale-skinned people looking at him with equal suspicion, so he backed his way out of the room and left.

He quickly returned to his tavern, focused on returning to Rory and the joyous news she had delivered. If a Moor was looking for him, then he suspected they would find each other soon enough. It would put him more on his guard, which was already in overdrive after Rory's news. He had to get her home and safe inside the massive walls of Southwell.

He blew into the tavern, taking the stone steps two at a time. Moving swiftly down the hall, he knocked heavily on the door to his room. No doubt, Rory would bolt it. He could hear voices inside, mostly hers, and assumed she was talking to the boys. The next thing he saw was her smiling face.

"Hi," she said, opening the door wide. "Look who's here."

Kieran entered the chamber, his gaze moving immediately to the other occupants. He saw Bud and David, sitting at the table eating, and someone else standing near the hearth. As recognition dawned, his jaw dropped.

"Yusef?" he said, disbelieving, his gaze then moving to a tiny old figure seated at the table. "Kaleef?"

Yusef appeared exhausted and unshaven but smiled warmly at his friend. The old alchemist did the same, waving a gnarled hand. Kieran moved into the room, shocked, and put a gigantic hand on Yusef's shoulder. Yusef returned the gesture, genuinely glad to see his English friend.

"My friend," he greeted Kieran. "I am so glad to see that God has protected you in your journey."

Kieran just stared at him. "You are the Moor who has been looking for me?"

Yusef nodded. "Old Kaleef and I have been following you for weeks. We had hoped to find you very soon."

The surprise of Yusef's appearance was replaced by a very strong sense of anxiety. There was obviously a powerful reason behind their appearance. Kieran's warm expression faded, his brown eyes focused on the Saracen.

"Why have you been looking for me?" his voice lowered. "Is something amiss?"

Yusef's warm smile faded and his eyes flicked to Rory and the two young boys. "Perhaps we should speak in private."

Kieran took him next door to the room where the boys were supposed to be sleeping. It was tiny but private. Shutting the door, he turned to his Saracen friend.

"What is going on?" he demanded quietly. "Why in God's name have you followed me for weeks?"

Yusef's smile was gone. "I had to locate you," he said. "I have news."

"It must be very important."

Yusef was exhausted; he sat heavily on the small bed in the room and removed his turban, wiping his brow with his hand. "Right after you left, a knight by the name of du Bois found me," he began. "Do you know him?"

Kieran nodded slowly. "Rhys is one of my closest friends. What did he say?"

"He told me that one of de Corlet's men broke faith and confessed all to the king, including the fact that you were not a traitor as de Corlet had told him." Yusef watched Kieran's expression tighten. "When Simon found out that the king knew of his lies, he fled. It is believed he has fled back to England, just as you are. I had to warn you, Kieran. You are both heading home and I did not want you to be caught unaware in case you came upon him."

Kieran stared at him, his jaw ticking faintly. "Do you know when he left?"

"I was given this information the day after you sailed, so I imagine that de Corlet departed around the same time you did."

Kieran lifted an ironic eyebrow. "If that is so, it is a wonder we have not met up at some point before this," he said slowly, eyeing Yusef. "Does Simon know I am returning home also?"

"I do not know. But if I could guess, I would say that he does not. How could he?"

Kieran shook his head, slowly. "He could not, unless he found out by happenstance." He took a deep breath, murmuring thoughtfully. "So Richard knows that I am innocent? Praise God."

"I knew you would want to know that as well."

Kieran sighed heavily, as if a great weight had been lifted. "Of course," he muttered. "I mean… well, it means a great deal. It means that I am not returning home with the cloud of treachery hanging over my head."

"It was unjust that you should."

Unjust indeed. Kieran chewed on that a moment before turning away, his mind rolling with tumultuous thoughts. He couldn't seem to wrap his mind around the implications, the ominous tidings to come. Simon was heading to England. He swore, at that moment, that if he ever saw Simon again, he would kill the man. No words, no greetings or threats. He would draw his sword and plunge it into the man's belly, taking great pleasure in watching Simon die. For all of the anguish and agony Simon had caused, Kieran would make the man pay a thousand times over. But before he got caught up in too much reflection, he turned back to Yusef.

He gazed down at the dark head, knowing how much the man had risked to come and find him. He was deeply touched and more than grateful. A lesser man would not have bothered. But Yusef was proving himself to be a man of great strength of character.

"You are a true friend," Kieran said quietly. "I want you to come back to England with me. I will provide you with lands and wealth of your own. When I tell my father what you have done, he will agree. Will you accept my gratitude?"

Yusef gazed up at him, his weary eyes glimmering. "You are generous, my friend. But I did not do it for reward. I did it because you are an honorable Christian who was turned upon by those you trusted. My commander, El-Hajidd, trusted you enough to carry his message of peace to your king. I have such respect for you as well."

"Does El-Hajidd know you are here?"

"He is the one that told me to come."

Kieran nodded faintly, feeling more gratitude than he could express; enemies who were no longer enemies. It spoke a great deal about the bond that was building between them, the trust that transcended race or religion. Kieran felt privileged to be a part of it.

"You may have been my enemy once, Yusef, but no longer," he said sincerely. "I would trust you with my life."

Yusef nodded, an exhausted but pleased gesture. "As I trust you with mine." He stood up, unsteadily. "Now that we have expressed our undying friendship and gratitude to each other, do you suppose that I could have something to eat?"

Kieran laughed and clapped the man on the shoulder. "Absolutely," he said, practically pulling the man to his feet. "The food is not as good as what you are used to in your land but it will do."

"It will have to," Yusef replied. "Anything but pork, of course."

"Of course." They emerged into the hall and Kieran turned to him. "There is something I would like to know, however. Why is Kaleef with you? Why bring a fragile old man?"

Yusef shrugged. "He has nothing left since his home was burned.

He wanted to come with me so I brought him. He says he has never seen green hills before and he hears that England is full of them."

Kieran lifted an eyebrow as they reached the door to his chamber. "Full, indeed," he said, hand on the latch. "But his presence is fortuitous. My wife has informed me that we are expecting a child and I will be comforted to know that Kaleef is with us."

Yusef smiled brightly. "That is good news, my friend. I congratulate you."

Grinning, they went back to the room where Rory, the boys and old Kaleef were. Warm conversation and food flowed for most of the evening, until Yusef was so exhausted that he could no longer keep his eyes open. He and Kaleef slept in the same room as Bud and David, who were a bit frightened by the two swarthy and unfamiliar men. Kieran had to convince the boys that the Saracens meant them no harm. Still, the children slept in the corner. Bud stayed awake, vigilantly, most of the night.

When Kieran and Rory were alone, he confided in her about the true reason for Yusef's appearance. She reacted as he knew she would; she threatened to kill Simon single-handedly.

CHAPTER TEN

One week later
London, England

IT WAS ONLY the second time Rory had ever been to London, but the skyline was nothing as she remembered. No Big Ben, no London Eye, no buildings of steel and glass that had become fixtures in modern London. As the barge they were traveling upon rolled slowly up the Thames, Rory was enamored with the Medieval sights at hand. It was truly an amazing experience.

It was a chilly day with a brisk breeze and big, puffy clouds scooted across the sky. There was a storm approaching from the west and the entire western horizon was blanketed with dark and angry clouds. But overhead, it was blue but for the breezy white clouds. Wrapped tightly against the elements, Rory was thrilled to have finally arrived.

Paris had been something of a disappointment; no Eiffel Tower or other buildings she was familiar with. But she did notice it to be a rather neat and continental city. Sure, there were some nasty areas, but the right bank of the Seine seemed to be clean and well-traveled. Kieran had picked a tavern overlooking the river about a mile south of Notre Dame Cathedral, which was standing but not nearly what Rory knew of it in her century. In fact, the entire city was somewhat backwater from what she knew until Kieran took her shopping the next day and she realized that Paris was a Medieval shopper's dream. Many merchant roads converged in the city and she bought more fabric, more skin oils and creams, more fragrances and more trinkets for Bud and David than she should have. They bought the boys small wooden swords and the kids were in high heaven. But Kieran liked to see her happy and, at this point in their travels, spending money was about the only thing that made her happy. She was exhausted and he understood that.

So they pressed onward the next day and took a boat from Calais to Dover, whereupon they switched boats and ended up on a barge that was to dock in London. It took the barge a few hours to move down the Thames and into the city.

Kaleef, Bud and David stood with Rory on the deck of the barge, watching the sights. Rory grew particularly excited when she caught sight of the Tower of London, which was absolutely nothing like the Tower she was used to. In fact, it took her a moment to realize what it was because it didn't have the shape or size of what it had in modern times. It had a massive curtain wall, of course, and the White Tower was obvious in the center of it, but it didn't seem to encompass nearly the acreage that it had in modern times. Clearly, it was a large castle but not nearly as large as it was going to be in the future. Still, it was a fascinating sight.

The docks of London were just to the west of the Tower and immediately before an enormous bridge that spanned the river. That, too, took Rory a moment to recognize; it was the London Bridge as she had never seen it. The barge docked on what looked like an actual pier and Rory was thrilled that she wasn't going to have to be carried ashore. Kieran and Yusef eventually joined the group, whereupon Kieran directed the two young boys to help with the baggage. Already, several dock hands were moving their trunks to the wagon that was waiting on the pier and the little orphan boys, now fatter with food, good treatment and rest, ran to assist. They were good little workers.

Yusef aided Kaleef down the gangway to the pier while Kieran took his wife in hand. Her boots, which she had worn since the day they had arrived at Nahariya, made big, booming noises as they made their way down the old, wooden gangway. Kieran looked at his well-dressed wife, clad in a beautiful, pale blue surcoat and matching cloak, and was deeply pleased with the vision. But the boots did nothing for her beauty.

"Lib," he said casually as they reached the pier. "Would you permit me to purchase proper shoes for you while we are here?"

She looked down at her work boots, the same boots she'd had since college. They were old, worn, but extremely comfortable. He had a point, however. They looked extremely out of place with the fine clothing Kieran had purchased for her. She pursed her lips wryly.

"Do I have to?" she asked.

He smiled. "I am offering to buy you something. Normally, the words are not even out of my mouth before you are agreeing. Why do you not want new shoes?"

She looked back at her boots. "Because I like these," she said softly. "They're something from home, something of mine. They're comforting."

He put his hand on her arm, rubbing her affectionately. "You do not have to dispose of them," he said gently. "But you have so many lovely new clothes and those shoes simply do not complement them."

She gazed up at him, knowing he was just trying to be kind. She wrapped her arms around his waist, laying her head on his chest as he enveloped her in his enormous arms.

"Maybe a new pair or two would be okay," she said. "But I would really like to keep my boots."

"I will bury you in them if it pleases you."

She giggled and he kissed the top of her head, releasing her and turning away to boom orders to some deck hands who were roughly handling their trunks. Then he turned to Bud and David, emitting a soft whistle and motioning for them to follow when he caught their attention. They went back up the gangway and went to the stern of the barge where Liberator and the ponies were tethered. Kieran took Liberator in hand while the boys each grabbed a pony. They led the animals off the barge while a deck hand pulled the cart off onto the pier.

Rory stood with Yusef and Kaleef as Kieran supervised the organization of their possessions. The boys were hitching up the pony cart, which had actually become more theirs than Rory's. They took great pride in tending the ponies and maintaining the cart.

Rory had been teaching them English for the past week and they were learning rapidly. Both boys were very intelligent and eager to learn. Little David especially had taken to Rory; he would sit on her lap and hold her hand, and she lavished affection on him. Kieran wasn't particularly thrilled that she was getting so familiar with servants but the few times he tried to bring it up, she had snapped at him. He knew her mothering instincts were kicking into overdrive so he finally gave up and left her alone. If she wanted to hug little David, who was truly an adorable child, then so be it.

Bud was a different story. He had come out of his shell in the past week, smiling more readily and learning English quickly, but he was clearly more comfortable with Kieran. He followed the man around, learning anything he could from the big knight, basically becoming Kieran's shadow. Even now, he helped Kieran count their trunks and ran to do the man's bidding when Kieran ordered the trunks loaded up on the cart secured to two big, hairy, draft horses. Kieran had grown up around pages and squires his entire life and knew how they should be treated, but even he wasn't hard pressed to admit that he was growing rather fond of Bud. He was a bright, serious child, eager to please.

Kieran had sent a man ahead to secure them three rooms at The Black Swan, a tavern where he had spent a good deal of time in the past when he visited London. Meanwhile, he put Rory and Kaleef in the pony cart while he and Yusef walked beside it, heading towards the Strand where the tavern was situated. He hadn't been home in three years and, already, he began to feel relief and comfort at the familiar sights. Now he was back in his element. He was home.

The streets were busy with people going about their business. Rory was enthralled with the unpaved dirt streets, the people, and the sheer magnitude of dirt all over everything. It was kind of like the Medieval faires that she had been to in the past, only smellier. Colors weren't vibrant; they were all muted and grayish because of the lack of modern pigment or finishes. Clothes seemed to be the same way; a few varying shades of browns or blacks or even reds. There weren't any particular styles of clothes for the most part; tunics, hose, rough surcoats for the peasants. She hadn't seen any fine ladies yet and she was eager to see what they were wearing.

As they traveled down the street, Rory noticed everything. Her archaeologist's instincts were going wild with the new sights and sounds. Kieran watched her and their surroundings closely; people didn't like to be stared at the way she was and he didn't want anyone to take her interest as a challenge. But he knew better than to discourage her. Dogs ran in the street and there was no sense of traffic control; people just walked where they felt like it. The scene was mildly chaotic.

Yusef, walking beside Kieran, was just as enthralled as Rory was only he was able to keep his wonder in check a little more than she was. Still, he'd never seen a city like this and he was awed.

"I have never seen so many Christians in my life," he commented, sizing up a wood and mortar, four-story structure that they were passing. He was amazed with all of the wood, so rare in his country. "Are all Christian cities so large?"

Kieran grinned. "Not all," he replied. "There are some remarkable cities in the Holy Land. What makes you so fascinated with this one?"

Yusef shrugged, watching a particularly lovely peasant woman walk by him with white skin and flaming red hair. "The people are colorful," he said. "In my land, everyone is dark. Here, there are people of many colors."

Kieran gave him a half-grin, glancing over to see that Rory was looking behind the cart, watching some activity. When he turned to see what had her attention, he couldn't make heads or tails of it. It was just the same busy London he was used to. He turned back to Yusef.

"We will stay here tonight and then head to Southwell in the morning," he said. "I will send word to my father that we are coming home. He will be thrilled."

Yusef gazed up at the puffy clouds. "What is your home like?"

"Big," Kieran promptly replied. "My family is very, very old; older than the Normans who conquered this land over one hundred years ago. We are descended from the kings of Mercia and when the Normans came, my ancestor was smart enough to work with them, not against them, and retain much of his holdings. Although my family ruled most of middle England and some of Kent for many years, we now have a section of land just north of Nottingham. It is a four or five day journey from London, longer if my wife stops to look at every little thing along the way. She is fascinated by everything."

Yusef looked over his shoulder at the exquisite woman. He had come to know her a little better over the past week of travel and was coming to think she wasn't such an aggressive, unruly woman as he originally thought. She was bright and quite humorous. Still, she had a very strange accent and there was something odd about her, something he couldn't quite put his finger on.

"Your wife is not from England?" he asked Kieran casually.

Kieran shook his head. "Nay."

"Where is she from?"

Kieran looked at him a moment, breaking down into a weak smile and looking away. "You would not believe me if I told you."

Yusef grinned. "Is she divine, perhaps?"

Kieran lifted an eyebrow, half-nodding, half-shrugging. "Not as much as she would like to think," he teased. "Her family is of Irish descent."

That seemed to satisfy Yusef somewhat. "I have heard the Irish are mad."

Kieran laughed. "Not all of them."

Yusef glanced at Rory again, who was saying something to Kaleef and pointing. "But I have also heard they are very strong," he said. "Your wife is a strong woman to have endured this journey."

Kieran's smile faded somewhat. "You have no idea just how strong she is," he said, suddenly serious. "She has saved my life and has made all things for me possible. Her strength goes beyond the obvious; it runs deep as I have never seen. I would trust that woman with my life a thousand times over and know that every time, she would risk all for me. I am here today only because of her and I owe her everything."

Yusef sensed a great deal of respect and adoration in that statement, but there was more to it. It was wider, deeper, and stronger. Most men did not speak of a woman that way. But Kieran obviously adored his wife, much more than Yusef could imagine. In that moment, Yusef's respect for Lady Hage grew simply because Kieran respected her so much.

"Then you are much fortunate, my friend," Yusef said.

"Aye, I am," Kieran sighed, glancing over his shoulder to see his wife carrying on an animated conversation with Kaleef. "But she still drives me daft at times."

They chuckled as they moved down the road, finally pulling up in front of a three-story structure that was built of stones and wood. It was crammed in between two other buildings in a long row of structures, some of them rather unsteady looking. As soon as the cart came to a halt, Rory leapt off but Kieran grabbed her before she could take a step.

"Stay with me," he instructed evenly. "You'll not go running amok, not here."

She pursed her lips impatiently. "I wasn't going to run amok."

He winked at her, taking her hand and tucking it into his elbow as he gave orders to the men that had accompanied them from the docks. Soon, things were in motion; trunks were being removed from the enormous horse cart and the door to the inn was open as men passed inside. Kieran entered the structure with Rory on his arm. Rory made sure the boys were behind them, safe, as they entered.

The main room of the tavern was long and dark. It looked as if it had been dug in a pit; the floor was at least two feet below the street level and a few stairs led down into the pit. They hadn't taken two steps when an older wench ran up to Kieran, gasping in recognition.

"Viscount Dykemoor!" she cried excitedly. "I heard that ye had gone with the king to fight the savages. God be praised for allowing ye to return home unharmed."

Kieran recognized the woman as the daughter of the tavern keeper.

"My thanks," he responded. "I have returned with my wife and friends. Go find your father and tell him that I have arrived."

The woman looked at Rory with shock, at Yusef and Kaleef with even more shock. After a lingering gaze, she turned and fled. Kieran watched her run off, knowing that she was racing to her father with tales of the savages Sir Kieran Hage had brought back with him from the Holy Land. There was a good deal of suspicion for dark-skinned people and Kieran knew he was going to face it more than once; he hoped that Yusef and Kaleef understood it as well.

Rory was more interested in studying the room and its occupants than concerned with Medieval prejudice. She held on to Kieran tightly, watching a particularly loud group in the corner, laughing and drinking. There was one woman and about five or six men; two of the men had their arms around the woman, who seemed to be enjoying their company tremendously. She was laughing and drinking. As Rory watched, one of the men put his hand down the woman's neckline and fondled her breast. He kept trying to kiss her as she talked to the others, but she was apparently uncaring or uninterested that the man was fondling her in public.

Rory raised her eyebrows and turned away; things like that happened in her time so it wasn't particularly shocking. The high-end clubs in Las Vegas had stuff like that all the time so she wasn't inordinately put off by the sight. But she was interested in the group of knights on the far side of the room against the wall. There were four that she could see, most of them sitting facing the door, which made it rather awkward to have a conversation. But like modern day cops, Medieval knights never sat with their backs to a door. The group was well armed, in well used armor and mail, and they had the remains of a massive meal spread before them. As she stared at them, they noticed her.

She abruptly turned her back on them, facing Kieran as she spoke. "There is a group of knights over there," she said, her big hazel eyes gazing up at him. "Did you see them?"

Kieran was focused on her. "Of course."

She grinned. "Stupid question," she muttered to herself, watching him smile. "Do you know them?"

He was still focused on her. "It has been three years since I have set foot on English soil," he replied. "I could be mistaken, but by my last recollection, black and gold standards meant Somerset."

"Friend or foe?"

"Most definitely foe."

The smile faded from her lips. "Do they know you? You're wearing your father's blue and gold."

He lifted an eyebrow at her. "If I understood some things from your time correctly, then I was mildly educated on what you called sporting teams."

She cocked her head in confusion at the change in subject. "Huh?" her brow furrowed, perplexed. "What about them?"

"They are competitive."

"Absolutely."

"And each of these teams had different-colored shirts to identify them."

"Right; we discussed that already."

"I know we did but I have a point to make," he said patiently. "Since these men are competitive, do you believe they know each other's colors on sight?"

She was beginning to understand where he was coming from. "They sure do."

"Then the answer to your question is yes, they know my father's colors on sight. The House of Hage is a powerful house."

She was beginning to have a sinking feeling. "Do they know you on sight?"

He sighed faintly, looking as if he were searching for the correct words. He put his hands on her upper arms, pulling her closer.

"My family has a very strong history of serving the kings of England," he explained. "My father was a great warrior and his father before him, serving Henry the First, Matilda, Stephen of Blois, and

Henry the Second. My father, in fact, was an advisor and champion to a young Henry the Second. They are the same age, or at least would have been if Henry was still alive."

Rory listened with awe at the legacy of the Hage family and the royals of England. "So what are you telling me?"

He fixed her in the eye. "There is much you do not know about my family so perhaps you should be aware, considering you are now a part of it." His voice was very low. "Although my father and Henry were friends when they were young, there was increasing dissention between them because Henry tried to manipulate my father into betraying Richard, the future king. My father, not appreciating how Henry tried to use him against a rival in an unscrupulous way, went to Richard of Aquitaine and told him of his father's plot. That forever sealed the rift between my father and King Henry, but it also cemented an alliance with Richard. That's a simplified version of what happened, but it is a sufficient explanation."

Rory's eyes were wide with the information. Some of the most famous figures in Anglo history were deeply involved with the Hage family and she was properly awed. In fact, it was difficult to wrap her mind around it.

"That's really amazing," she breathed. "So you've always served Richard, then."

He nodded. "Aye. And everyone knows it." He tipped his head in the direction of the other knights. "And to answer your question, most fighting men know me on sight. As Richard assumed the throne, I was one of his champions. I led the king's armies in many a battle against brother or father."

She regarded him a moment, thinking her husband was a far greater man than she had suspected. She had known the man was a friend of Richard's and a great warrior, but it seemed to go beyond that and it was a stunning realization. But along with those thoughts came something else.

"I'm just curious," she said carefully. "How do you feel about a king who has never really lived in England? Doesn't he live in Aquitaine?"

Kieran smiled ironically. "I serve England's king. It does not matter where he lives. He is still my king. And my friend."

She smiled and let the subject drop. Any more questions out of her mouth might sound like a challenge and she was in no way challenging him. But she was increasingly concerned about the rival knights on the opposite side of the room.

"So what about those guys?" she nodded her head in their direction. "Are they going to try and attack you?"

He smiled. "I doubt it," he said. "I've not given them a reason to."

"Do they really need a reason in this day and age?"

He kissed her on the tip of her nose, turning her around by the shoulders as the tavern keeper approached. The man was round and surprisingly well dressed, with a bald head and bright blue eyes. He smiled happily at Kieran.

"My lord Dykemoor," he greeted. "It has been a long time. Praise God that you have returned from the Holy Land."

Kieran nodded in response to the man's greeting. "I am here for the night and require three rooms," he said. "My wife requires a bath and your finest meal."

The man nodded eagerly, his jowls shaking. "Of course, m'lord." He began yelling to the cluster of women behind him, who bolted into action. Then he turned back to Kieran. "Please sit and enjoy drink while we prepare your rooms."

Kieran began pulling off his gloves, pointing to two tables near the window. "Let us sit," he said to his wife and Yusef. But he spoke over his shoulder to the tavern keeper. "Bring food with the drink. My wife is famished and requires pickled lemons."

He was smirking at Rory, who made a face at him as they went to sit. She was increasingly famished these days, not strangely, mostly for pickled lemons. Kieran had little difficulty locating pickled lemons in Paris but he'd not found any since that time and knew he'd better find her some or she would likely skin him alive. It was all she talked about.

They took the two tables near the window. Yusef and Kaleef sat with Rory and Kieran while the boys sat at a small table that leaned dangerously. The youngsters had big, wide eyes at the tavern and big, wide eyes when the innkeeper brought them a big loaf of bread all their own. Kaleef and Yusef could not drink the fermentation of grapes or wheat, so the innkeeper provided boiled fruit juice instead. Rory wanted it, too. She wasn't too keen on drinking wine or ale these days. He brought her some with rose petals floating on the top.

In the next several minutes, the innkeeper and his daughter brought bread, butter, some kind of fruit and honey compote, mutton that was stewed in gravy, and boiled vegetables. They were so boiled that it was difficult to tell what they were. But the man came through in the clutch. He presented Rory with pickled onions, peas and cucumbers, which he called briny vegetables, and something else brand new to England.

He brought forth a big earthenware jug, sealed, which he opened at the table. Rory peered inside, her head blocking out everyone else's view of what it held. Whatever it was smelled both sweet and sour, so she stuck her fingers in and pulled out a citrus segment. She smelled it; it smelled very sweet and tart. Popping it in her mouth, she crowed with delight. It was an orange that had been soaked in sweet wine, honey and cinnamon. It was absolutely delicious and she wrapped her arms around the jug and refused to give it back to the innkeeper. He graciously left it while Kieran laughed at her.

While everyone else ate mutton and bread, Rory ate pickled onions, peas and cucumbers and the delightful orange segments. She held out a piece of orange to Kieran, dropping it in his open mouth and giggling when he pretended to eat her fingers. He chewed, nodding with approval.

"Delicious," he offered, lifting an eyebrow at her as she shoved more in her mouth. "For a woman who swore she would not eat anything of my time, you are proving yourself to be a liar."

Rory giggled, licking the juice off her fingers. "I know," she agreed. "I don't care. Can we take this with us?"

Kieran shook his head at her, chuckling. "If you wish."

She did. She shared her fruits with the boys, who had never had such treats. David in particular wanted more but Bud was seemingly satisfied with what he had. In fact, the boys had more food between them than they had ever known in their lives, eating until they were stuffed. When the meal was almost over, Kieran called Bud over to his table.

The boy came obediently and stood next to Kieran expectantly. Kieran held out a big cup of wine and the boy looked at him questioningly. Kieran smiled and put it in the lad's hands. Bud understood the honor and the implication and took a big drink, smacking his lips. Rory looked up from her oranges long enough to scowl.

"Kieran," she scolded. "He's just a kid. Don't give him wine."

Kieran lifted an eyebrow at her. "He has grown up at St. Victor's," he told her frankly. "He has been drinking wine since he was born. Is that not correct, Bud? *Vous avez bu du vin puisque vous étiez bébé.*"

Bud nodded eagerly, smacked his lips, and took another big drink of Kieran's wine. Kieran laughed at the boy, took his cup back, and indicated for Bud to go back to his brother. Bud wiped his mouth, smiled, and retreated.

Rory watched the exchange, shaking her head. "You're going to turn him into a child alcoholic," she muttered. "We're going to have to put him in rehab."

Kieran wasn't sure what an alcoholic was, or rehab, so he just grinned. "You worry overly, Mother."

She smirked at him, turning back to her beloved orange segments. She was thrilled to be eating fruit. The diet of the Medieval period was sorely lacking in fresh produce so she was thrilled to have something citrusy. As she happily licked her fingers, laughing at David when he tried her briny onions and cucumbers and puckered up his face, she suddenly noticed that Kieran's expression had turned to stone. The man was looking over her head, suddenly rising to his full height. At six feet six inches, he was an incredibly imposing man. Startled, Rory turned around to see what he was looking at.

Somerset's knights had risen from the shadows and were moving across the room towards them. Rory's jovial mood was gone as Yusef bolted to his feet because Kieran had, prepared for a fight. Frightened, Rory stood up as Kieran pulled her back, out of the way. She scooted around the table and went to the boys, pulling them back out of the line of fire. Her eyes were wide with terror as the four Somerset knights approached Kieran.

"Hage," the knight in the lead spoke as if Kieran's name was the vilest word in the English language. "I thought it to be you when you walked in the door but I could not be positive. I am not sure if you are aware, but it seems that trained beasts followed you back from The Levant."

His men laughed rudely at Yusef and Kaleef's expense. Kieran didn't show any emotion whatsoever.

"You would know something of trained beasts, of course," he said. "You married one."

The knight's smile vanished. "I shall be sure and inform my wife's father what you truly think of her," he growled. "Welsh warlords are not known for their understanding. Once slandered, you make an enemy for life."

"I shall take that chance."

The knight regarded Kieran with his dark, wicked eyes before turning his gaze to Yusef. He looked at the man as one would look at a snake. "He does not belong with good Christians," he spoke to Kieran. "I am offended by his presence. He and those like him should be in the livery with the rest of the animals."

"He stays."

Rory watched the exchange with growing fear. It was Kieran and Yusef against four fully-armed knights. It wasn't like she could call nine-one-one or run for the cops; there were no cops in this time. Law was in the hands of the people for the most part. These men could kill Kieran and there would be no justice, no one brought to trial. But more than that, she would be without him. The man who was literally a part of her soul would be gone. She would be dead along with him.

And the baby… he would never know the strong, wise, amazing man who was his father. Panic began to set into Rory's mind, thinking quickly. Like two dogs preparing to fight, she wanted to turn a hose on them. But there were no hoses. Her heart began to thump faster and faster and her palms began to sweat. Wild thoughts began to pop into her head to create a distraction; she took the first thought that popped into her head. There wasn't time for second or third options. She nudged Bud. when he turned around, she silently urged him to follow her lead.

Leaping onto the small, rickety table that the boys had eaten their meal on, she began to stomp and clap in rhythm… stomp, stomp, clap… stomp, stomp, clap. When the boys picked up her rhythm, she suddenly yelled to the crowded room.

"Do it with me!" she shouted. Stomp, stomp clap… stomp, stomp, clap. "Do it loud!"

Bud was the first one to take her lead strongly. He jumped up onto the nearest table, stepping in someone's meal as he did so. He was stomping and clapping as loud as he could. David was, too, stomping and clapping fearfully because Rory and Bud were. The kid had no idea what was going on. Rory drew on her cheerleading roots, four years of the extracurricular activity, and the familiar chant that echoed through a million high school stadiums on Friday nights throughout the United States. It was the only distraction she could come up with and she began to sing out the words.

"Buddy you're a boy make a big noise, playin' in the street gonna be a big man some day.

You got mud on yo' face, you big disgrace; kickin' your can all over the place, singin' we will, we will rock you! We will, we will rock you!"

By this time, she had the entire tavern stunned, watching her as if she had lost her mind. But it had worked the desired effect. Kieran and the Somerset knights simply stared at her, no longer focused on each other.

Rory jumped off the table and began waving her hands, encouraging people to stomp and clap with her. Although they were timid at first, it was well-known that Medieval people enjoyed entertainment and they enjoyed participating in songs. They were always up for a good time. This was a heck of a song and, in little time, she had the entire tavern stomping and clapping.

Thrilled that her audience was with her, Rory leapt onto the nearest table and belted out the second verse.

"Buddy you're a young man hard man, shoutin' in the street gonna take on the world someday, you got blood on yo' face, you big disgrace, Wavin' your banner all over the place. We will we will rock you, sing it, we will we will rock you."

She was able to get the crowd to pitch in on the chorus. Bud, picking it up quickly, was singing at the top of his lungs, running around the room like a miniature cheerleader, very surprising for the usually reserved boy. The entire room was stomping and clapping so hard that flotsam was floating down from the beams on the ceiling. Feeling the power from her audience, Rory launched in to the last verse.

"Buddy you're an old man poor man, pleadin' with your eyes, gonna make you some peace some day. You got mud on your face, big disgrace, somebody better put you back into your place. We will we will rock you, sing it, we will we will rock you!"

The energy level of the room was reaching titanic proportions. Kieran was watching, rather dumbfounded, and two of the Somerset knights were even stomping and clapping along with her. The crowd was going crazy for Rory and her cheerleader-on-caffeine tactics. But suddenly, she threw her hands up to immediately silence the crowd. After a few lingering stomps and claps, they shut up, a hushed silence falling over the crowd to see what she was going to do next.

Rory's head was lowered, her eyes closed. She began to sing facing her feet, the lyrics soft and sweet. Drawing on her experience in her high school chamber singers, she had a lovely alto voice, which grew increasingly louder as the lyrics progressed. She had the entire tavern enthralled, including her husband, as she sang a song that Freddie Mercury would make famous in the far distant future.

"I've paid my dues – time after time – I've done my sentence – but committed no crime –
And bad mistakes – I've made a few
I've had my share of sand kicked in my face –
But I've come through,

We are the champions – my friends
And we'll keep on fighting – till the end –
We are the champions –
We are the champions
No time for losers
'Cause we are the champions – of the world –

I've taken my bows – And my curtain calls –
You brought me fame and fortune and everything that goes with it – I thank you all – But it's been no bed of roses – no pleasure cruise –
I consider it a challenge before the whole human race – and I ain't gonna lose,
We are the champions – my friends
And we'll keep on fighting – till the end –
We are the champions –
We are the champions
No time for losers
'Cause we are the champions – of the world!"

When the song was finished, no one dared move. The entire place was as still as stone. Rory stood on the tabletop, gazing over the room with increasing embarrassment, thinking that they hated her song. But when the crowd realized the song was over, they burst out in such loud applause that Rory had to cover her ears. The entire room was quaking with shouts and applause.

Rory jumped off the table and raced over to where Kieran was still standing, still in the company of the Somerset knights. As the crowd roared their approval and began to bang their cups, knives and plates against the table for an encore, Rory grabbed Kieran by the arm.

"Come on," she hissed, breathless. "Let's get up to our room and bolt the door before they realize we're gone."

Kieran was looking at her with a good deal of amazement from what he had just witnessed. But he was confused by her request.

"What…?" his brow furrowed. "What do you…?"

"Please!" she whispered urgently, her hazel eyes suddenly verging on tears. "Let's get everyone up to their rooms and bolt the doors before those knights come to their senses."

Suddenly, he could see what she was doing. Honestly, when he first heard the clapping, he thought she had lost her mind. But he quickly realized she had done it to distract the building hostilities. He felt like an idiot for not having understood that before. But watching her perform, he saw a side of her that he had never seen before, something that was both shocking and deeply attractive. He knew she was talented but he had no idea just how talented. The woman had dimensions he couldn't even fathom.

"As you say, sweetheart," he murmured. "Take the boys and go upstairs. I will be up shortly."

But she didn't let go. "No, Kieran," she said insistently. "Come with me now. Please."

He patted her hand reassuringly, looking to Yusef, a few feet away. "Go with Yusef," he tried to pass her off to the Saracen. "Take Kaleef and the boys and go upstairs."

"But, Kieran…!"

"Please. Do not argue with me."

"I'm not leaving you!"

His jaw ticked, not a good sign. "Do it now or you will not like my reaction."

She opened her mouth to reply when a fist suddenly came flying at Kieran's face, sending him reeling. Rory shrieked. Running on instinct, she grabbed the nearest thing on the table, which happened to be a big, wooden pitcher. She swung it with all her might at the Somerset knight and hit him in the side of the head. He teetered back as Kieran righted himself and charged forward, throwing a massive fist and shattering the man's nose. Blood spurted and the knight went down.

Yusef was moving into action as the room suddenly erupted with screams and people scrambling. He pulled Rory back, away from the flying fists, and tackled the nearest Somerset knight as Kieran went after another one. Kaleef and the young boys were backed into a corner as the room deteriorated into a massive brawl, and Rory stumbled over to them.

"We need to get clear of here," she said to them, taking little David by the hand and gesturing to Bud to take charge of Kaleef. "Follow me."

The four of them moved for the stairs, trying to stay clear of flying tables and chairs. It was like an Old West bar brawl only worse; these people were biting and gouging eyes along with throwing punches. By the time Rory and her little group reached the stairs, she noticed that several men in the room had jumped into the fight. Only one Somerset knight was left standing, and that man was having the stuffing beaten out of him by Kieran. Not strangely, the men who had jumped into the brawl were also fighting each other. Punches and stools were being thrown like crazy. The room was being destroyed as Rory pulled David, Bud and Kaleef up the stairs.

Rory paused about halfway up the staircase, urging the others to head to the top. She had to watch Kieran, to make sure no one was taking out a sword to stab him in the back. Not that she could do much from her perch on the stairs so she began to move back down the steps, inching towards the fight that had now broken through the front window.

Kieran finished off the Somerset knight by picking the man up and tossing him across the room. He barely had time to recover when two men nearby charged him; one caught him in the shoulder and the other man caught him in the abdomen. Annoyed, he grabbed the pair by their hair and smacked their heads together, sending them crashing to the floor. He spied Rory on the stairs and he began to charge towards her.

"Go," he boomed. "Up the stairs."

The sheer volume of his voice startled her. He sounded furious and she had no idea why.

"You don't have to yell!" she hollered back.

He opened his mouth but got hit from behind, almost sending him to his knees. A group of men were fighting behind him and someone got shoved into him, clipping him behind the knees. Kieran turned to the group, clobbering two of the men and sending the others scattering when they saw how furious he was. Kieran's anger was unleashed and he was obliterating anyone, or anything, that got in his way. Then he swung to his wife, his face taut with rage. Rory saw the expression and she knew, for her sake, that she had better do as he told her. She bolted up the stairs, taking the boys and Kaleef with her into the nearest open room when she reached the top. She slammed the door behind her and bolted it.

Kieran mounted the stairs two at a time, storming up the steps until he reached the top. Lashing out a massive boot, he kicked the door in, shattering the wood. Splinters rained down as Rory and the boys cowered in a corner. Old Kaleef sat calmly on the bed, watching the events fold out before him. He was the only one in the room not wrought with terror.

"She is with child, my lord," Kaleef reminded him steadily. "If you beat her, you risk the child."

Kieran acted as if he had not heard him. He charged into the room, grabbed Rory by the arm, and pulled her back out into the hall. She stumbled behind him as he towed her down the short, uneven corridor and into a room at the far end. The door shut with a bang, the sounds of a bolt being thrown echoing in the sudden stillness of the corridor.

Once inside the chamber, Rory yanked herself free of Kieran's grasp and ran to the other side of the room. Truth be told, she was terrified. But she was also furious in her own right. As he swung to face her, jaw ticking, she jabbed a finger at him.

"Don't start with me," she demanded, taking the offensive. "I made an ass out of myself trying to distract those Somerset knights so that they wouldn't kill you, but you still wouldn't leave. You just stood there in all your manly glory because to turn away from a fight is considered cowardly. Well, I don't consider it cowardly; I consider it smart. I'm not going to let you yell at me when all I was trying to do was save your life."

Kieran stood by the door, grinding his teeth as he listened to her speech. After a moment, he began to rip his gloves off, tossing them angrily onto the bed.

"I can save my own life," he growled. "I do not need or want your protection. You do not seem to realize that every time you disobey me, every time you put yourself someplace where you should not be, you divide my attention and make it possible for someone to catch me off guard. As I was standing there arguing with you, Somerset's man was able to throw a fist into my jaw. It could have just as easily been a knife to my chest. And it would have been your fault."

Her face turned red and she was gearing up for a serious retort. But as Kieran watched, her face crumpled and she turned away from him in hysterical tears. Kieran's fury drained out of him in an instant. Grunting with remorse, he sighed and made his way towards her.

"Do not weep," he muttered regretfully. "I did not mean it."

"Yes, you did," she wept. "You were trying to hurt me and you did."

He sighed again, with great guilt. "I was not attempting to hurt you," he said hoarsely. "But I am angry. I am angry because your stubbornness could have gotten us both killed. Sweetheart, I do not give you directions simply to hear myself talk. I do it because it is important.

You must understand that."

"And you must understand that I'm not some weakling Medieval woman who can't think for herself," she fired back. "I don't need you to boss me around like I'm mindless chattel. Is it so hard for you to treat me like a partner and not a possession?"

"This has nothing to do with that. You are not a warrior and you must trust that I know more than you do with regards to personal safety."

"I know enough that I was trying to distract those knights so you could get away. And you just stood there!"

He could see that this wasn't a battle he was going to easily win. Rory simply didn't understand that she needed to listen to him for her own health and safety. She was very much the modern woman who took care of herself and tried to help others. Her assimilation into Medieval society wasn't going as smoothly as they would have hoped and he couldn't figure out if it was because he was resisting her or if she was resisting him.

"I do not know what to say except I am sorry your feelings are hurt," he murmured. "I love you, Lib. Never doubt for a moment that you are the most important thing in the world to me. I understand you were attempting to assist me downstairs but you must understand that I do not need assistance, mostly because if you are involved, I spend my time worrying about you. Divided attention, in my profession, can be deadly."

She wasn't going to let him off so easily. When he tried to gently take her in his arms, she yanked away and stumbled over to a small table and chair against the wall. Sitting heavily in the chair, she wept hot tears into the wall.

"Go away," she sobbed. "Go downstairs and get yourself killed. I don't care anymore. You're hateful, Kieran, just hateful."

Kieran stood there, watching her weep, feeling like an ogre. She was sobbing heavily, so hard that she ended up vomiting up all of the wonderful orange segments all over the floor. He didn't care if she didn't want him to touch her. When she started heaving, he went to her, pulling her hair out of the way and holding her steady as she lurched. She tried to smack him, to push him away, but she couldn't do that and vomit at the same time. When she was finished expelling everything in her stomach, she began to weep louder.

"Oh, my God," she gasped miserably. "I've made such a mess. I can't… can't…"

Kieran had had enough. He picked her up and carried her to the bed, laying her down and throwing himself down beside her. His arms went around her tightly, enveloping her against his massive body. Rory struggled for a few seconds before succumbing to the inevitable. He was alive and warm against her, and she now wept for an entirely new reason. She was just glad he was alive.

"You're the most important thing in the world to me," she sobbed. "Why do you think I was trying to help you?"

He knew that but he didn't have anything to say about it. "Calm yourself, sweetheart." His lips were by her ear, his voice low and soothing. "Everything is all right now. Just calm yourself."

Rory was exhausted. She put her hands up to her face, covering it, wiped out from the day's events, the pregnancy, the weeping. She quieted quickly as Kieran held her and drifted off into a fitful doze. Kieran thought wryly that she must have been thoroughly exhausted because she didn't even inspect the bed for bugs. He held her, both arms wrapped around her body and a massive hand on her forehead, stroking her gently.

"Sleep, sweetheart." He kissed her gently. "All will be well on the morrow."

She snored in response.

CHAPTER ELEVEN

Belvoir Castle, Lincolnshire
England

JOHN LACKLAND, PRINCE of England and the surviving brother of Richard the Lionheart, was, in truth, a man of few words. Being the youngest in a family of aggressive loudmouths had left him a rather edgy and quiet man, not given to fine speeches or big demands. He simply gave orders to those around him, who moved heaven and earth to ensure that his wishes were met. Not because they loved the man. They did it because they were aggressive and full of ambition, and John had the power and wealth to ensure their dreams were achieved.

Simon de Corlet sat across the table from the prince. It was a gloomy day, the rain coming down in silver sheets and thunder clapping steadily. The solar of Belvoir Castle was moderately warm and well lit, considering John wasn't fond of darkness. There was danger in darkness. The prince eyed de Corlet across the taper-lit table.

"Your tale is an amazing one, I must say," John said slowly. "You have told me, in essence, that El-Hajidd presented the Christian armies with the Crown of Thorns worn by Jesus Christ as he was being put to death by the Romans? I am most eager to see this holy relic."

Simon was nervous. Sometimes John heard only what he wanted to hear, not what had actually been said.

"It was a gift, Your Grace, to prove that he was sincere in his desire to seek peace with the Christian armies," Simon replied evenly. "As I told you, the gift never made it to Richard. It is with Sir Kieran Hage and I do not know his whereabouts."

John's dark, droopy eyes gazed steadily at Simon. "You told my brother that Hage was a traitor. But one of your men told Richard that you had lied and that Hage was not a traitor at all."

Simon could not hold the man's gaze. "Aye, Your Grace."

"So you fled home. Quickly, I might add."

"I traveled as swiftly as I could in order that I might tell you what has transpired," Simon's head came up. "Kieran Hage has the relic. If he is able to present it to the king, then hostilities between the Muslims and Christians will cease. Victory will not be ours."

"And my brother will be known as the king who brought peace to the Holy Land."

"Aye, Your Grace," Simon said honestly. "But more than that, he shall return home as a saint, acclaimed as the greatest king to have ever ruled England. Peace shall be known in The Levant but not victory."

John's expression darkened and he turned to his wine, drinking moodily. "I do not expect that all of the Christian kings will side with him," he muttered. "Philip Augustus, Guy de Lusignan… they do not want peace. They want conquest and glory."

Simon nodded. "Indeed they do, Your Grace," he replied. "But your brother is persuasive. Even if he agrees to peace and pulls his armies out, there will still be those who will continue the fight. But Richard will be seen as the peacemaker and the people will love him."

John's pale features tightened. "If Richard returns home a saint, then my struggles against him will be more difficult."

"The people will side with a saint and will look at you as evil for opposing him, Your Grace. Your cause will be ended."

John's jaw ticked and he pushed his bejeweled cup aside. He clawed at the tabletop a moment, his mind torn with thoughts of victory and defeat. He had been battling his brother for so long that he knew of no other way. He looked up at Simon.

"It is possible that Kieran Hage has already presented my brother with this gift?" he ventured.

Simon nodded. "It is possible, Your Grace," he replied. "The last time I saw him was in Nahariya. I told him that he could not return to

Richard. But when I was betrayed to the king, it is possible that Hage was able to present the gift. It is possible that Richard holds the Crown of Thorns already."

John sat back in his chair, his dark eyes dull with uncertainty and anger. "The House of Hage is seated at Southwell Castle," he muttered. "I know the family well. Jeffrey Hage served my father."

Simon wasn't sure what to say to that so he said nothing. He watched John rise from his cushioned chair, his skinny legs supporting a short and skinny body. The prince made his way to the lancet window that overlooked the bailey of Belvoir, watching the rain pound in the courtyard below. He clasped his hands behind his back, fidgeting with his spindly fingers.

"Perhaps I should pay a visit to Sir Jeffrey Hage," John said slowly. "Perhaps he should know that his son is a traitor, having met with the Saracen armies in private in order to betray Richard."

Simon wasn't following the prince's train of thought. "For what purpose, Your Grace?"

John wasn't quite sure, either. But it seemed like a good plan. "The House of Hage is a very old, very proud family. To have a traitor in their midst… a son betraying a father… perhaps Sir Jeffrey will understand my resistance to my father. Perhaps he will understand my cause if he believes his son has become loyal to me."

Simon's eyebrows flew up. "Kieran loyal to you?" he scoffed. "Never would that man swear fealty to you. He hates you." When John turned sharply to him, he added nervously. "Your Grace."

John's dark eyes glittered wickedly. He had been playing these games since he had been five years old. Thanks to his mother and father, he understood the games well.

"We shall see," he said quietly.

ꕥ

KIERAN AND HIS party were a day out of Southwell. Traveling had been wet and wild, rain pounding one day and then windy and cold the next.

Before leaving London, he had sent a messenger ahead to Southwell to announce his arrival and he had also purchased a larger wagon to accommodate Rory's increasing collection of trunks. He gave the pony cart over to Bud and David completely and purchased an enclosed cab for Rory to travel in. It was a well-made carriage that came with a big, white horse to pull it. He hired a driver at the livery where he purchased it and in little time, they were heading north to Nottingham.

One more purchase they made before leaving was a horse for Yusef. He wasn't fond of the big chargers, or even the Spanish Jennets, so Kieran had to go to three or four liveries before they found a horse that Yusef found acceptable. He was looking for an agile Arabian but settled for a long-legged Spanish Jennet, a lovely caramel color with a black mane and tail. Kieran assured Yusef that once they reached Southwell, the man could have his pick of the Arabians that Kieran had shipped home during the course of his three years in the Holy Land. He had something of a collection of the beautiful animals. Southwell stables had at least twelve of the horses and probably twice as many offspring of crossbreeds between Arabians and hearty English warmbloods. Kieran's instructions to his father were to breed the beasts and sell them for a hefty profit which, Kieran was sure, his father had gleefully done.

On this cloudy, misty morning, Rory sat in her cab, wrapped up in heavy cloaks against the chill, teaching English to little David. He had learned many words and was starting to string them together in sentences. Kieran rode at the front of the group while Kaleef rode just behind him, driving the little pony cart. Rory's cab came next with the hired driver followed by Bud driving the big wagon. Yusef rode alongside Bud, making sure the boy didn't get into any trouble. It was an odd caravan but one that Kieran was extremely proud of. He was returning to Southwell with a wife, friends, servants, and a multitude of possessions. He always thought he would return at the head of his army, but that was not to be. Not that he was disappointed; quite the contrary. It was just not as he had expected.

Kaleef was behind him, singing softly as the ponies trudged over the muddy road. Kieran turned to look at the old man, who seemed truly happy in spite of the fact that he had been burned out of his home and forced to trek thousands of miles to a faraway enemy country. Kieran thought back to that time before, when history had taken another turn, the day when Simon's assassins had wounded him and he had made his way to Kaleef, looking for help. They'd had a conversation while Kieran lay dying, something that Kieran remembered even now. *I sense your work on this earth is not yet complete.* Even then, the old man had been intuitive. Odd how he found the old man with him now and Kieran had to wonder if it wasn't for some greater purpose. Kaleef was a great healer. Perhaps he would be needed again to heal Kieran in the future. Or even Rory.

Thinking of his wife made him rein his horse around to the cab she was riding in. He directed Liberator next to the cab, peering in to see her sitting huddled up with young David, both of them under heavy blankets. When Rory caught sight of Kieran, she smiled at him.

"Hello there," she said brightly. "How's it going?"

He flipped up his visor, returning her smile. "All is well," he replied to her modern-day greeting. He had learned to figure them out. "How are you feeling?"

She shrugged. "Okay, I guess," she said. "Just tired. How are you?"

His smiled broadened. "I am always well as long as I am with you."

She smiled coyly, batting her eyelashes at him dramatically. "You always know the right thing to say, you smooth-tongued devil."

He laughed. "I would sing to you as well if I knew how. But it would seem that you are the entertainer in our family."

She wasn't sure what he meant at first. But a split second later, she remembered her floor show at The Black Swan. Since that day, they'd not spoken of it and she figured it was better to let some things lie. That particular moment in time was a sore point for them both. But he had brought it up so she wriggled her eyebrows at him.

"Oh, yeah," she sigh. "I'd almost forgotten about that."

"I have not. But given the emotions of that night, I did not want to bring it up too soon and risk upsetting you."

"Me upset?" she looked at him, surprised. "You're the one that was yelling at me, not the other way around."

He lifted an eyebrow at her. "This is a line of conversation that neither one of us can win, so I suggest that we not pursue it." He pushed his helm back and scratched his forehead. "I did want to tell you how impressed I was with your singing ability, Libby. You are a woman of many talents."

Her smile was back. "Thank you, but I really wouldn't call that singing. I was just trying to create a distraction so you wouldn't get gored."

He wasn't going to get into that subject with her again, so he continued to focus on her singing skill. "Sing something for me now."

"Now?"

He nodded, his gem-clear brown eyes glittering at her. "I wish it."

She had to chuckle at him; he was very decisive about his wishes. So she thought a moment, the smile on her face broadening as she sang the words softly.

"I made it through the wilderness; somehow I made it through…
Didn't know how lost I was until I found you.
I was beat, incomplete
I'd been had, I was sad and blue…
But you made me feel
Yeah, you made me feel
Shiny and new…
Like a virgin, touched for the very first time; like a virgin, when your heart beats next to mine…"

Kieran was enjoying the sweet, gentle words in her seductive voice until she came to the last strain. Then his eyes flew open wide and his jaw went slack when he understood what, exactly, she was singing about. When Rory saw his reaction, she shut her mouth and began to giggle uncontrollably, falling back against the back of the cab. Kieran reined Liberator next to the cab and stuck a massive arm inside the open window.

"Come here, you naughty wench," he growled. "I am going to blister your backside."

She screamed with delight, scooting to the other side of the cab as he grabbed for her. Her giggling turned into loud laughter as he made another swipe at her through another window. David, inside the cab, tried not to get run over by Rory as she moved around. He sat against a corner and grinned.

"Kieran, stop!" she commanded after a good deal of chasing. "You're scaring David."

Kieran leaned low on Liberator, sticking his head in one of the windows to see if what she said was true. But David was grinning, squealing when he saw Kieran reaching for him. He grabbed the boy by the foot and David giggled hysterically, clutching at the seat to prevent being dragged out the window. Rory leapt to the rescue but the moment she came close, Kieran let go of David and grabbed her by the wrist.

"Ah *ha*!" he boomed. "Now I have you."

"You cheated!" She beat at his hand. "Let me go!"

He shook his head. "I will not," he said. "Kiss me and I may consider it."

"I'm not going to be blackmailed into kissing you."

"You have no choice. Do as you are told."

"No!" she refused, even as he pulled her to the window and tried to kiss her. She put her free hand out and pushed his face away. "You're not getting a kiss."

Kieran was having a hard time keeping a straight face. When Liberator startled because of all of the struggling going on, he was forced to release Rory to regain control of his charger. She stuck her head out of the window as he was struggling with the horse and stuck her tongue out at him.

"Them baggy sweat pants and those Reeboks with the straps," she taunted him with a fairly risqué rap song. "She turned around and gave dat big booty a smack! Hey! She hit the floor, next thing you know, Shawty got low, low, low."

She made sure to turn around and slap her rump so he could see it. Then she started doing some crazy dance in the cab. David was laughing at her, as was Yusef; no matter what he thought of the bold and aggressive Lady Hage, she was quite funny even if he had no idea what she was singing about. Only Kaleef seemed to be oblivious to what was going on, driving his pony cart ahead of the group and singing to himself. When Kieran regained control of Liberator, he dismounted the charger and tied him to the back of the wagon. His wife was still inside, bopping around to a rap song, when he threw open the door and yanked her out.

Rory screamed as he threw her over his massive shoulder. He planted a trencher-sized hand on her backside and she howled, banging on him. He held her so her belly wasn't against his hard armor, which made it rather awkward to maintain his hold on her once she started fighting back. He was about to smack her again when they heard sounds of distant thunder. The humor on his face abruptly vanished and, alert, he stopped the horseplay and turned in the direction of the coming sound.

Rory heard it, too, and slithered to the ground, still in his grasp. She looked up at him and, seeing his tight expression, began to feel some fear.

"What's wrong?" she asked, pressing close against him. "Who is it?"

He shook his head. "I do not know." He turned her around, quickly, for the cab. "Get inside and stay there."

She resisted slightly. "But, Kieran, if it's…"

He grabbed her by the shoulders and forced her to look at him. "With God as my witness, if you argue with me about this, I will lock you up once we reach Southwell and throw away the key. You will listen to me and you will do what you are told for once in your life. Is this in any way unclear?"

She gazed up into his eyes, knowing that she needed to comply. The last time she resisted his attempts to get her to safety, he had been caught in a brutal fight. She knew that next time, he might not be so lucky. She needed to trust him and do what he told her to do so he was not distracted by arguing with her when people were out to kill him. So she fought down her natural instincts and nodded obediently, patting him on the cheek.

"It's perfectly clear, baby," she murmured. "I'll get back in the cab and stay there."

His hard expression wavered somewhat. "Thank you."

She smiled at him and quickly scooted to the cab, jumping in and slamming the door. Kieran, rather shocked that he hadn't had to bully her into submission, was better able to focus on the coming thunder. As he made his way back to Liberator, he could see many, many horses and men in armor approaching from the north.

He mounted Liberator and rode out to meet them.

☙

KIERAN KNEW THE identity of the army within the first few moments of his approach. Although they were well on the horizon, he could see the blue and gold as he drew closer. When three knights broke off from the cluster of mounted men and charged towards him, he knew his brothers on sight and his heart began to race. He actually had a lump in his throat. As the chargers drew near, he suddenly reined Liberator to a halt and bailed off. Dropping the reins, he began to walk, very quickly, towards the approaching trio.

In rapid succession, the knights pulled their chargers to a halt and began to jump off. The first man to reach Kieran threw him in such a bear hug that he nearly sent them both toppling. Suddenly, the other two knights were upon them and arms were going around everyone. They were hugging and slugging and somewhere in the middle of it was booming laughter.

Rory saw her husband being mugged by three other knights, not particularly concerned about it because no one seemed to be drawing weapons. They were slapping each other around and hugging, and she could hear the laughter as she approached. Yusef called a halt to their party when they drew close, watching Kieran from a short distance away as he was greeted by people he apparently knew. Kieran was suddenly ripping off his helm and his smile positively lit up the sky. Rory could see his joy from where she remained in the cab and it made her smile as well. But there was no way she was leaving the cab until he told her to.

Yet, in spite of his joy, he hadn't forgotten about her. He grabbed the two nearest men and began dragging them over to the carriage. The third man followed, slapping Kieran and grabbing him around the neck joyfully. By the time the four of them reached the cab, Rory was smiling broadly. She had never seen Kieran so happy.

"Lib," Kieran yanked open the door to the cab and nearly ripped it off its hinges in his excitement. "Come out, sweetheart. I want you to meet my brothers."

Rory climbed out of the cab. Clad in a silky red surcoat and her hair in a couple of sweet-looking braids, she was utter eye candy for the Hage brothers. One by one, the helms came off and she found herself gazing back at men that, to varying degrees, looked like her husband. They were studying her quite intently and she tried not to look at anything other than their faces, although the lure to inspect their armor and weapons was nearly too much for her to take. She smiled at the curious, friendly and joyful faces.

Kieran went to her and put his massive arm around her shoulders, presenting her for inspection to his brothers. "Gentle knights," he gazed down at her, relishing the particularly important moment. "This is my wife, the Lady Rory Elizabeth Hage. She will answer to Libby. Lib, meet my brothers; Christian, Sean and Andrew."

He indicated right to left and Rory smiled broadly at the Hage brothers; Christian was a little taller than Kieran, rather slender as compared to the other three, and with a head of unruly bright red hair and Kieran's brown eyes. Next to him was Sean; Sean was built like Kieran, extraordinarily handsome, with cropped light brown hair and clear brown eyes. The man was definitely a looker. Last was Andrew; he was stocky, broad, with nearly-shaved auburn hair.

"It's wonderful to finally meet you," she said. "Kieran has told me a lot about you."

Her accent threw them for a loop. They looked at Kieran in surprise and he understood their silent questions.

"She is from the west of Ireland," he told them, eyeing Rory. "She knows that she sounds odd. I am endeavoring to break her of the habit so she can speak normally."

Rory scowled at him. "That's a terrible thing to say in front of your brothers," she hissed. "They just met me and you're telling them I'm odd?"

He grinned at her, hugging her. "'Tis well enough that they learn it right away," he said, winking at his brothers. "But they should also know that I worship and adore you, Lady Hage. You are most worthy to be part of this family and due all respect."

Sean was the first one to push forward, taking her hand gently. "Welcome, Lady Hage," he said. He had a wonderful, deep, soothing voice. "We are honored."

Rory's smile was back. Sean was an absolute doll and she liked him right away. He wasn't nearly as tall as Kieran, perhaps three or four inches shorter, but he was big and muscular like his brother was. He also seemed genuinely sweet.

"Thank you," she said sincerely.

He smiled at her and moved aside as Christian, the taller brother, stepped forward. Rory had to crane her neck back as she looked at the man. Kieran was six inches over six feet and Christian was taller than he was, so she guessed the man was somewhere around six feet eight inches. He was extraordinarily tall, with a rather lanky body, but he had that Hage square-jawed look. He smiled at Rory and dipped his head.

"Lady Hage." He had the deepest voice she had ever heard. "It is a pleasure."

Rory nodded in acknowledgment as the last brother approached. Andrew seemed to be quite a bit younger than the other three. Upon closer inspection, she noticed that he had very dark hazel eyes and pale skin with freckles on his face. He was a good looking man but when he smiled, she saw a big chip on his front tooth. He took her hand as Sean had done.

"Lady Hage." He actually kissed her fingers. "I wish you and my brother much happiness."

Rory smiled at the man. "Thank you," she said, looking around the group. "I'm very happy to be here."

They were staring at her, inspecting her, as new family members often do. Christian finally snorted and turned to his brother. "She is far too good for you." He slugged Kieran on the arm. "I will make it my goal in life to steal her from you."

Sean pushed himself in between Christian and Kieran, taking Rory by the hand and tucking it into the crook of his elbow.

"If you barbarians are going to start fighting, I'd better remove the lady," he said, leading her out of the line of fire. "Please give this woman a demonstration on the idiocy of this family. Well? Go ahead and brutalize each other."

Kieran's brow furrowed as Sean took Rory a few feet away. He followed and reclaimed her. "Give her back to me," he scolded lightly. "You are already married."

Sean laughed. Rory watched him, sensing that he was a very gentle, low-key man. "Is your wife at Southwell?" she asked him.

He nodded. "My wife and my daughter," he replied, watching Kieran's face light up with surprise. "The child was born last year. She's beautiful, Kieran. We named her Eleanor, after mother."

Kieran clapped his brother on the shoulder in sincere congratulations. "Well done," he murmured, his eyes glimmering with warmth. "She will have a cousin join her this fall."

The news sent the brothers into a flurry of congratulatory hugs and slugs for Kieran. Then they turned on Rory and she was rather startled when they all descended on her with happy kisses to the cheek. Christian nearly knocked her over in his enthusiasm. Kieran shoved his tall brother back by the head.

"Back, you animal," he growled good-naturedly. As Christian grinned, Kieran indicated the others in his party. "I want you to meet my Saracen friends. These men have risked their lives for me so that I might return home and I want you to give them all due respect. Look not to their skin color; look to their character and heart, for I would not be here if it were not for them."

The smiles and joviality began to fade as the Hage brothers beheld Yusef. Up until this point, they had been focused on Kieran and his wife. Now they gazed at Yusef, who dismounted his caramel-colored horse and stood there, allowing the knights to become used to the sight of him. There was no animosity sensed, only varied degrees of curiosity. Sean was the first one, as usual, to approach him.

"My lord," he greeted, unsure what more to say. "If my brother holds you in such high regard, then I will as well. You are welcome at Southwell."

Yusef nodded at the square-jawed brother who looked a good deal like Kieran. Christian and Andrew greeted him as well, with more confusion than anything else, but they were polite. They were all big, white, well-fed men. No one bothered to greet Kaleef at all, for the old man still sat upon the pony cart, watching the situation warily. Lacking any more to say, Kieran gestured at the cab.

"Let us escort my wife back to the safety of Southwell," he said. "I am sure she is anxious to stop traveling."

The brothers went to collect their horses, who were wandering around the area, nibbling on foliage. Kieran lifted Rory into the carriage, kissing her sweetly. She clutched his hand before he walked away.

"Your brothers seem really sweet," she said quietly.

He smirked at her. "Perhaps to you," he said. "But I assure you, they are ferocious in battle."

She lifted her eyebrows and sat back in her seat. “I have no doubt.”

He winked at her and shut the door. Rory watched Kieran and his brothers rally the army as her little party fell in somewhere in the middle of it. It was a big mass of mounted men and Rory found great interest in the horses, tack and what the soldiers were wearing. Yusef ended up riding next to her, inside the swarm of white soldiers, and she looked up at him, concerned for the dark man in a land of white people. Although the Hage brothers seemed to have accepted him right away, Rory knew a little of prejudice given that she grew up in Southern California. There were a multitude of races and she had heard and seen something of discrimination in her life. She suddenly felt very protective of Yusef, the man who risked everything to save a man he knew by reputation only.

“Yusef?” she called to him.

He paused and smiled politely at her. “How may I serve you, Lady Hage?”

She looked up at him through the cab window, not sure how to voice what she was thinking. “Are… are you all right?”

He cocked his head curiously. “What do you mean?”

“Are you well? Do you feel well? Happy? At ease?”

His expression rippled with confusion. “I am well. Why do you ask?”

She gazed up at him, thinking he had no idea what she was talking about. Perhaps she should just let it go.

“I just wanted to make sure,” she said. “You’re in a strange country with people who are technically your enemy, so I just wanted to make sure you were okay.”

Some of the smile returned to his face. He began to understand what she meant and he was oddly touched. “It is kind of you to ask, Lady Hage,” he said. “I am well.”

Rory let the subject go, sitting back in the cab and pulling David onto her lap. The little boy fell asleep against her for the rest of the afternoon. She slept with him.

CHAPTER TWELVE

THAT NIGHT, THE army camped about fifteen miles from Southwell, amassed in a big group with blazing fires and the smells of cooking meat. Rory hadn't really been around the heavy smells of roasting, fatty, animal flesh and she quickly realized that the smell made her very nauseous. It was a heavy, cloying smell. She wouldn't even touch the mutton that had been freshly cooked, so Kieran broke out the earthenware jug that was about a quarter full with the wonderful orange segments and some bread and butter. That was about all she would eat. After all of the trouble he went to, she was exhausted and wanted to go to bed.

She slept with David and Bud, and Kieran spent all night talking to his brothers just outside the tent where Rory and the boys slept. A fire blazed warmly and the Hage boys drank and talked, mostly about Kieran's sojourn to the Holy Land.

Kieran eventually informed them of the secret meeting with El-Hajidd and Simon de Corlet's treachery. Although he told his brothers that it was a secret peace meeting, he did not mention the gift that would seal the bargain. The Crown of Thorns did not yet make it into the conversation, mostly because Kieran wasn't sure how his brothers would take that particular bit of knowledge. But he also made it very clear that the king knew that he was not a traitor, courtesy of an informant, and that it was Simon who had been branded both liar and traitor. At the end of the conversation, he informed them that Simon was thought to have returned to England to escape the king's wrath.

The knowledge that Simon was somewhere in England brought great ire from Christian in particular. The man tended to be the most volatile of the four and he swore he would seek out de Corlet and deliver the man a painful death. Andrew, the youngest, went along with his brother while Sean, perhaps the most politically informed of the group, sat mostly silent. Sean, as an agent for Richard and William de Longchamp, was essentially a spy. He knew more, and saw more, than most. While Christian and Andrew planned a slow and agonizing demise for de Corlet, Sean turned to Kieran.

"I've not heard any rumor of de Corlet's return," he said quietly. "But trust me when I say that I will find out what I can."

Kieran looked at his brother; eighteen months younger than him, the two had always been inordinately close. He'd missed Sean a great deal and he respected and admired his brother tremendously. While Kieran went with Richard to The Levant, Sean had stayed home to fight for Richard's cause on English soil. It was, in Kieran's opinion, the more difficult battle.

"Where is the prince right now?" Kieran's voice was low.

Sean inhaled thoughtfully. "As of one month ago, he was at Belvoir Castle."

Kieran was silent a moment. "Sean," he said softly, slowly. "There is something I did not tell you about my meeting with the Saracens," he moved closer to his brother as Christian and Andrew continued to drink and spew threats. "There was a deeper purpose to that meeting, one that is at the heart of everything. You see, El-Hajidd presented me with a gift for the Christian kings, something of such great Christian significance that it would provide no doubt as to the Saracen sincerity. This gift is why Simon spent nearly a week attempting to assassinate me before I was able to leave the Holy Land."

Sean's dark eyes glittered in the weak firelight. "What is this gift?"

Kieran thought on where to begin. "Let me give you a brief history lesson and then perhaps you will understand better," he began. "When our Lord Jesus Christ died on the cross at Mount Calvary, his body was taken and prepared for burial by Joseph of Arimathea among others. 'Tis said that after the resurrection, Marc collected not only the shroud of Christ's burial, but the diadem of thorns that had been cast to the floor of the vault when our Lord's body had been wrapped. As you know, Jerusalem was under Roman control and no place for Christians. Especially those close to Christ. Joseph traveled north in his ministry, carrying with him the shroud and the crown, until he came to Tyre."

Sean nodded slowly, increasingly enthralled. "Go on."

Kieran did. "While in Tyre, he stayed with an innkeeper and his family. Romans abound, however, and the innkeeper saved Joseph's life against a band of particularly cruel soldiers. In thanks, Joseph gave the pious man one of the only possession of value he had; the Crown of Thorns. The innkeeper kept the crown and passed it down through generations of his family. Eventually, the family converted to Islam, although the crown was still kept sacred. When the Crusades came, the patriarch of the family buried the crown to keep it from being destroyed by vengeful fanatics. Even as the family fought against the Christian knights, the crown was still kept hidden until the coming of Guy de Lusignan and Frederick of Barbarossa."

"And?" Sean was on the edge of his seat.

Kieran was fixed on him. "The family had risen to prestige within the ranks of Saladin's warriors, including the eldest son and heir. When the collapse of Acre became apparent over two years of continuous fighting, the heir attempted to negotiate a truce without Saladin's consent. Saladin, of course, was reluctant to a surrender of any kind, but El-Hajidd, the heir apparent of this family, was convinced a peaceable treaty was necessary in order to preserve what was left of Saladin's forces. As a show of good faith, he extended the Crown of Thorns, the relic his family had kept safe for over one thousand years, as a peace offering, something the Christians would value above all else."

By this time, Sean was gazing at him with some shock. "And you accepted the crown?"

"I have it in my bags."

Sean struggled not to let his jaw drop. He stared at Kieran with the most awe-struck expression. "God's Blood, Kieran," he hissed. "If this is true, then you hold the greatest holy relic to ever exist. What are you planning to do?"

Kieran cocked an eyebrow. "My goal was to live long enough to bring it home. Now that I am here, I am not sure what to do. I would seek advice from you and Father to this end."

Sean was still dumbfounded. Across the fire, Christian and Andrew had deteriorated into drunken revelry. Kieran watched his inebriated younger brothers a moment before returning his focus to Sean. The second eldest Hage brother caught Kieran's attention and, after a moment's pause, simply puckered his lips thoughtfully.

"Father will have something to say about this, to be sure," he finally said. "That and the fact you have taken a wife without his permission."

The corner of Kieran's mouth twitched. "He will fall in love with her as I have."

"He will want to know about her family."

"I told you. Her family is Irish nobility. The name is Osgrove."

Sean just shook his head. "I am not as confident as you, Brother," he said. "She is a beauty, no doubt. I've never seen finer. But in Father's world, as long as she is from a good family, she can have the outward appearance of a horse."

Kieran snorted. "He cannot do anything about it regardless of how he feels. Libby is pregnant with the next Earl of Newark and Sherwood whether or not he likes it."

Sean inhaled deeply, thoughtfully, eyeing his brother as he did so. "He always expected more from you than the rest of us," he said quietly. "Unless your Libby is a Princess of Ireland, I am not entirely sure he will approve.

"That is his misfortune."

They wisely moved off the subject and on to other things. As Christian and Andrew eventually passed out from too much alcohol, Kieran and Sean stayed awake the rest of the night, talking quietly until dawn.

THE NEXT MORNING, Rory was introduced to the power, wealth and majesty of the Hage family.

The morning was foggy and she awoke nauseous. As the Hage army began to dismantle the tents and servants began to pack up their goods, Rory stood near her carriage with David and Bud, watching the activity and thinking that everyone pretty much looked like they had just walked out of a Medieval faire. Those Renaissance-type festivals were fairly accurate with their dress, weapons and other articles, because everyone around her looked just like what she had seen. She wished Dr. Dietrich and Dr. Peck could see what she was seeing; they would have been amazed. She doubted Bud could have survived without coffee, but it would have been one heck of an adventure. As she watched Kieran and his brothers give orders and make sure the army mobilized, she found herself swept up in this world she now found herself a part of.

Everything about it was different from what she knew to varying degrees; for instance, the grass beneath her feet was wild and thicker than modern-day, cultivated grass. The roads were only roads in the literal sense and not the even, well-made and paved paths that she knew. The heavy rains that they had been having for weeks had created mini-lakes along the road to Southwell and the ride was bumpy and rough.

Feeling nauseous as she did, she eventually grew ill in the rocking and rolling carriage and got out to walk. Kieran, at the head of the column, found out by a message passed up through the ranks and he reined Liberator around and thundered back along the army until he came to his wife's carriage. She was slugging through mud and water, her skirts hiked up around her knees, but she was walking very determinedly. When Rory saw Kieran approach, she put up a hand to stop his rebuke.

"Save it," she told him. "I can't ride in that thing anymore. It's making me sick."

He reined his horse near her, trying to be gentle. "Sweetheart, I know you do not feel well, but we will not reach Southwell until tomorrow if you walk. You must ride."

She shook her head. "Uh-uh," she snorted humorlessly. "Not in that thing."

"Would you at least ride in the pony cart?" he asked nicely.

"Maybe." She looked up at him. "Where's Yusef? I haven't seen him this morning."

"He is riding at the head of the column in a place of honor."

She twisted her lips doubtfully, moving closer to him. "He may not be comfortable with that," she said quietly.

"Why not?"

"Because he's a stranger in enemy lands," she explained.

When Liberator realized Rory was beside him and tried to shove her with his big head, she poked him in the nostril and he snorted unhappily.

"Gross!" She wiped off her snotty finger, returning her focus to Kieran. "Did you ask him if he wanted to ride with you or did you just tell him to?"

Kieran had no idea what she was driving at as he tried to comfort his pouting charger. "He understands that I am putting him in a place of honor."

Rory gazed at him a moment longer before shaking her head doubtfully. "I'm not sure about that," she said. "He may not be comfortable in the middle of a bunch of white English soldiers who don't know him as well as you do. They may be cruel to him. They don't understand his ways and they might make him feel bad. It's called discrimination."

Kieran really didn't get her concern but he tried to humor her. "Then what would you have me do?"

"Ask him where he wants to ride next time. Don't tell him; ask him. Let him do what he is most comfortable with."

Kieran was trying to understand; he really was. But it was difficult. Rather than argue with her, he simply agreed so she wouldn't grow upset.

"As you wish," he said. "Now, back to the pony cart. Will you at least ride with Kaleef? You know that you should not be exerting yourself so."

Rory glanced back behind the cab to see the old man driving the little pony cart. Bud was riding with him. With a shrug, she stopped and waiting until the pony cart caught up to her. Kieran had Bud get out and Rory took his place as the pony cart continued to move. Bud climbed up on the bench seat of the carriage next to the driver. With everyone shuffled around and settled, Kieran left his wife with a wink and returned to his post at the head of the army.

Rory watched him go, admiring the way he rode Liberator, the power and strength that radiated from the man. She was in the middle of the Hage war machine and trying to analyze it clinically, from the shoes they wore to the weapons they brandished. She found it rather fascinating that the entire army was mounted, which gave her an inkling as to how wealthy and powerful the Hages were. Most armies were foot soldiers with just a few mounted officers and knights. But she was surrounded by at least three hundred mounted men. It was impressive and, if she were to admit it, a little intimidating.

The fog began to lift by mid-morning and the deep green landscape began to come into view. It was fairly flat topography but for a few rolling hills now and again, lush and dotted with sheep. Rory was riding fairly comfortably beside Kaleef when she began to hear a buzz going through the men. The chatter was growing but she couldn't quite catch what they were talking about. Kaleef suddenly nudged her, pointing to the northeast. Straining her eyes, she eventually saw what had the men so excited. It was an awesome sight to behold.

Southwell Castle appeared on a distant rise, a massive castle of pale-colored stone that reflected the weak sunlight like a beacon. Rory stared at it, studying the structure, as they drew closer and she began to see that Southwell wasn't only a castle; it was an entire city. The castle proper was on the top of a gentle rise, an enormous four-story keep like the ones at Rochester or Hedingham, planted at the crest of the hill. As they drew closer and she could see the architecture, she noticed that the walls of the keep had what was called "blind arcading"; a series of arches applied to the façade as decoration. The Normans were particularly fond of that kind of architecture but she'd never actually seen it in such a perfect state; it was extremely impressive. Other than the huge, block-like keep, she could only see walls; miles of them, concentric walls that encircled the hill and then another set that enclosed a portion of the city. It looked like what the ancient fortress at Mycenae must have looked like. It was absolutely enormous.

"Oh, my God," she breathed, studying the castle as the light grew stronger and the structure suddenly looked as if it were made of gold. "Look at that."

Kaleef's old eyes focused on the distant city. "It looks like Paradise."

She nodded, her eyes never leaving the vision. "And Kieran is going to inherit the whole thing," she breathed, shielding her eyes from the sun. "Amazing."

Kaleef looked at her, noting how entranced she seemed. He continued to gaze at the woman; her perfect skin, perfect face, perfect teeth. There was nothing imperfect about the lady. She was also, clearly, very misplaced with her strange speech and forthright behavior. He'd known that from the beginning. Her odd songs and peculiar mannerisms spoke of a difference even more pronounced than his was. He continued to study her, the faint cosmetics on her face that were so strange yet so appealing, the way her eyebrows were perfectly shaped over her perfect eyes.

"Lady," he said softly.

"Hmmm?" Rory answered, still staring at the castle in the distance.

"Where is America?"

Her head snapped to him, the hazel eyes focusing. She was afraid to answer him, having no idea where he had heard of America. Kaleef could see her hesitation, her fear.

"When you came to me for help when you were injured," he reminded her, "you told me that you were from America. Where is this place?"

Rory suddenly remembered that conversation, that dark night. It seemed like a million years ago.

"It's across the sea, to the west of Ireland," she said. But when he had no real reference point, she illustrated with her hands on her lap. "Here's England, here's Ireland, and then all the way over here is America."

Kaleef digested that. "I have never heard of this country."

She looked at him, wondering just how much to tell him. He seemed the quiet sort, a very old Middle Eastern man misplaced in the world of the English. She felt sorry for him, just as she felt sorry for Yusef. But she was misplaced, too, and, in that sense, she felt a kindred spirit with him.

"That's because it hasn't been discovered yet," she said softly. "Kaleef, are you really an alchemist?"

His dark eyes regarded her. "I am what I am."

He was being evasive with her, probably out of fear. "Look," she put her hand on his wrist. "I want you to understand that your secrets are safe with me. I would never betray you. You can trust me and I hope I can trust you, because the things you and I talk about can never be repeated to anyone other than Kieran. He's the only one who wouldn't think we were witches and try to burn us at the stake."

Kaleef regarded her a moment longer, distracted when the pony cart hit a particularly deep rut and the ponies struggled to pull it free. When they were moving again, he turned back to her.

"My knowledge is not limited to the mysterious," he finally said. "I was a healer, once, and a very good one. But I knew there was more in this world that we did not understand and was yet to be discovered. I have discovered many wonderful things that others might consider blasphemy."

Rory thought back to how the old man had given Kieran potions to suspend his bodily functions and caused the man to sleep for eight hundred years. Even to this day, no one had done what Kaleef had in his little hut with all of his mystical and odd ingredients. The man, as far as she was concerned, was a genius.

"I know," she murmured. "Succotrine aloes, zedoary gentian, saffron and rhubarb."

Kaleef looked at her as if she had just struck him. He began to grow very nervous and Rory's hand tightened around his wrist.

"Don't be frightened," she whispered. "Kaleef, I swear I will take your secrets with me to the grave but I have to say, what you have discovered is the most miraculous thing I've ever heard of. I've always wanted to talk to you about it."

He was less nervous but still shaken as he tried to drive the ponies and look at her at the same time. "Who told you this about me?"

"Kieran."

"How does he know?"

She wasn't sure how she could adequately explain everything. She took her hand off his wrist and sat back against the bench. "Because you saved his life, once. You are the reason he is living today."

Kaleef shook his head. "I have never saved your husband."

She cast him a long glance, a gentle smile on her face. "You and I are going to have a very long talk one of these days about the amazing properties of your potions. I think you'll find it very interesting."

They fell into contemplative silence as they approached the mighty castle of Southwell. As they drew closer, Rory became more and more enamored with the sight. The city loomed before her in all of its Medieval glory and pageantry, with its people and massive walls and banners snapping on the parapets in the wind. It was at that moment that Rory began to understand that she was really, truly entrenched in another period of history other than the one she was born into.

She had arrived.

CHAPTER THIRTEEN

Jeffrey Hage, Fifth Earl of Newark and Sherwood, was everything Rory had imagined he would be. He wasn't particularly tall, perhaps around six feet, but he was a big man with wide shoulders and enormous hands. He was also quite handsome even at his advanced age, with heavy, dark brows and a salt and pepper beard on his face. He was still hugging Kieran by the time Rory pulled up with the carriage and wagon bearing their belongings, joyfully kissing his son and praising God for his safe return. The old man was obviously thrilled. But the joy was short lived; the moment Kieran pointed out Rory, Jeffrey's good humor fled. Rory could only make out a few sentences before the explosion.

"Who is she?" Jeffrey asked, stunned, his gaze on Rory several feet away.

Kieran had his arm around his father's shoulders. "My wife, the Lady Rory Elizabeth Osgrove Hage."

Jeffrey's heavy eyebrows flew up. "Your wife?"

"Indeed."

"Where is she from?"

"West of Ireland."

"We will have no Irish bastards in this family!"

From that point, the conversation and the situation deteriorated. The joyful homecoming was ruined. Rory and Kaleef remained on the pony cart while David and Bud remained in the carriage, fearful of all the yelling going on. Yusef, having dismounted his horse several minutes earlier, came to stand next to Rory as they watched Jeffrey Hage rant. He was screaming at his son in a massively booming voice. Jeffrey told Kieran how stupid he was. He pointed out how disappointed he was in his son. Kieran took the barrage of insults with his usual stoic demeanor. He didn't try to argue with his father or interrupt. Kieran simply let the man have his head.

But Rory wasn't stoic; she was growing increasingly emotional watching Kieran's father yell at him. Sean stepped in at some point to try and soothe their father, but Jeffrey literally shoved the man aside as he bellowed at Kieran. Kieran remained silent and composed, even when Jeffrey jabbed a big finger at him and thumped him in the chest. Sean and Christian stood next to their brother in mute support while Andrew made a futile attempt to calm their father. It was an ugly, chaotic scene and, somewhere in the middle of it, a couple of the lesser Hage knights were disbanding the army. They didn't want the vassals to be witness to a family feud.

But Jeffrey Hage and his sons remained steadfast. Rory watched, disgusted and nauseous, until she was unwilling to witness the shouting any longer. Jeffrey Hage was a horrible, horrible man as far as she was concerned and she suddenly bailed out of the pony cart, practically running for the great gates of the ward. Yusef ran after her.

"Lady Hage!" he called. "Where are you going? Lady Hage!"

Rory broke into a dead run, heading for the gates. She had no idea that, behind her, Kieran caught a glimpse of her racing for the open gates and he made a break for Liberator. His father grabbed him by the front of his tunic to prevent him from following. Kieran cuffed the man to the point where Jeffrey lost his balance and fell to one knee. Instead of the Hage brothers going to the aid of their father, they were all racing for their steeds. Jeffrey Hage struggled to his feet, shouting his anger to all of his foolish, disobedient sons, but none of them were listening. They were all scrambling to follow Kieran as he raced after his wife.

Having closed behind the incoming army, the great gates lodged within the massive gatehouse of Southwell were cracked open enough to only allow one person at a time to enter. Rory darted through the opening and bolted off the road, into the town that literally butted right up against the inner wall. By this time, she was weeping hysterically, exhausted, pregnant and despondent over Kieran's father's reaction. All she wanted to do was get clear of the fighting, to cease being the cause of the friction. Her emotions were on edge and she didn't have as much control as she normally had.

The town of Southwell was a maze of small alleys and streets, of homes and merchant stalls. It was actually fairly well developed for a Medieval town and Rory ran down a few little alleys until she came to a dead end that backed up against the inner wall. There was a stable next to the wall. She ran into it, looking for some kind of shelter. There were a few stalls with wide-eyed goats and a loft. She spied the small ladder that led up to the loft and climbed up.

It was a rickety, old loft full of freshly cut hay. Sobbing, Rory threw herself down on a pile of the stuff, feeling it cushion and poke her weary body. She'd been traveling for weeks, eight hundred years from her time and a thousand miles from that rocky beach at Nahariya. She may as well have been on the moon. She lay there, staring at the unevenly-thatched roof and thinking of her life for the past several weeks; the two orphan boys she was coming to love, Kaleef and Yusef, and a husband she loved more than words could express. But apparently, their marriage had been a very bad thing, indeed, at least as far as his father was concerned. Kieran had worked so hard to achieve his goals in life; he was proud, honorable and compassionate. She just couldn't stomach the thought that, after everything, his father would think him stupid or irresponsible. All because of her.

Several more minutes of painful sobbing saw her fall into an exhausted sleep.

☙

KIERAN AND SEAN had been searching for Rory for nearly an hour. Yusef was with them. Having lost Rory nearly the moment she entered the town, he had returned to the castle to collect his horse. Along with Christian and Andrew, they were blanketing the town, a town they knew particularly well. As young children, they used the town as their private playground, so they knew all of the nooks and crannies.

Few things had changed in the town since Kieran had left. Even so, he hadn't been able to locate his wife and was growing increasingly apprehensive. He and his brothers had upended the five taverns in town, interrogating the patrons and turning any sleeping rooms upside down. Soon, the whole town of Southwell was aware that Sir Kieran Hage, newly returned from the Crusades, was searching for his errant wife and citizens of the town began searching for her of their own accord. It helped that Kieran had promised a huge reward.

Andrew, accompanied by Yusef, went off towards the south end of town to search. As the afternoon drew into evening, Kieran, Sean and Christian left the very last tavern where they had given the barkeep a few coins to aid in the search for Lady Hage. The barkeep knew everyone in town and usually had his finger on the pulse of any information. Plodding back to the chargers through the darkening streets, Kieran finally allowed his despair to swamp him. He couldn't resist it any longer; it had been a long and stressful trip only to return home to a ranting father and a distraught wife. He suddenly slumped forward in the saddle, dropping the reins and wiping his hand over his face in a weary, defeated gesture. Liberator, without Kieran's strong hand reining him, came to a confused stop. Sean and Christian came to a halt beside him.

"We shall find her," Sean assured him quietly. "She is hiding, somewhere. She cannot have run far."

Kieran sighed heavily, rubbing his eyes exhaustedly. "I know," he muttered, blinking his eyes and trying to focus on his next course of action. "But it does not erase the fact that even when I find her, she will be shattered. What woman would not, given the way Father acted?"

Sean refrained from "I told you so"; Kieran didn't need to hear that. "She will recover," he said. "Remember that Father did not like Margaret when I married her, either. Her family was not good enough, he said. Do you recall? It took him a year to warm to her and when Ellie was born, he fell in love with them both."

Kieran's jaw ticked as he stared moodily out into the darkness. "But Maggie is a Bigod," he said. "She is from one of the finest families in England so his argument of her being from an inferior family was baseless. Libby is… she is from minor nobility. But she is the most brilliant, courageous and beautiful woman I have ever met. She has risked her life for me and I owe her everything."

Sean glanced at Christian, who was looking at his eldest brother's lowered head. It was clear that he was sympathetic. Sean and Christian exchanged glances.

"What would you have us do, Kieran?" Christian asked. "Shall we continue to search?"

Kieran shook his head vaguely. "There is nothing more to do unless we want to tear this town apart house by house," he muttered. "I am confident Libby is in no danger; we would have heard the screams. She is, if nothing else, loud and demonstrative. She is hiding somewhere, licking her wounds, and I will find her."

"And then what?" Christian pressed quietly.

Kieran lifted his big shoulders. "I do not know. I will not force her to live where she is not comfortable. If Father cannot come to terms with our marriage and treat her civilly, then I will have no choice but to occupy Peveril Castle. I will not stay where my wife is not welcome."

Sean's brow furrowed. "Peveril?" he repeated. "That places is an outpost and unworthy of you."

Kieran looked at him. "It is mine, given to me upon my birth through Father. It is still a royal outpost for the king with royal troops. I will take my wife there and we will raise our family."

Sean sighed heavily and looked away. "Do not do anything rash, Kieran. You have only just returned and I do not want to lose my brother again so soon. At least let us speak with Father and try to rectify this situation."

Kieran didn't reply; he simply leaned forward on his saddle horn, exhausted. Sean nodded at Christian. The younger Hage brother took the hint and began to move away, returning to the castle. Sean reined his charger next to Kieran and lowered his voice.

"Christian is going to return and speak with Father," he said quietly. "I will stay with you if you wish and continue the search for your wife."

Kieran thought on that a moment before shaking his head. "Nay," he said after a moment. "I will search for my wife alone. Return to Maggie and give her my love. I will return as soon as I can. Make sure that Kaleef and the two young servant boys are well taken care of, if you please."

Sean clapped him on the shoulder and was gone, following Christian up the dark streets back to the gatehouse of Southwell. Kieran remained still for a moment before collecting his reins and pushing forward.

He took a different path than his brothers. He reined Liberator into a series of small streets that butted up against the inner wall of Southwell. He simply plodded along, looking into any little open door or crevice, hoping to spot that beautiful chestnut head. He was feeling increasingly despondent, so incredibly sad on her behalf. His father's ranting was nothing new to him; he'd been dealing with it since he had been a child. Jeffrey Hage was a cruel, competitive man. Kieran knew that, but Rory didn't. He should have been more sensitive to that.

He ended up near a dead end. He could see down the alley and it was dark and cold. He was about to turn away when a small boy suddenly appeared. Kieran reined Liberator back so the horse wouldn't snap at the child, but the little boy kept coming towards him. Kieran finally held out a hand.

"Stop," he commanded. "My horse may injure you if you come any closer."

The boy stopped and stared at the horse as if it had fangs. Kieran looked at the child. The boy was fairly well bundled up against the cold, so he wasn't an orphan. Someone took care with the child. Kieran started to rein Liberator around, muttering to the child as an afterthought.

"You haven't seen a strange woman around here, have you?" he grumbled.

"Oy!" the kid piped up.

Kieran paused, peering more closely at the child. "What did you say?"

The boy threw an arm out, pointing behind him. Seized with the possibility, Kieran dismounted Liberator in a hurry and approached the child.

"Did you see a finely dressed woman?" he asked, eager.

The boy nodded and began to run. Kieran ran after him. They ended up at a small stable that butted against the inner wall of Southwell and the boy jabbed his finger at the leaning structure. Kieran sized it up.

"In there?" he asked, pointing to the stable.

The kid nodded emphatically. Kieran put a trencher-sized hand on the boy's head, dwarfing him, and gave the kid a gold coin. It was more money than the child had probably ever seen in his life. Silently, Kieran entered the dark structure.

It was shadowed and eerie. The first things Kieran saw were two goats, looking up at him with big, curious goat-eyes. With the utmost quiet, Kieran proceeded to peer into the four stalls of the stable. They were cluttered with hay and other implements, but he had yet to see anything human. Puzzled, he stood back and assessed the room when his gaze moved upward and he noticed the loft.

There was a small ladder in the corner that led up to the loft. With extreme care, he made his way slowly up the ladder, his senses alert, as his head finally emerged into the second level. His eyes moved over the hay-filled area but he didn't see anything other than dried grass. It was very dark and he took another step on the ladder, gaining a better look. Still, all he could see was hay. Puzzled, discouraged, he was about to turn away when his gaze fell on a foot.

But it wasn't any foot. It was a big, ugly boot that he recognized. Relief such as he had never known swept him and he very nearly fell off the ladder as the wave of comfort and joy washed through him. Creeping up the ladder, he moved across the loft, towards the boot, on his hands and knees. Rory was lying on a small pile of hay, wedged between the wall and the hay. Her foot was the only thing visible. And she was sleeping like the dead, snoring softly.

Kieran looked at her, a lump forming in his throat. Truth be told, he was exhausted himself. He had tried so hard to keep Rory happy and soothed during this very difficult transition, but she still wasn't settling in. He knew it was very hard for her and the addition of an unexpected pregnancy was only making it worse. Still, he would be lost without her. Those few hours she was missing were the worst of his life. He felt like a failure that she had been so despondent it had caused her to flee. Removing his helm, he crawled into the space between Rory and the wall, and lay down beside her. The moment he touched her, the tears came.

Rory woke up to the sounds of sniffles. Her eyes rolled open to the sight of Kieran lying beside her. The moment their eyes met, he threw his arms around her and burned his face in her neck, sobbing quietly.

Rory was startled. She wrapped her arms around him and held him as closely as she could. She didn't even stop to wonder how he had found her; it never crossed her mind. All that mattered was that the man, her rock, was weeping.

"Baby," she whispered into the top of his dark blond hair. "What's wrong? Why are you crying?"

He couldn't even answer her. He just held her tightly, weeping into her neck. But very quickly, he composed himself, wiping his face furiously with one hand while holding her with the other. Rory lay silent as the man pulled himself together after his painful outburst. She stroked his face, his hair, kissing his forehead until he was strong enough to look her in the eye.

"I am sorry," he whispered. "Forgive my weakness."

She kissed his cheek tenderly. "I'm the one who should apologize," she murmured. "I've made your life miserable since we appeared on that rocky beach in Nahariya. I've done nothing but complain and cry and behave horribly. I'm sorry I ran away; I just couldn't watch your father scream at you anymore. I just snapped."

A big hand was stroking her cheek. "I understand," he said softly. "I am so accustomed to his rants that it did not occur to me that it would take a toll on you. I apologize for his hateful words. Realizing he has hurt you… it shatters me. We will leave Southwell tomorrow and go to my holding of Peveril. I will not permit my father to spout abuse and hurt you."

She smiled sadly. "I'm a big girl. I can take it. I promise; no more running. I didn't mean to scare you so badly. I just couldn't stand watching him yell at you. I felt like I just needed to get out of there."

His expression tightened. "He has been yelling at me all my life. It is the way of things."

"It's wrong, Kieran."

"It is his way."

Rory felt so sorry for the man. She knew what it was like to have an abusive parent. Her mother had been the same way; never happy with her only child, constantly brow-beating her for improvement. Rory kissed him, firmly, and Kieran responded ferociously. He loved her so strongly that words could not express the strength of the emotion. Rolling Rory onto her back, his big hands moved over her torso, his mouth moving to the swell of her bosom. He pinched her nipples gently through the fabric, listening to her groan. Then he took a full breast in his hand, squeezing carefully.

"You are still wearing your bra," he murmured against her lips.

She laughed, shaking with mirth as he fingered the underwire. "I can't help it. I don't feel dressed unless I have it on."

"It is too much of a barrier between your flesh and mine," he growled. "I suppose you have those odd undergarments on as well."

She continued to giggle. "Yes, I am wearing panties."

He growled and tossed up her skirts, putting his hand over her mouth when she squealed. As she continued to giggle, he pulled off the lacy white panties, wedging his enormous body between her legs and putting his mouth on her groin.

"I cannot taste your flesh with those oddities against your body," he growled, grabbing her behind the knees and lifting her legs. He suckled and lapped the tender flesh of her inner thigh. "I must have my fill of you."

Her giggles were fading as his mouth moved to the sensitive core between her legs. He began to suckle on the pink folds and she grasped him by the hair.

"Kieran," she half-hissed, half-moaned. "Don't…"

He ignored her, feeling her squirm in his hands. "You'll not tell me no, Lib, not ever."

She was quickly succumbing to his wicked tongue. "But… this is just weird. I'm pregnant and…"

He kissed her pink folds gently, his hand moving to her still-flat belly, and he kissed the soft flesh reverently. "I know," he whispered. "I would taste where my son has been conceived, where our love has come to fruition. I can never be closer to you or to him than at this moment. Do not deny me that."

Rory's head came up and she looked at him, wedged down between her legs. She watched him as he kissed her belly and lay his great head against it. Tears sprang to her eyes.

"That's the sweetest thing I've ever heard," she sniffled. "I love you so much."

He didn't say anything; he just lay there with his head against her stomach. When he did speak, his lips were against her flesh.

"Nothing my father says can hurt us or break us," he murmured. "We are strong, you and I."

Rory lowered her head, staring up at the dark rafters of the stable. "We are strong enough to have defied time and history," she murmured. "I suppose your father is small potatoes by comparison."

His head came up, the brown eyes gazing steadily at her. "What is potatoes?"

She half-grinned, running her fingers through his cropped hair. “Never mind,” she said. “It wouldn’t mean anything to you, anyway. I guess I just meant that your father is small in comparison to whatever Fates have brought us to this point in time. Your father couldn’t break us if he tried.”

Kieran kissed her belly one last time and sat up, looking around for the white panties he had tossed aside. He found them behind him and retrieved them, sliding them awkwardly up her legs as she giggled. When he had them secure, he just sat there and looked at them.

“I sincerely hate those,” he muttered.

She laughed, sitting up and pulling her skirts down. “Why?”

“Because they are odd.” He wriggled his eyebrows. “But they are strangely enticing at the same time. I cannot make up my mind.”

She couldn’t argue with him. They sat there a moment, gazing steadily at each other. Kieran finally reached out and cupped her chin gently.

“Are you ready to return to Southwell?” he asked.

Her smile faded. “Yes,” she said reluctantly. “But I made a fool of myself running off like that.”

He shook his head and held out a hand to help her to her feet. “You did no such thing,” he said. “My brothers were as worried for you as I was.”

Rory let him help her down the ladder, emerging into the dark stable below. Liberator was just outside the stable, munching on a big pile of hay that had fallen from the loft. Kieran made sure the horse was stable before lifting Rory into the saddle. He mounted behind her, holding her safe and secure as he directed Liberator back to the gatehouse.

☙

“I SHALL NOT hear rebuke from my own son.” Jeffrey thrust a big finger in Christian’s face. “You always were a fool, Christian. If you married a lowly peasant, I would understand. But I expected better of Kieran.”

Tall, flame-haired Christian was the most like his father out of the four Hage brothers. He was hotheaded and brash, often speaking before thinking. But he understood his father better than the other three and was usually the best one to reason with him for that fact. At this moment, however, Jeffrey did not want to be reasoned with.

"The man has just returned home from the great Quest," Christian stated, his tone somewhat taut in the face of his father's insult. "You have not seen him in three years and the first words out of your mouth are labeling him foolish and stupid? Is that really what you think of him?"

Jeffrey's jaw ticked. "He should not have married without my permission."

"That does not make him foolish or stupid."

"Aye, it does!" Jeffrey stomped about in the lavish solar of Southwell, a room that was resplendent with the riches of the Hages; tapestries, plate and other utensils lined the walls and hearth to an obvious degree. "He knows better. Why should he behave so?"

"Because he loves her," answered Sean as he entered the solar, pulling off his big, leather gloves. He moved for the pitcher of wine on the nearby table. "According to Kieran, she is brave and intelligent. And, as we all saw, she is extremely beautiful. It was only natural that he succumbed to her."

Jeffrey didn't like it when his sons banded against him, which was often. "So you defend him as well?" he snarled. "I should have expected it. You always defend him and he always defends you. But I care not what you say; he should not have married that Irish rubbish."

Sean sighed heavily, turning to look at his father with his wine in hand. "If I were you," he said evenly, "I would not call the woman rubbish in front of Kieran. He is likely to take your head off."

"I shall disown him!"

Sean drank his wine, snorting into the cup. "As if he needs you," he said. "The man has more wealth than you do. He just doesn't flaunt it so lavishly."

Near the door, Christian nodded. "Peveril Castle and the fiefdom of Dykemore and Sewall, and the heir apparent to the earldom of Newark and Sherwood," he reminded his father as if the man did not already know. "He also inherited all of the lands from Warrington to Liverpool, the Hawkesbury baronetcy, through mother's Jenkinson relations. He is far wealthier than you, Father, and far more influential."

Jeffrey knew that. He also didn't like to be reminded. "He'll not get the earldom if I disown him," he snapped. "It will go to Sean."

Sean shook his head and took another drink. "Do not think to hand me that mess of titles so easily," he said. "I have the baronet of Walcot. I am quite content."

It was unfortunate that the sons had to treat their father with such callousness but not too unfortunate considering all the man had ever done was pit one against another. But Eleanor Britton du Reims-Hage's common sense and good graces had been inherited by her boys. They knew their father for what he was; an over-emotional, brilliant, deeply family oriented bully. It was a strange paradox.

Jeffrey watched Sean pace the room with a cup in hand while Christian simply stood his ground near the door. Realizing that he was not supported in his reaction to Kieran's marriage, Jeffrey slowly sat behind the massive oak desk that had once belonged to his grandfather. It was a heavy, carved thing, massive in size. It was the desk of a powerful earl.

"Still," Jeffrey muttered. "I expected more from Kieran."

The calm expression on Sean's face faded as he turned to his father. He watched the man a moment, unable to control the anger that was building within him.

"You expected more?" he muttered bitterly. He moved towards his father. "Let me tell you something about Kieran and let us pray that you can understand my words; the man is returning home a hero. He fought with Richard for three years in the godforsaken lands of The Levant to make you and his family proud. He was so great that whilst he was there, he earned a reputation for himself that Saladin himself had heard of. It was so great, in fact, that when the Muslims were prepared to extend an offering of peace to the Christian armies, they contacted the only Christian they felt they could trust by reputation alone, Sir Kieran Hage. My brother was asked by the Muslim commanders to relay their peace offering. And you expect more from the man? He is greater than you could ever hope to be and I, for one, am extremely proud of him. I love and respect my brother even if you do not."

By the time Sean was finished, Jeffrey was gazing at the man without his usual belligerence. It was rare when Sean became upset and Jeffrey took notice, even if it was difficult for him to rein in his pride. Meeting Sean's intense gaze, he was the first to lower his eyes.

"Kieran is my son," he said hoarsely. "Of course I love and respect him."

But Sean wasn't finished yet. "You had better," he growled. "And let me tell you something else; Kieran has returned home because his men, friends he trusted, turned on him out of jealousy and tried to kill him. He came home to seek counsel and protection, and all you can do is scream at him like a fishwife for having married a woman he is in love with. You make me ashamed, Father; you make me horribly ashamed of the way you have treated him."

Jeffrey's dark brow furrowed with outrage. "What do you mean there are men attempting to kill him? Who is trying to kill him?"

Sean wondered if his father had even heard the rest of what he had said. In the long run, he supposed it didn't matter much. He had his attention now.

He told Jeffrey everything.

CHAPTER FOURTEEN

RORY WAS WILDLY uncomfortable being in the bailey of Southwell again. When Kieran rode into the bailey, several men ran out to greet him. They took hold of Liberator and Rory looked down to see many hands raised to her, offering to help her from the horse. Kieran didn't hesitate in lowering her into the waiting sea of arms.

He dismounted behind her and took her by the hand, leading her across the dark bailey. Rory was somewhat in awe of her surroundings; there were torches everywhere, big burning things that lit up parts of the bailey like streetlights. Men on the battlements had torches as well, with the addition of dogs on leashes. Rory peered at the dogs through the darkness; they were tall, skinny dogs with long snouts. Greyhounds, she thought with amazement. She pointed up to the battlements.

"You have watchdogs?" she asked, incredulous.

Kieran glanced up to the parapets. "Better than soldiers," he commented. "They smell changes on the wind and see things that men cannot. I took two dogs with me to the Holy Land for that purpose alone."

"What happened to them?"

"Richard is fond of dogs as I am. He confiscated them and now they are the property of the king."

She grinned as his expression slackened in a defeated gesture. They made their way across the vast and dusty bailey which, oddly enough, had two massive oak trees growing in it. One was next to the keep and the other was on the east side of the ward near the stables. They passed under one of the enormous oak trees as he took her to the steps that led into the keep. As was common at the time, the stairs were wooden and retractable, leading up to a second floor entrance. There was also a great stone forebuilding around the stairs, like a stone porch, that protected it during times of siege. If worse came to worse and the bailey was breached, they would close off the stone porch to protect the stairs. In a worst case scenario, they would simply burn the stairs to prevent an enemy from gaining access to the keep.

Kieran took her inside, up the stairs, emerging into the second floor. Rory, forgetting her apprehension, was completely fascinated with her surroundings. They had entered a tall-ceiling entry hall with thick-planked wooden floors. To the right was a doorway leading into a big room and a short corridor stretched out before them; she could see another enormous room at the end of the corridor. To her left was a wide, squat and steep spiral staircase that disappeared into the floor above. Great iron sconces were bolted to the stone walls, each one of them blazing with a torch spitting out black smoke. The entire vision was creepy, fascinating, and totally Medieval. The place smelled dusty, smoky, with a faint hint of grass.

"Wow," Rory breathed as she looked around. "This place is amazing."

Kieran smiled at her as a man approached him from the room down the corridor. It was a servant, an old man with stringy white hair and a hump in his back, clad in a blue-dyed wool tunic, hose and funky shoes with weird toes. Rory peered closely at the man as he approached Kieran and bowed deeply. She noticed that the shoes were made from wood and some kind of material, not leather. They were kind of like slip-on, canvas tennis shoes. She was intently inspecting the shoes when the man spoke.

"My lord Kieran," he said happily. "God be praised for returning you safe from the land of the savages. Welcome home, m'lord."

Kieran nodded. "My thanks." He indicated Rory, who was still staring at the servant's shoes. "This is my wife. You will treat her with all due respect."

The servant turned his attention to Rory and the first thing she noticed about the man was that he had a big cataract in the left eye; the iris was milky. He smiled at her, with all of the three teeth in his head, and bowed deeply.

"Lady Hage," he greeted. "We are honored."

Rory smiled at the old man. "Thank you."

Her accent caught the old servant by surprise; Kieran could read it in his face. "She is Irish," he explained, rather distractedly. He was looking around, peering into the room to their right. "Where are the others I brought with me this afternoon? The Saracens and the boys?"

"The Saracens are in the knight's quarters, m'lord," the old man replied. "Sir Sean directed that they be given their own rooms. The boys have been shown to their room as well."

Kieran nodded. "Excellent," he replied. "You will spread the word that they are my guests and to be given all due honor."

The old man nodded crisply. "Aye, m'lord."

Satisfied that Yusef and Kaleef and the youngsters were taken care of for the moment, his thoughts began to turn to his own bedchamber. Now it was his turn to be taken care of.

"Is my room ready?"

The old man nodded again, indicating the stairs. "It is, m'lord," he replied eagerly. "Your baggage was brought up this afternoon."

Kieran began to remove his gloves. "Good," he said, pulling at the fingers. "Where are my brothers?"

"In the great hall with your father," he replied. "They asked to be notified when you returned."

"Then tell them I am returned. My wife and I will take sup in my room tonight."

The old servant fled to do his bidding. Kieran removed his gloves and indicated the stairs to Rory.

"My lady?" he smiled. "Shall we retire?"

Rory looked dubiously at the stairs; they were ridiculously steep, but wide. She wondered how in the heck she was going to make it up the steps in her long dress. With a shrug, she gathered up her skirt and carefully mounted the steps. Kieran was right behind her. They wound their way up to the third floor and Rory stopped on the landing.

"Now where?" she asked.

He pointed up the stairs. "Keep going."

She did. They reached the fourth and top floor and she came to a halt on the landing.

"Well? Don't tell me to keep going."

He snorted and pointed to his right. "Nay," he said. "In here."

They were in a small landing with two doors; one to the left and one down a small corridor to the right. Kieran pushed open the massive oak and iron door to the right and suddenly, an entirely new world opened up.

It was like a scene from a fairy tale; a massive fire blazed in a hearth that was taller than she was. Huge amounts of heat and smoke blazed into the room. The room was lavishly appointed. In fact, it looked more like a museum display. The bed was a massive four-poster deal with heavy curtains hanging from it. Next to it, instead of the traditional rushes, were enormous animal skin rugs. There were three of them, all identical cowhide and very beautiful. There was a magnificent table to her right, underneath the window, that had two equally beautiful chairs. Trinkets, knickknacks, chests, and other treasures were strewn around the room in organized Medieval chaos. The hearth for that gigantic fireplace had several bejeweled plates lining the mantel. Rory stood there with her mouth hanging open as Kieran moved around her, throwing his gloves on the table and pulling off his helm. She heard him sigh heavily.

"God's Blood, 'tis good to return home," he exclaimed. "I did not realize how much I missed it until now."

Rory just stood there, overwhelmed with everything around her. She finally let out a strangled yelp.

"Ahhh!" she half-spoke, half-yelled.

He looked at her. "What is wrong?"

The oddest expression creased her face. Her eyes bulged and she grinned humorlessly. "Look at this place!" she cried with feigned dramatics. "It's… it's unbelievable. I've never seen such lavish Medieval wealth."

He looked around, not quite sure what she was saying. "What do you mean?"

"I mean that it looks like the Emperor Caligula lives here." She turned to him, amazement on her face. "I've refrained from asking this question because it really isn't any of my business, but the entire trip home from Nahariya, you were throwing money around like you own a treasury. Just how rich are you?"

His brown eyes twinkled as he turned away and began to remove his tunic. "You are correct, madam. It is none of your affair."

She wouldn't let him off so easily. "I know I'm being nosy as hell, but where do you get your money? Do you rob people?"

He laughed and pulled the tunic over his head. "Nay, I do not rob people." He bent over to pull off the chain mail hauberk. "My family is wealthy. I have inherited much of this wealth."

"Will you please tell me exactly how wealthy?"

"Why?"

"Because I just want to know."

"Does it make a difference in how you feel about me?"

She shook her head and turned away from him. "Of course not," she said softly. "But the majority of Medieval people don't live like this. Kieran, you live like a king."

He pulled off the mail coat and tossed it on the table, proceeding to removing the rest of his clothing and watching his wife as she walked to the bed, inspecting the fabric of the curtains. Then she yanked them back, gazing at the well-appointed bed. She began to pull it apart, examining each individual piece and holding it close to the light of the fat taper near the bed. He sighed heavily as he pulled off his heavily-padded linen tunic.

"As Viscount Dykemoor and Sewall, I inherit the revenue from the lands left to me from my father's father," he said quietly. "I have also been left the expanse of land between Warrington and Liverpool from my mother's family, including three baronetcies. Since those are heavily populated and rich lands, I am due the revenue from those as well, including a portion of the port revenue from the docks at Liverpool. I also hold three castles; Peveril, which is garrisoned for the king, meaning that Richard pays me for the garrison, plus Bucklow Castle and Rainhill Castle from my mother's family holdings."

She digested that. "Tell me your full title, including all of the little things you don't consider important."

He seemed reluctant. "I told you all of this before."

She shook her head slowly. "No, you didn't. Not everything."

He hesitated a moment before proceeding. "I am Viscount Dykemoor and Sewall. I also hold the titles of Baron Hawkesbury, hereditary Lord of Deus Mons, Baron Mere and Heyrose, and Guardian of the King's Gateway. When my father dies, I shall become the sixth Earl of Newark and Sherwood." He lifted his hand in a resigned gesture, letting it slap back against his thigh. "Is there anything else you wish to know?"

Her eyes glittered as she processed the full extent of his nobility. "Yes," she said slowly. "How tall are you and how much do you weight?"

She was toying with him, not taking him or his titles seriously. He appreciated that; most women treated him like God Descended when they discovered the extent of his wealth and titles. But not Rory; she didn't care about his wealth or titles. She only cared about the man himself. He could be a pauper and it wouldn't matter. He put his hands on his hips.

"I am six and a half feet tall and I weight more than twice what you do, so do not make light of either attribute," he growled, although he wasn't serious. "So if you truly wish to know how wealthy I am, I will not tell you. But I will tell you this; thanks to my mother's family and King Richard's generosity, I have more lands and wealth than my father. I do not believe he has ever quite forgiven me for that."

She watched him closely a moment, her smile fading. She moved towards him, her thoughts turning to Richard and the Crusade for some reason. His tremendous wealth brought about darker facts and reasons.

"Do you remember what I told you when we first met?" she asked softly, putting her hands against his bare chest when he pulled her into an embrace. "About Richard being captured and held for ransom by Leopold of Austria?"

Kieran's expression darkened as he recalled the conversation they'd had. It seemed like a thousand years ago but, by their timeline, it was really only a couple of months ago. He remembered his outrage and frustration as she had told him what was to happen to Richard in the future.

He nodded slowly. "I recall."

Her fingers caressed his flesh gently. "It took Richard's supporters over a year to raise the money to free him. In fact, his mother, Eleanor, pawned the crown jewels. The ransom demand was one hundred and fifty thousand gold marks."

"She will not have to pawn the crown jewels," he said. "I can supply them with the money in a day."

Her touch grew firmer, her eyes imploring. "That's what I thought," she murmured. "Kieran, I'm not so sure you should. If you do, you could change the course of history. I'm not sure how to explain this, so bear with me. For all intents and purposes, you were dead two months ago. At least, you were no longer a factor in the history of the world. No children, no wives, nothing. I would assume that meant Sean inherited the title of Earl of Newark and Sherwood."

Kieran nodded thoughtfully. "Aye, he would have."

"Then any children he had would be his heirs."

"Correct."

She sighed, trying to put her thoughts into focus. "But that's all changed," she said. "Now you're back, you're a major player in England's history, and I'm back with you. Not only that, but I'm pregnant with what will presumably be another earl of Newark."

"I understand your reasoning."

"Good," she continued. "Here's the problem. You weren't even supposed to be here but, for some reason, we were both brought back to your time. We were both brought back for a reason so powerful that Fate or God or whoever you believe in realized they had made a mistake and brought you back to accomplish something that will change the course of history. The problem is this; we don't know what the purpose is and I'm terrified that if we change it too much, the world as I know it will cease to exist. I might even cease to exist. I might not even be born. Does that make any sense?"

His expression darkened as he understood her line of thinking. "So what are you attempting to say? That I should not pay the ransom for Richard?"

She sighed, laying her head against his bare chest. "I'm just saying that if we change things too much, I might disappear. I'm here for a reason, but I don't know what that reason is. You're here for a reason. Maybe it just revolves around the Crown of Thorns; maybe that's the only reason you've been brought back. But why me? Why am I here? And will I do something inadvertently, with all of my historical knowledge, that will change history forever?"

He held her close, his face on the top of her head. "I do not know how to answer your questions," he murmured. "You are far more knowledgeable about this than I am. But I will say this; the thought of losing you scares me more than anything else on earth. I would stay locked in this room the rest of my life if the alternative meant I would lose you."

She lifted her head from his chest, gazing up into his strong, handsome face. "I don't think we need to do that," she said. "I'm just saying that we should probably think about it very carefully before we do anything at all, including bailing out Richard."

He nodded, studying the fine lines of her face, the way her big hazel eyes reflected the light. "Agreed," he said, leaning down to kiss her. "Do you think we need to analyze my need to take a bath?"

She chuckled and pulled away. "God, no," she said. "I think we need to scrub you down."

He snorted, watching her move away from him to remove the heavy cloak she was wearing; it was covered with hay. Then he moved around the bed to the other side of the room. Looking up from picking the hay off her cloak, Rory noticed there was a doorway that he disappeared through. Curious, she skittered after him.

She emerged into a smaller room set into the corner of the massive keep. It took her no time at all to see that it was a privy, and a big one. There were two toilets cut into one wall, which was actually just a big stone seat with two holes chiseled into it. And the other side of the room had an enormous copper tub that was lined with linen. There was a basin and pitcher, plus a big screen made out of carefully-woven grass to shield the bather. Rory stood there with her mouth open.

"Oh, my God," she gasped, putting her hands on her hips as she inspected the room. "A master bathroom."

He looked at her as he sat on a stool and began to pull off one of his boots. "Sean and his wife have the adjoining chamber," he said. "I allow them to use this room also."

She could see the second doorway in the chamber, connecting it to the other bower. The door was half-open and she could see a nice room beyond but not nearly as lavish as Kieran's. She watched him as he removed the other boot and stood up.

"Do your brothers ever get… well, jealous of everything you have?" she asked.

He shook his head. "They have a good deal themselves. Sean is Baron Walcot, a gift I bestowed upon him before I went to The Levant. The Walcot baronet was mine, through my mother, but I gave it to Sean because he deserved it. The Walcot baronet brings in about thirty thousand marks a year, making Sean a very rich man. Both Christian and Andrew have lands as well. In fact, Christian is the sole heir to the lands of the Wyvern, which are the most mystical and revered lands in the ancient kingdom of Mercia. Those lands are rich with farmers and stock. Therefore, think not that my brothers are destitute, because they are most certainly not."

She shook her head in awe. "How is it that one family has so much?"

"I told you; we are descended from the kings of Mercia. When the Normans came, we were able to keep most of our lands in exchange for loyalty."

She went to sit on the stool that he had vacated, watching him move for what looked like a small door in the wall. She thought it was a dumbwaiter, although she'd never heard of such a thing in Medieval England. But, sure enough, he slid open the door, bellowed "water", and shut it. Then he went to the basin and poured water from the pitcher into the big, marble bowl.

"What is that thing you just shouted into?" she asked.

"What?" he looked to see what she was pointing at. "That is a lever; there is a shelf in there that, when pulled by a winch, lifts items from the ground floor up to this room."

She leapt up and ran to it, sliding the door open and peering inside. "It is a dumbwaiter," she commented. "I'll be damned. I've never heard of one in a castle from this era."

He knew she was mumbling more to herself than to him, inspecting everything with her scientist's mind. He washed his hands, his face, just as several servants entered the chamber from Sean's room, carrying with them buckets of steaming water. Rory moved out of the way as the servants moved quickly and efficiently, filling up the giant, copper tub in little time. As she sat on the stool in the chamber, watching the activity, she noticed that the same servant who had greeted Kieran downstairs had entered their bedchamber with a giant platter of food. The servants all left as quickly as they came, shutting doors behind them. Abruptly, Rory and Kieran were alone again.

Kieran was already stripping off his breeches. They ended up in a pile on the floor and he sank into the tub, sighing heavily as he settled down. Rory rose off the stool and went over to the tub, inspecting it and him.

"Do you want some help?" she asked. "I have a bunch of soap and oils that you can use."

He began splashing water all over his head, sending droplets onto Rory. "Nay, madam," he said. "I do not wish to smell like a woman."

She chuckled and stepped back, out of the line of splashing water. "It doesn't all smell like flowers," she said. "I have a bar of soap that smells like sage and pine."

"I am content as I am."

He might have been but she wasn't. Rory disappeared into their chamber, hunting down the trunks that had been completely emptied. She began to search for the contents and discovered them all neatly stacked on the shelf in one of the two enormous wardrobe cabinets in the room. The soap she was searching for was a milky-colored lump with flecks of green. Laying her hands on it, she took it back into the privy chamber.

Kieran was still splashing water all over his head. Rory went up to him, grabbed him under the chin to force his head up, and began lathering up his head.

"What are you doing?" he demanded, though he didn't pull away. "I told you that I did not want to smell like a woman."

"Shut up," she said lightly. "Splashing water all over you isn't going to do a bit of good. You're not really clean unless you've used soap. It gets rid of the dirt and bacteria."

He groaned as she scrubbed his head. "Good God," he growled. "I've not needed soap for thirty-two years and…"

"Enough," she snapped, moving to soap up his neck and shoulders. "I've been dealing with your sweaty, dirty body for weeks now and I think I deserve a clean husband for once."

He just growled, but now it wasn't so entirely angry. She was soaping his shoulders and back, massaging him at the same time, and he was quickly succumbing to her. The woman had magical hands. She moved around to his chest, soaping him, rubbing him, and Kieran could feel himself growing hard. There was such powerful chemistry between them that his physical reaction to her was almost instantaneous.

"You are a tyrant, Lady Hage," he muttered.

"I know." She came around front, washing his face. "Stop pretending that you don't like it."

"Get in this bath with me."

She saw that twinkle in his eye, the familiar sexual desire. She shook her head. "Not now," she said, splashing water on his cheeks. "Let's get you clean first and then I'll think about it. Stand up."

He did, with a full-blown erection in her face. Rory just shook her head at him again, trying not to giggle as she soaped around it. She moved from his belly to his back to his buttocks and down his muscled legs. Kieran's erection never went down and she finally succumbed to her own lust for her husband's hot body and soaped his testicles, pleasuring his massive member with her mouth until he begged for mercy. When he climaxed, she let him spend himself on the swell of her breasts.

Exhausted, sated to the bone, Kieran collapsed back into the bath and lay back against the slope of the tub, his head resting on the back. Rory wiped off her breasts with a corner of the linen he was going to use to dry himself.

"You are a witch, Lady Hage," he groaned, satisfied. "You cast a spell upon me and I can only think, hear or taste of you."

She smiled at him, rinsing her hands in the bathwater. "So I'm a witch and a tyrant, am I?" she said. "You must think very highly of me."

He grinned, his eyes still closed. "You are also my angel," he murmured. "I worship you."

She laughed softly. "Nice save, buddy." She leaned over the side of the tub and kissed him; he put his wet hand against her back affectionately. "Do you want me to shave you?"

He sighed heavily. "Perhaps later." He opened his eyes and looked at her. "I told Brethel to bring food. Has it arrived yet?"

She nodded. "They brought it when they brought your hot water."

"Good." He rubbed her back fondly, drinking in her sweet, rosy-cheeked face. "Perhaps we should eat first and retire early. Tomorrow will be a…"

He was cut off by many voices, male voices, he recognized. Rory didn't even have time to stand up before the Hage brothers burst into the chamber via Sean's room. As Rory rose to her feet, Sean smiled sweetly at her, took her hand to help her stand, and kissed her on the cheek.

"Lady Hage," he greeted kindly. "It is good to see that you are well."

She nodded gratefully. "I am, thank you," she replied. "I'm sorry to have caused so much trouble."

Sean's dark eyes glimmered at her. "No trouble at all, my lady," he said and turned to his brother. "Why are you up here? We were waiting for you in the hall."

Rory stood back as Sean, Christian and Andrew clustered around the tub. Kieran looked up at his brothers with irritation on his face.

"Can a man not have some time alone with his wife?" he demanded. "If I wanted you here, I would have sent for you."

Sean snickered as Christian and Andrew looked rather dumbfounded. They all looked at Rory, standing primly several feet away from the tub. Then Kieran's words finally occurred to Christian.

"God's Blood," he muttered, turning away from the tub and dragging Andrew with him. "We have interrupted them."

Kieran reached out and grabbed his brother by the leg before he could move away completely. "Fortunately for you, you have a keener sense of timing," he said. "Five minutes earlier and I would have taken your head off."

As the brothers snickered, Rory turned beet-red and fled the bathroom. Kieran was on his feet, sloshing water out of the tub.

"I was jesting, sweetheart," he called after her, grabbing the linen towel slung over the woven partition. "Do not be angry."

She called something back to him that none of the brothers, save Kieran, understood. It was an insult he would not repeat and wriggled his eyebrows at his brothers.

"The child has made her extraordinarily sensitive," he explained. "I must watch what I say or she will fly into a rage."

Sean nodded in understanding. "As did Maggie. Great Gods, I remember those days with fear and awe."

"Then perhaps you can help me navigate these unfamiliar waters," Kieran said as he wrapped the towel around his waist and moved into his big, warm chamber with his brothers on his heels. He saw Rory standing in front of the wardrobe, tucking away the sage and pine soap. "I was jesting, sweet. I am sorry if I upset you."

She closed the doors to the wardrobe and faced the group. "Don't worry about it," she said, studying the trio of unfamiliar faces. "Besides, I just thought you'd like to be alone with your brothers."

Kieran smiled at her, dropping the towel right then and there. She tried not to blush as he went to the other wardrobe and threw open the doors, looking for something to wear. It apparently didn't bother him that he was stark naked with his brothers and wife in the room. Worse than that, his erection hadn't died down completely and Rory found herself wishing the floor would swallow her up. She reopened the wardrobe that had her possessions in it and pretended to busy herself as Kieran found a pair of leather breeches and pulled them on. Meanwhile, Christian and Andrew were over at the food on the table, throwing off the cloth and inspecting the offerings. Kieran caught sight of what they were doing.

"Get back, you hounds," he admonished. "My wife has not yet eaten. You can scavenge her leavings."

Out of the corner of her eye, Rory saw that he was at least partially dressed and she reemerged from the wardrobe and shut the door.

"It's all right," she said. "I'm really not that hungry."

Kieran went to her, bare-chested and delicious, and led her over to the table, shoving his brothers aside. He sat her gently.

"Eat," he kissed the top of her head.

She reached up and touched his big hand as it rested on her shoulder. "Do you think Bud and David can come up and eat with me? They're probably really scared, being in a strange place and all. Please?"

Kieran couldn't deny her, although his family might think he'd gone mad. No sooner had he sent a servant to collect the boys than his father was suddenly bursting into the room.

"Here you are," he boomed, shoving open the door. "I found myself alone in the hall and assumed you were all up here."

Rory was startled by the door flying open and the big, booming voice. When she saw who it was, she immediately lowered her head. She was terrified that any words exchanged with the man would have her throwing punches at him. So she kept her head down and shoved a piece of white cheese into her mouth.

But Jeffrey ignored her completely. He went straight to Kieran. "What's this I hear that de Corlet tried to murder you?" he demanded. "And this story of a holy relic; Kieran, is it true?"

Kieran scratched his head and went in search of a tunic. "Aye," he said simply, finding a soft, unbleached, linen tunic and pulling it over his magnificent chest. "It is true; all of it."

Jeffrey's brown eyes flickered dangerously. "That petty bastard," he growled. "I will gather a thousand men and lay siege to his father's home. I'll wipe the man from the earth!"

Kieran held up his hands. "That will not be necessary," he said. "But I do need your advice. You must keep your wits about you and not think with your sword."

Jeffrey opened his mouth to retort but thought better of it. Taking a deep breath, he clasped his hands behind his back and made all attempts to look composed. Kieran, eyeing his father, pulled on another pair of boots.

"Do you know the entire story or must I repeat it?" he asked, somewhat subdued.

Jeffrey, too, was calming. "Sean told me everything."

"What did he tell you about the holy relic?"

Sean, standing over near Rory, spoke up. "I told him everything you told me," he said. "Father knows that the savages used you as a peace envoy to Richard. He knows that Simon tried to kill you because of it. He knows you brought the relic home."

Kieran looked at his father. "As I told Sean, my only goal was to make it home alive," he said. "Now that I am here, I would seek your advice on what to do with the relic. It is no longer a gift of peace. That opportunity is long gone."

Jeffrey appeared thoughtful, seriously pondering the problem. "Are you sure the savages did not lie to you? Is it really Christ's Crown of Thorns?"

Kieran's reply was to turn for the wardrobe that held his belongings. He opened the doors and began rummaging around, drawing forth a big, leather satchel. Rory, on the other side of the room, recognized the bag as he laid it on the bed. The first thing he pulled out of it was something she identified immediately; his journal.

It brought her back to the day when they had first discovered Kieran's suspended corpse. His possessions had been hastily buried with him, including the journal, and Rory had latched onto it right away. Because of the age of it at the time, it had been difficult to read the parchment pages. They were old and brittle. But she had read enough to know that Sir Kieran Hage was a man among men. She had fallen in love with him before she even met him. As she saw Kieran lay the journal out, she rose from the table and went over to the bed.

Rory picked up the journal as Kieran dug around in his satchel and pulled forth the box he had been seeking. Plain, unassuming, made of precious wood and woven fibers that she assumed to be papyrus or something like it. It was about nine inches by nine inches, perhaps three inches high. Kieran lifted the latch on the top and opened the box, peeling back the rough linen and revealing the treasure inside.

By this time, Jeffrey and the three Hage brothers were leaning over the bed to get a glimpse of what the box contained. They could all see the rather pathetic bundle of vines, faded and hardly spectacular. Long thorns that looked more like small branches adorned the circlet, some of them having broken off during the passage of time. Rory remembered thinking the first time she saw it that it hardly looked like something of such powerful holy significance. But the aura radiating from it, the feeling when she got when she looked at it, told her otherwise.

The first thing Jeffrey did was reach down in an attempt to pick it up. Rory's scientist instincts kicked in and she smacked his hand away.

"No," she grabbed the box and held it tight against her chest. "Don't touch it. It's over a thousand years old. If you touch it, it'll fall apart."

Jeffrey looked at her; it was the first time since entering the room that he had acknowledged her. His jaw began to flex and he suddenly thrust a finger in her face.

"Listen to me, lass," he hissed. "I make the rules here. I can do whatever I want without the likes of you telling me otherwise."

Rory's eyes narrowed. "You can't touch this," she growled. "It's old and fragile. You can look all you want, but don't touch it."

"You'll not tell me what I can or cannot do in my own home!"

"Do you want to look at it or do you want to argue with me?"

Jeffrey looked at Kieran, his eyes wide and accusing. "You will allow her to speak to me in this manner?"

Kieran met his father's gaze steadily. "Speak to you in what manner? She has said nothing horrific or disrespectful. She simply asked you not to touch it because it is very fragile."

Jeffrey's mouth popped open. Sensing an explosion, Sean, Christian and Andrew exchanged nervous glances. Rory saw their expressions and swiftly sized up the situation. She could choose to butt heads with the man or she could kiss his ass. She suspected that, being the earl, he would respond far better to a supplicant lady. As much as it would kill her to pacify him, she suspected that Kieran would rather have her behave submissively than duke it out with his father. For Kieran's sake, she would try to ease the situation. She really didn't want to spend the rest of her life battling with the man. Before Jeffrey could respond, she spoke.

"I'm sorry if I was disrespectful," she forced out the words. "I didn't mean to be. But you have to understand that this relic is extremely fragile and can't be touched. Look at it this way; the last person to touch this, other than the Muslims, was Joseph of Arimathea. Before him, it was Christ."

Jeffrey wasn't following her but he wasn't yelling at her, either. Rory put the box back on the bed and pointed at the wreath. "Look here," she indicated. "See the dark stains on the end of these thorns that stick out on the interior of the crown? That's the blood of Christ; the real blood. You don't want to wipe that off, do you? We need to leave the imprint of Christ on this. It's the only physical evidence we have of the man. We… we need to treat this like it's Jesus' body. Would you put your hands all over Jesus and lift him out of a box?"

Jeffrey's angry gaze moved between the box and Rory. He finally settled on the contents of the box for several moments before turning back to Rory.

"How do you know so much about this?" he asked, still not entirely friendly.

Kieran answered. "She is most knowledgeable in matters of the Church and her word is beyond question," he said, realizing his father and Rory had not yet formally met. "Father, this is my wife, the Lady Rory Elizabeth Osgrove Hage. She will answer to Libby. Her family hails from County Connaught."

Rory decided to throw caution to the wind. She figured she had nothing to lose by being nice to the guy, so she smiled at Jeffrey. "It… it's an honor to meet you, my lord, and to be a part of this family."

She certainly was a beautiful woman. Jeffrey stared at her as she smiled, thinking he'd never seen such a lovely lass. There was something about her beauty that softened him, made him feel slightly giddy and weak in spite of his strong opposition to the marriage. He hadn't felt that way since he'd been a young lad. He found himself focusing on her completely.

"Tell me of your family." He crossed his big arms expectantly.

Rory didn't hesitate; she knew that if she did, it would look like she was lying. Just as Kieran had said, her lineage was obviously extremely important to Jeffrey and she was somewhat prepared. Pulling on everything she had ever learned about the Irish, she just started talking.

"My family descends from the high kings of Ireland," she said as if she had been reciting such a thing all her life. "We are born directly from the great high king, mac Murchada, chief of the Clan Tomaltaigh. My uncle, Uriah, is a great overlord and a very educated man. My father is a great warrior. Is there anything else you'd like to know?"

As Kieran stood beside his father and grinned at his wife's strong stance, Jeffrey seriously pondered her words.

"Who is your father?"

Rory thought on the father she'd only met once in her life; she had been the result of her mother's one night stand with a married Marine sergeant. "His name is Lucas," she replied evenly. "I'm an only child."

"Do you have lands? Property?"

She did look at Kieran, then. She didn't want to lie too much and back herself into a corner. She already felt bad enough about elaborating on her lineage. "No," she shook her head. "Everything was confiscated and my father fights for our liege." Well, he sort of did. He was in the Marines and he did what the President of the United States told him to do.

That seemed to throw Jeffrey for a loop. He cleared his throat loudly and looked at Kieran, suddenly nervous as if he thought she might blame him for the English confiscating her family's lands. He was suddenly anxious to be off the subject.

"Very well," he said, turning back to the box on the bed. "Tell me what else you know of this diadem."

Rory's attention moved to the box also, thankful that he wasn't pressing her further about her family. "That's about all I know," she replied. "It's extremely fragile and Kieran has gone through hell to bring it back to England. Now, the question is what to do with it and I think I have a suggestion."

All of the men looked at her. "What is your suggestion, sweetheart?" Kieran asked.

She looked up into the expectant faces, thinking hard on what she was about to say. Frankly, she was surprised they were allowing her to speak up in this extremely male-dominated society. She tried to be very respectful, not wanting to come across like she was smarter than the rest of them. It would be a sure-fire way to garner resentment and she really didn't want to do that. She realized that she very much wanted Kieran's family to like her, including his blow-hard father. Or, at the very least, accept her.

"This gift was meant for Richard, for the Christian armies, as a peace offering," she began, scratching her head. "If I recall, Prince John has a fairly adversarial relationship with the Church right now. He doesn't like them and they don't like him. It hasn't reached its zenith yet but that will come and he'll make a complete ass out of himself. Anyway, my suggestion is this; present the diadem to the Archbishop of Canterbury as a gift from Richard the Lionheart. It'll cement Richard's relationship with the Church, make him look like a holy hero, and further cement a wedge between John and the Church."

They were staring at her like she was speaking in tongues. Some of Rory's confidence slipped and she looked at Kieran. "Right?" She wanted reassurance.

Kieran gazed at her a moment longer before looking to his father. "A brilliant plan," he said. "Do you not agree?"

Jeffrey's gaze was still lingering on his son's wife and her incredibly odd speech and bizarre words. He looked at his son. "What did she say?"

Kieran put his arm around his father's shoulders. "She said that I should present the diadem of Christ to Hubert Walter as a gift from the king. It will present Richard as a strong supporter of the Church and a devoted servant of the Pope."

Jeffrey pondered the situation, now made clear to him by Kieran's understandable words. Rory watched his face, finally speaking to

Kieran as she nodded her head at his father.

"Maybe your father should present it," she said, somewhat exaggeratedly, hoping he'd take the hint. "It would bring the Church's blessing to the entire family."

Kieran took the hint. "Absolutely," he agreed, removing his arm from his father's broad shoulders. "Perhaps we should all go to Canterbury as a family and present it. What say you, Father?"

Jeffrey was looking at the crown now, his brown eyes glittering with thought. Sean, Christian and Andrew watched the man's expression, wondering what he was thinking. He could be a difficult man to predict, especially in light of the fact that the reasonable suggestion was made by a woman. Rory was feeling increasing apprehension. She looked around the bed to the faces of the Hage men, seeing both approval and hesitation. When she came to Sean, he smiled faintly and winked at her. She smiled back.

Jeffrey, arms still crossed, moved away from the bed and began to pace pensively.

"The Hage family has always been a supporter of the king and the Church," he said thoughtfully. "If we were to present this holy relic to the archbishop, it would bring unimaginable honor to us. All of us, united, presenting this most remarkable gift would bring us glory as we have never known. And Kieran will be there to confirm that it is, indeed, the Crown of Thorns that Jesus Christ wore upon his crucifixion, rescued from the savages that have overrun Jerusalem. Kieran saved Christ's crown and now it is where it belongs; in England!"

He was growing more and more elaborate with his speech. Rory looked at Kieran to see his reaction but Kieran was focused on his father.

"Then we ride for Canterbury?" he asked.

Jeffrey turned to face his sons, his face alive with pride and excitement. "We leave on the morrow," he said decisively. "We will take a thousand men with us to show the strength of the Hages. And when we approach the cathedral at Canterbury, it will seem as if God's mighty army has…"

He was cut off by the sounds of alert going off on the walls outside. Kieran and his brothers rushed to the windows which overlooked the gatehouse and the road leading into the city. Although it was dark, they could see a faint black tide on the horizon, spreading out like ants. Flickers of light signified torches, an ominous sight. Kieran knew, even in the dark, the sight of an army approaching. Kieran shouted down to the sentries.

"Who is it?" he bellowed.

The sentries on duty shouted up to him. "A messenger has come, my lord," one man called up to him. "The prince has come to see Lord Jeffrey."

Kieran looked at his father with some shock. "John is here?"

Jeffrey looked equally shocked. "That skinny bastard?" he spat. "I do not want him on my lands. I will…"

Sean cut him off, looking to Kieran as he did. "We need to mobilize the men and close the gates," he said as Christian and Andrew raced from the room, already knowing what must be done. "Is there any possibility that the prince knows you are here?"

Kieran shook his head. "It is doubtful though not impossible," he said. "We stopped in London before coming north and I had an encounter with Somerset knights. It is possible word of my return made it back to the prince."

"But that doesn't make any sense." Rory spoke up before she could stop herself. "The guard on the wall said that the prince was here to see your father. If the prince knew you were here, wouldn't he say that he was here to see you?"

Kieran nodded in agreement. "He would," he said, looking between his father and Sean. "It is my suggestion that we welcome the prince's visit and make no mention of my return home, at least not yet. I am curious as to why the prince is here."

Jeffrey took a calming breath, eventually nodding. "Agreed," he said, moving for the door. "The man has never paid me a visit in his life. He must have a very good reason and I, too, am curious to know it."

The men were moving out of the chamber and Rory spoke up again. "Can I say something?" When they turned to look at her, she tried to look as respectful as possible. "Please?"

Kieran's expression was warm. "What is it, love?"

She clasped her fingers at her mouth thoughtfully. "Is Simon a supporter of the prince?"

Kieran lifted an eyebrow. "I never knew him to be. But, then again, I did not know the man was capable of turning against me. Anything is possible."

She nodded as if to agree with his assessment. "Since we know he fled the Holy Land about the same time we did, is it possible he made it home before us and went straight to the prince?" She dropped her hands, shrugging faintly. "He could have told John anything about you, including the fact that you have a holy relic. Who knows? Maybe this visit has something to do with Simon's return."

Kieran and Sean looked at Jeffrey. "It is as good a possibility as anything," Sean said. "Perhaps Simon went to John with the same lies he told Richard."

Jeffrey's eyes were fixed on Rory. He regarded her for a moment before turning away, heading from the door.

"Then we shall be vigilant," he replied firmly. "I will tolerate no slander of my son within the walls of Southwell."

Jeffrey and Sean quit the room but Kieran paused, returning to Rory and taking her in his arms. He held her tightly.

"Stay here," he murmured, kissing her tenderly. "Finish eating and go to bed. I will come to you when this is finished."

She looked at him, her eyebrows flying up. "Are you kidding? Do you really think I'm going to sleep when Prince John is here? My God, Kieran, the man is legendary, even in my time."

The warmth faded from his eyes. "You are, under no circumstances, to leave this room in any way. Do you comprehend?"

She pursed her lips in an exaggerated pout. "Not even a peek?"

"If you peek, I will spank you so hard that you shall not be able to sit until this child is grown."

Her pout grew. "You're mean!"

He kissed her nose, her mouth, swiftly and let her go. "Aye, I am." He jabbed a finger at her. "But you will listen to me or you will pay the price."

She made a terrible face at him, sticking out her tongue. His firm stance fractured and he laughed at her, shutting the door behind him.

With a grin on her face, Rory went to the window to watch something no modern person had ever seen. She was so excited that she was nearly beside herself, in spite of the fact that John was not a particularly favored historical figure. She found herself wishing that Dr. Dietrich and Dr. Peck were with her just so they could experience the magic, too. Dave Peck, in particular, would have gotten a huge kick out of all of this.

The arrival of a legendary Medieval prince.

CHAPTER FIFTEEN

JOHN WASN'T PARTICULARLY pleased that Jeffrey Hage ordered his entourage camped outside of Southwell's city walls. The fact that Lord Hage made no effort to house him in the keep did not sit well with him, either. More than that, two of the powerful Hage brothers, Andrew and Christian, rode out to meet him with a heavily-armed escort and refused to allow any more than twenty of the prince's men into Southwell. That included advisors as well. And with that final insult, John was furious. But amidst the fury and posturing, Andrew and Christian were the first to see Simon de Corlet in the prince's entourage. While Christian ran a tight escort around the prince, Andrew rode back to tell his father and brother.

Kieran honestly wasn't surprised to hear of Simon's presence. It simply confirmed what they had been speculating all along, that Simon had fled Richard's rage and returned to England. It also confirmed that Kieran didn't know the man at all; Simon had always seemed quite loyal to Richard. Then again, he'd always seemed quite loyal to Kieran. But Simon's appearance did, indeed, prove something else; the reason for John's visit undoubtedly had to do with Kieran. And Kieran was going to be ready for him. The advantage of surprise was most definitely his.

As Kieran went to find Yusef, Jeffrey and Sean went to the great hall, a separate building from the keep, to await John. Now, their plan was set as the reason for the prince's visit was no longer unknown. Jeffrey, being rather devious-minded, made sure the fire in the hearth was low, rendering the hall rather cold, and the only refreshment provided was ale. No wine, which would have been much more appropriate. He didn't want the prince to feel welcome in the least. In this cold, cavernous and inhospitable hall, they waited.

It took some time for the prince and his entourage to reach the inner bailey of Southwell. For every one of the prince's guard, there was a Southwell man and it was a tense ride into the inner sanctum of Southwell's complex. There was a good deal of threatening posturing going on, making for slow going. The prince's entourage was permitted to enter the hall along with Southwell's fully-armed escort. The tension was palpable.

The prince entered the dark and dreary hall. He was wrapped tightly against the chill so the event of a cold chamber didn't particularly bother him. He was, however, incensed at the lack of hospitality and serving women to choose from. Everyone in the country knew of his appetites and expectations. Men hid their wives and daughters from him but, somehow, he still managed to take what he wanted. It had, therefore, become common practice amongst the nobles to ensure a plethora of serving women to entice the prince, hopefully away from their wives and daughters. As long as the wench had an ample bosom, the ploy usually worked.

Jeffrey was seated at the end of the massively long table that sat near the hearth in the enormous room. Sean stood next to him, watching the man he had desperately come to hate. John knew Sean on sight and knew he served his brother. There was little doubt in the prince's mind that this Hage brother was a spy but the prince would not waste his energies on the man. At least, not at the moment. Men like Sean Hage tended to trip themselves up at some point. When he did, John would be there to pounce. The prince approached the table, most uncustomarily. He was, in fact, used to being greeted upon his arrival and escorted in. But the Hages had made sure not to extend the usual courtesies which bordered on insubordination.

"Jeffrey Hage," John rolled the name off his tongue. "'Tis a proud and mighty name you bear, son of Mercia."

Jeffrey remained seated, spying Simon standing a few feet in back of the prince. "Your Grace," he greeted in his deep, rumbling voice. "Your visit is something of a surprise. Is there a purpose?"

John almost smiled. The man was not one for pleasantries or courtesy. He was straight to the point. The prince motioned to his retainers, who quickly moved to pour him ale. He sat on the bench near Jeffrey, eyeing the man with the piercing brown eyes and attempting to decipher his level of hostility. Drinking the ale, he made a face and pushed it aside.

"Do you not have wine, Hage?" he demanded. "You provide me with this horrific swill?"

Jeffrey fixed him in the eye. "We are all out of wine," he said flatly. "Would you be so kind as to tell me the purpose of your visit, Your Grace?"

John's rage was building. With an unhappy sigh, he reclaimed the ale cup. "I have come to do you a favor, Hage. But I am not so sure that I will do this given your bad manners," he said, watching for a reaction. He received none. "I have come to help you."

"Help me?" Jeffrey repeated. "How, and why, would you do this?"

John motioned to Simon, who removed himself from the group and moved forward, his gaze darting back and forth between Sean and Jeffrey. He nodded at Sean.

"Greetings, Sean," he said quietly. "It has been a long time."

Sean, Kieran and Simon had fostered at Kenilworth Castle as children. They had all known each other for years. It was difficult for Sean, given what Kieran had told him, to behave civilly towards the man. He wanted to break the man's neck.

"Simon," he replied, nodding faintly. "I see that you have returned from the Holy Land alive."

Simon nodded. "Indeed," he replied, looking down at the prince and seeing that the man's attention was on him. It was apparent that John was expected him to lead the conversation and Simon grew unnerved. "I have returned bearing dismal news, I am afraid. That is why I sought the prince, in fact. I did not feel that I should deliver this news alone and the prince has agreed to accompany me."

Jeffrey looked at Simon as if the man were the lowest form of life.

He resisted his natural instincts to insult him. Instead he waited to see what the man would spout. He sincerely hoped the man would dig his own grave. If even half of what Kieran had told him was true, then Simon was lucky to be alive at this moment. He was fortunate he hadn't been gutted the moment he set foot on Hage lands.

"News?" Jeffrey repeated. "News of what?"

Simon looked at him. "Of Kieran, my lord."

"Oh?" Jeffrey's eyebrows lifted inquisitively. "What of my son?"

Simon looked at the prince for support. "I... I am afraid that something tragic has happened."

"What do you mean tragic?" Sean demanded. "Is he dead?"

Simon took a deep breath, knowing he needed to speak out before the Hages grew further agitated. He could already see an extreme lack of patience in their expressions.

"Nay, he is not dead," Simon replied steadily. "But I am afraid the man has lost his mind. He's gone mad and has attempted to betray Richard."

Sean looked at Jeffrey, who was staring at Simon with a piercing gaze. "Explain your slanderous statement, de Corlet," he rumbled.

Simon was intimidated by the tone but continued. "It would seem that Kieran, for reasons unknown, has attempted to betray Richard," he said. "I was witness to the man's secret meeting with Muslim generals, men who wanted Kieran to betray and murder the king in the hopes that the Christian armies would weaken. I myself witnessed Kieran accepting a gift in payment for this deed. Richard sent men to find Kieran but the man managed to evade all patrols. I am fearful that he will return to England to wreak havoc."

Jeffrey and Sean simply stared at Simon, digesting his tale. It was Jeffrey who finally shifted in his seat, stroking his chin wearily.

"I see," he muttered. "And how did you happen to witness this secret meeting?"

Simon shrugged. "I have known Kieran for many years," he said. "The man had been acting strangely, secretively. I began to grow suspicious. So I followed him one night and was witness to this exchange."

"Did you confront him?"

Simon shook his head. "From my vantage point, I heard what was said. I did not need to confront him." He lifted an eyebrow. "Your son has allied himself with the enemy, my lord. I felt it my duty to return home to tell you."

Jeffrey cocked his head. "Why was it necessary to return home to tell me?"

Simon faltered somewhat. "As I told you, I feared he would return to England to spread lies and wreak havoc. The prince supports my assertions and it is he who has brought me here to tell you of this tragedy. Kieran Hage is no longer loyal to Richard; he has tried to kill him. The prince offers you his condolences and support in this matter."

Jeffrey lifted an eyebrow, casting John a long glance. The prince was gazing back at him smugly. "No doubt," he muttered sarcastically, returning his attention to Simon. "And this alleged gift that was presented to my son in exchange for his turning against Richard; do you know what it was?"

Simon took a deep breath, eyeing John as he did so. "I was told it was a holy relic."

"Who told you this?"

Simon faltered. He'd not thought this far ahead in the conversation and mentally scrambled to attain a believable reply. "I… I heard some of the Saracens speaking, men who had presented the gift to Kieran. They told him it was a relic of Jesus Christ."

Jeffrey pondered that a moment, sitting forward on the table and folding his big hands. It was clear he was deliberating all of the information presented. Sean stood silently next to his father, his powerful gaze never leaving Simon. But Sean remained as quiet as the grave. He would let his usually hotheaded but extremely wily father handle the situation. All Sean wanted to do was throttle the man.

"So you have come to tell me that my son is a traitor to Richard's cause," he said.

"To all of England, my lord," Simon insisted. "The sands of The Levant have done something to his mind. He is not the same man you knew."

Jeffrey grunted. "So you fear he is returning home to wreak havoc?"

"Aye, my lord."

"What kind of havoc?"

Simon blinked as if startled by the question. "I would not know, my lord," he replied. "But the man is unstable. There is no telling what he will say or do."

Out of the darkness, a figure moved, so swiftly that no one saw the movement until it was too late. Kieran descended out of the shadows and landed a crushing blow against Simon's jaw, so hard that as Simon sailed over the table, three teeth landed on the wood. Kieran vaulted over the table and went after him, sending John and his retainers scrambling for cover. Finally, it was the confrontation that Kieran had been waiting for. Punishment was at hand.

"Unstable, am I?" Kieran grabbed Simon and punched him in the face so hard that the facial bones shattered. "A traitor, am I? Considering one of your men confessed your lies and treachery to Richard, I would say that you are the only traitor in this room. Richard put a price on your head so you fled home to spread lies about me."

Simon was bordering on unconsciousness as Kieran pulled him up from the floor and drove another fist into the side of his head. That blow knocked Simon out completely and he was a rag doll in Kieran's hands. Kieran tossed the man across the room, like a dead body, and the room suddenly became alive with swords being drawn. As the prince's men and Southwell troops engaged, John was screaming in the middle of it, demanding he not be harmed. He screamed at some of his men to save Simon and several of them rushed Kieran, who was unarmed.

Sean intercepted three of the prince's guards, joined by Andrew. Yusef, who had been in the shadows with Kieran listening to the lies, ran to Kieran as the room deteriorated into chaos.

"We are unarmed, my friend," he said, watching the fighting. "Perhaps we should acquire weapons."

Kieran was as furious as he had ever been in his life. Listening to Simon's lies firsthand had put him over the edge. A few of the prince's men were down on the floor, gravely injured, and he went to collect weapons they no longer needed. With a broadsword in hand, he was extremely formidable. But he didn't particularly want to fight. He wanted everyone in the room to understand that he was not the traitor Simon had painted him out to be. More than anything, he wanted to be vindicated. He leapt onto the feasting table with Yusef behind him, bellowing for calm.

"Cease!" he roared, holding up his enormous hands. "Southwell troops, you will cease!"

At the booming command of Kieran Hage, the room ground to an unsteady halt. Men were lying on the floor groaning and the prince, with several of his advisors, was huddled in a far corner. Kieran's gaze fell on the prince as the man cowered in the shadows and he leapt off the table with Yusef in tow. As he approached, the prince held out his hands.

"You cannot harm me, Hage," he practically screamed. "I am the king's brother. You cannot harm me!"

Kieran stopped several feet away, his features taut and his chest tight with anger. "I have no intention of harming you," he said. "But I want you, and every man in this room, to hear the truth of what transpired so that you will understand I am not a traitor. Simon's poisonous lies will no longer be tolerated."

John didn't lower his hands but his fearful gaze moved between Kieran and the dark-skinned savage at his side. "What… what truth?"

Kieran looked at Yusef, who stepped forward and bowed traditionally to the prince. "Sharif," he gave the traditional Muslim greeting. "I am Yusef Ibn Ahmed Ibn ad-Din, a general to the great El-Hajidd, advisor and chief general to the great Sala' a-din. Many knights have fought for the Christian kings but there was one man, Sir Kieran Hage, who distinguished himself from the rest. Even our Muslim commanders knew of Sir Kieran's reputation for justice and honesty. It was for that reason that my commander called a secret meeting with Sir Kieran Hage to offer a truce to the Christian armies. As a show of good faith, he extended the Crown of Thorns worn by Jesus Christ as a peace offering."

John was still cowering in the corner but the naked fear had somewhat left him. "That… that is an amazing tale," he said, although he'd already heard all of it. He presumed his best defense at the moment was to plead ignorance to whatever he could get away with. "Sir Kieran was most honored by the Muslim armies, then."

Yusef nodded, looking over his shoulder at Simon, on the other side of the room and still unconscious, before turning back to the prince. "Sir Simon was part of that delegation as well," he told the prince. "I saw him myself, for I was a member of the Muslim delegation. Simon was present when the terms for the treaty were relayed to Sir Kieran. What Sir Kieran did not know was that jealousy and treachery burned in Simon's heart, and Simon made many attempts to murder Sir Kieran. When his attempts failed, he told King Richard that Kieran had betrayed the Christian armies by secretly meeting with the enemy."

John pushed himself out of the corner, moving oddly sideways towards the entry to the hall. He was trying to leave and not being entirely unobvious about it.

"Then Simon lied to me as well," he announced. "Had I known that, I would have never come here. I would have ignored him."

Kieran knew that John was just trying to cover himself. He tossed aside the broadsword in his hand, feeling rather drained and empty after his rage. The entire situation was more or less coming to an unexpected head and he found himself emotionally exhausted. But Yusef took the opportunity to speak to all concerned.

"Sir Kieran is a noble man who has been set upon by wolves," he said strongly, making sure everyone heard him. "Sir Simon spreads lies of betrayal where none exist. You must know of Sir Kieran's innocence in all things."

John was practically at the door. "I believe you," he said. "But what of the relic? What happened to it?"

Kieran was still standing over by the corner where the prince had been cowering. "I have it," he replied, somewhat wearily. "It is in my safekeeping."

John stopped creeping for the door. "What do you plan to do with it?"

Jeffrey, still at the table in spite of all of the fighting that had gone on around him, stood up. "The Hages will gift it to the Church," he said firmly, moving towards the prince. "It will be our gift to England. My son has saved this holy relic from the savages and it is our duty to present it to the Church where it belongs."

John looked rather stricken. "But…" he stammered. "But this gift was meant for Richard. If Richard is not here to accept it then, as his brother, it is only right that I should accept it in his stead."

The mood of the room suddenly changed. It was odd and strained, confused even. Kieran, seeing that the quest for the relic could go in an entirely different direction, opened his mouth to refute the prince. But Yusef was first to reply.

"The relic was meant for all Christendom," he said. "It is not meant for any one man."

John's brow furrowed. That dark, greasy, mono-brow lowered angrily. "But you said yourself that your general meant it for Richard," he said. "What do you expect Richard to do with it? He would have returned it home to England where it belongs."

"It goes to the Church," Jeffrey put in before anyone else could answer. "I will take it to the Archbishop of Canterbury myself. But until then, it is in safekeeping and warrants no further argument."

John was clearly unhappy. "It should be in the charge of the royal family."

"Yet it is not." Jeffrey gave the man a powerful scowl. "If you have nothing more to say, then I would ask you to leave Southwell and return to wherever it is you came from."

They were extremely bold words to the prince. As Kieran watched his father's body language and listened to his speech, he wasn't even sure if he would have spoken so brashly to a royal. But Kieran knew that his father saw Henry in John, the friend he once had, the manipulator he had grown to hate. Jeffrey was used to speaking his mind with the royals.

But John's mouth flew open, aghast. "Are you ordering me out of Southwell?"

Jeffrey moved towards him. "Get out of here before I take you over my knee. It should have been done years ago."

John's outrage knew no bounds. He began to yelp and snort, cuffing one of the advisors standing close to him when he realized the man was attempting to usher him out of the hall. He struggled against his men.

"This is not finished!" he screamed. "This is not finished at all!"

Southwell men, including Andrew and Christian, escorted the prince and his entourage back to their horses. Kieran, Sean, Yusef and Jeffrey stood and watched from the doorway as John threw himself down on the dirt of the bailey and pitched one of his legendary fits.

They were so involved in watching the prince twist and foam that no one noticed Simon rising from the floor on the other side of the room. He was smashed and disoriented, but not completely senseless. He staggered to his feet and shuffled over to one of the king's guards, lying dead on the floor. Yanking the man's broadsword out of his stiff hand, he headed for the Hages.

Jeffrey suddenly grunted. Startled by the sound, Kieran, Sean and Yusef turned to see Simon with his hand on the hilt of a sword that had been driven into Jeffrey's back. Horrified, Kieran reached out and grabbed Simon around the neck, snapping it before the man could draw another breath. As Simon fell dead to the floor, never to rise or spread lies again, Kieran was grabbing his father, holding the man close as Sean pulled free the sword.

Kieran had never known such anguish. As his father bled bright red blood onto the dirt floor of the great hall, it suddenly reminded Kieran of a time long ago when he, too, had bled bright red blood onto a cold dirt floor. He could only think of one thing as he looked up into Yusef's shocked face.

"Get Kaleef," he breathed.

☙

FROM HER VANTAGE point, Rory had a perfect view of the gatehouse of Southwell and the road leading to it. The road wound its way from the plains beyond, through the town, and up to the enormous two-towered gatehouse. After Kieran left, she pulled up a stool and sat, watching the scene unfold below.

The prince arrived with a cluster of men on horseback. She couldn't see well enough in the darkness to make out what the soldiers and knights were wearing as far as tunics or banners, but it was really something to see. The men on horses were dressed in heavy armor and the dogs on the parapets were barking furiously at the intruders. The gatehouse, lit up by dozens of enormous torches, closed its fanged portcullis slowly behind the incoming party. Rory could hear the ropes and chains creaking as the wheels were turned. She watched, fascinated, as an entire Medieval world came to life before her eyes.

Shortly after Kieran left, Bud and David appeared in her room, escorted by the long-haired old man that had originally greeted them when they had first entered the keep. She hugged David happily and even Bud seemed glad to see her. From what the old servant told her, the boys had been in the knight's quarters and Sir Kieran had ordered them brought to his chamber. Rory was thrilled and thanked the servant, who left them alone and shut the door. As the boys sat down and cleaned up the rest of the food, Rory continued to watch the activity below.

Once John's escort passed through the gatehouse, there really wasn't much more to see. There were a lot of soldiers upon the parapets and a lot of dogs pacing with them as they walked their posts. She could see the city beyond, the torches burning to illuminate homes and streets, and she could catch whiffs of cooking smells. But they were mostly smells of roasting meat, which made her nauseous, so she tried not to smell too much. Just when she was considering turning away from the window and going to sit with the boys, there was a soft knock on the door.

David and Bud looked at her expectantly. Rory rose from the stool and went to the door, a bit apprehensive. She didn't open the door, somewhat fearful of what might be on the other side.

"Who is it?" she called.

There was a slight hesitation. "I am Lady Margaret, Lady Hage," came a soft, female voice. "Sean's wife."

Rory unlatched the iron bolt and opened the door. A very slender, very pale young woman with enormous green eyes stood there, smiling timidly. On her hip was a little girl, about a year old. Rory smiled at the pair.

"Hello," she said to the woman. "It's nice to meet you. Who is your little friend?"

The Lady Margaret de Russe Bigod-Hage gazed back at perhaps the loveliest woman she had ever seen. The lady was tall and lush, with a curvy figure, long chestnut-colored hair that she allowed to flow free and big hazel eyes. The woman's stunning beauty was something of a shock. And she had no idea what the lady meant with her very odd question until Rory reached out to touch the baby's hand. Margaret hastened to answer.

"This is my daughter, Eleanor," she replied. "It is a privilege to know you, my lady. I was so happy to hear that Kieran had returned from the great Quest with a wife."

Rory motioned for Margaret to enter. The tiny woman slipped into the room and Rory shut the door behind her. They turned to each other, Margaret far more timid than Rory. In just those first few seconds, Rory could see that Margaret was a very proper Medieval woman in every way. She was extremely polite, her hair was pulled back into an elaborate bun on the back of her head, and her surcoat was very conservative and even somewhat loose to avoid flaunting her figure. She was also quite pretty in a pale, ethereal sort of way. Rory studied the skin of her face, something that had never seen modern cosmetics or moisturizers. Her skin looked a little oily, minor acne on her chin, but was otherwise clear. Overall, Margaret seemed rather fragile and Rory knew she would have to be careful with her. From outwards appearance, a twenty-first century woman might frighten this one to death.

"So, Lady Margaret," Rory began, trying to be careful in her speech and manner. "How long have you and Sean been married?"

"For five years, my lady," Margaret replied politely.

Rory took a second look at her, trying not to be obvious about it. the young woman couldn't have been more than sixteen or seventeen. "How old were you when you were married?" she couldn't help the question.

"I had seen twelve summers, my lady," she replied proudly. "Sir Sean and I had been betrothed since I was a child."

Rory stared at her, doing the math in her head. Kieran had mentioned that his brother was only a year and half younger than he was, which meant Sean was around thirty years of age. He was twenty-five when he married Margaret, who was only twelve at the time. Pedophilia is alive and well in Medieval England, she thought. Still, she knew it was the custom. No one thought twice about it.

"Congratulations." She didn't know what else to say. "And congratulations on Eleanor. She's beautiful."

Margaret looked at the brown-eyed little girl, smiling hugely. "Ellie is my love," she said. "She is a very good child, very bright."

"I can see that," Rory said, laughing when the baby grinned a big four-toothed grin at her. "She looks like you."

Margaret's smile vanished. "Oh, no, my lady," she insisted. "She favors her father greatly."

Rory lifted her eyebrows, knowing in Medieval society, the world revolved around the man. She nodded as if to concede the point. There were two enormous chairs of stuffed cowhide over near the blazing hearth and she indicated for Margaret to sit.

"Tell me about yourself, Lady Margaret," she said as they sat down opposite one another. "Where did you grow up… I mean, foster?"

Lady Margaret shifted Eleanor to her lap and Rory found herself inspecting the woman's surcoat. It was finely made with incredibly detailed stitching around the bodice. Someone had taken a lot of time and effort with it. But Margaret seemed oblivious to the fact that Rory seemed to be staring at her breasts.

"I was fortunate enough to have fostered at Berkeley Castle," she said proudly. "My father is Edward Bigod, half-brother to the Earl of Norfolk. I was born at New Buckenham Castle, my father's holding."

Talk about powerful family ties, Rory thought. She smiled politely. "Do you have any sisters or brothers?" she asked, simply to keep the conversation going.

But Margaret shook her head. "Alas, I do not. My father is extremely disappointed he has no sons."

There was really nothing more to say to that so Rory spoke on the first thing that popped into her mind. "Do you have any hobbies?"

Margaret cocked her pretty blond head. "Hobbies?"

"Talents. Skills. Do you draw?"

Margaret smiled brightly. She had nice, straight teeth that were slightly dingy. "Indeed I do, Lady Hage," she replied. "I sew. Why, I sewed this dress."

She indicated the embroidery that had Rory so fascinated. It really was stunning work. Rory looked closely at it. There were flowers and bees in an intricate pattern.

"It's gorgeous," she said sincerely. "You do beautiful work."

"My thanks, Lady Hage."

The conversation died slightly. Rory was running out of things to ask about when Margaret piped up.

"Do you have also skills, Lady Hage?" she asked politely. "Surely you must be very accomplished to have married Sir Kieran."

Rory suddenly felt like the most useless person in the world. She couldn't sew or speak five languages like some Medieval women, or even play an instrument, but she could draw. And she could sing. Okay, so she didn't feel entirely useless.

"I can draw and I can sing," she announced. "And I can cook."

Margaret looked startled. "Cook?"

Okay, maybe that wasn't the best thing to say. Proper Medieval women really didn't cook, but she had already admitted it.

"Yes," she admitted to it. "I can cook. I'm a great cook and Kieran is very proud of me."

It could have been interpreted as a rebuke, but Margaret didn't take it that way. Her timid smile returned. "I… I have always wanted to learn," she confessed. "I have been taught to run a household and I understand the art of maintaining kitchen stores, but I have never learned to cook. At Berkeley, they would not let us into the kitchens when the cooks were at work."

Rory smiled. "I'll teach you," she said. "It's really very easy."

Margaret appeared intrigued if not reluctant. "Do you believe I can learn? Is it difficult?"

Rory waved her off. "For a smart woman like you? You'll be great at it."

Margaret giggled as if she were planning something bold and crazy. "As you say, Lady Hage," she said, not completely understanding the odd speech patterns but understanding enough that she was coming to like Lady Hage very much. "I would be grateful for your tutelage."

Rory just smiled at her, thinking the poor, little thing really was timid. God help her if she hung around Rory for too long; she would either shrivel away with shock or learn how to stand up for herself. Rory watched the pale, lovely girl, wondering which it would be. The conversation began to drag again and Rory looked around the room, trying to think of something more to say.

"Well," she began, grasping for thoughts. "Uh… this is a pretty big keep. Who else lives here?"

Margaret stepped up with the answers. "Sean and I have a room on this floor, next to Kieran's room," she told Rory what she already knew. "There is another room next to ours, a very small room, which is Andrew's. Below us are chambers for Christian and Lord Jeffrey. Oh, and a small chamber for Charlotte."

Rory cocked her head. "Charlotte? Who's that?"

"Christian's betrothed. She only came to live with us a few months ago."

"Oh," Rory replied. "I haven't met her yet."

Some of the smile disappeared from Margaret's face. "And you shall not, more than likely," she said. "Christian does not like for anyone to speak with Charlotte."

Rory's face screwed up with confusion. "Huh?" she said. "Why not?"

For the first time since introducing herself, Margaret appeared uncomfortable. "Lady Charlotte was a betrothal that Lord Jeffrey insisted upon," she lowered her voice, speaking hesitantly. "She is from the de Longley family in Northumbria, the Lords of Northwood. Christian does not want a bride. He forbids anyone to speak to her."

Rory's confusion grew. "Why not?"

Margaret shrugged. "I do not know," she said honestly. "But he forbids anyone to speak to the girl. I've only seen her twice since her arrival. Christian keeps her closed up in her chamber. He and his father fight about her all of the time. Christian wants her sent home and Lord Jeffrey refuses."

Now Rory's confusion was turning to outrage. "Are you kidding me?" she exclaimed. "He keeps that woman locked up and won't let anyone talk to her?"

Margaret nodded, somewhat intimidated by Rory's sudden angst. "She is not a woman," she said. "She is only thirteen years old."

"What?" Rory shot to her feet. "She's a little girl, for God's sake. And she's been kept locked up for months?"

"Aye, Lady Hage," Margaret replied, completely fearful of the woman's reaction.

Rory opened her mouth to vent her outrage, but looking at Lady Margaret's frightened expression stilled her. The woman looked like she was about to faint dead away. So she visibly cooled, although her mind was racing.

"Well," she forced herself to take a deep breath. "I will have to ask my husband about that. It doesn't seem right to me."

Margaret was greatly relieved that Lady Hage was calming. She rocked the baby in her lap. "It is Sir Christian's wish," she replied.

Rory cast her a long look. "We'll see about that," she muttered. A thought suddenly came to her. "You said she's downstairs, directly below us?"

"Aye, my lady."

Clever, if not disobedient thoughts came to Rory's head. "I haven't been shown the keep," she said, almost innocently. "Would you mind showing me around?"

Margaret stood up, looking somewhat fearful. "My husband instructed me to stay here with you. We are not allowed to leave our rooms, my lady."

Rory was going to be a very bad girl. "You can just show me this floor and the floor below. We won't leave the keep. That's what they're most concerned with, isn't it? That we don't leave the keep?"

Margaret was distressed, growing more distressed as Rory moved to the door with the apparent intention of leaving.

"Nay, my lady," she ran to the door, bouncing poor Eleanor around. "We must not leave. They would become very angry with us."

Rory opened the door, revealing the darkened landing beyond. She put up a hand to soothe Margaret. "We're not going anywhere," she insisted. "I just want to see this floor and maybe the floor below."

Margaret began to plead with her when, suddenly, sounds of shouting and activity began to filter up from the floor below. It sounded like a lot of scuffling going on, the shouts of servants, and somewhere in the middle of it, Rory swore she heard Kieran's strong, steady voice. But then there was a resounding bang, loud enough to cause both ladies to startle and, without further communication between them, they both raced back into the bedchamber and shut the door. Rory threw the bolt and turned to Margaret with big, stunned eyes.

"What in the world was that all about?" she half-gasped, half-demanded.

Margaret looked terrified. "I do not know, my lady."

Rory stood by the door, listening for more sounds, but began to realize that if there was trouble, they could come up the stairs and enter her chamber through Sean and Margaret's room. She motioned quickly to Margaret.

"Go to your room and make sure all of the doors are locked," she instructed, watching the woman flee. "Come back here when you're done."

Rory continued to stand beside the door, listening. She had her head against the wood, which is why she nearly fell over with a concussion when someone pounded on the door.

"Libby?" it was Kieran.

She threw open the door, the joy on her face turning to horror when she saw the blood on him. "Oh, my God," she quickly rose to panic. "What happened? Where are you hurt?"

He shook his head and put his bloodied hands on her to steady her. "Not me," he insisted. "My father. Come with me."

Shaking and frightened, Rory did as she was told.

CHAPTER SIXTEEN

RORY HAD TWO years of Pre-Med in college before switching majors. She had thought, long ago, that she wanted to be a doctor and even became a certified Emergency Medical Technician. But the lure of Biblical Archaeology had changed all that. Still, she knew quite a bit about medicine but she felt disoriented and out of her league when she entered Jeffrey's chamber. There was a trail of blood on the floor where his sons had carried him to his bed. Rory followed the trail until she came to a very pale man upon his bed, bleeding heavily.

Kaleef was in the room but Jeffrey was conscious, refusing to allow the dark-skinned old man to touch him. There was quite a bit of chaos going on as Kieran and Sean tried to convince their father to allow the old man to work while Andrew advocated his father's wishes. Christian had his father propped onto his side, holding a rag up against the bleeding wound. He stayed out of the argument going on over his head, having his hands full with a gushing injury.

Rory was a little wide-eyed at everything going on. She tugged on Kieran's arm. "Why am I here?" she hissed.

Kieran's face was pale, his features strained. "You know something of medicine, do you not?"

She looked around the room hesitantly, at all of the stressed faces, and her gaze returning to her husband. "Yes," she replied. "But you have more experience tending battle wounds than I do. What in the hell happened to your father?"

Kieran didn't answer her question. He glanced over at Kaleef. "Kaleef can save his life," he grumbled. "But my father will not let the man near him. He believes Kaleef is a savage."

Rory gazed up at Kieran, hearing the desperation in his voice. Once,

Kaleef had saved Kieran's life. Both Rory and Kieran knew what the old man was capable of, but no one else did. They had no idea that the tiny old man's knowledge spanned mysticism and medicine, encompassing things that weren't even known yet in modern times. He had the ability to suspend a life and then heal the body. The man had the ability to work miracles.

Pained to see the desperation on Kieran's face, Rory made a bold decision. She left her husband, pushing past the servants and family crowded around the bed, and knelt down by Jeffrey's head. Her face was inches from his as she spoke.

"Listen to me," she half-hissed, half demanded, grabbing the man's bloodstained hand. "If you want to live, you'll let Kaleef tend you. Right now, you're bleeding to death. There's no time for this bullshit and stubbornness. Kieran wouldn't suggest letting that old man tend you if he didn't know for a fact that he had the ability to save your life. Do you really think he'd let some fool near you? Don't you trust your son more than that?"

Jeffrey was pasty and in pain. He closed his eyes against Rory's words as she spoke to him, but as she finished, his brown eyes opened. He was looking at her and Rory impulsively reached out, touching his bearded cheek.

"That old man saved Kieran's life once," she murmured. "I know because I was there. I saw it. Your son was dead and that man brought him back to life. He has that gift. You must let him examine you."

Andrew had been listening to her. He knelt down next to Rory, focusing on his father. "Do not listen to her," he insisted fearfully. "If you do not want the savage to touch you, then he shall not. We have sent for our surgeon. He will be here soon."

"Your father will be dead soon," Rory snapped, looking at the scared young man. "If you want your father to live, then you'll tell him that he has to let Kaleef look at him. It's his only chance to survive and time is trickling away the more we argue about it."

Andrew was terrified. He looked back at Rory, a woman he did not know but a woman his oldest brother desperately loved and respected. He could see strength and confidence in her. Still, he was afraid for his father. He was afraid of the unknown.

Rory could see his dilemma. She held the young man's gaze a moment longer before returning her focus to Jeffrey, grasping his hand again and squeezing it.

"My lord?" she whispered earnestly. "Will you please let Kaleef examine you? I would really like for you to meet your grandson in the fall."

Jeffrey's eyes flew open and he stared at her with a piecing gaze very reminiscent of Kieran. Kieran, in fact, had knelt down behind his wife, his enormous hand closing over hers as she squeezed Jeffrey's fingers.

"Please," Kieran begged in a whisper. "I swear this man can help you. I would not trust your life to someone whose skills I did not greatly respect."

Jeffrey gazed at his eldest son, his son's strange but beautiful wife, and closed his eyes. But as he did so, he nodded his head, briefly, but it was enough. Kieran bolted to his feet and waved over Kaleef, who was escorted through the servants and knights by Yusef.

"Do what you can for him." It was a plea. "I would be grateful."

Kaleef didn't bother looking at the sons of Jeffrey Hage who were surrounding him. He went to work, rolling the man onto his stomach so he could gain a better look at the puncture wound to his back. Rory and Yusef jumped in to help him, making sure Jeffrey was comfortably moved. But Jeffrey was in agony lying on his stomach so Kieran and Sean lent their assistance, positioning their father so that he was not in excruciating pain.

Kaleef lifted the tunic, exposing Jeffrey's back. The broadsword had entered his lower back, just above the pelvis on the left side. It was a clean cut that was bleeding profusely. After a few moments of visual examination, he turned to Kieran and Sean, standing next to him.

"From the manner in which your father is bleeding, vital veins have been cut," he said quietly. "I do not have any of my instruments or medicaments with me. They were burned in Nahariya."

Rory jumped into the conversation; she'd had Anatomy as part of her Pre-Med studies and understood some of what was going on. "If a major artery had been cut, he'd already be dead," she said. "But you need to go in and sew up whatever is bleeding, and do it fast."

Kaleef nodded firmly. "I will need a needle and thread, a goodly amount of alcohol, and the sharpest dagger you can find. Bring it to me now so that I may save this man's life."

Sean and Christian scattered, sending servants running for the requested items. Meanwhile, Rory was looking at Jeffrey, thinking that they had no anesthesia to offer him. The thought of digging into his back while he was conscious made her squeamish but she knew there was little choice. She turned to Kaleef.

"What options do we have to put him to sleep while you operate?" she asked.

Kaleef was in the process of very closely inspecting the oozing puncture. He lifted his head, looking at Rory curiously.

"Sleep?" he repeated. "He will not sleep."

"Sorry, that's not what I mean," she tried again. "What I meant was, are there any options to take his pain away while you work on him? Maybe poppy?"

Kaleef shook his head. "I have no poppy."

Rory thought quickly. "If I remember correctly, ether won't be discovered for another seventy-five years yet," she muttered to herself, wracking her brain to come up with something that could ease Jeffrey's pain. "How about hemlock? That has sleep-inducing qualities, doesn't it?"

Kaleef's dark eyes glittered dully. "If I had my own medicaments, I could provide the lord with something for his pain," he said softly. "I do not believe the Christians have these ingredients."

"But they have a surgeon," she insisted. "He must have something you can use. If you can get ahold of opium, that would do it."

Kaleef shrugged just as a burly man entered the room, shoving the servants aside and calling for hot water. He froze when he came to the bed with Jeffrey upon it, staring at Rory and Kaleef as if they were from Mars. His fat, ruddy face grew more inflamed at the sight.

"Be gone!" he boomed, waving his arms. "Move aside!"

Kieran was suddenly in the man's face. "This is my wife," he growled. "You will keep a civil tongue in her presence. She is here to help my father and so is the man with her. You will give them all due respect and assist them or you will leave this place and never return."

The burly surgeon looked rather startled to see Kieran Hage. He hadn't heard that the man was returned from the Quest and his attitude changed dramatically. "My lord Kieran," he offered and stepped back, bowing apologetically. "I did not know you were returned, my lord. Praise God that you did not suffer in your journey."

Kieran eyed the man he had known the majority of his life. The surgeon was arrogant and brash, but knowledgeable. His tight manner softened as he turned to Rory and Kaleef. "This is Marcuson," he indicated the big, hairy man. "He is Southwell's surgeon. Tell him what you need and he will ensure that you receive it."

Kaleef was literally half the size of the man; a tiny, shriveled old man with a leather-like face against a bull of a pale-skinned man. As he gazed up at the fat Englishman with some trepidation, Andrew suddenly cried out.

"He is not breathing!" He was kneeling at Jeffrey's head, his young face full of panic. "He has stopped breathing!"

Everyone in the room whirled to Jeffrey's still form, startled by the cry. A couple of the serving women, standing near the door, began to wail. Rory was the first one to react. She ran to Jeffrey, trying to flip him onto his back. "Help me!" she cried. "Turn him onto his back!"

Without question, Kieran, Sean and Christian moved in swiftly, rolling Jeffrey onto his back as Rory held his head and neck carefully. Once the man was flat on his back, Rory adjusted Jeffrey's head, tipped it back slightly, pinched his nose and blew into his mouth. As the room watched in shock, she counted to five, blew into Jeffrey's mouth, and repeated the process five times. Then she leapt up onto the man's chest and put her ear against it, listening.

No one had any idea what she was doing, least of all Kieran. Everyone was looking to him for answers but he had none to give. All he knew was that his wife possessed knowledge about medicine that he could never hope to understand. He knew he had to let her do whatever she was doing because she was trying to help his father. He kept telling himself that. But when she suddenly sat up on Jeffrey's chest and brought a fist onto his sternum, hard, even he began to wonder if she'd lost her mind. She was beating the man right in front of them.

Rory began CPR, her hands folded against Jeffrey's chest and counting out each thrust she delivered. After four rounds of five-counted thrusts, she scrambled back over to Jeffrey's head and blew in his mouth in the same counted fashion. The vision was growing increasingly disturbing for those who did not know what she was trying to accomplish. Finally, Sean hissed to Kieran.

"What is she doing?" he asked.

Kieran, eyes riveted to his wife, shook his head slowly. "I do not know," he admitted. "But whatever she is doing, you must let her complete it."

Rory moved back and forth between chest compressions and breathing, counting everything out with even, measured strokes. No one dared offer to help. But after five rounds of the breathing and chest compressions, Marcuson finally boomed up.

"She is killing him," he declared, turning to Kieran. "Will you let her kill your father?"

Kieran was on edge after what had happened that night. His patience was gone and he could not withstand a personal attack on Rory. He moved for the old surgeon menacingly but was intercepted by Sean. Kieran glanced at his brother's pleading face and calmed somewhat, although he was still righteously angry.

"Another word and I will throw you from this keep," he rumbled. "She is not killing him. She is attempting to help him."

The old surgeon wisely kept his mouth shut but he was not convinced. He was horrified at what he saw, more distressed that the Hage brothers were allowing it to go on. He was, therefore, pleased when Andrew rushed up to Kieran, horror on his face.

"Stop her," he begged. "You cannot allow her to kill father!"

Kieran could see how distressed everyone was. He was distressed, too. But because he trusted his wife, he was permitting her to continue. But these people did not know her as he did, of her amazing abilities and altruistic deeds. His gaze moved between his brothers and Rory, who was still working furiously on their father. With a faint sigh, he finally moved towards the bed as his wife alternately blew in his father's mouth and pushed on his chest.

"Lib?" he said hesitantly. "What are you doing? Kaleef must…"

She cut him off as she straddled Jeffrey's chest and resumed thrusting. "He can't work on a dead man," she grunted as she worked. "I'm trying to get him breathing again."

Kieran still wasn't clear. "But what are you doing?"

"CPR," she grunted again, turning to look at his perplexed face. "It's called Cardiopulmonary Resuscitation. I'm trying to get his heart and lungs working again."

She said it loud enough that nearly everyone heard her. Then she suddenly stopped and put her ear against his chest again, listening. Kieran leaned closer as if he could hear whatever she was listening for. She lay there, concentrating, until a smile slowly creased her lips. Then she put her fingers on Jeffrey's neck, feeling for the pulse. Satisfied, she sat up and held out a hand to Kieran, who helped her climb off his father's chest.

"He's breathing on his own and I can feel a pulse." She looked at Kaleef. "Whatever you're going to do, you'd better do it fast. His pulse is weak and his breathing is shallow."

Kaleef's dark eyes glimmered at her and she swore she saw a flash of a smile. Perhaps, in this lady, he saw someone as strange and talented as he was in the medicinal arts. He understood her where no one else could. He moved past her, rattling off orders to Yusef and Marcuson. The men went to work on Jeffrey as the rest of the room seemed fixated on Rory. She noticed that everyone was staring at her as if she had just resurrected a corpse. But she realized that, to them, she had. She had just accomplished something very strange and very wonderful. Andrew was suddenly beside her.

"You..." He had an incredulous expression on his face. "You brought him back to life."

She shook her head. "Nothing so amazing," she said. "It's a simple technique, really. It's not magic, I promise."

Andrew wasn't convinced. "But he was dead," he insisted strongly. "He was not breathing and you gave him life again."

Rory was growing the slightest bit uncomfortable; she didn't like the implications. She didn't want people to think she was a witch. "Trust me, he wasn't dead," she replied. "He was still very much alive. I just helped him to start breathing again. Sometimes great trauma to the body can shock it and... well, believe me, he wasn't dead. He was very much alive."

"She works miracles," Sean said, his dark eyes glittering with renewed respect. "My brother has married a most amazing woman and I, for one, am very grateful. Thank you for your skill, Lady Hage."

She smiled thankfully at Sean's gracious statement. It didn't make her sound like she had the powers of darkness over life and death. Looking over her shoulder, she could see that Kaleef seemed to have enough help with Jeffrey. She didn't really think she could help him through Medieval surgery, anyway. The mere thought made her queasy. She turned back to her husband.

"I am really exhausted," she said quietly, pressing her weary body against him. "I would love it if I could just go to bed now."

Kieran put his powerful arm around her shoulders and, without another word, whisked her from the room. Those left behind were still attempting to process the amazing skills of Kieran's very strange and beautiful new wife. But for Sean, Christian and Andrew, a serious respect for the woman began to bloom. As far as they were concerned, she had brought their father back to life.

Maybe she really was as wonderful as Kieran said.

CHAPTER SEVENTEEN

THE NIGHT THAT Jeffrey had been injured, Rory had gone to bed and slept for almost a day. Kieran had kept everyone away from their bedchamber, including asking Sean to move Margaret and Eleanor to another floor, so that Rory wouldn't be disturbed. She was exhausted and pregnant and he wanted to make sure she had all the rest she needed. The entire trip had been exhausting her and he was anxious for her to recover and to settle in to some semblance of normalcy.

Jeffrey, surprisingly, survived his surgery and they moved him into Sean and Margaret's room while Sean and Margaret took his room on the third floor. The fourth floor of Southwell's keep had become the infirmary, a floor where no one was allowed to speak in tones over a whisper. The servants had taken to wearing something that looked like socks on their feet so they wouldn't make noise as they went about their duties. Kieran, even though he was settling in to life returned to Southwell, still managed to check on his wife every hour just to make sure she was all right. To help ease his mind, Margaret offered to sit with her, an offer he gratefully accepted.

As far as Simon was concerned, they had left his body in the great hall until the early morning hours. The prince had long since left, leaving four dead men and Simon behind. He made no move to claim them. So very early on the morning after Jeffrey's injury, Kieran, Sean, Christian and Andrew entered the great hall to clean up the mess from the fight. With the dead bodies inside, the servants wouldn't go near the hall. With help from several of their soldiers, they cleared out the bodies and took them into town to the large cathedral, Southwell Minster, for burial. Kieran left Simon's body with the priests and never looked back. He was finished with the man and the chaos he had created. Although they had a friendship that went back to when they were children, he couldn't even mourn the loss of a friend. That friend he knew, once, had died years ago. The man he left at Southwell Minster was someone he didn't know.

So he pushed it all behind him; the murder attempt, the assassins, the turmoil in the Holy Land. When Simon died, it all died with him.

Nearing the evening of the second day since his return, Kieran was on the grounds with Sean, Christian and Andrew, walking the vast area of Southwell and making note of any changes that had occurred since he had left. He walked with his brothers, talking and laughing, being followed closely by Bud, David and Yusef. Yusef was getting quite an education on English fortresses and they were not surprise to note he had a great deal of architectural knowledge, which he discussed very intelligently. Yusef was polite and flexible, and the Hage brothers were starting to warm to a man they had once considered their enemy. They were coming to understand why Kieran held him in such high regard.

As Kieran strolled the walls of his ancestral home, he felt an amazing amount of peace and contentment. He hadn't realized how much he had missed England and his family, and he couldn't help but remember how close he came to not seeing this place again. He would have thought that the fantastic path he had taken to return to England would have been a dream except for the fact that Rory was with him. She was the reason he was back, the entire reason for his existence. He loved her more, worshipped her more, with each passing moment. Even as he walked the parapets of Southwell with his beloved brothers, his heart and mind were up in the room on the fourth floor of the keep with his wife. He kept glancing up to the keep as if to see her through the very walls.

As the sun was setting, Yusef brought up the subject of the Arabians Kieran had shipped home from the Holy Land. That set off a cavalcade of praise regarding the stud qualities of the two Arabian stallions that had survived the trip home. Yusef very much wanted to see the horses; Christian and Andrew were more than eager to show him. Kieran and

Sean remained on the walls as Christian, Andrew, Yusef and little David went to see the horses. Bud, fascinated by the soldiers walking their patrol with the big, skinny dogs, remained on the wall and followed one of the soldiers as he went about his watch.

Kieran and Sean watched the child follow the man and his dog along the wall walk. Sean's gaze eventually moved from the boy to his brother, who was still watching the lad in the distance. He studied his brother a moment, a man he had missed terribly over the past three years. But as he gazed at his brother, he realized that something was different about the man. He'd noticed it from the start. He wasn't sure what it was, but there was a definite difference.

"You have changed," he said quietly, watching as Kieran turned to look at him. He smiled faintly. "I do not know how, but somewhere, somehow, you have changed, Brother."

Kieran lifted an eyebrow, returning his brother's smile. "Three years in The Levant is enough to change any man."

Sean shook his head. "It is not that," he grasped for words, leaning back against the battlement behind him. "There is something else. I am not sure what it is, but I believe it has something to do with your wife."

Kieran's smile faded. "What do you mean?"

Sean cocked his head, his smile fading completely. It was clear there was much on his mind. "Where did you meet her?"

Kieran was prepared for the question. "Her brother was my friend. Upon his deathbed, he asked that I take care of his sister. Unable to deny a dying man, I agreed to marry her."

Sean stared at him, hard. "If I were an idiot, I would believe that. But I am not. I know you too well, Brother. No dying man on earth could have convinced the brother I knew to agree to a marriage. There is something you are not telling me about your very odd yet beautiful wife, Kieran. She behaves in ways I have never seen and she knows things that no earthly person should know. I am hurt that you do not trust me enough to tell me the truth about her."

Kieran stared at him. Then he looked thoughtful, turning away and leaning on the battlements, gazing off across the darkening landscape. The sun was almost set upon the western sky and he watched it a moment, studying the pink and purple horizon, pondering his brother's query. His thoughtful expression turned painfully pensive, almost confused.

"Have I ever lied to you, Sean?" he finally asked.

Sean replied without hesitation. "Never."

"And if I tell you something in confidence, you will never repeat it?"

"I will take it to my grave."

Kieran looked at him. "I believe you. And you know the same can be said for any confidence you may bestow upon me."

"I would trust you with my life a thousand times over."

Kieran inhaled deeply, contemplatively. He gazed out over the purple-shadowed landscape once again. "Then I will tell you the truth because, at some point, it may be necessary to enlist your help regarding matters about my wife," he said. "You saw what she did to Father."

"She gave him life again."

Kieran shook his head. "Nay, she did not, but it may appear that way. There are those who might not understand her skill and believe she is a witch, or worse. She is none of those things."

Sean leaned on the battlement next to him, his focus on his brother. "So tell me the truth."

Kieran scratched his head and smiled ironically. "You will find it difficult to believe."

"After what I witnessed last night, I would believe anything."

Kieran never honestly thought he would be facing this situation. He never expected to tell the story of how he and Rory really met. But gazing into Sean's eyes, the same color as his, he realized he was about to tell the man the truth. In fact, he found that he very much needed to tell someone.

"Very well," he turned and faced his brother, leaning a big shoulder against the battlement. "But you must keep in mind that every word I tell you is God's honest truth. I did not imagine it, dream it or otherwise. It happened. I would not lie to you."

"I know that."

"And I am not mad, either."

Sean grinned. "That is a matter of opinion."

"Do you want to hear this or not?"

Sean forced aside his smirk. "I do. Tell me."

Kieran took a deep breath, wondering where to start. "I told you that Simon had tried to kill me after the secret meeting with El-Hajidd." He watched his brother nod and he continued. "The truth is that his assassins did reach me. They gored me in the belly and it was a mortal wound. But the owner of the hostel where I was staying sent me to seek an old man who was known for his amazing healing gifts. That man was Kaleef."

Sean's brow furrowed. "The same man who worked on father?"

Kieran nodded. "Kaleef used to be a healer long ago but his interests moved into the world of alchemy. He delves into the world of eternal youth and other mystical things. When I appeared at his doorstep, he knew that time was running out for me so he did the only thing he could do. He put me into an eternal sleep that slowed my body processes down enough so that I wouldn't bleed to death."

Sean was watching him closely. "He… he put you to sleep?"

Kieran nodded slowly, watching his brother's reaction. "Remember I told you that Kaleef was experimenting with the secret to immortality and eternal youth? He was able to put me into a manner of deep sleep while he administered another potion that stopped my bleeding and allowed my wound to heal. Now, the problem was this; there was no way to awaken me from this sleeping state except by the strongest of human emotion. A kiss from the one who loved me best. And that is where Rory came into my life eight hundred years into the future."

He watched Sean's expression as he launched into the tale of his experience with the twenty-first century. He watched his brother's face as he told the man about cars, buses, airplanes, department stores, toilet paper and electricity. He watched Sean's features pale as he spoke of returning to this time from a lightning blast and how he surmised that God must have brought him back for a reason. He suspected that the Crown of Thorns, the core of all of his problems, was the true reason he had returned. He had to finish what he had started, which he assumed to be presenting this most holy of relics to the Church for safekeeping. He had been called home to return it to the faithful. He could think of no other explanation.

Sean didn't say anything when Kieran was finished. He fell into a deep silence, staring at his boots and pondering what his brother had just told him. Kieran watched Sean's lowered head, knowing his brother did not believe him but that he was unwilling to tell him so. In truth, he didn't blame the man; it sounded crazy. So he leaned back against the wall and shook his head.

"I do not blame you for your disbelief," he said. "Even as I repeat the story, it sounds as if a madman is speaking. But I swear to you, as I live and breathe, that it is the truth. I could not concoct a story like this from my imagination; I am not that clever. Furthermore, I have proof."

Sean lifted his head, gazing somewhat apprehensively at his brother. "Proof?"

Kieran nodded slowly. "Come with me."

☙

KIERAN'S CHAMBER WAS dark except for a small taper giving off light on the table against the window. Margaret sat by the weak light, looking up from her sewing when Kieran and Sean entered. She smiled brightly at her husband and he returned her smile, stroking her cheek as he followed his brother into the room. Kieran paused in front of his sister-in-law.

"Has my wife awoken?" he whispered.

Margaret shook her head. "Nay." She set the sewing down in her lap. "She has barely stirred all day."

Kieran went over to the bed, pulling back the heavy curtains and peering inside. He was surprised to see Rory's sleepy, smiling face gazing up at him. He smiled broadly at her, putting a massive hand on her forehead.

"So you are awake, are you?" He sat down next to her. "You have been asleep almost an entire day and night."

Rory yawned and stretched. "I heard your voice when you came in," she said. "How is your father?"

Kieran's smile faded somewhat. "He lives," he replied. "How are you feeling?"

She thought on his question. "Hungry," she replied. "Is it time for supper?"

He leaned down, kissing her cheek. "What do you feel like eating?"

She wouldn't let him straighten up. Wrapping her arms around his neck, she held him close. "No meat," she said. "Is there any fruit? And I'd like vegetables that haven't been boiled to death. Carrots would be good."

"And white bread."

"Yes," she insisted. "And I would love any kind of cakes or cookies."

He shook his head. "There are no cookies, at least not as you know them."

She grinned at him, rubbing her nose against his. "I can make some," she said. "You have oatmeal, honey, eggs and flour, right? I could make awesome cookies with that."

He grunted. "It is unseemly for my wife to be seen working the kitchens."

"Please?"

He sat up, taking her with him. When he stood, he swept her up in his arms. "Absolutely not," he said, turning to face the room. "Greet Sean and Maggie, sweetheart. Maggie has been watching over you all day."

Rory's arms were around Kieran's neck, her head on his shoulder. "Hello, Sean." She smiled sweetly at the knight, then looked at Margaret. "Thank you for sitting with me today. I'm sure you had better things to do."

Margaret stood up, smiling. "I had nothing better to do, Lady Hage," she said. "Are you feeling better?"

Rory nodded. "Much better, thank you." She pushed herself out of Kieran's arms, standing stiffly as she turned to her husband. "I think I'd like to take a bath and eat."

Kieran cast a glance at his brother. "In a moment," he said. "I want to show my brother something."

Rory was already moving for the wardrobe, not entirely cognizant of the greater implications of what he was saying. "Show him what?" she asked, opening up the doors, suddenly distracted by the peg and hole joints of the large doors. Even half-asleep, her scientist's mind picked odd places to kick in and she picked at them a moment before returning her attention to the contents of the wardrobe. "Baby, where are Bud and David?"

Kieran moved for his wardrobe. "Bud is upon the walls with the sentries and David is with my brothers."

She stopped what she was doing and looked at him. "You left Bud with strangers?"

He lifted an eyebrow at her. "My men are not strangers."

She frowned at him, shaking her head in disapproval but refusing to respond for lack of a good argument. She continued to dig around as Kieran opened the doors to his wardrobe.

"Maggie," he said casually, turning to look at his sister-in-law as he removed one of his satchels. "I have not seen my niece since my arrival. Are you keeping her from me a-purpose?"

Margaret looked stricken. "Of course not, Kieran," she gasped, setting her sewing on the table and practically bolting for the door. "I shall bring her right away."

"Good. I should like to meet her."

Margaret fled as her husband lifted his eyebrows at her hasty departure. When he turned to apologize to his brother, Kieran jerked his head at the partially-open chamber door.

"Close the door," he said quietly.

Sean suddenly realized why Kieran asked to see the baby. It removed Margaret from something Kieran did not want her to see. Sean went over to his brother as the man set a large satchel upon the bed and began digging around. After a bit of maneuvering, he suddenly pulled forth a package wrapped in linen. He unwrapped the fabric, exposing the American blue jeans and extended them to his brother.

Sean just stared at them. Rory happened to look up from searching for the lamb's wool shift she loved so much and noticed that Kieran was showing his brother the jeans. Startled, she rushed over to the bed.

"What are you doing?" she asked him, looking nervously at Sean. He didn't answer her right away and she touched his arm. "Kieran?"

"I am proving to my brother that I am not mad," he answered, looking at her. "And that you are not Irish."

Rory didn't know what to say. She glanced at Sean, who was seriously contemplating the jeans. After some hesitation, he took them from his brother's grip and unrolled them. He laid them upon the bed and visually inspected them before fingering the brand at the top, the rivets. As he continued to inspect them, Kieran took out the construction boots and mock turtleneck shirt that had made the trip through time with him. Sean barely looked at the shirt but, as Kieran had, paid great interest to the steel-toed work boots.

He picked up the shoes, turning them over and over, fascinated and confused by the rivets and modern laces. He picked at the soles, peered inside the shoe. There were tags inside and printing. He scratched at it to see if it would come off. Finally, after several minutes of inspecting the shoes, he looked up at his brother.

"God save us," he breathed. "Kieran, I truly thought you were mad. But looking at these items… I cannot dispute your story. I have never seen anything like this."

"Nor will you again."

Sean struggled to come to grips with a miracle. "And you say that Simon mortally wounded you?"

Kieran nodded faintly. "Had time taken its normal path, I would not be with you right now. You would not know I was dead until years later when I simply did not return home."

That thought distressed Sean a great deal; it was obvious in his expression. "But you are here." He shook his head, baffled. "For some reason, you have returned. God's Blood, is this really true? Did this really happen to you?"

Kieran smiled faintly. "If you do not believe the evidence in your hand, Libby has clothing items as well. She is, in fact, wearing two of them."

Sean looked at Rory curiously but she backed off, knowing that Kieran meant her bra and panties. She put up her hands. "No way." She looked at her husband. "I'm not showing him what I'm wearing."

Kieran laughed but Sean didn't get the joke. Kieran shook his head at his brother and tried to use his hands to describe what his wife was wearing.

"These garments go… well, they go here," he motioned to his chest. "And then there are others that cover… they cover around here."

Rory had enough. She went to her husband and held his hands still. "Never mind," she told him, lifting her eyebrows at him to suggest if he continued, he would be in a good deal of trouble. "He doesn't need to know and I'm sure he doesn't care."

Kieran stopped his charades game, fearful of an angry wife. He raised his eyebrows at his brother as Sean grinned.

"Nay, Lady Hage, I do not need to know," Sean assured her. "But I find my brother's story quite fascinating."

Rory simply nodded, not knowing what more to say to him. She really wasn't comfortable that Kieran had told him their story but there wasn't anything she could do about it now. Slowly, she returned to her wardrobe and finally found the soft, white shift she was looking for. When she came back over to the bed where Sean was still sitting, she saw that he had removed one of his massive boots and had put on a construction boot. Kieran was explaining the advantages of such a shoe as she came upon them.

"I'm going to take a bath," she told him. "Can you please find Bud and David and bring them up here? I don't want them running around in a strange castle. Too many things can happen."

Kieran put a massive hand on her head, pulling it to his lips for a kiss. "Aye, Mother," he said patiently. "I shall send for the boys. But keep in mind that they must grow up sometime. You cannot keep them against your bosom forever."

She frowned at him. "They're still children," she insisted. But even as she said it, she was suddenly reminded of what Margaret had told her about Christian's child bride locked up in her chamber below. "And speaking of children, what's this about Christian keeping his betrothed locked up and not letting anyone speak with her?"

Kieran had no idea what she was talking about but Sean did. He paused as he tied up the shoe. "Who told you this?" he asked.

Rory was about to tell him but thought better of it. She didn't want to get Margaret in trouble if, in fact, she wasn't supposed to say anything. "It doesn't matter," she said. "Is it true?"

Sean glanced at Kieran before refocusing on the shoelace. "That is Christian's affair," he replied evenly. "We do not interfere."

"Christian is betrothed?" Kieran interrupted before Rory could speak.

Sean nodded. "To the Lady Charlotte de Longley, an heiress from the Lords of Northwood. She came to Southwell about three months ago."

"But she's kept locked up and Christian won't let anyone speak to her," Rory jumped in. "Why in the world does he keep this girl isolated?"

Sean finished tying the shoe. "That is his business, Lady Hage," he said, putting his foot on the floor and inspecting the fit. "As I said, we do not interfere."

"But she's only thirteen years old." Rory wouldn't let the subject go. "That's cruel and abusive. He can't keep her locked up like a prisoner."

Kieran didn't know the story behind his brother's betrothal but he could see that Rory was growing distressed about it. He put his arm around her shoulders and squeezed her.

"Go tend to your bath, sweetheart," he said, trying to both distract and soothe her. "If it will ease your mind, I will speak with Christian about his betrothed."

"Please do." She looked up at him. "He can't keep that girl locked up unless she's crazy or something. It's just cruel."

"I understand," he said patiently. "Go and take your bath. Bud and David will be here when you finish."

Sensing there was nothing more for her to say about Christian, Rory obediently retreated into the big bathing chamber and, as Kieran had done, opened up the dumbwaiter and shouted for a bath. Back in the bedchamber, Kieran and Sean went back to discussing the remarkable shoes with the steel toes. But Kieran knew, even as he praised the quality of the shoe, that the issue with Christian's betrothed was likely to become a sore subject if he didn't do as he promised. He would have to speak with Christian about the situation.

Otherwise, he knew his wife well enough to know that there would be trouble.

CHAPTER EIGHTEEN

THE NEXT DAY brought snow and sleet like Rory had never seen. Growing up in Southern California, she was only marginally familiar with snow as it pertained to skiing at local resorts, so the storm that blew in overnight was something to behold.

The morning started out innocently enough. She and Kieran had slept wrapped up in each other as they usually did but when dawn came and he tried to disengage himself, she refused to let him go. He was so warm that she fought him tooth and nail, so he relented and stayed in bed with her a while longer. Rory was clever, however, and knew that once she started touching him intimately, he would stay until his lust was satisfied so she burrowed beneath the soft linen coverlet and pleasured him with her mouth until the man could take no more. He rolled her onto her back, quietly, and made love to her as the sun rose amidst the storm clouds.

When their bodies cooled and their passion was satisfied for the moment, Kieran pulled back the great curtains, immediately looking over to Bud and David, sleeping in piles of linens and furs next to the glowing hearth. He and Rory had kept quiet through their lovemaking purposely so they would not wake the boys. Kieran still couldn't convince her to let the boys sleep with the rest of the pages but until such time as he could do that, he was not about to sacrifice his bedroom behavior towards his wife. The compromise was to stay as quiet as they could even though, for Rory, it was difficult. Kieran either kissed her or had her suck his fingers the entire time because if her mouth was occupied, it was more difficult for her to make noise.

After Kieran left to join his brothers in the hall, Rory fell back asleep for a short time before waking surprisingly bright and alert. She hadn't felt so good in weeks and she threw back the coverlet, hooting at the chill of the room. A glance over at the hearth showed that Bud and David were gone, so she guessed they had gone with Kieran. Eager to look around Southwell for the first time since her arrival, Rory ran to the bathing room and shouted down the dumbwaiter.

Kieran had already told the servants that his wife would bathe daily, so they were prepared. It was only a matter of minutes before the first servants appeared bearing hot water. So they filled up the tub, she bathed and went through the daily ritual of washing her panties, and then used the sesame oil to soothe her skin. She honestly couldn't remember her skin ever being so smooth and soft; water without chemicals and oils without preservatives had advantages.

Because of the snow, she dressed in the warmest thing she had. Her panties had dried by the fire, which Kieran must have stoked into a serious blaze before he left, so she put on her panties and bra, followed by a pair of soft, linen pantalets that her husband had purchased for her in Paris. She thought the pantalets were kind of goofy looking but they protected her skin against the shifts and surcoats, which could be rough. There were no fabric softeners. And there were no real undergarments for her torso underneath the shift other than corsets, which she wouldn't wear. As she put the shift on and the lovely orange surcoat made of heavily-brocaded linen, she smoothed the garments down and was beginning to feel the expansion of her belly. She rubbed her hand over the small bulge right around her belly button, feeling the evidence of the pregnancy for the first time. She was both thrilled and terrified.

Her long chestnut hair had undergone a transformation over the past seven weeks. With no hair products like mousse or gels or shampoos or hairsprays, her hair was taking on a natural curl all its own. Rory had no idea her hair had curl to it but the lack of modern products and the pure water she had been washing with had brought the quality to light. To accentuate it, she had taken to sleeping with her hair rolled up in strips of cloth she had torn from the towel she owned. It was an idea she had, since she was without her curling iron, and

Kieran had laughed at her the first time she had done it. But he found the result so beautiful that he couldn't keep his hands out of her hair.

So she unrolled the rags in her hair and ran a comb through it, creating a lustrously full head of curls. Then she used the comb to make them long and spiral, shaping them around her hand. Pulling the section over her forehead back and securing it with a real tortoiseshell comb, she finished off with a few of the precious cosmetics they had purchased in Tyre. And with all that done, Rory was finally ready to face Southwell.

Once she opened the chamber door, a blast of freezing air hit her in the face. Shuddering, she hunted down the cloak she had stolen from Hut's hostel on that night so long ago, the off-white wool that was incredibly warm. She had practically slept in the thing during their travels and she had grown attached to it. Since she hadn't really been out of the keep since their arrival, she moved slowly and cautiously. Her intent was to explore but if anyone saw her, she would use the excuse that she was looking for her husband. There was a certain thrill in exploring the massive stone keep by herself.

The fourth floor was empty. She peeked inside Sean and Margaret's room where Jeffrey lay sleeping. There was a male servant at his side and she slipped away unnoticed. She also peeked inside a narrow door that led into a very small, very messy chamber that she assumed was Andrew's. It smelled like a teenage boy lived there. Moving down the steep stairs, she ended up on the third floor where the floor plan was pretty much identical. There was a room in front of her that would have been directly below Kieran's bedchamber and then another chamber down a short corridor to the left. She noticed servants coming out of the door down the hall and disappearing into what looked like a slit in the wall. When she walked down to take a look at it, it was actually an opening for an extremely steep set of stone steps leading down into the darkness. She had no idea what lay beyond. Too intimidated to take the stairs, she moved to return to the main spiral staircase when her gaze fell on a narrow door just to the left of the servant's staircase.

It was bolted from the outside; she could see the big, iron bolt wedged into a socket. She gazed at the door, realizing that Christian's betrothed must be inside. Hesitantly, she approached the door and put her hand on it, wondering if she should knock. Everyone had told her that it was Christian's business. It had been made clear to her. But she couldn't stand the thought of a thirteen year old caged up like a criminal because the man she was betrothed to had no interest in her. It was cruel and horrible. More than that, it was barbaric and inhumane. In her world, they threw people in jail for this kind of thing. Waffling with indecision, she finally threw caution to the wind and unbolted the door.

Pushing it open timidly, she stuck her head into the room. There was a small corridor leading from the door into the room itself and all she could see beyond was part of a small window and little else. Now that she had the door open, she thought she'd better announce herself.

"Uh… Lady Charlotte?" she said timidly. "Hello? Lady Charlotte?"

Not a sound stirred in the room. Rory ventured in hesitantly, pushing the door open a little more. "Lady Charlotte?"

Still no response. She took a couple of steps in when, suddenly, a figure emerged from the portion of the room she couldn't see due to the angle of the small corridor; a small, angelic-looking girl with long red hair looked at her, rather stunned. She had something in her hand that Rory couldn't quite make out, but she was more concerned with the expression on the girl's face. She looked terrified. Rory smiled weakly.

"Hello," she said. "My name is… Libby. I am Kieran's wife. Kieran is Christian's older brother."

The girl blinked in confusion. "Sir… Sir Kieran?"

Rory nodded. "Yes," she replied. "We just returned from… well, he just returned from the Holy Land. He was fighting with King Richard."

The girl was so pale and weak looking. "Why have you come?" she asked fearfully.

"To introduce myself. I heard you were here."

The girl emitted an odd choking sound. "I am a prisoner," she hissed. "No one… no one will speak to me. I am caged like a beast."

Rory felt genuinely sorry for her. "I've heard that," she said softly. "I intend to speak to my husband about it. This… this just isn't right."

The girl blinked, tears suddenly swimming in her red-rimmed eyes. "I just want to go home," she whispered. "Why will they not let me leave if they do not want me?"

Rory was feeling worse and worse, having no real answer. She was about to speak again when the girl suddenly screamed and raised whatever was in her hand. It looked like a very large needle, something used for sewing. Before Rory could get out of the way, Charlotte stabbed her in the arm with it. Rory jumped back, yanked the needle from her arm, and raced for the door.

But Charlotte was running after her, screaming. The two of them reached the door about the same time and struggled with it; Rory to get out of the room and shut the door and Charlotte to escape. It was an odd and desperate struggle until Rory finally shoved the girl back and moved from the room, pulling the door shut behind her. Heart thumping painfully against her ribs, she threw the bolt.

It had been a frightening experience. Rory was panting with fear, staring at the door and listening to Charlotte howling on the other side. But she didn't want to be standing outside of the door when people came running to the screams, so she ran back to the main stairs and disappeared down to the floor below.

Her heart was still thumping painfully as she struggled to calm herself. Because of the thick stone walls, Charlotte's screaming barely went beyond her room. Rory couldn't hear it on the floor below. Struggling to swallow away her fright and guilt at having been doing something she shouldn't have, she tried to look composed as she looked around the level, noticing what appeared to be a parlor or solar in front of her. She entered the room, seeing that it was, indeed, a solar, and a very lavish one at that. She was admiring the colorful and functional tapestry on the wall overhanging two lancet windows when the door in the entry hall suddenly banged open.

Men and loud voices entered. Rory recognized Kieran's voice immediately. She turned to the solar entry to see men entering, shaking snow off their shoulders and armor. Servants were suddenly running at them, assisting them with the snowpack on their mail and wiping up the quickly melting snow at their feet; wet wood tended to be slippery and swell. The servants were efficient and silent as Kieran, still talking to Christian, began removing his gloves and then caught sight of his wife.

She smiled at him when their eyes met. Kieran's brown eyes twinkled as he entered the solar, pulling off his remaining glove.

"So you are awake?" He bent down and kissed her on the cheek with his cold lips. "I thought for sure that you would sleep another day away."

She shook her head, letting out a little hoot of shock as his freezing nose grazed her. "Awake and hungry," she said, rubbing her cold nose. "I hope you don't mind. I haven't really seen Southwell and I was just looking around."

He shook his head. "Not at all," he said. "I can give you a tour if you like."

She latched on to his elbow, smiling sweetly. "I would love it," she said, noticing how cold he was. "But don't you want to warm up first?"

He shook his head. "I had forgotten the misery of cold winters," he said frankly. "I never enjoyed snow as it was but, right now, I am wishing for the heated sands of the Holy Land."

She laughed at his comment. "What about Kaleef and Yusef? They've probably never seen it before."

Kieran snorted. "Kaleef refuses to touch it. He says it is the Devil's tears. Yusef, however, is more courageous; he actually tasted it."

"Where are they?"

He tipped his head in the direction of the door. "Out in the bailey," he replied. "At least, Yusef is. Kaleef is still in the knight's quarters and Yusef is trying to convince the old man that the snow will not harm him."

Rory chuckled. "I'll have to go outside and see it for myself," she said. "Maybe I can get him to come out. By the way, where are Bud and David?"

His smile faded. "You are not going to like it."

She went from smiles to suspicion in an instant. "Why not?" she demanded, scowling at him. "What did you do with them?"

He cocked an eyebrow. "I did not do anything with them," he said flatly. "And before you become angry, know that it is what they wanted."

"What did they want?"

"To spend time with the sentries on the wall. David is fascinated with the dogs. He wants to know if he can have one."

"What did you tell him?"

Kieran just shook his head. "I am finished telling them anything," he grumbled. "Every time I do, it is wrong in your eyes. I would tell him that he cannot have a dog but you would tell him that he can. And, of course, he would get his dog."

Rory could see his frustration. Laughing, she fell against him and wrapped her arms around his torso, smiling sweetly into his cold-pinched face.

"I love you," she murmured. It was a truthful statement, yet she was also saying it because he was perturbed and she hoped to ease him. "You're a sweet, wonderful man."

He lifted an eyebrow as he wrapped her up in his massive arms. He knew she was attempting to soothe him and he weakly resisted. "Hmmm," he grunted. "I will say this; our son will be raised the way I wish for him to be raised. I will not allow you to turn my son in to a coddled weakling."

She struggled not to laugh at him. "Treating children kindly and gently when they are small is not coddling."

"He will leave to foster when he is five years of age and I will hear no argument from you."

Her expression turned threatening. "You are not sending my son to foster when he is five years old," she informed him. "Maybe when he's twelve; even then, I'm not sure about that. Why does he even have to go away at all? Why can't he stay here and learn from you?"

Kieran sighed heavily. "I can see that I will have to steal the boy away in the dead of night or surely you will never let him go."

She pursed her lips angrily at him and he brushed her nose with his lips, kissing her cheek when she turned away petulantly. But as she tried to pull away from him, he saw something on her upper arm and his good humor faded.

"What is this?" he fingered the small bloodied stain. "What happened?"

Rory had no idea what he was talking about until she looked and saw the small bloodstain. Her first instinct was to lie to him to protect herself, but she found that she could not. She could never lie to the man no matter what the circumstances.

Christian was standing over Kieran's left shoulder, speaking with a servant. She eyed the tall, redheaded Hage brother a moment before answering.

"I've been very bad." She looked up at her husband. "You're going to be really mad at me but before you explode, please know that I am very, very sorry and I meant no harm."

He looked at her quizzically. "What did you do?"

She pressed closed to him and lowered her voice. She didn't want Christian to hear. "I went to see Christian's betrothed," she said, rubbing the bloodied spot. "The girl attacked me."

Kieran stared at her a moment before letting out a hiss and rolling his eyes. "What did she do to you?"

He was pulling the cloak aside to get a look at her arm and she hastened to assure him that it wasn't bad. "She stuck me with a needle," she said quickly as he grabbed her arm to get a better look. "I'm fine. But that poor girl… she just screamed and ran at me."

He inspected her arm and the bloodstain. Then he gave her a very reproachful expression.

"You were told that it was not your business," he growled.

She nodded her head vigorously. "I know you did and I'm really sorry," she said quickly. "I should have listened to you but the idea that some young girl was locked away just seemed too cruel. So I went to see her and she seemed so despondent. Before I could really talk to her, she attacked me. Please know that I meant well."

His jaw ticked and he shook his head as if at the end of his rope. "You always mean well, Libby. But the truth is that, in spite of what you are told, you always do as you wish. Do you think you know so much more than the rest of us?"

His words hurt her, right or not. She averted her gaze, unable to look him in the eye. "I don't think that," she whispered. "It's just that poor girl is locked up and that's barbaric. It's no wonder she's acting crazy. Your brother can't just leave her there to…"

"She is locked up because she *is* mad." His fury was gaining speed. "I spoke to Christian about it. But rather than wait for me to tell you the truth, you took matters in your own hands with complete disregard for what you were told."

Rory was growing hot. "That's not true," she fired back. "And I don't think she's really mad. I think she's just stir-crazy because she's been locked up against her will. How would you react if you were locked up in a strange place by people you didn't even know? You'd be crazy, too."

Kieran's brown eyes were blazing. "You have absolutely no respect for me or anyone else, so I can only assume you think we are all idiots because we do not have nearly the knowledge or education that you do. Do you always assume you are the smartest one in the room and know better than the rest of us fools?"

It was the last straw. Rory burst into tears and fled the solar. Kieran didn't do what he'd always done before; he didn't follow her. He watched her run up the stairs and let her go. As much as he regretted hurting her feelings, he was convinced that she had to learn a lesson. The next time she disregarded what someone told her, it might cost her greatly. Maybe even her life.

He turned to Christian and told him what she had done.

☙

A HALF HOUR later, Kieran showed up at his chamber bearing a massive tray of food. It was a peace offering even if he wouldn't admit it.

He just couldn't stand it. His strong stance had lasted all of thirty minutes and then he had caved, going to the kitchens himself to retrieve food and taking it up to his pregnant wife. When he entered the room, the fire was burning low and it was cold. Even though there were oilcloths over the windows, freezing air still blew inside. He set the food down on the table and went to the hearth, throwing more peat and wood on it and stoking it up into a bright blaze. Brushing off his hands, he made his way to the bed.

Rory was lying on her side, facing away from him. Leaning over to see if her eyes were opened, he realized that she was sniffling in her sleep. Her lips were parted in sleep and she was snoring softly. He touched her head, feeling like a lout that he had scolded her but he knew it was for her own good. Still, he had been angry and, perhaps, was more condescending than he should have been. He kissed her gently and pulled the edge of the coverlet up over her against the cold room.

He went to his wardrobe and quietly opened it, searching for a warmer pair of gloves. As he searched, his leather-bound journal caught his eye and he looked at it a moment, realizing the last time he has written in it had been before he had met Rory. A lifetime ago.

He pulled the journal out and hunted around for the quill and ink. They were in his satchel, carefully wrapped. Forgetting about the search for the gloves, he went over to the table beneath the lancet windows and pushed the tray of food aside, setting the journal on the surface. He opened it to the first clean page, the fine parchment of a soft yellow color, and prepared his quill, sand and ink. His gaze drifted to his wife, sleeping soundly on the bed, as he collected his thoughts. Then he began to write.

He wrote of everything that had happened since the moment Simon's assassins caught him unaware. He wrote of his encounter with Kaleef, his awakening in Rory's century, and their adventures. He wrote of his reappearance in his time, with Rory by his side, and the knowledge that he had returned to accomplish something great, something historic. His reflections and opinions were in every page, every situation. But one thing was clear as he wrote; he adored the woman who woke him from his eternal sleep, the one he had yelled at less than an hour ago and the one who was sleeping in his oversized bed.

He wrote of the son she carried, the one who had defied time and history to be born. He hoped the child would be a great knight, with his wife's intelligence and his strength. He could close his eyes and see the boy, a handsome lad in the image of his father. He was so caught up in his reflections and his writing that it took him a moment to notice that someone was standing next to him.

He looked up to see Rory leaning over him, trying to read his careful, scripted letters. When their eyes met, he smiled.

"How do you feel?" he asked.

"Fine," she said. "But I'm hungry. Thanks for bringing me food."

She went to pull out a chair but he stopped her, wrapping an enormous arm around her waist and pulling her close. He pressed his face into her torso, deriving great comfort from the feel and smell of her. Rory leaned against him, her gaze somewhat guarded as she gazed down at him.

"Look," she said before he could speak. "If you're going to yell at me again, don't bother. I've learned my lesson."

He gave her a gentle squeeze. "Sweetheart, I am sorry if I hurt your feelings," he said. "I was harsh and I apologize."

She lifted her shoulders. "I guess I had it coming," she said. "You were right. I just do what I want to do. I heard about a girl locked up and I immediately thought the worst. But I still really feel that she's not crazy, just desperate from being locked up. Anyone would be."

He sighed, his great head against her breasts. "I have discussed this with Christian," he murmured. "He has promised to take the matter under consideration."

It was probably the best she could hope for so she didn't push further. She wrapped her arms around him, feeling so very fortunate to have such an understanding, compassionate husband who forgave easily when he could have righteously remained angry with her.

"I love you," she murmured, laying her cheek against his cropped hair. "You're too good to me."

He squeezed her gently. "You are my angel."

She kissed the top of his head, ready and willing to forget the subject. She looked down at the page he had been carefully scribing. The letters were very elaborate and she read through them slowly.

"What are you writing about?" she asked.

Arm still around her, he looked down at the page. "Everything that has happened to me since Simon's assassins caught up to me," he replied. "I am also writing to my son."

She smiled at him. "That's sweet," she said. "What are you telling him?"

He looked at the page, lifting an eyebrow. "That his mother is a disobedient wench." When she giggled and pretended to slap him, he grinned. "I am writing about my feelings for him, I suppose. My joy and expectations."

"He's not even born yet and you already have expectations?"

"Every parent has."

"I don't suppose you've named him already, too. I probably don't have a say in that, I would guess."

He looked up at her, smiling. "You may give your opinion, madam. But I will make the decision."

She laughed at him, shaking her head. "I thought as much," she said. "Well, what's it going to be? I like Christopher or James. I even like Henry."

He lifted an eyebrow. "Well enough names," he said. "But it is a tradition in my family to name the firstborn son after the grandfather of choice. I would choose my mother's father; he was a great man. He meant a great deal to me."

"What was his name?"

"Tevin."

"Who are you named after?"

"Tevin's father, Kieron d'Mearc. He was a great knight during the reign of Henry I and held the title Viscount Malden, heir to the Earl of Essex."

Rory took his hand and put it on her belly. It was gently bulging, hardly noticeable, but the firmness was obvious. Kieran smiled at the first physical proof of his child, leaning down to kiss it. He looked up at Rory, who smiled in return.

"Then Tevin it is," she said softly.

He finished writing in his journal as Rory ate the contents of the food tray. Unfortunately, writing became prohibitive when she was finished with her meal because she kept inspecting the quill, the ink, the pages of the journal, and making it generally difficult. He finally gave up and put the quill down, pulling her onto his lap and holding her close, thinking of their future.

The reality was that he was home where he belonged, Rory was with him, and he was more content than he had ever been in his life. Jeffrey seemed to be healing from his wound and Simon was dead. Everything was as it should be in an ideal world. And even though Kieran was content, there was still a nagging thought in the back of his mind.

He had returned to his time for a reason. And he knew, deep down, that the ancient circle of vines in the little box in his wardrobe was the reason. He was expected to do something with it, or to it, and was terrified that he wouldn't be able to discover what it was. He was terrified that if he wasn't able to do whatever he needed to do fast enough, God would give up on him and send Rory back to her time and return him to that bleeding, dying mess he had once been. He was terrified he would waste his second chance.

His life, and Rory's life, centered around the diadem of Christ.

CHAPTER NINETEEN

Early October
Year of our Lord 1192 A.D.

IT WAS THE moment they had been waiting for.

Kieran was in the solar with Andrew when the cry from the sentries went up. The brothers looked at one another and, in a rush, sprinted to the front door and took the old, wooden stairs leading down to the bailey much too fast. Kieran, in fact, nearly tripped over his brother when Andrew stumbled at the bottom. Slapping his youngest brother on the back of the head, he pushed past Andrew and met Sean as the man entered the bailey on his sweating charger.

The day was cool and crisp but the weather had been unseasonably dry. At mid-afternoon, gray clouds were beginning to gather overhead but they didn't smell of rain. It was simply gloomy. As Sean reined his red charger into the bailey of Southwell, the beast kicked up clods of dirt against Andrew's legs.

"So you have decided to come home, have you?" Kieran teased the man as he climbed off the horse. "It has been so long that your daughter believes I am her father. Well? What do you have to say for yourself?"

Sean had been in London for four months, completing his tasks for de Longchamp. Kieran knew the man brought the very latest news with him but they spared a moment for pleasantries. Sean flipped up his visor, grinning at his brother.

"While you stay here warm and cozy in Mother's bosom, some of us are actually concerned with the direction of the country," he teased in return. "We must discuss the most important items first; are you a father yet?"

Kieran lifted an eyebrow but his smile grew. “Dear God, nay,” he shook his head. “Libby is ready to explode. I have never seen anyone so miserable.”

Sean laughed. “Well do I remember that wait, old man. Is she well?

“She is marvelous. But she cries at the change of the hour and is generally miserable. Sitting is uncomfortable and walking is exhausting, so these past few weeks have been long and weary.”

Sean clapped him on the shoulder. “Take heart,” he assured Kieran. “It shall be over soon.”

Kieran nodded his head in a weary gesture as Andrew joined them. Now that the pleasantries were over, they focused on the news Sean bore.

“What is the latest from London?” Kieran lowered his voice as they made their way towards the keep.

Sean began removing his gloves. “As we had hoped,” he said. “Richard is on his way home. The last word we had, he was leaving Corsica. That was two weeks ago. God willing, he should be in home in a month.”

Kieran was silent a moment, thinking of what he knew; that Richard would be taken hostage before he could make it home. He would have to discuss it with Rory to see what the timeline was for the occurrence, but from what she had told him, it was sometime before Christmas of this year. He was edgy as he thought on it, wondering for the hundredth time if he shouldn’t have sent his own men to Richard to escort the king home by a different route. But Rory wouldn’t let him do it. She was fearful of the course such action would take. Would it alter history enough to the point where she would vanish? It was her increasing fear, altering the natural course of history to the point where she would have never been born. Kieran had to agree; he didn’t want to upset the balance, either. As much as he loved his king, he would rather have his wife alive and by his side.

“Richard will be going to his holdings in France,” Andrew broke into his thoughts. “He will not be coming back to London.”

Kieran nodded. "Aye, he will," he replied confidently. "He knows that his brother thirsts for his throne. When Richard arrives on English soil, we must be prepared to fight for him."

Andrew snorted. "Why?" he shook his head. "He will not kill his brother. He may imprison the man, but he will not kill him. We will be fighting a fool's war."

"We will be fighting the king's war," Kieran reminded him. "Think of the alternative. If John gains control of this country, all we know and love will be lost. It would not do well for our family."

Andrew pursed his lips, nodding reluctantly at what he knew was the truth. Over the past several months, John's campaign against the Hages had increased substantially. It all centered around the Crown of Thorns, something John coveted greatly but Jeffrey held fast to. Because of John's propaganda, the Holy Church had found out about the relic and now they, too, were demanding it be turned over to them. Jeffrey, still weak from the wound that had almost claimed him those many months ago, swore he would take it to Canterbury himself when he was well enough. But that time had not yet come and the Church was increasingly impatient. Meanwhile, John hadn't forgotten about it; he wanted that crown with a seething envy. Knowing this, the Hages had become increasingly guarded against John's supporters. All Hage lands were now heavily patrolled and protected.

"So what do we do?" Andrew finally asked. "Do we just wait for Richard's return?"

"For now," Sean said. He was weary from his time away from home and was increasingly focused on seeing his wife and child. "De Longchamp told me to come home. He will be paying us a visit soon, as will many other of the king's supporters. They will want to council with Kieran and Father."

Kieran remained silent on the matter, his mind turning to the events he knew were going to happen. He wondered if it was wise for him to sit in council with de Longchamp. As the three brothers neared the keep entry, Christian suddenly appeared in the doorway and threw his arms around Sean, picking the man up and shaking him.

"Great Gods, Christian," Sean grunted as his happy brother set him to his feet. He slugged Christian in the chest. "The last time you did that, you cracked two of my ribs."

Christian beamed. "I was hoping to beat my record," he said, rubbing the spot where Sean hit him. "Father heard the sentries. He wants to see you right away."

Sean nodded wearily. "Can I at least see my wife first?"

As if she heard him, Margaret came barreling down the spiral stairs with little Eleanor in her arms. Squealing with delight, she threw herself into her husband's arms, weeping and laughing happily. Kieran smiled as he watched the exchange when another vision on the stairs caught his attention. Looking up, he found himself gazing into the face of an angel.

Rory was moving down the stairs far more slowly. In a voluminous, white gown made from soft wool that was gathered just underneath her breasts, she did, indeed, look like an angel. Long sleeves trailed well past her hands and her enormous belly was evident. Kieran went to the steps, helping her down the last few. As was usual when Kieran came within close proximity to her, he put his hand on her belly and kissed her forehead. He always had his hands on her belly, as if they were magnetically joined.

"Sean has returned safely," he told her. "He brings news."

Rory was one of those women who truly had the pregnancy glow. She was round-cheeked and rosy, and Kieran fell more deeply in love with her every time he saw her. She had the biggest belly he had ever seen, however, but Kaleef assured him that the pregnancy was progressing nicely. Still, she was miserable and he sympathized with her a great deal. He had turned into what he had once accused her of being; a coddling mother. He coddled her, catered to her and loved her like no husband ever had or could.

Rory knew how fortunate she was and she thanked God every day for the man. He was amazing. But having spent the past two hours trying to take a nap, she was not in a particularly good mood as she accepted his kiss. She was exhausted and grumpy, and completely non-sociable. She eyed Sean.

"I'll bet he has news and probably not good news, either," she muttered, crabby as hell, watching the man get reacquainted with his daughter. "But I'm glad he made it home all right. Oh, God, I have the worst heartburn. I feel like my throat is on fire."

Kieran put his arm around her shoulders. "Let us go and sit down. Sean can tell us about his trip."

She shook her head, the familiar pout coming to her lips. "I don't want to sit down." She suddenly fanned herself furiously. "I'm having hot flashes, too. I need to go outside and get some air before I burst into flame."

Kieran dutifully escorted her to the door, taking her out onto the landing outside. But she wanted to go down into the bailey so he carefully escorted her down to the dirt. Once in the brisk air, she stood there a moment and breathed deeply. Kieran stood next to her, watching her with a faint smile on his lips.

"Better?" he asked.

She nodded. Her luscious hair was pulled to the nape of her neck, a lovely ponytail hanging down her back. She looked so sweet and angelic and he was captivated. But she spoiled the vision by belching.

"Oh, God," she breathed again, putting a hand to her chest and burping most unladylike. "I just want this to be over with."

Kieran's smile broke through. "Kaleef says that Tevin should come any day now," he assured her. "It will be over soon."

She looked up at him. "And that's another thing," she said, her eyes suddenly filling up with tears. "There's no hospital or doctor or anything even remotely modern. I've got to have my baby in that stupid castle with some alchemist as my doctor. I'd do better with a witchdoctor. What happens if something goes wrong? What are we going to do?"

Kieran heard this same worry every other day. He, too, was terrified by the thought but there wasn't much either of them could do about it.

"Would you rather have the midwife from town?" he asked.

She shook her head vigorously. "No," she replied flatly, wiping her eyes. "Kaleef is more knowledgeable. I don't want that crazy old woman touching me; she burns sage to ward off the evil spirits of death."

She wriggled her fingers dramatically as she spoke the last few words and he struggled not to grin. "She has a solid reputation for bringing mother and child through unscathed," he said evenly. "She delivered Sean's child without incident."

Rory sneered at him. "It's Maggie's child."

Kieran didn't want to get into an argument with her. He went to put his arms around her to offer some comfort but she pushed him away.

"Don't touch me," she scolded. "You're too hot and I'm burning up already."

"You are a cruel woman, Lady Hage, denying my affections."

"It's not your affections I'm denying but your body heat."

He couldn't help it; he snorted. "You like it well enough when our chamber is freezing and you put your cold feet on my legs."

She made such a face at him that he burst out laughing. Rory grinned reluctantly and fell against him in spite of her recent objections. He wrapped his arms around her and kissed her.

"I want to walk around," she told him. "Kaleef said that can help the labor get started."

He nodded, taking her hand. "Very well. Let us walk."

So they did. Around and around and around in the bailey. Bud and David, who now had a permanent home upon the battlements with the sentries and the dogs, saw them walking around and came to join them. Both boys had learned a great deal of English over the past several months and could converse quite well in the language. David took Rory's free hand as they continued their walk around the bailey while Bud walked behind them with his very own greyhound puppy.

Rory listened while Kieran kept up a running chatter about the trip he would like to take in the summer when the baby was old enough. He wanted to take her on a tour of his castles to the north so she could see his holdings. She knew he was talking simply to keep her mind off her misery but it wasn't working; her ankles were swollen, her back was killing her, and the baby was sitting so low in her pelvis that it was agony simply to move. To make matters worse, she had trouble breathing when she lay down because the child was so big that he pushed on her diaphragm. All in all, she would be glad when it was over. But she was terrified for the event itself.

It wasn't labor that scared her so much; she wasn't particularly afraid of the pain. She was afraid of the lack of medical knowledge in case she or the baby went into distress. She glanced at Kieran as he spoke of Peveril Castle. She was afraid for him most of all. She didn't know what would become of the man if something happened to her. They were so attached to each other that she feared for his very life if she were to perish in childbirth. It was something that had been haunting her for a while now. As Bud's greyhound suddenly bounded off and the boys went in hot pursuit, she took the opportunity to bring the subject up.

Kieran was watching Bud trap the dog as David tried to grab it. He snorted his approval. "Bud is an intelligent boy," he said, gesturing to the pair. "He cornered the dog so his brother could get hold of the leash."

Rory watched the boys, hands to her back as she tried to support her aching muscles. "He's always shown a lot of intelligence," she said, eyeing him. "In fact, I was thinking something about the boys."

He was still watching them. "What about them?"

"I was thinking we could adopt them."

He looked at her. "Adopt them? You mean as our own?"

She nodded. "Why not? They're like family, anyway. Why can't they become our sons?"

His brow furrowed. "Because they are servants, Libby. You cannot make a prized stallion out of a donkey."

Her mouth flew open in outrage. "That's a horrible thing to say," she hissed. "They're intelligent, bright boys and I love them. I want to be their mother which means that you are going to be their father."

She emphasized the "you" by jabbing her finger at him. Kieran found himself backing down from another argument. At this point in her pregnancy, her mood swings could be so severe that she would take a dagger to him if she didn't like his attitude. So he nodded his head, putting up his hands in surrender.

"Very well, sweetheart," he said with veiled impatience. "Do not trouble yourself. Let us speak more about it after the baby is born. Agreed?"

She was still frowning, rubbing her back furiously. "There's nothing to discuss. I want to adopt them."

"Whatever you wish, sweet."

Satisfied, she resumed walking, her hands on her back. Kieran walked next to her, noticing that she was seriously working her back muscles. He was about to ask her if she was doing well when she interrupted his thoughts.

"There's something else I want to talk to you about," she said.

He nodded. "Of course. What is it?"

She paused a moment as they passed by the northeast tower, the one tower of the bailey that didn't have a city butting up against it. It was such a massive tower that it held the armory among other smaller rooms. The puppy suddenly zinged passed them, followed closely by Bud and David, and they watched as the boys chased the dog into the stable area.

"I guess they didn't catch the dog after all," she commented.

Kieran grunted. "Apparently the dog is the more intelligent of the three."

She grinned, eyeing him as they continued to walk. "I want you to promise me something," she said.

"Anything."

She paused and turned to look at him. "I want you to promise me that if something happens to me in this birth that you won't waste your life grieving." She was suddenly very serious. "You and I have something that no one else has ever had; a love that has carried us through time and history. Nothing can separate us but death. If that happens, I want you to promise me that you won't grieve forever. I want you to live and love again. I want you to be happy again."

He gazed back at her, unable to stomach the thought of losing her. He was prepared to give her a glib answer but he couldn't muster the strength. Instead, morose thoughts swamped him and he shook his head, averting his gaze.

"I do not want to discuss this," he said, moving away from her as if to resume their walk. "You are going to be fine and my son will be fine. There is nothing to worry over."

She watched him walk away and slowly began to follow. "I'm sure there isn't but, just in case, I want you to promise me that you won't throw yourself on your sword in grief. Please?"

He just shook his head and continued walking. Rory picked up the pace but as she did so, the painful muscles in her back suddenly radiated through her belly. It wasn't a strong pain but it was different from what she had been feeling lately. She paused, feeling the pain radiate down her thighs before fading and she wondered if it wasn't the start of something. The Braxton-Hicks contractions she'd had for the past month had felt different. They had almost been unnoticeable but for a tightening around her belly. But these were different.

Excitement and terror filled her. Suspecting that the walking was doing its job, she caught up to her husband and they walked for another hour.

ଓ

BY MIDNIGHT, RORY was in the full throes of labor. The long and tedious wait for the child was in full swing.

Margaret never left Rory's side. Her labor had been very different. She had spent nearly two days in bed laboring to bring forth little Eleanor. The midwife from town wouldn't let her get out of bed, so there was no walking around as Rory was doing. More than that, Sean stayed in the solar downstairs with his brothers and his father while the women did the work upstairs. It was considered unseemly for a man to be with his laboring wife. But Rory had insisted Kieran remain with her early on and, not wanting to upset her, Kieran had stayed. Even now, well after midnight, he walked with his laboring wife around the fourth floor, trying to keep her calm.

Rory was calm enough but her pains were growing worse. She refused to sit down because it hurt so much with the baby pressing down, so she walked the floor and grunted when the contractions would hit. Margaret sat and watched nervously while Kaleef brewed something in a cast iron pot that hung from an arm over the fire. Over the past several months, he had collected a variety of herbs and flowers in preparation for this moment, knowing he would be called upon to ease Lady Hage's labor pains. He was prepared.

"Libby," Margaret said timidly. She had long since become familiar with Rory and they were good friends. "That pain was close upon the heels of the previous one. Perhaps you should lay down now."

"Not yet," Kaleef said steadily. "It is not time yet."

Rory growled with frustration. "How do you know?" she fired at him. "How do you know anything? Have you ever had a baby before?"

Kieran had her by the arm. "Come along, sweetheart," he tried to get her moving. "It would not do to kill Kaleef before the baby is born. We need him."

"Oh, shut up," she growled at him, taking a few steps. Then she suddenly stopped and her eyes watered. "Can you please rub my back? It hurts so bad that I can't stand it."

"Of course, sweetheart. Let us go and lie down."

He took her over to the bed and helped her to lie down. Rory rolled on her left side, curling up as much as her colossal belly would allow, as Kieran got into bed beside her and began rubbing her lower back. When another contraction hit, he paused, feeling her entire body tighten and closing his eyes at the pain she was surely experiencing. But he resumed rubbing, leaning over to kiss her head now and again, thinking he would much rather be downstairs with his father and brothers. As much as he loved Rory, this process was terrifying and foreign. More than that, he just couldn't stand to see her in so much pain.

It grew worse when she began to softly weep as the contractions grew stronger. She never uttered anything louder than a quiet grunt, but he could tell her pain was growing severe. He continued in back-rubbing mode for quite some time, kissing her tenderly on the temple and hoping to give her some comfort. Margaret retrieved a moist cloth and wiped Rory's face to keep her comfortable while Kieran continued to rub until his hands were ready to fall off. Rory lay unmoving, rolling with the contractions, until shortly before dawn, she let out a loud gasp.

"Oh, my God," she rolled onto her back. "There's so much pressure in my pelvis that I can't stand it."

Kaleef suddenly stood up from his stool. "It is time," he announced, hobbling over to the bed. "My lord, you will leave. Let us do our work."

Rory clamped down on Kieran's hand. "No way," she exclaimed. "He's not going anywhere."

Kieran put a big hand on her forehead. "Have no fear," he murmured. "I will not leave."

Rory smiled wearily at him and he kissed her gently. "I am anxious to meet Tevin," he whispered. "Are you ready?"

She nodded, puffing out her cheeks. "I'm ready."

Margaret helped her lift her knees and pulled up her damp shift, exposing Rory from the waist down. Kieran may have been willing to stay with his wife but he was unwilling to watch the birth of his son. He held Rory's hand but kept his attention on her face, not wanting to see the great mysteries of life going on below her waist. As a particularly strong pain gripped Rory, Kaleef and Margaret could see the top of a dark, little head struggling to make its way into the world.

"He is coming, Libby!" Margaret cried excitedly. "When you feel another pain, push hard!"

She did. Another pain hit her and Rory nearly folded herself in half pushing the baby forth. Kieran put his arm behind her back, supporting her as she struggled. Rory pushed as hard as she could, never uttering more than a weak grunt as she worked. Between her legs, Kaleef grabbed hold of the dark head to help.

"Push hard, my lady," he commanded. "Push!"

Rory obeyed. It was significantly easier with Kieran's support on her back and Rory grabbed her knees, pulling them up to her chest and struggling to bring forth her child. She was nearly bent in two. The pain was intense but she worked through it, focused on freeing the baby from her body. She was almost finished and that knowledge renewed her spirit. She wanted to see her baby as badly as Kieran did.

But it wasn't an instantaneous process. Unfortunately, an hour of pushing barely moved the child and Kaleef was doing everything he could to help the baby come forth. He was beginning to suspect there was a problem but he didn't want to alarm Kieran or his wife. He kept encouraging Lady Hage to push and she did, but she was growing exhausted. At some point, Kieran's head came up from where he was huddled against his wife's head and his eyes found Kaleef. The old man saw terror there, coming from the bravest man he had ever known, and it prompted him into action. He didn't say a word as he wedged his fingers into Rory's body, hoping to get a better grip on the baby's head and help pull him free.

Rory gasped when the old man put his fingers into her, crying out in pain when the pressure became unbearable. Kieran gripped her tightly as she yelped, feeling more terror than he had ever known. He could see that Kaleef was doing something to her but he didn't want to look too closely; he really didn't want to know. All he knew was that Rory was in extreme pain, the child seemed to be stuck, and Kaleef was attempting to solve the situation. Finally, the old man looked up from what he was doing and focused on Rory.

"My lady," he said grimly. "With your next pain, you must push as hard as you can and do not stop. The child is wrapped up in himself and he must come forth or he will die."

Rory's eyes flew open wide, horrified at the assessment. But the moment the next pain hit, she let out a yell and pushed as hard as she could. With Kaleef pulling, the child slipped forward. Rory didn't stop pushing but she was growing weak. Her strength was waning and soon, she wouldn't be able to push at all. Kaleef knew this; he did what he had to do. He beseeched Kieran.

"Put your hand on the top of her belly and push," he commanded. "Do it now!"

Kieran was terrified but he did as he was told. He put his hand on her belly just below the ribcage and pushed strongly. The action helped Rory a great deal and she took another deep breath, pushing through a pain that seemed continuous. Kaleef pulled and adjusted the baby and, just when Rory was out of strength, the baby suddenly slipped out.

Rory collapsed in Kieran's arms, gasping for air. But she wasn't so out of it that she didn't realize the baby wasn't crying.

"The baby!" she gasped. "Is he okay?"

Kieran was close to panic as he watched Kaleef work on the child at the end of the bed. Margaret stood next to him, handing him linen towels, her eyes swimming with tears. If Kieran had believed Margaret's expression, then he would have thought his child to be dead. He couldn't take the silence.

"Kaleef," he said hoarsely. "The child…?"

Kaleef suddenly picked up the baby and, with a hand holding the baby by the ribcage, patted him strongly on the back. The baby let out a thin wail and Rory burst into tears.

"Is he okay?" she begged her husband, tears streaming down her temples. "Tell me!"

Kaleef lay the baby down on the bed and ran a brisk hand over its feet. The baby's cries picked up and it began to wail lustily. Rory's weeping increased as the baby's grew louder.

"You have," the old man wiped the child off with some warm water that Margaret provided, "the largest baby I have ever seen. No wonder it was such a difficult birth; the size is astonishing."

"Is it male?" Kieran was still in panic mode although it was beginning to occur to him that an unhealthy child would probably not be screaming so loudly.

Kaleef suddenly lifted the baby up, showing the red, screaming face to the worried parents. "It is," he announced. "Congratulations on your enormous son."

Rory lifted her arms up and wrapped them around Kieran's neck. He buried his face in her neck, silent tears of joy and relief pouring from his eyes. After a moment, he pulled back, kissing her furiously over her face and lips.

"He is well," he reassured her over and over. "Do not be troubled any longer; he is well."

Rory gazed into his eyes, wiped the tears from his face. "I think you're more worried than I am," she laughed as she put her hands on his damp cheeks, returning his sweet kisses. "I want to hold him."

Kieran looked at Kaleef and Margaret. "My wife wants to hold our son," he announced. "Hurry and give him to her before she snatches him herself."

By this time, Margaret had the baby and was cleaning him up for presentation to his parents. Kaleef was busy delivering the afterbirth, which Rory could feel but wasn't particularly pained with. She was more interested in getting her hands on her son. Margaret finished with the snug swaddling and brought him over, smiling as she extended him to Rory.

"He is so beautiful, Libby," she said softly. "He looks a great deal like his father."

Rory accepted the baby, cradling him against her bosom and getting her first look at his little face. He was pinched and red, and had an enormous cone head, but he was absolutely gorgeous. She started crying all over again. Kieran hovered over the two of them, his arms around her, pulling back the swaddling so he could get a better look at his son's face.

"God help us," he murmured lightly. "He looks just like my father."

Rory giggled through her tears, touching the baby's face, being rewarded with fussing and weak cries. "He's perfect," she whispered, opening up the swaddling more so that she could count his fingers and toes. "Look at his hands; they're so beautiful."

Kieran had moved beyond his emotional outburst and was now utterly fascinated by the boy in front of him. Never in his life had something meant so much to him; he couldn't put the moment into words. The love that he felt for Rory had come to fruition and the result was living and breathing in front of him. Little Tevin Jeffrey Lucas Hage was easily close to ten pounds, a very big and fat baby that had his parents absolutely enamored. Kieran knew, as he watched the red little face, that he had been given the most precious gift in the world. Perhaps this was why he and Rory had been returned to his time. Perhaps it all centered around little Tevin, the child who, in theory, should have never been born.

Kieran left his wife and son sleeping soundly as he went down to the solar where they were already celebrating Tevin's birth. Jeffrey was so thrilled to have a grandson to carry on the Hage name that he became ragingly drunk and passed out just before noon. But Kieran stayed awake with his brothers, with Yusef, discussing plans for the future as well as running trivial subjects around the table. It didn't matter what they talked about; all that mattered was that life went on at Southwell as a healthy heir was born.

Kieran even brought Bud and David into the hall and gave them both a cup of wine to celebrate the birth of their baby brother. He knew he would be their father eventually. Gazing into their big blue eyes and intelligent faces, he realized he wasn't all that distressed about it. He loved them as Rory did.

Sometime around dusk, he made his way wearily back to his fourth floor chamber only to find Rory sitting up, nursing Tevin. Margaret was with her, helping her with the baby, but she quickly fled when she saw Kieran. With an exhausted smile, Kieran stretched out on the bed next to them, watching the baby tug at his wife's full breast and never in his life experiencing something so tender or emotional. It was the most wonderful thing he had ever seen.

When she began singing softly to him in her sweet, pure voice, his emotions got the better of him and tears streamed down his temples as he watched the baby nurse.

"If I give my heart to you
I must be sure
From the very start
That you would love me more than her
'cause I couldn't stand the pain
and I would be sad if our new love was in vain."

He fell asleep with his arms around them both.

CHAPTER TWENTY

Four months later

IT WAS AN oddly bright February day, a cool breeze blowing cotton-puff clouds across the expanse of blue sky. In the bailey of Southwell, Rory and Margaret sat in the weak sun near the keep and watched as little David chased Eleanor around in circles. At two years old, Eleanor was a beautiful girl with Sean's good looks and a brilliant personality. And she adored David; they played like siblings.

Rory sat with Tevin on her lap, grinning as David would poke Eleanor and she would scream with delight. Then David would run at Tevin and make faces at him, turning the baby into a kicking, grinning fool. Tevin was an enormous baby with his mother's chestnut hair color, his father's handsome features, startling green eyes and, Rory thought, he was, perhaps, the most beautiful baby ever born. He was bright, chubby, smiled easily and ate constantly. He was the absolute apple of his parents' eyes.

Contrary to the usual behavior of Medieval fathers, Kieran did not leave the childrearing to others. He was very much a hands-on father and he emerged from the great hall this day, spying his wife and son across the bailey and making his way towards them. David saw him coming and ran to him. The boy found himself up in Kieran's arms and upside down. David giggled uncontrollably as Kieran came upon the women and shook him playfully before setting him on his feet. Then the man extended his arms for the baby.

"Give me my son," he commanded.

Rory smiled as she stood up and handed him the boy. Kieran kissed his son, kissed his wife and put his arm around her shoulders. She gazed up at him adoringly as he talked to the baby, unable to remember when a husband and child had not been the center of her life. True, accepting a world with no electricity, running water, bathrooms or cell phones had taken some getting used to. In fact, she was still getting used to it. She had gotten over her phobia of bugs and had simply learned to be vigilant rather than panicked about it. No blow dryers, spas, hair salons, Saks Fifth Avenue or shoe stores. But gazing at Kieran as he crooned to his son made it all worthwhile; she didn't even think of those modern conveniences any more. They were places that she only visited now in her memories.

"He needs to be fed," she told Kieran. "He's going to start getting cranky."

Kieran acted like he hadn't heard her. "I do not know who he gets his green eyes from," he commented, touching the baby's cheek. "But he clearly looks like me."

Rory snorted. "He's your doppelganger," she said. "I've never seen a baby look so much like his father. I was just an incubator."

"I do not know what your words mean."

She laughed. "It means that I don't see anything of me in Tevin other than my hair color," she said. "And he gets his green eyes from my mother. They're exactly the same color."

Kieran looked at her, grinning, before turning back to his son. As he fussed over the boy, Sean walked up beside him and picked up his daughter. Eleanor wanted to kiss Tevin, so Sean leaned her over so she could kiss the baby. Rory watched the scene, so very content with her life. It was sweeter than she could have possibly imagined.

"So what are your plans today?" she put her hands on her hips, focused on Kieran and Sean.

Kieran looked up at her. "I have no plans."

She shook her head. "Don't feed me that line. You and your brothers have been huddled in the great hall all morning. You have something up your sleeve."

Sean looked at Kieran, having no idea what she just said. The woman had phrases and language skills that they were all still trying to comprehend although, after all these months, they were getting better at it. Kieran merely shrugged in a "whatever" gesture and Rory sighed with exasperation.

"What I mean is that you guys have plans you're not talking about," she clarified. "What's going on? Does it have something to do with that rider than came from London yesterday?"

Kieran didn't look at her and neither did Sean; they pretended to be busy with the children. But Kieran looked up, catching sight of something on the opposite side of the bailey and pointing.

"Look," he said casually. "There is Christian and his young lady."

He was attempting to steer her off the subject and doing a poor job. Rory knew what he was up to but she dutifully looked in the direction of the great hall where Christian and Charlotte were walking in the sun. She shook her head at the sight of the tall, redheaded brother and the small girl who had barely gone through puberty.

"I'm sorry," she turned back to her husband, muttering more to herself. "Call me new-fashioned, but there's still something wrong with a twenty-six year old man and a thirteen year old girl. In my day, they called it pedophilia."

"What?"

"Never mind. I suppose I should be happy that he decided to finally let her out of her cage."

Kieran cocked his head. "They look quite content together. I do not see your concern."

She knew he didn't understand her reserve and there wasn't much more she could say about it even though it had taken Christian months to let the girl have contact with the outside world. She stopped trying to escape almost immediately and since that time, Christian hadn't seemed so opposed to the match. Still, Rory let the subject drop for the moment. She knew that both Kieran and Sean were tired of hearing her harp about something called a pedophile, although they had no idea what that was and Rory couldn't adequately explain the concept so they could understand it. So she moved closer to Kieran, wrapping her hands around his forearm as he held the baby. She gazed up at him.

"So what's going on?" she lowered her voice. "Please tell me."

He didn't say anything nor did he look at her. He was focused on the baby. Then he started walking, pulling her along with him. They traveled around the northwest side of the keep, towards the stables, listening to Eleanor's screams of delight in the distance as David resumed teasing her. Rory listened to the cries, grinning, as Kieran shifted the baby to one arm and took hold of her with the other.

"Acre has fallen," he said, not looking at her. "The Christian armies have been victorious and thousands of men are now returning home to England. It is a great victory for Richard."

Rory nodded thoughtfully, noting that the timeline that she had knowledge of and the new timeline seemed to have remained the same. She knew this moment would come and she was vastly relieved. But something else also occurred to her.

"Does Yusef know?" she asked quietly.

Kieran shook his head. "He does not know of his army's defeat but I will tell him as soon as time permits."

"Where is he?"

Kieran wriggled his eyebrows. "With that woman from town, I would presume," he said with some distain in his voice. "He seems very fond of her."

In spite of the serious subject matter, Rory smiled at his snobbishness. "She is the daughter of the richest man in town. Her father sees nothing wrong with Yusef courting her so I'm not sure why you have a problem with it."

"He spends much time with her."

"And I repeat; why do you have a problem with it? The man has got to make his own life here in England. He has a right to a wife and children just like you."

"I can select a more suitable woman for him."

Rory lifted an eyebrow at him. "You selected your own wife. Why can't he?"

Kieran didn't want to get into the same argument with her. They'd spent the past several weeks in debate over the suitability of the daughter of the richest tavern owner in town and cultured, handsome Yusef. Rory saw nothing wrong with it, as she genuinely liked the woman, but Kieran thought he could do better. So he avoided responding to her altogether.

"There is something more to the news we received." He wisely veered the subject back to their original focus. "Richard is missing."

She was successfully diverted. "We knew he would be."

"Indeed," Kieran's jaw flexed and he suddenly seemed disquieted. "God's Blood, Lib; it was difficult for me to not react to the news. I felt so… so guilty. Almost as if I was an accomplice somehow."

Rory squeezed his hand. "You're not an accomplice."

"I should have sent my own men to escort him home."

"You couldn't have," she said, but stopped and looked at him. "Kieran, if you had, there's no telling how history would have been changed. You couldn't do anything about it."

"Perhaps not." He didn't like her answer but knew she was correct. He lifted an eyebrow at her. "I will confess something, however. Up until the moment de Longchamp's man delivered the news, I had my doubts of your information. I thought that, somehow, you would have been wrong and Richard would have made it home without complication. You will forgive me; I should have never doubted you."

She smiled faintly. "I forgive you," she replied. "Has a ransom demand been sent yet?"

He shook his head. "Nay," he replied. "To be truthful, we do not even know for certain if he has been kidnapped. He has simply not returned to his holdings in France yet as we have anticipated. It has been several months since he left The Levant so de Longchamp's assumption is that the king has either been killed or kidnapped."

She looked up at him, squinting in the weak sunlight. "I think it's safe to say he's been kidnapped."

"I do not doubt you."

"So what are you going to do?"

Kieran paused, turning to look at her. Rory's gaze moved between her husband's brown eyes and Tevin's bright green ones as he gazed at his mother. She had to smile at the two relatively identical faces looking back at her.

"I must go to London to meet with de Longchamp," Kieran said, watching Rory smile at the baby.

She stopped smiling and looked up at him again. "I figured as much," she muttered. "But don't offer to pay the entire ransom, okay? Remember what we discussed. The timeline of Richard's release can't be altered. If it is, there's no telling how it will affect the future."

"I am aware of our discussion on the subject."

"So don't go offering your entire fortune for the man's release."

"I will not offer all of my coinage."

"Good." Satisfied, Rory moved on to the next thing on her mind. "Can Tevin and I come?"

"Nay," he said shortly.

"Why not?"

He sighed. "Because it is not safe for the baby to travel. You know this."

Her features moved into the familiar pout. "But I don't want to stay here without you."

He gave her a very impatient look. "Libby, there are some things I must do without you. This is one of those things."

She frowned, averting her gaze and looking at her feet. Kieran watched her fidget angrily but, to her credit, she kept her mouth shut. He felt himself softening.

"'Tis not as if I want to leave you or Tevin," he comforted, reaching out to finger a tendril of her hair. "I never want to leave either of you. But it is far safer if you stay here. I must know that you are safe while I conduct business."

She still wasn't convinced. "You need to bring me," she insisted. "I know what's going to happen and you may need to consult with me about things. You know as well as I do that Richard's situation can't change until it's meant to change. He can't be released early or, God forbid, die too soon. We really need to keep a close watch on this situation or the world as I know it will change. Everything will change."

He studied her a moment, digesting her words. "Then tell me," he said quietly. "Tell me everything you know about the situation so that I may know it also."

She shook her head. "No."

"Why not?"

"Because I'm going with you."

He nodded as if he just understood her completely. "So you would use this information as leverage to get your way."

Rory opened her mouth to argue with him but shut it almost immediately as she realized he was right. She was doing exactly what he accused her of. So she lowered her head, kicked at the dirt beneath her feet, and remained silent. Kieran watched the top of her chestnut head, wound in a gorgeous bun at the nape of her neck, and began to feel himself relent further.

"Sweetheart, I know that we have not been separated since the moment we met," he said. "I understand your anxiety. I have a great deal of my own and I do not want to leave my wife and son. But you must understand that it is far more important to me that you remain at Southwell, safe, while I conduct business. As much as I will long for you every day, I also know that my mind will be eased considerably knowing you are safe and knowing that we will see each other again very soon. Does that make any sense?"

She nodded, still staring at her feet. But then she looked up at him, the hazel eyes moist and pleading. "We were returned to this time for a reason, Kieran," she reminded him. "I know we say that over and over, but it's true. It's not just that you were returned, but I was returned with you. Maybe my role in all of this is greater than yours simply because of the knowledge I have. It's not that I don't want you to go without me because I'll be lonely without you or I just don't want to be left behind. It's because I feel like I have to. I need to."

He gazed steadily at her. "You will not be lonely without me?"

She broke down into a grin. "You know what I mean." She poked him in the arm. "And don't change the subject. Why do you always assume it's you with the biggest mission on earth and not me as well? Please, baby, I really need for you to think rationally about this and not just like a Medieval knight who's trying to protect his lady."

Tevin was beginning to fuss and Kieran, rather than hand him back to Rory, began to bounce the baby gently. It was clear that he was pondering her statement.

"If you go with me," he finally said. "The baby must not come. I do not want to risk his life unnecessarily."

Rory looked stricken. "I'm not leaving him. I can't; I breast feed him."

"Then it is more important for you to stay here with him."

"But…"

Kieran cut her off. "You may go but he must stay. Make your choice."

She pursed her lips in frustration. "You know my choice will be to stay with him."

He simply shrugged, his bouncing increasing as the baby's fussing grew louder. Rory watched the pair a moment before finally holding up her hands.

"Here," she grumbled. "Give him to me. I have to feed him."

Kieran kissed his son's cheek and handed him over. Without a word, Rory headed into the keep. Kieran watched her disappear into the forebuilding as his brother came to stand next to him. Together, they watched Rory's shapely backside move from view.

"Did you tell her?" Sean asked quietly.

Kieran inhaled deeply, puffing his cheeks out as he turned to face his brother. "I told her of Richard's disappearance," he said. "She knows we must go to meet with de Longchamp."

"You did not tell her about the crown?"

Kieran shook his head slowly. "I did not tell her that I am taking the Crown of Thorns with me," he said quietly. "She does not know that I intend to use it for Richard's ransom."

"We do not even know if he had been kidnapped. He could be lost or delayed somehow."

Kieran fixed his brother in the eye. "Trust me when I say that the man has been kidnapped. A massive ransom demand will be forthcoming and I intend to offer the Crown of Thorns in exchange for his release." He paused a moment, thinking on his wife, his son, the life they had come to know since returning to his time. "I have always wondered on the purpose that Rory and I were returned to my time. She and I have been over it innumerable times, attempting to determine why we were brought back together. I have always suspected it has something to do with the Crown of Thorns but to what extent was the mystery. And then it occurred to me; Richard will be kidnapped. From what my wife has told me, it took over a year to raise the money for his ransom and, even then, it was because his mother pawned the crown jewels. Perhaps that is not necessary now; perhaps that is what this crown was meant for – to buy the freedom of a king. What could be more valuable than a holy relic?"

Sean didn't doubt what his brother apparently knew. "In exchange for the life of a king, I should think it would be a fair trade," he said softly. "But the question remains; will your wife agree?"

Kieran lifted an eyebrow. "Agree or not, it is my decision. She will have to accept it."

"Did you discuss it with her?"

"I did not. And you will not, either."

Sean lifted an eyebrow. "Are you afraid she will prevent you from doing it?"

Kieran lifted his shoulders. "She is fearful that anything I do will change the course of the future and, consequently, the world she knows. But my fears are for my world and the world I know. I want our children to grow up in a land that knows peace and prosperity. What I do, I do for Tevin and Eleanor, and for any other children to follow. I do this for our family."

Sean sighed faintly. The concept of Rory being from the future and the amazing trip his brother had taken through time and history was still difficult for him to grasp even if he did believe it. "Perhaps you should discuss it with her nonetheless," he suggested quietly. "She has proven to be wise and insightful."

Kieran vacillated between a strong, husbandly stance and that of a submissive man. "My decision is made. She will simply have to go along with it."

Sean cast him a long and doubtful glance. One of Rory's colloquialisms popped into his mind, something he understood from almost the moment she had said it months ago. It seemed particularly appropriate at this moment.

"Bullshit," he snorted.

ଓ

"A MASSIVE ARMY departed Southwell three days ago. They are heading for London."

John sat in the great hall of Winchester Castle, a home that had belonged to the kings of England since being built at the time of the Norman invasion. Surrounded by the luxury of the royals, he was crowded by the servants waiting for his command, the soldiers sworn to guard his hall, and the courtiers that hovered around him like giddy children. But at this latest news, he leapt out of his chair, his dark eyes glittering at the scout he had sent to watch Southwell over three months ago. Finally, the news he had been waiting for had come.

"Did Kieran and his brother ride with the army?" he demanded.

The messenger nodded. "With my own eyes did I see them, Your Grace. Sir Kieran Hage was at the head of the army."

John clapped his dirty hands together. "He rides to de Longchamp," he said, his devious mind working furiously. He eyed the messenger in mid-thought. “A massive army, you say? How big?”

“Over a thousand at least, Your Grace.”

“Did you see Jeffrey?”

The messenger shook his head. “I only saw the four Hage brothers, plus a host of other knights, Your Grace,” he replied. “Sir Jeffrey was not among the warriors.”

John lifted an eyebrow. “You are certain of this?”

“Certain enough, Your Grace,” he replied. “As soon as the army left, the castle was locked down. I have no way of knowing how many men were left in the fortress considering the size of the army that left. Southwell could not be manned by more than a few hundred.”

The prince digested that statement, turning back for the cushioned chair that sat close to the hearth. He was a small man with a small mind and cold bones. His hands turned into fists as he approached the chair, shaking them in the air and speaking to no one in particular.

“I have waited over a year for this moment,” he hissed, sinking against the cushions. “Kieran Hage has not left the safety of Southwell since January last.”

“His wife delivered a son in October, Your Grace,” one of his thin, badly-smelling courtiers put in. “Our spies informed us that he would not leave her.”

John held up a finger. “But he has left her now,” he muttered thoughtfully. “He is going to see de Longchamp regarding my brother. There could be no doubt. Together, they will undoubtedly try to determine the best way to pay the ransom for Richard.”

“Hage has more wealth than the crown, Your Grace,” the same courtier snorted. “He is undoubtedly bringing chests of gold to pay for the king’s release.”

John glanced at the man. “Undoubtedly,” he agreed, lifting a finger in thoughtful pause. “More importantly, however, he has left something behind at Southwell that belongs to me.”

“What is that, Your Grace?”

John lifted a greasy eyebrow. “The Diadem of Christ.”

The dirty courtier shook his head mockingly. "With only a few hundred soldiers to protect the castle?" he clucked mournfully. "Whatever will become of them if someone breaches the walls?"

The prince's thoughtful expression faded, being replaced by something dark and sinister. "He should have thought about that before he refused to give me the diadem," he replied. "I have already proven that I can capture a king. Now I will capture the diadem given to him by the savages of The Levant and prove to the Hage family that they cannot deny or defeat me. I shall win in the end."

Whispers of approval went up through the room as John rose from the chair and began to pace the floor, accepting the praise that was forthcoming. He extended his arms, like Christ bestowing a blessing.

"Is it not God who said that His punishment shall be swift?" he asked the crowd. "The diadem of Christ was meant for England, not the Church. It is meant for me. Kieran Hage had no right to keep it from me so I shall undo his wrongful deed. And he shall know the meaning of punishment when I raze Southwell and take what is rightfully mine."

The dirty courtier lifted an eyebrow. "I hear that Lady Hage is a woman of unparalleled beauty. Perhaps she would make an excellent guest to ensure Kieran's behavior."

John looked interested. "Perhaps this shall not be an entirely unpleasant undertaking, then, if I am able to obtain Lady Hage's company." He whirled to the messenger, still standing where he had left him. "Rouse the troops. The full army shall ride to Southwell and, before the week is out, I intend to have both the diadem and Lady Hage in my possession."

The messenger scattered, as did several soldiers around the room. John turned back to his courtiers, accepting the congratulations on his brilliant plan.

CHAPTER TWENTY-ONE

NO TELEVISION, NO newspapers, no smarmy gossip magazines. Rory sighed as she sat in the great chamber she shared with Kieran, watching her son sleep in his elaborate bassinet just a few feet away and bored out of her mind. She wanted something to read, something that wasn't considered an invaluable piece of art with carefully scripted letters, but there wasn't anything like that available. She needed something to do these days. She had tried sewing but she wasn't very good, so she had taken up drawing and working out to pass the time. But that only occupied some of her time. And with Kieran away, not only did she have the adjustment period of being without him, she had to find things to accomplish so she wouldn't shrivel up and fade away. Life in Medieval times was nothing as she knew it and it was still a struggle, after all of this time, to adjust.

Gazing from the lancet window into the spring countryside beyond, she sighed again, her thoughts turning to her husband as they so often did. She knew he had to go away and she furthermore knew he had to go without her. She couldn't leave the baby and she couldn't bring him along, traveling on a long journey where bad things could happen. Kieran had left almost two weeks before, taking Kaleef, Yusef and Bud with him. Even with the thousand-man army, his brothers and friends alongside, the fact remained that she didn't want Kieran traveling without her. She felt some odd need to be with him to protect him, even though she knew he was perfectly capable of protecting himself. She also felt left out.

They had never been separated, not since the moment they first met. But there was a first time for everything. With yet another heavy sigh, she turned away from the window and thought about going for a run around the castle. Her intention to continue her twenty-first century habits had been an entirely new experience for everyone. There was no way she could run in the fine, Medieval slippers that Kieran had purchased for her so the only other alternative was her big, worn work boots, which weren't exactly conducive to running. Worse still, there were no workout clothes, gyms, or anything remotely similar. So she had borrowed a pair of Kieran's linen breeches, the kind worn underneath leather breeches and under chain mail, and borrowed a big, linen tunic from him, and had taken to running around the castle in this peculiar outfit with her work boots leading the way.

After the first time she had done it, Kieran had heard such an uproar from the castle that he had asked her not to do her peculiar ritual in public anymore. It was too unseemly and people simply didn't understand her. So Rory had taken to running up and down the stairs in the keep, something that was quickly halted by Kieran when she accidentally slipped on one of the steps and nearly broke her neck. He didn't understand her need to work up a sweat and their discussion had turned rather heated, ending up with her in tears.

So he relented and told her she could run up and down the retractable wooden stairs on the exterior of the keep because they were less dangerous and also because they were shielded by a forebuilding. That way, no one could see his wife running up and down the steps like a madwoman. It had been a compromise for them both. She still grinned when she thought of Kieran and Sean watching her run up and down the stairs with strange looks on their faces. She knew they thought she was, indeed, mad.

Lost in thought about her attempts to work out and keep busy, Rory wandered over to Tevin's crib and gazed down at the fat, little cherub. He was such a good, beautiful baby and she leaned over, pulling the blanket up over his shoulders. She smiled as she thought of him learning how to eat solid food. She had been feeding him porridge and mashed vegetables for the past few weeks and he was doing admirably well. In fact, he would open his mouth to anything that came near it, beef included. Kieran let him suck on salty morsels of beef, gnawing on bones with his six new teeth. Rory hadn't been entirely sure about the venture but Kieran could not have been prouder of the boy. His little man was growing up.

Jeffrey was proud, too. The Hage patriarch seemed to have accepted Rory into the family when she delivered a massive, healthy son. Ever since Tevin's birth, he had been respectful and almost affectionate with her. It was typical male Medieval behavior towards a woman and she knew it. Once she had proven her worth, she was accepted into the family. Jeffrey's kind behavior was odd and she wasn't sure how to act towards him. Since her father had never been a part of her life, Rory had never known a father-figure so the concept of a father-in-law was foreign. She was polite and kind, but she couldn't seem to generate any real affection for the overbearing, arrogant man.

Tevin was busy sleeping and she wandered away from the crib, her gaze falling over the ornate wardrobe in the room. Medieval cabinet-making was something of an art form and the doors to the wardrobes were carved and lovely. She walked past her wardrobe, running her hands over it, before moving to Kieran's. She opened up the doors, greeted with his messy pile of clothes, but she could smell him in the piles and she picked up a couple of garments, inhaling her husband's distinctive scent. It was enough to set her heart fluttering with longing and excitement. His satchel, the one he had traveled with to the Holy Land and the one that contained the Crown of Thorns, caught her attention as it was half-buried at the bottom of Kieran's laundry pile. Rory couldn't help but notice that it seemed rather flat. Curious, she pulled it out from underneath the clothing.

The journal he kept was still in it. Rory pulled it out, setting it carefully on the bed, as she dug her hand around in the satchel for the plain and simple box that contained the Crown of Thorns. But it clearly wasn't in the satchel and, curious, Rory began to hunt around for it in the bottom of the cabinet. A simple hunt began to turn into an earnest one and, soon, all of Kieran's clothes were on the floor in a big pile as she plowed through the cabinet in search of the sacred box. When the entire cabinet was cleared out and nothing else remained, Rory struggled not to panic.

"Oh, my God," she breathed, looking around the room. "Where did he put it?"

She was muttering to herself, looking under the bed and peering into any corner or crevice she could think of. Within little time, she had pulled the entire room apart and her panic had reached epic proportions. God help her, she knew where it was. If it wasn't in the room, there was little doubt where it would be. Kieran wouldn't have let it out of his sight in any case. It therefore stood to reason that…

"He took it with him," she almost cried with the realization. "Oh, dear God, he took it with him. He must have."

She did, in fact, shed a tear. It was more for the fact that she knew what he was going to do with it than for the fact that he had it and didn't tell her he was taking it. She knew, without a doubt, that he was going to present it as payment for Richard's ransom demand. There was absolutely nothing else he could do with it and no other reason why he should take it. He didn't tell her because he didn't want her to stop him. She had asked him once not to pay for Richard's ransom with his own money, thereby possibly altering the timeline and, consequently, history. But they had never discussed offering the crown for the king instead. Never once. She couldn't believe he hadn't discussed it with her. She couldn't believe that he felt the king's return was more valuable that altering history and, consequently, her very life. The thought was painful and heavy.

With tears in her eyes, she sank onto the bed, wondering how much time she was going to have left with him and with Tevin. They had always discussed the greater purpose for them both having returned to Kieran's time. Maybe Kieran thought that perhaps this situation, Richard's kidnapping, had been that purpose. And maybe the crown, intended as a gift for the king once, would now buy his freedom. She could see his logic perfectly.

Trouble was, she didn't know if that was the case.

ᏣᏰ

TEVIN WAS FUSSY.

He wasn't exactly crying but he was making a singsong screeching noise as Rory walked the great hall with him, bouncing him around and trying to distract him. David followed her. Wherever Tevin went, he usually followed like a magnet. David would make faces at Tevin, who would laugh momentarily before screeching again and trying to smack David in the face with his fat, little hands. Rory eventually handed the baby to David and the little boy walked very carefully with him, talking to him in his sweet, little French voice. But the savage beastie would not be soothed so easily, so David finally sat on the floor and put Tevin between his legs, finding a piece of kindling and a small pebble to bat around. That held Tevin's attention while Rory stood a few feet away and supervised.

"He misses his father," Jeffrey said as he came up behind her, watching David play with Tevin. "He has not seen him in several days and feels his absence."

Rory turned to Jeffrey. "I feel the same way," she replied, smiling wanly. "When do you think they'll be back?"

Jeffrey shrugged, his clear brown eyes fixed on David and Tevin near the fire. He was almost back to his old self after his bout with death but it had definitely taken its toll; he was not particularly robust and slept a great deal. He chose not to go to London with his sons because he knew that he could not keep up with them, which was something of a blow to his ego.

"It depends on many things," he told her. "If the weather is fine, perhaps it will only take a month or so. If it is not, then it will take longer. And, of course, depending on what business de Longchamp has for them, it could take several months. We will not know until they are sighted on the horizon."

It wasn't much of a comforting answer. Rory sighed with dismay and turned back to the boys. Tevin was now trying to crawl away from David, screaming when the boy wouldn't let him get away. Rory moved from Jeffrey and scooped up her son, kissing his little cheeks as he squirmed.

Margaret entered the hall with Eleanor at that point. The little girl raced across the room to Rory and Tevin, grabbing at the baby's fat feet and giggling when he kicked. Charlotte, Christian's pale and lovely betrothed, entered shortly thereafter in the company of a few servants, taking a seat at the table and waiting patiently for the meal. Even though Rory and Margaret had made every effort to integrate her into life at Southwell, she was still standoffish and somewhat of a loner, so they left her alone for the most part and hoped she would eventually warm up.

Margaret smiled as she walked upon the group, her eyes falling on Tevin's chubby face.

"Tevin seems in fine form this eve," she commented. "He appears happy and healthy."

Rory lifted an eyebrow. "He's been screaming constantly."

Margaret held out her hands. "May I hold him?"

Rory handed over the squirming bundle. "Be my guest."

As Margaret hugged the baby and cooed to Tevin, Rory moved back towards the scrubbed table where Jeffrey was now sitting. Servants had laid out a lovely spread; there was a big ham which tasted a lot like modern ham, plus green peas, beans, and several loaves of bread. Since Rory knew something of cooking, she had spent time in the kitchens when Kieran wasn't around and couldn't catch her at it, directing the cook and helping her make dishes that weren't so darned boiled or spiced. Medieval people went crazy with spices and for good reason; things went bad quickly and they often used the spices to cover up the rotting taste.

Rory was, therefore, extremely careful about what she ate. Mostly, she ate what was fresh and seasonal, and she loved her briny vegetables. Kieran imported briny peas, cucumbers and onions from London by the barrel. There was also a fishpond on the grounds so she had her choice of fresh fish.

She had also been active in experimenting with what ingredients were available to use them in modern recipes. About halfway through her pregnancy, Rory had developed a terrible sweet tooth and was dying for cake. Kieran had objected at first to her spending time in the kitchen, but she nearly took his head off one day so he backed off and let his pregnant wife play in the kitchens if it pleased her. She had white flour, eggs, butter, cream of tartar (a byproduct of wine making, she discovered), shortening made from animal fat, and milk. What she needed was white sugar which, at this period in time, was not widely known, yet not impossible to get.

She had Kieran send a missive to the same man that supplied them with briny vegetables from London, asking for him to send as much sugar, or "sweet salt" as it was known, as he could get his hands on. A big bag of the stuff arrived over a month later and Rory was thrilled. With no chocolate and no vanilla, she used lemon juice in her cake and frosting and was able to make a fairly rich and delicious cake. She'd had a fat slab of it but the rest was devoured by Kieran and his brothers before anyone else could have any. So she made another one and carefully guarded it no matter how much the brothers begged. Lemon cake became all the rage at Southwell.

Tonight, the talented Southwell cook had made another cake from the remaining sugar, only this one had apples, raisins, cinnamon and cloves with a kind of white ganache on it. Under normal circumstances, it wouldn't have lasted five minutes on the table, but with the Hage boys away, it sat untouched and reminded everyone of their absence. Along with the cake and centerpiece ham was fresh fried fish from the pond, rolled in flour as Rory had shown the cook and fried in fat. There was no vegetable oil so she had to compromise with the lard.

Rory sat with Jeffrey and Charlotte, eating ham, fish and peas while Margaret walked the floor with Tevin, Eleanor and David. Jeffrey ate with his hands but Rory had long since gotten over Medieval table manners. She found herself eating with her hands, too, because spoons and knives were heavy and unwieldy. It was dirty but she figured it was no big deal since everybody else did it, too. Still, she kept a little bowl of water nearby to wash her fingers in. She couldn't stand sticky fingers.

As the evening wore on, Margaret eventually walked Tevin to sleep so Rory excused herself from the table and took her snoozing son from the hall. It was cool and dark outside as she crossed the bailey towards the massive keep, thinking to herself that it was at night when she felt the weight of the Medieval world most heavily; men upon the battlements with torches and dogs, soldiers going about their rounds, and an odd sense of being locked away from the world. It wasn't like she could take a leisurely walk into town after dinner. Straying from the castle, out into the unprotected world beyond, was unheard of. Still, there had been a few times when Rory had strayed into town purely for curiosity's sake. Kieran had caught her twice. The second time, he took her over his knee and spanked her. But it wasn't enough to dampen her spirits. There was a tavern in town that had spectacular mulled cider and it was her husband's fault for taking her there in the first place. She loved that cider.

The keep was dark and quiet as she put Tevin to bed. Once the baby was down, she turned away from the bassinet only to be faced with a big, lonely, empty bed. No Kieran. Her heart sank a little more. She wasn't sure she could face that big, empty bed tonight. Not that she had much choice, but she just wasn't ready to face it yet. She felt the distinct need to get away somehow, to occupy her mind to keep it off her missing husband. A thought occurred to her as she remembered the mulled cider in town. Kieran wasn't here to scold her for leaving the castle. Perhaps she could slip into the town, have her delicious, warm drink, and return before anyone missed her. It was a not-so-brilliant idea that she talked herself into.

Putting on one of the heavy cloaks with the fur lining that Kieran had given her, she called down the dumbwaiter for the old cook. The woman sometimes sat with Tevin when Kieran or Rory couldn't be with him and, having nine children of her own, she knew something of babies. Rory trusted her. Once the woman showed up, Rory told her she would return shortly but didn't tell her where she was going. She didn't want the woman to alert anyone. But the cook wasn't curious and happily sat beside the sleeping baby as Rory slipped from the room.

The compound of Southwell was cold and dark but for the intermittent torches upon the walls. Rory felt like she was escaping her parents to go clubbing as she dodged a couple of soldiers and slipped from the postern gate near the kitchen. There was something wicked, disobedient, dangerous and exciting about what she was doing and she knew that Kieran would kill her if he ever found out. She was on the north side of the wall, slipping on the muddy slope as she made her way back around to the south side of the structure where the town lay nestled against the old stone walls. Once she reached the edge of the berg, she lost herself in the dark and narrow streets.

From having traveled the town with Kieran several times, she was relatively familiar with the layout. The tavern she was looking for was near the road the led into the castle, so she jockeyed through the narrow alleys and avenues until she came to a larger road that would take her to the tavern. A dog almost bit her and an escaped goat tried to ram her, but she escaped unharmed and laughed at her luck. The streets were fairly vacant, which wasn't unusual at this time of night, by the time she reached the tavern.

The innkeeper knew her on sight as Sir Kieran's wife. He greeted her immediately and took her to a warm corner near the kitchen. The man was fat, missing most of his teeth, but he could make a killer cider and if he thought it was odd that the Lady of Southwell was alone, he never said so. He presented Rory with a big mug of the mulled cider and a type of bun with cinnamon, nuts and honey. It was very good and Rory spent the next couple of hours drinking the cider and chatting with the innkeeper. After the austere conditions of Southwell where her only companions were Jeffrey and Margaret, she found the earthy personalities of the innkeeper and his wife refreshing.

Rory was enjoying herself so much, in fact, that she never heard the cries go up from the sentries on the wall of Southwell or the thunder of an approaching army. She sat tucked back in the inn, warm, dumb and happy, oblivious to what was going on outside. It only began to occur to her that something was wrong when the strong smell of smoke began to waft in through the windows and people in the inn began to chatter and run. By that time, it was too late; Southwell was sealed up tightly and Rory was caught outside the walls.

She wasn't truly panicked until she stepped outside and saw a massive army infiltrating the town. She knew what enemy soldiers did to hapless peasants and townsfolk caught in their path, and this army didn't look like the merciful type. They were beginning to light some of the homes near the walls of the fortress on fire, mostly so they could burn down the structures and move their siege engines or ladders up to the walls. Rory had been well educated on the tactics of a siege; as an archaeologist and history major, she was more knowledgeable than most. And she knew she had to get out of the danger zone.

Racing back into the tavern, she didn't see the innkeeper or his wife. It looked as if everyone had fled. Rory dashed out the back of the structure and into an alley, only to nearly be run over by the townspeople fleeing the attack. She bolted to her left, hoping to make it back to the postern gate, which would undoubtedly be locked and manned. The Southwell soldiers would recognize her and let her in; that is, providing she survived. She was terrified.

Racing down the alley, she had to intersect with a major avenue before she would be able to lose herself in the maze of small streets and alleys nearer to the fortress. That meant she would be exposed to the incoming army for a time, as the avenue led directly off the main road to the castle. But she had to take the chance. As she prepared to bolt across the avenue, she was almost run over by a knight on a huge, black charger.

The horse snapped and kicked out at her, and Rory screamed in fright as she tried to turn around and go back in the direction she had come. But the knight on horseback was fast. He noticed her fine cloak instantly and, being a trained observer, immediately followed. He knew she was no ordinary peasant and curiosity, more than anything, demanded he follow.

Rory soon had what she had feared; a pursuer. So much for trying to stay out of sight. But she would not give in so easily and ducked into a narrow walkway between two buildings. The knight could not pursue on his steed but he did not give up. He paused a moment to determine in which direction she was heading and moved to cut her off.

He almost succeeded, too, but Rory heard the horse coming and she shifted back on her path, racing in the other direction. When the knight realized he'd been fooled, he spurred his charger down the road and parallel to Rory's path. Rory thought she was being clever by backtracking again and ending up back near the tavern. But the knight was clever, too. Just as she emerged from a small pathway, he was there to grab her.

He had her by the neck with a big, leather glove and Rory fought viciously.

"Let me go!" She swung her fists at the hand holding her. "Let me go!"

The knight didn't reply nor comply. He shifted his grip on Rory and got her by the arm, yanking her up over his lap. Rory yelped in pain as her arm was practically wrenched from its socket, grunting when she was thrown over his thighs. She twisted and fought, but he managed to hold her fast with one hand while directing the charger with the other.

Terrified nearly out of her mind, her struggles turned violent. Even as he directed the horse out of the town, Rory swung her legs around, trying to kick the horse, anything to distract the knight so she could break free. He ended up winding his hand in her hair to hold her fast, yanking on it when she grew particularly severe in her struggles. At one point, she whacked the horse in the hindquarters with a foot and the horse reared up and danced around. Bracing herself against the saddle, she shoved hard in the hopes of breaking free. The horse bucked, she pushed, and she and the knight went flying off onto the soft, damp grass.

The knight landed on top of her, knocking the wind out of her. Rory lay in the grass, gasping for air, as the man pushed himself up. The first thing he did was throw up his visor and glare at her.

"Foolish wench," he snarled. "You will pay for that."

Stunned and gasping, Rory tried to get to her hands and knees. She flopped backwards, away from the knight, trying to crawl away.

"Leave me alone," she hissed. "Leave me alone or my husband will kill you."

The knight made a swipe for her and missed. "You will not escape me, wench."

Rory kicked at him and he grabbed her foot, tripping when she struggled and ending up on top of her again. Rory shoved at him, getting a good look at his features for the first time, and stopped shoving. Looking back at her were very familiar eyes.

It was Bud Dietrich.

Or, at least, the man looked like Bud. There was no one else in existence who had such ice-blue eyes and such a square-jawed, strong face. There was joy and comfort in the realization, but there was also astonishment. Rory's eyes widened and her mouth popped open in surprise.

"Bud?" she whispered.

The knight's icy eyes gazed at her a long moment before reaching out to grab her by the wrist. He hauled Rory to her feet.

"Who are you?" he demanded. "And no lies, 'else my justice shall be swift."

Rory rationally knew that he wasn't Bud, but he sure looked like him. She was torn and bewildered by the sight, confused as hell. Everything she'd ever heard about reincarnation or past lives suddenly popped into her head, a screaming mass of information that she struggled to shove aside. It's not Bud, she told herself. It's not him!

"My name is the Lady Rory Hage," she told him as evenly as she could. "My husband is Kieran Hage. I know you've heard of him."

The knight's eyes glimmered strangely and he looked oddly torn himself. He looked the woman up and down, noting her fine clothing, her exquisite face. She was a fine beauty, indeed, more than a fitting bride for the mighty Hage family. But the fact that she had been running around alone in the town had him puzzled. Suddenly, his anger wasn't so great. He simply looked stunned and suspicious.

"Hage?" he repeated. "You are Kieran Hage's wife?"

Rory nodded, trying to yank her hand out of the man's grasp. "Yes," she grunted as she futilely yanked again. It never occurred to her that she should not have told him who she was. She thought that Kieran's name would strike fear into the man's heart and he would instantly release her. "Let me go and I won't tell him that you tried to abduct me."

The knight's grip wasn't lessening; if anything, it tightened. He suddenly yanked her towards him, twisting her wrist. Rory yelped in pain as she ended up pressed rather closely against him.

"No lies, woman," he growled. "I told you I would…"

"I'm not lying," she insisted hotly. "My name is Rory Hage and if you don't let me go, I'll make sure my husband breaks every bone in your body before he cuts your head off. Let me go!"

The knight didn't obey. He held her tightly, a thousand thoughts rolling through his head. If what the lady said was true, he had the key to the siege of Southwell within his grasp. It was a huge stroke of good fortune. And he was sure the prince would be very interested to know of the woman.

Very interested, indeed.

CHAPTER TWENTY-TWO

"LADY HAGE," THE prince's voice was soft, seductive. "I had heard you were an exquisite beauty. I can see that the rumors were true."

Rory could hardly believe the situation she found herself in. It was dark in the wide and elaborate tent, with small braziers with glowing peat set intermittently in the area to warm up the space. The entire tent was as lavish as anything she had ever seen, with heavy, hide-covered chairs and a carved oak table that must have taken a dozen men to move. As she sat on a very soft chair somewhere in the middle of the tent, a man who had been introduced as John Lackland stood near the door, his dark eyes appraising her.

As Rory gazed back, she could see that every bad thing ever said about the man was true. He reeked of filth and evilness; she could just feel it. All of the carvings or paintings she had ever seen of the man didn't do him justice. He was nothing like the homogenized artist's portraits. He looked like a serial killer.

She tried to stay clinical about meeting him. She tried to stay calm as he moved closer. She inspected his long, thin fingers, his surprisingly rotund body, and the oddly smooth skin on his cheeks and neck. No stubble, no scars. The man had a lovely complexion. He had dark, stringy hair that framed his rather thin face and one droopy eyelid that gave him a rather dimwitted appearance. But she knew he wasn't dimwitted; the man was legendary in his cunning and she was truly in awe. But she was also scared to death. It was well documented what the man was capable of.

John entered the room silently, almost as if he floated over the fine carpets that covered the grass beneath the tent, before coming to rest in front of Rory. The weight of the moment wasn't lost on her and she fought to keep her panic down. She may as well be facing off against Genghis Khan for all of the terror she felt.

"It is a pleasure to meet you, Lady Hage," John said pleasantly, his gaze devouring her. "I understand that you returned with your husband from the Crusades. Odd that you were in The Levant; what were you doing there?"

Rory realized she was trembling. She also realized he was looking for an answer. "I, uh, accompanied my brother there," she replied, quivering, and then added almost as an afterthought: "My lord… uh, Your Grace."

John smiled faintly, revealing yellowed teeth. "Your brother took you on a military quest?"

Rory tried to stick to the story that she and Kieran had told everyone. "My parents are dead. I had no one else, so I went with my brother."

John digested her statement, scrutinizing her closely. "Where are you from, Lady Hage?"

She sighed faintly, miserable, not wanting to divulge too much. "From… from Ireland, Your Grace."

John nodded as if he understood completely. "That explains much," he muttered to perhaps the half-dozen advisors that were standing in the shadows behind him. "She has the beauty of the Irish and the foolishness of them as well."

The men behind the king tittered and Rory lowered her gaze at the insult. Unsure as to what the prince's intentions were, she thought, perhaps, her best option would be to try and take control of the situation and hope that she could negotiate her way out of this. She could hear Kieran in her mind, over and over, *you will stay with me for your own safety*. The man was always insisted she stay with him, or his brothers, never straying alone. For a modern, independent woman, she had resented what she saw as a controlling measure even though she knew, deep down, that it was for her own good. But she realized now, too late, that he'd truly meant to protect her. This was a perfect example. She should have never strayed from the castle. God help her, she knew it. And now she was in deep, horrific trouble.

"Your Grace," she spoke boldly, hoping she could assert herself and convince the prince of her wishes. "As pleased and honored as I am to meet you, I really must ask that you allow me to return to the castle. I have a baby who needs me and I really must get back to him."

John just looked at her. Then, his thin eyebrows lifted. "Ah, yes," he nodded as if suddenly remembering. "The child. I had heard that you bore your husband a son."

She nodded. "May I please return? The baby will be awake for his midnight feeding soon."

John looked as if he were actually considering her request. Could it really be that easy? she thought anxiously. But she never, for a moment, truly believed that.

"I would be happy to consider your request, Lady Hage, if you will do something for me," the prince countered.

Rory was torn between fear and agreement. "What would that be?"

John's warm expression faded as he gazed into her eyes. Rory had difficulty looking into his droopy-eyed faced. He was a genuinely unhandsome man.

"All of this can be avoided, you see," he explained as he waved his hands around at the tent, the people behind him, "if you will simply help me gain something that your husband holds. That is why I am here, you know. Your husband has something that belongs to me and I want it."

"What is that?"

John's joviality faded entirely. "When he returned from The Levant, he brought back with him something that was meant for the English crown. I want it."

Rory was genuinely puzzled. She had no idea of John's demands to Kieran the night he had come to Southwell those months ago, the night when Simon had died. She had no idea the prince had become obsessed with the Crown of Thorns. It was something that Kieran had never discussed with her, as he didn't consider it of particular concern to her. She was understandably confused.

"What did he bring home?" she asked.

John watched her face as she spoke, watching the soft pout of her lips. He had already decided the moment he laid eyes on her that he was going to have this woman. The more she spoke, the more he wanted her.

"I believe your husband calls it Christ's Diadem," he said. "Do you know of this object?"

Rory didn't know why but, at that moment, she felt like everything was lost. Any hope she had of being released was just torpedoed. Her first reaction was to deny any knowledge of it but, on second thought, it might work better if she told him the truth. It might get the prince off of Southwell's front door and back to London to where Kieran was with a thousand-man army. It was a calculated risk and she decided to go with it. She couldn't truly be in any worse trouble than she was. At least, she hoped not.

"I know of it," she replied. "It's not here. Kieran took it with him when he left for London to see de Longchamp."

She watched the prince's expression as he stared at her, pondering her reply. "Are you sure of this, my lady?"

She nodded. "Absolutely. He never lets the thing out of his sight. When he left for London, it went with him. It's not here."

John smiled, a gesture that Rory found frightening. The smile grew and Rory's trepidation exploded. Suddenly, the king was turning to the men behind him, his arms out wide as if to embrace the whole lot of them. He began laughing a weird snort-type of laugh. Rory had never heard anything like it and it was horrifying.

"He has it with him," he announced to the group. "Did you hear?"

The men nodded in various degrees of excitement, including the knight who looked exactly like Bud. Rory could see him back in the group, unemotional, watching her carefully. The prince began doing some odd dance across his carpets, turning to Rory after the first few crazy steps. He acted like a mental patient.

"A perfect situation, truly, my lady," he said happily. "Your husband has something that belongs to me. I have something that belongs to him. I think he will easily give me my crown in exchange for his wife. Do you not agree?"

Rory's jaw dropped open; she couldn't help it. But she honestly wasn't surprised. She felt about a thousand times stupider than she had when she had first entered the tent; the prince didn't miss the golden opportunity presented.

No fanfare, no beating around the bush – he saw the value of holding Rory to gain Kieran's compliance and Rory just hung her head. The tears were there but she fought them off, feeling sick and hollow and deeply sorrowful. She couldn't believe she had gotten herself into such a horrific mess.

She wondered if Kieran would ever forgive her.

☙

Tower of London
Two weeks later

"KIERAN!" ANDREW WAS taking the stairs two at a time as he moved to the fourth floor of the White Tower at the Tower of London. In his hand, he held a long, yellowed scroll and he extended it to his brother as he entered the small, well-lit room in a corner turret.

"This just arrived by messenger for you," he told him.

Kieran was standing over a table with a large vellum map on it, pocked by years of commanders and kings pouring over it, marking their positions throughout England, France and the rest of the continent with great iron pins. Richard had used it and Henry before him. William de Longchamp sat next to the table, an old man who had seen much in life, as he and Kieran debated Richard's current status. It was all they had spoken of for nearly a month, the whereabouts of the monarch and the general theories related thereto.

The missive was an interruption into their latest conversation as Kieran took it from his brother.

"Who is this from?" he asked before he looked at the seal, knowing that curious Andrew would have already inspected it.

But Andrew's face showed no joy or curiosity with the missive. In fact, he looked rather hesitant and Kieran had no idea why until he uttered one word.

"John," he said softly.

Kieran wasn't so quick to panic. Calmly, he inspected the seal and noted that it was, indeed, the prince's mark. There was no reason for him to be apprehensive as he slid his finger along the edge of the vellum to break the seal.

"He is probably demanding the diadem again," he grunted. "This will make four such demands in the past year. I have yet to respond to any of them."

Andrew leaned against the wall, crossing his arms. "He is having quite a tantrum, isn't he?"

Kieran snorted in agreement as William spoke up. "The diadem of thorns?" he clarified.

Kieran nodded as the parchment popped open. "I told you he wants it badly," he said. "He insists that it belongs to him."

Old William simply rolled his eyes, reaching for his pewter chalice of ruby red port. "Everything belongs to him," he muttered into his cup. "The entire world belongs to him. That is why we find ourselves in this predicament."

Kieran grinned as he moved away from the table and began to read. Andrew wasn't paying attention to him, looking at the map table instead, until Kieran suddenly came to a halt somewhere near the lancet windows that flooded the room with cool, white light. As Andrew looked up at his brother, he noticed that the man seemed to have lost his coloring. Concerned, Andrew pushed himself off the wall.

"Kieran?" he ventured. "What does it say?"

Kieran's hand was over his mouth as the other held the missive, now shaking. He turned away from the window, eyes still glued to the parchment, and ended up stumbling back against the wall when he tried to walk. His reaction had Andrew moving to him and William out of his seat.

"Kieran?" Andrew pressed. "What is wrong?"

Kieran tore his eyes away from the missive and looked at his brother. He couldn't even speak; he simply extended the missive to Andrew. His brother took it, deeply concerned, and began to read. About halfway through it, his eyes widened and he suddenly shouted.

"Bastard!" he yelled. "How… how in the hell did this happen?"

Kieran was almost beyond rational thought. He stood there with his hands to his mouth, his brown eyes wide with shock. William, leaning heavily on his cane, moved to Kieran and put a concerned hand on the man's shoulder.

"What has happened?" he asked quietly.

Kieran was trembling. He took his hands away from his mouth, struggling to focus. "The prince has sent me a missive to announce that he has my wife." His voice was hoarse.

"Your wife?" William repeated. "Why does he have her?"

Kieran shook his head. Then he snorted and dropped his chin to his chest, overwhelmed with the news. "The missive was another demand for the diadem, as I suspected," he mumbled with great irony. His great head came up. "But this time, it is John who holds the power to force me to comply. He proposes an exchange – my wife for the Diadem of Christ."

Andrew was livid. He threw the parchment on the dusty wood floor of the chamber and stomped to the door like a madman.

"I shall gather the army, Kieran," he announced. "We shall be ready to leave by sunset."

Kieran could only nod as his brother stormed off, cursing to the rafters. They could hear him as he moved back down the stairs. William stood there with Kieran a moment before going to retrieve the fallen parchment. He hobbled over with his cane and slowly reached down to pick up the missive. After reading it thoroughly, he set it on the table and passed a concerned glance at his young friend.

"He wants the diadem badly," he commented. "I would not have suspected him to resort to this kind of treachery."

"And why not?" Kieran half-muttered, half-demanded. "He is capable of worse."

William knew that, perhaps better than anyone. "He says that he has taken her to Winchester," he said, almost casually. "What do you intend to do?"

Kieran was struggling with his composure and his panic. But he couldn't hold it back entirely and sank into the nearest chair. He put his hands over his face.

"How?" he breathed, removing his hands after a moment. "How did he get to her? Southwell is locked tight. There is no way he could have gotten inside to get her. And what of my son? Where is he? He does not mention my son."

"He does not mention him because he does not have him," William was trying to reassure him. "He would have said so. You know John well enough to know that he would gloat."

Kieran was sick to his stomach, feeling more anguish than he ever thought possible.

"Dear God… Libby," he breathed, raking his fingers through his hair nervously. "How did John get to her? Why did I have to hear this from him and not my father? Where has my father been during all of this?"

William could see how devastated Kieran was, which was something of a shock considering that Kieran was the strongest man he knew. He had spent the past month hearing of Kieran's wife and child, a woman he clearly loved and a child he worshiped. He'd known Kieran for years and had never seen the man so happy or strong. This latest missive was a blow and William could see that Kieran was struggling not to crumble.

"Your father must have a good reason," he said, trying to sound firm. "Get hold of yourself, man. You will be of little help to your wife if you fall apart. She needs your level head."

Kieran glanced up at the old man, knowing his words were true. But it was easier said than done. Still, he had a point and the more Kieran thought on it, the more enraged he became. It shifted his focus off of his devastation and spurred him into action. He suddenly bolted from the chair, almost knocking William off his feet. He reached out to steady the old man apologetically, but William did nothing more than wave him off.

"I have been shoved aside by better men than you," he quipped, a grin on his old lips. He could see Kieran's expression soften in appreciation and he gave the knight a gentle shove. "Go and do what must be done. I will be here when you return."

Kieran nodded, suddenly looking hesitant and sorrowful. "The diadem," he said. "As much as I revere Richard, my wife's life is worth more to me. I am afraid that I must retract my offer of the diadem to pay for Richard's ransom."

William nodded. "I knew that your offer was rescinded the moment you read John's missive," he replied. "Moreover, we do not yet know if Richard has been kidnapped. We've not received a ransom demand yet."

Kieran thought back to everything his wife had told him, events that were now coming to pass. "You will," he muttered. "When you do, I will provide fifty thousand crowns for his return. Remember that."

"Fifty thousand crowns?" William repeated, incredulous. "Are you so certain of this, Kieran?"

Kieran nodded. "Do not ask me how I know because you would not believe me," he put a giant hand on the old man's shoulder. "I will contribute what I can towards the king's release. But for now, I must go retrieve my wife. That is my more pressing task."

"Go," William ordered softly. "Give John what he wants and regain your lady."

Kieran simply nodded, his mind moving in a thousand different directions. The diadem, the very reason he believed that he and Rory had been returned to his time, was going to be used for a purpose unlike any they had envisioned. The path they were on was taking an odd and unpleasant turn.

Descending the Tower stairs, he ran into Andrew again as he neared the entry level. Andrew had, in his hand, a missive from Jeffrey Hage. It had just arrived, minutes after the missive from John. Kieran didn't have to guess what it said; he already knew. At least he thought he did. With shaking hands, he opened it.

When he read the part describing Tevin's safety and constant appetite, he openly wept.

☙

WINCHESTER CASTLE HAD been built in 1067, a year after William the Conqueror had taken control of England. It had been the seat of government for quite some time until the government was moved to London, so it was a strong and well-historied castle. It was also impenetrable, dank, gloomy and cold, smelling of dirt and rot and ghosts. It was a horrid and creepy place.

It had been Rory's home for almost two weeks. As she sat by a thin lancet window, gazing into the cloudy countryside beyond, her dulled mind mulled over the past thirteen days and what had brought her to this point.

When she'd realized the prince intended to abduct her, she had turned into a wildcat. She'd tried to escape and ended up slugging it out with the Bud look-alike knight, a man who was strong and muscular for his average frame. But the man had finally subdued her and had taken her to another tent, where he tied her up and left her sitting on wet grass for the remainder of the night. When the army had pulled out at dawn, she had gone with them. But it had been kicking and screaming the entire way.

Traveling with Kieran, in spite of the primitive conditions, had been a cakewalk compared to traveling as a prisoner of the prince. The ropes she had been tied with irritated her damp skin and she had ridden in the back of a wagon, tied up, for days. The only time she was untied was to allow her to eat and relieve herself, and then she was tied right back up again. The welts around her wrists were bleeding and, she was sure, were becoming infected. More than that, she traveled in the clothes she had been captured in. And although they were well made and fine pieces of clothing, they weren't holding up well over the days of travel. By the time they reached Winchester, they were damp, dirty and reeking. Rory had never been so miserable in her entire life.

At Winchester, she was locked in a room in the oddly shaped keep, an extremely small chamber with a stool in it, a filthy disgusting vessel she assumed was a chamber pot, and nothing else. It was horrifying beyond belief. But she was grateful that they had at least untied her; the wounds around her wrists and ankles were in various degrees of irritation and she had a nice infection going on her right ankle.

With no antibiotics, she was very concerned that the infection would rage out of control. When they brought her food on the second night of her arrival at Winchester, it included a big loaf of yeasty bread. She soaked the bread in the wine that accompanied the meal and applied it to the wound, hoping the alcohol and bread would kill whatever was breeding on her skin. It didn't cure it but it seemed to ease it.

Oddly, the prince had stayed away from her. From everything she'd read about the man, she had expected a daily rape attempt. But he'd stayed away and she was very curious as to why; thankful at the reprieve, but nonetheless curious. When her thoughts weren't full of fear for the prince's appearance at any moment, they were centered around Tevin and Kieran.

She wept almost hourly for the baby. Although Tevin had started eating solid food, he was still nursing and she was deeply fearful and concerned over his health. Never mind that her breasts had been painfully engorged for about a week before finally drying up; her little boy was without her and she missed him with wild desperation.

But one thought kept her sane. She knew Margaret and knew the woman would stop at nothing to ensure that Tevin remained happy and healthy. That was a great comfort to her, knowing he was undoubtedly very well taken care of. But almost more than her fears and concerns for Tevin were her fears and concerns for Kieran. She knew that the prince had sent word to him of her abduction and she knew that Kieran was more than likely already on his way to Winchester to negotiate her release. She was vastly fearful for her husband, knowing he would move heaven and earth to rescue her, including giving up the Diadem of Christ. There was no doubt in her mind that Kieran would hand it right over. She sincerely hoped it would be that simple to gain her release but, somehow, she didn't think so. Something told her to expect the worst.

Rory still couldn't believe she'd gotten herself into such a predicament. She promised God that if she made it out of this safely, she would never again disobey Kieran or do anything foolish. Her situation was stupidity in the worst way because it could have been avoided. Now, Kieran and his family were at the mercy of the prince, and it was all her fault.

Leaving the window, she huddled up in the corner of the room and fell into a fitful sleep. With no bed in the room, she had slept on the floor since her arrival and was somewhat becoming used to it. When she awoke on the morning of her fourteenth day of captivity, she awoke to a stiff body and an aching right leg. Lifting up her skirt, she could see faint red streaks running up her leg from the wound that didn't want to seem to heal. She knew immediately that it was some kind of blood poisoning.

"Oh… no," she breathed, fingering the puffy wound and examining the red streaks. "God, please no. Please don't let this be as bad as I think it is."

Her leg was hot to the touch and she had never felt so much panic in her life. If untreated, a systemic infection could kill quickly. Looking over to the remains of her meal from the previous night, there was a small amount of wine left in the cup. Rory picked at the sloppy scab on her ankle and peeled it off, exposing puffy pink tissue beneath. Taking the wine, she poured it directly into the open wound. She didn't know what else to do.

It stung like crazy but she bit her lip, refusing to cry out. Eventually, the sting faded and she sat on the floor with her leg extended, letting the air get to the wound. She tried to think of everything she could about natural medicine and what could be done to ease the infection. But all she could think of at the moment was wine and the alcohol in it that killed germs, but what she had was different from common germs. She had an infection.

Focused on her leg, she was startled when the door to the chamber suddenly opened and an older woman appeared. Rory didn't say a word. She hadn't seen the woman before and she glared balefully as the woman suddenly entered the room and began snapping orders to servants out in the hall. There was a great deal of activity that Rory couldn't see and the next person who entered the room was the knight who looked so much like Bud.

He had been her jailer since the moment of her capture. She didn't even know his name; he'd never said more than two words to her. But he was always around, bringing her meals and lingering near the door. He didn't seem particularly hostile but she knew he was there to make sure she didn't escape. He stood back out of the way as several servants rushed in and, suddenly, the little chamber was awash with activity. Rory huddled back against the wall, uncertain, angry, ill and fearful of what was going on.

A big tub was brought in and there were piles of material and other items being brought into the room. Several servants began filling up the tub with hot water; Rory could see the steam rising. As she watched from her perch against the wall, a tub was filled, bedding was put on the floor, and someone even brought in a bucket of smoldering coals meant to give off heat. The mature woman snapped orders, shoved people around, and finally got the entire room organized with a great deal of help. Then she chased the servants out, politely asked the knight to leave, and turned her focus to Rory once the door was shut.

Rory was still glaring up at her. The woman didn't say a word, patiently extending her hand; the implication was obvious. Ill, exhausted and dirty, the lure of the hot tub was too much to resist and Rory stood up on unsteady legs, ripping off her dirty clothing and throwing herself into a tub that, she realized as she sank into it, was full of floating rose petals. It was warm and wonderful and sweet. Settling down in the tub was the most profound physical experience of her life; greater than an orgasm, or at least it felt like it at the moment. The hot, delicious water covered her and she doused herself completely, losing herself in the joy of a simple luxury.

The mature woman produced a cake of whitish soap with rose petals flaked into it. She began to lather up a stiff horsehair brush with the soap but Rory, still without saying a word, reached out and took both the soap and the brush from her. She didn't want anyone bathing her, least of all one of the prince's servants. With the soap in one hand and the brush in the other, she scrubbed her entire body furiously, including her hair. As primitive as it was, it was better than the spa treatment at a five-star resort. Once Rory rinsed all of the rose soap from her hair, she felt like a new woman.

Not needed, the mature servant stood near the door in complete silence, watching Rory bathe herself. It was a little voyeuristic but Rory couldn't have cared less. She was simply glad to be clean. Even her leg felt better, having been soaked and scrubbed. The red streaks were still there but they hadn't gotten any worse. As she ran her fingers over the red streaks on her leg, the mature woman suddenly vacated the room and shut the door softly behind her.

Rory was glad to be left alone, examining her wound and hoping she could control whatever bacteria was growing with regular dousing of wine or maybe packing it with salt. There wasn't anything else she could do or use, and she didn't want to tell anyone for fear that the prince, who had so far left her alone, would be reminded of her presence. Maybe he had forgotten about her, although she knew that wasn't the case. Still, she was grateful he hadn't shown his face.

The door to the chamber opened again but Rory didn't look up. She was still examining her ankle and assumed it was the mature serving woman. But a whiff of stench hit her nostrils a split second before a voice reached her ears.

"Lady Hage," the voice was male and horrific. "I find you most compromised. I should have knocked first, I suppose. How rude of me."

Startled, Rory swung around and water sloshed out of the tub. John was standing only a foot or so away from her. His droopy-eyed gaze was lascivious and terrible. Rory's heart began to pound, terrified by the look in his eye. Everything she had feared suddenly came crashing down around her and it was difficult to maintain her composure.

"What are you doing here?" she blurted, furious and fearful.

John smiled seductively. He began to toy with the tassels on the sash binding his tunic. "I came to see how you were faring." His eyes were riveted to her naked body beneath the waterline. "I fear I've not been a very attentive host; illness has kept me away from you. My sincerest apologies."

"Illness?" Rory was backing away, moving against the opposite side of the tub as he came towards her. "Don't come near me if you've been sick. I don't want to catch anything. And a good host wouldn't be coming into the room of a bathing guest."

John laughed softly, pulling on the edge of the sash. It came untied and he let it fall to the ground. Rory nearly vomited when she realized what he was doing. He began to pull the edges of his tunic apart.

"I thought we could become better acquainted," he purred.

Rory didn't care if she was naked or not. There was a huge piece of drying linen to her right and she suddenly bolted out of the tub, yelling as she grabbed the linen.

"I don't want to become better acquainted with you," she clearly informed him. "Get out of here!"

John lifted his eyebrows, still pulling the tunic off and still advancing towards the tub. He wasn't deterred in the least.

"It is an honor to become acquainted with a prince," he told her. "I will be king someday. You will have the comfort of knowing a king found pleasure with you."

Rory was outraged, moving away from him as he came around the side of the tub. She was wrapped up tightly in the linen, trying to stay one step ahead of him.

"You're not going to touch me," she hissed. "My husband is going to kill you when I tell him what you tried to do."

That seemed to ease John's amorous intentions. His soft expression hardened and he stopped his advance. "He cannot lay a hand on me," he growled. "I am Richard's brother and by virtue of my birth, untouchable to man. If I see something that I want, I take it; daughter, wife or mother. It matters not to me. If I want you, I shall have you and your husband cannot do anything about it."

Rory's mouth was dry with fear. "Touch me and I'll kill you, you bastard," she snarled. "Get out of here before you get hurt."

John's anger was overtaking his lust. "You threaten me?"

"Absolutely!" she shouted. "If you thought I'd be an easy conquest, think again. You'll get the fight of your life."

The prince stared at her. Rory watched his dark eyes shift with the concept of his unwilling quarry. His jaw began to tick.

"Get in that tub," he rumbled. "If you do not, I shall make you wish you were never born."

"Never," she seethed.

"Do it!"

His high-pitched yell startled her but Rory kept her head about her, moving away from him as he began his advance again. He was beginning to tremble, his jaw working furiously as he advanced on her.

"Get out," she growled in return. "Get out or I swear you'll be sorry."

Threats from a woman were too much for John to take. With a

howl, he threw himself at her. Rory was fast but there was nowhere for her to run; the chamber was too small. In little time, he had her by the arms and was shoving her over to the tub. Terrified, Rory struggled to fight him off and keep the towel on her at the same time. But the towel fell away and John made a grab for her full breasts. With a yelp, Rory batted him away but he had a good grip on her. The two of them struggled viciously until Rory backed up against the tub and tripped on it. Falling backwards, she smacked her head on the wall.

Stars burst before her eyes and, for a moment, she was stunned senseless. It was enough of a break for John to yank off his tunic and pull his hose down, releasing his enormous and lopsided member. Saliva dripping from his lips, he fell to his knees and roughly pulled Rory's legs apart. He was preparing to ram himself into her tight body when Rory suddenly came around, saw what he was doing, and brought a knee up that caught him right in his aroused groin. John screamed and collapsed on the floor.

Rory was in full-blown panic mode. She scrambled out from under him, trying to shake the cobwebs out of her brain, when John reached up with one hand and grabbed her bad ankle. The pain was excruciating and she screamed, falling to the floor as he grabbed at her with his other hand, digging his nails into her tender flesh and bruising everything he touched.

"After I take my pleasure with you," John breathed as his saliva dribbled onto her skin, "I shall have you killed for your insolence. Do you hear me, you worthless, foolish whore? I will kill you!"

Rory was in a haze of panic. She knew he meant every word and she further knew that, at this moment, it was her survival against his. Rory wasn't one to give up or surrender; she had every intention of living a long and healthy life. She had been brought back to this era with a purpose. So much had happened since she and Kieran had appeared on that rocky beach in Nahariya; a love that had defied all odds to flourish and thrive. She could see Kieran's face, hear his gentle laugh and feel his loving touch. No, she wasn't ready to give up yet, certainly not to a spoiled prince who would make a terrible king. She didn't even care about the consequences of her actions at the moment. All she was concerned with was surviving and seeing her husband and son again. It was all she ever wanted. She had to live.

John was coming close. Rory's flailing hand came into contact with the stool she had been sitting on, the only piece of furniture in the entire room until just a few minutes ago. She felt the leg in her hand, hard and solid. She knew what she had to do. It was her survival against his.

Gripping the leg, she swung it at the prince's head with all her might. Even when he fell off her, she swung it again and again, frantically beating the man's head in and watching his brains bleed out on the floor. When the panic faded and the blood spattered, and she realized he was never going to get up again, it suddenly occurred to her what she had done. The bloody stool fell to the floor.

Realization turned to horror. She had just accomplished everything she had feared, everything she had instructed Kieran not to do. She'd spent the past fourteen months terrified that somehow, someway, Kieran was going to do something inadvertently to change the future. Her future; the world she knew and came from. But in a sickening twist of fate, she was the one who ultimately accomplished, in one swift and panicked action, that which she had feared more deeply than death itself. She had just irrevocably changed the course if history with a stool. She had just killed the next King of England.

Her mind began to short circuit. She could see the dead prince on the floor but she refused to believe what her eyes were telling her. It was like she was unable to process the truth. The door to the chamber opened and the knight who looked so much like Bud was standing in the doorway, shock all over his face at the scene before him. But Rory couldn't summon the energy to defend herself. She just stood there, unmoving, feeling oddly unstable as the world around her began to rock.

It was then that she noticed the chamber turning peculiar shades of gray. It was almost like she was looking at the walls from underwater; they were undulating, turning darker. It gradually occurred to her that they weren't turning darker; *she* was. She was fading. A glance to her hands showed the truth; like a ghost, she could see through them. Her greatest fear was coming to pass as somehow, someway, she had altered the future.

Generations of those who came before her were now altered, DNA that used to exist no longer existing. Somehow it carried down family lines as those who should have been killed as the result of John's reign and subsequent English history were no longer dead. Those who should be living were no longer living. Her world was changing before her.

"No!" she suddenly cried, trying to grasp for walls that were no longer solid, now like clouds. Her hands slipped through them. "Please don't let me die! Please… don't let me go! I don't want to go!"

The walls faded into oblivion and Rory with them. The sounds of her cries echoed off the old stone, still remaining, even though her body had vanished like a puff of smoke. In seconds, she was gone and the future world as she knew it also vanished. All that was left was a dead prince and a knight with a gaping mouth.

The knight with the ice blue eyes would swear to the day he died that Lady Hage had been but a dream. He couldn't explain it any more than that, not even to her devastated husband when the man had shown up with an entire army to retrieve her. The woman had disappeared right before him.

But Kieran knew what had happened. God help him, he knew.

CHAPTER TWENTY-THREE

Six months later

Present time; the University of California at San Marcos

BUD DIETRICH HAD entered the class towards the end, watching the lovely professor at the head of the class discuss the Methodology of Preliminary Excavation. It was a lower level class that was packed full of archaeology and anthropology majors, young kids with bright minds and big dreams. Bud tucked himself into the back of the class, seating himself at a desk as the class ended and the students filtered past him. A few greeted him, knowing Dr. Dietrich on sight. The man was practically a legend around the school. Big digs and a big reputation followed Bud wherever he went.

But he wasn't thinking about digs or reputations at the moment. His gaze was fixed on the pale woman who was putting her papers back into her briefcase at the front of the class. As the last few students trickled out, he rose from the desk and made his way to the front of the class. He smiled faintly when big hazel eyes noticed him.

"Hi," he said.

Rory neatly put the last of her papers in the case and closed it. "Hi," she responded.

He watched her lowered head as she fumbled with her purse, opened drawers and put pens away.

"Got time for lunch?" he asked.

She shook her head. "No," she replied. "I've got papers I need to grade before my six o'clock class."

Bud wriggled his eyebrows. "Running a little late on that, aren't you?"

Rory was forced to agree. "Yep," she shrugged. "But I'll get them done. I always get them done."

Bud sighed faintly, watching her lethargic and unenthusiastic body language; ever since that incident on that rocky beach in Nahariya, Rory hadn't been the same. Having Kieran Hage killed in front of her by a lightning strike had a devastating effect on her. At least, it was the general opinion by all who witnessed the event that Hage had been vaporized. But Rory told a different tale, one so amazing that the only person she had told it to was Bud. Anyone else would have thought she had lost her mind.

Everything about her tale had been vivid to the last detail, a story that had been so great and fantastic that it was beyond the wildest novels. She'd even had a baby in this crazy tale, a son to carry on the Hage name. She and Kieran had been deliriously happy. Trouble was, the entire happening was impossible. Somehow, the lightning strike had affected Rory's mind and that crazy tale had come forth. But she did have a rather odd rope burn on her ankle, an infected wound that had looked strange and raw. Bud still didn't know how she could have gotten it. All she would tell him was that it was because Prince John had tied her up.

He tried to push all of that out of his mind as he attempted to convince her to have lunch with him. He didn't like to leave her alone these days because she was so emotionally brittle.

"I promise that lunch won't take long," he encouraged her. "I have a request from the higher-ups I'd like to talk to you about."

Rory stopped putting things away and looked at him. Her lovely face was without color, devoid of joy.

"What request?" she demanded.

He sighed again. "Can we talk about it over lunch?"

Her features tightened. "No. Tell me now."

He scratched his crew-cut blond hair. "Dr. Buitoni is taking a leave at the end of the semester. His wife is sick, you know. He wants to spend some time with her. They want to know if you'll take his class."

Rory frowned. "He teaches Medieval History."

Bud nodded slowly, averting his gaze. For some reason, he just couldn't look at her. "With your expertise in the field, they were hoping..."

She slammed the drawer on the desk and cut him off, grabbing her purse and her briefcase as she pushed past him. "No," she said firmly. "I'm not going to do it."

Bud tried to stay calm as he followed. "Rory, honey, Medieval History is right up your alley. You know it like..."

She suddenly stopped, whirling on him. "No, I don't know it, Bud," she hissed. "You know I don't know it anymore. What the history books say happened in Medieval England is not the history I know. I told you that. It's not the same. It hasn't been since that day in Nahariya."

They'd had the same argument for the past six months. It never got any better. She wouldn't return to the dig in Nahariya, instead choosing a professorship at the university. The love she'd had for excavation and archaeology seemed to have gone out of her and she pigeonholed herself in a classroom. So the university had put Dr. David Peck in charge of closing down the Nahariya dig and offered Bud an opportunity to go to Cyprus on a high-profile excavation.

But Bud had turned the offer down simply so he could remain with Rory. He was deeply worried for her with everything they had been through. He just couldn't leave her but, at times, it was trying. He grunted softly to her statement, with lagging patience.

"Honey, whatever made you think that John Lackland lived to be king, spawning generations of Plantagenets from his paternal line, is just some wild dream you had," he repeated what he'd told her many times. "Do you know what a horrible king he would have been and how England would have gone to the dogs? It would have been devastating. Whoever murdered that man did the world a favor."

"It was *me*," she hissed deliberately, her hazel eyes flashing. "I've told you a hundred times that it was me. I did it. I changed history!"

Bud sighed and averted his gaze, scratching at his head again. He just didn't know how to respond to her when she got like this.

"That's impossible and you know it," he told her. "I just don't know what to do anymore. Something has happened to you and I just can't fix it."

Rory stared at him, feeling that familiar sick feeling come over her again. The guilt, the anguish, the sorrow… she sank down into the nearest chair, feeling overwhelming desolation. She felt like a fool, the one person in the history of mankind who had actually changed the course of history and no one believed her. Maybe it was a good thing. She was guilty as sin and paying the price every morning that she woke up in this horrible modern world without Kieran beside her.

"John had a son who reigned as Henry the Third," she muttered. "Henry had a son named Edward the First who was arguably the greatest king in English history. And Edward had a son who…"

"John wasn't king, honey." Bud crouched in front of her, gazing up into her beautiful, weary face. "He was murdered before Richard returned from the Crusades. When Richard died, the royal line came from his oldest living sibling, Matilda, who married Henry the Lion, Duke of Saxony and Bavaria. Her eldest son was Henry V, Count Palatine of the Rhine who would go on to be the future King of England. The entire English line descended from him. Do I really have to explain this again?"

Rory looked at him, her eyes brimming with tears. "That's not what happened," she whispered. "Bud, you remember Kieran, right?"

"Of course."

"And you know he was a knight from Richard's Crusade, put into a suspended state by an alchemist until I woke him up."

Bud averted his gaze, scratching his neck as he thought on his answer. "I know you believed that's who he was."

"Are you seriously telling me that after everything we went through, you still don't believe he was who he said he was? I thought you believed, Bud. I really thought you did."

Bud opened his mouth to reply but a soft knock on the classroom door interrupted him. Both Rory and Bud looked up to see a man in a dark suit standing in the doorjamb. He smiled weakly when Rory and Bud looked at him.

"I'm sorry to interrupt," he said, taking a step into the room. "I was told I could find Dr. Rory Osgrove here."

Rory stood up, quickly wiping the tears from her eyes. "I'm Dr. Osgrove," she replied. "How can I help you?"

The man stepped into the vacated classroom, echoes from his expensive shoes bouncing off the ceiling. He was dark-haired, middle aged and very corporate looking.

"My name is Marc Tillery," he introduced himself. "I'm sorry if I'm intruding, but I've tried calling a few times. I've even sent a couple of emails but I got no response."

Rory cocked her head, her brow furrowed with faint recognition. "Emails? I don't think I…"

He interrupted. "I work for the firm Trent, Rosskopf, Sheppard and Jones in Los Angeles," he said. "I represent some international clients that…"

It was Rory's turn to interrupt him. She pointed a finger at him. "I recognize that name," she said. "You sent me a couple of emails about representing an international client who wanted to get in touch with me."

"Right," he nodded quickly. "It began to occur to me that in sending you those emails, it sounded like one of those internet investment scams so I thought I'd better come personally."

Rory nodded her head, somewhat suspicious yet not without interest. "You're right. It did sound like a scam," she said. "The emails were pretty vague and generic. I just deleted them."

Marc grinned. "I figured as much." His gaze drifted over the very pretty if not somewhat exhausted-looking woman. "I know they were vague, but I didn't want to put too much into writing. Emails can be hacked and all. But it's not a scam, believe me. In fact, it's all very strange but totally legitimate so I was hoping to have a moment of your time to explain."

Rory shrugged. "Sure. Go ahead." She caught sight of Bud from the corner of her eye and introduced him. "This is Dr. Dietrich. He's a colleague. It's okay to talk in front of him."

Marc greeted Bud, his gaze returning to Rory. He stared at her a moment before chuckling. "Oh, boy," he looked around for a chair and ended up sitting at one of the desks in the front row. "Where to start? I have to tell you that in my entire fifteen years in law, I've never quite seen anything like this. This is a first."

Rory set her purse and briefcase down on her desk. "A first for what?"

Marc leaned back on the chair, contemplating how he was going to explain everything. "Well," he began. "First of all, I was contacted by a colleague of mine in London, a barrister by the name of Joseph Saladin. He is a partner in a high-powered firm in London that only works with the crème de la crème of British society. You know; the old nobility and barons and such. The firm has been around for about three hundred years. One of Joseph's clients is an old family; like, over one thousand years old. He says they can trace their lineage back before the time of the Norman Conquest. Anyway, this family is one of the few left in England who still hold any power and property. They contacted Joseph to see if he could find someone to track you down."

About midway into Marc's explanation, Rory's heart began to race. The more he spoke, the more lightheaded she seemed to become. By the time he finished, she was sitting on the desk and gripping the sides of it so she wouldn't slide off.

"Me?" she repeated. "Why would they want to contact me?"

"Because," Marc continued, "they apparently have a document that is about eight hundred years old with your name on it."

Rory was having difficulty breathing. She didn't dare look at Bud, fearful of what she would see in his face. She began to shake uncontrollably.

"What..." she began, swallowed, and started again. "What is the document? What does it say?"

Marc shook his head. "That's the big mystery," he replied. "Nobody knows. It's been a family heirloom for eight hundred years, sealed up and addressed to you."

Rory struggled to maintain her composure. "Maybe... maybe it's to someone else named Rory Osgrove, somebody who lived eight hundred years ago."

Marc sighed and nodded his head. "That would make sense except it's addressed to Rory Elizabeth Osgrove, daughter of Lucas, American, Year of our Lord Twenty and Twelve. The only Rory Elizabeth Osgrove, daughter of Lucas, that we could find is you." He sat forward, shaking his head in disbelief. "Completely disregarding the fact that someone knew about America eight hundred years ago, why in the hell did someone eight hundred years ago write to a person living in modern times? It doesn't make any sense."

Rory just stared at the man. Beside her, Bud was watched her pallor go from pale to paler. He knew the color was gone from his face, too, because the crazy story she had told for the past six months suddenly wasn't so crazy any longer with this bizarre little twist. He was fairly shaken himself and the message didn't even involve him. Clearing his throat softly, he turned to Marc.

"Where is this letter?" he asked.

Marc's dark eyes moved to him. "The family has it," he told him. "They made it very clear that they would not let it out of their possession. So my job is to find who it is addressed to and bring them to London. The problem is, I don't even know if Dr. Osgrove is the intended person. There's no way to prove it. Is it all some peculiar coincidence?"

Rory wasn't looking at him any longer; she was staring off into space, a dreamy expression on her features. There was something of longing and disbelief and joy there. She didn't say anything for several long moments. When she did speak, it was in a voice barely above a whisper.

"The name of the family is Hage, isn't it?" she murmured.

That brought Marc to his feet. "How did you know that?"

She looked at him, then, a faint twinkle to her hazel eyes. "The man who wrote it is Kieran Hage, Viscount Dykemoor and Sewall. Is that confirmation enough that I'm the person addressed on the letter?"

Now it was the lawyer's turn to look shocked. His wide-eyed gaze moved between Rory and Bud. "Then you know about this?" he asked, awed. "Who in the hell told you?"

She shook her head. "No one told me," she murmured, suddenly feeling calmer and more at peace than she had in six months. She should have expected that Kieran would have tried to communicate with her beyond the grave. Closing her eyes, she could see him again, smell him, and feel the texture of his skin. Her heart was aching with joy and longing so strongly that it brought tears to her eyes. "But I can prove that it's mine."

Marc continued to stare at her as if she had just grown another head. At a loss for words, he simply shook his head. "With that knowledge, I'd say it's proof," he agreed, eyeing her. "Care to tell me how you knew?"

She smiled, some color coming back into her cheeks. She suddenly didn't feel so alone or horrible any longer; there was so much elation in her heart that she wasn't sure she could contain it. She desperately wanted to get her hands on that letter, more than she had wanted anything in her life. "You wouldn't believe me if I told you," she said sincerely. "So when do we leave for London?"

"Whenever you're available."

"I'm available now."

Marc nodded, a bit surprised by the swiftness of her reply but pleased nonetheless. "All right, then. I'll call Joseph and tell him we're on our way."

Within twelve hours, Rory, Bud and the lawyer found themselves on a red-eye to Heathrow.

ଓ

RORY'S FIRST LOOK at Southwell had her wiping silent tears from her eyes. It was vaguely the castle she remembered, but the guidebook said that somewhere around the sixteenth century, the Hage family got the bright idea to add a wing on to the keep. Then, one hundred years after that, they added a Georgian façade which altered the entire character of the place. It was no longer the stark, imposing and warring fortress that Rory knew. It was a palace with big rooms, wide halls and gardens. Southwell had evolved.

In the rented Vauxhall sedan, Rory sat in the front seat while Bud sat in the back. Marc was driving. The road through Notthinghamshire was a two lane, little road with big hedgerows on either side; the village of Southwell was barely visible through the foliage but the castle was a clear view up on the rise. Bud leaned forward, his chin nearly on Rory's shoulder.

"So this is Southwell, huh?" he asked.

She nodded, her eyes drinking in everything. "This is it."

"Is this how you remember it?"

Rory set the guidebook on her lap, dashing away an errant tear from the corner of her eye. She had refrained, since the moment she had returned to that rocky beach in Nahariya, from doing any research or reading on Southwell or the Hage family. She didn't want to know what happened after she had left, mostly because she knew how much it would shatter her already-shattered emotions. She had decided early on that it was best just not to know what had become of those she loved. There was nothing she could do about it, anyway, and to know the fate of Kieran and Tevin would only wrack her with anguish.

For her own sanity, she didn't want to know. But now, with Southwell looming large before her, she had decided to pick up the guidebook and read what she could. She thought it might be wise so she wasn't blindsided by anything. But her heart was pounding and her hands shook, feeling more apprehension than she ever thought possible.

"No," she replied to Bud's question. "I mean, the walls look the same essentially, but everything else has changed dramatically. Even the town; it used to butt up against the walls, but now the walls are clear and the village has moved away. It's kind of weird."

Bud's chin came to rest on her shoulder as he jockeyed to get a better look. "It's a massive place."

Rory's gaze lingered on the stone walls that were faded and mossy with age. Other than natural anxiety, she wasn't sure what else she was feeling… sadness? Excitement at having returned? Anguish because this was the last place she saw Kieran and Tevin? She wasn't quite sure yet but, at the moment, the predominant emotion she was experiencing was awe; awe that Southwell was still standing after all of these years. The place was immortal.

Tillery sat in the driver's seat, hearing the soft rumblings of conversation but not really hearing what was being said over the drone of the radio. The whole situation was odd for him but it was also very intriguing. The more time he spent with Dr. Osgrove, who seemed like a genuinely sane and sweet woman, the more interested he became in the case. She still wouldn't tell him how she knew about the letter or how she knew so much about who wrote it; she simply said that he wouldn't believe her anyway. But the truth was that, at this point, he'd believe anything. The entire situation was just too weird to believe.

Southwell had a car park to the west, a neatly graveled area where a few cars were already parked. Southwell Castle was still inhabited by the Hage family yet great sections of it were open to the public. As Rory discovered, they also had weddings and other events in the castle to help pay for the undoubtedly massive upkeep.

As the car came to a halt, Rory bolted from the car without her coat and just stood there, looking at it. Bud climbed out behind her, collected her jacket, and held it as he walked up behind her. Together, the two of them just stood there and stared at the structure; Rory because she was feeling an overwhelming sense of anxiety and Bud because he was, frankly, curious about her reaction.

Marc locked the car, put on his coat, and walked up beside the pair. He stared at the castle because they were. Overhead, fat, dark clouds threatened rain and he glanced up, wondering when they were going to get soaked. He could smell the rain.

"Shall we go in?" he encouraged them. "My colleague should already be here."

As if on cue, a man in an expensive, camel hair coat stood beneath the gatehouse, waving an arm at them. Marc waved back and began walking towards the man. Bud took a few steps to follow, noticing Rory was still rooted to the spot. Her expression was odd. He put a hand on her elbow, gently pulling her forward.

"Come on, honey," he said softly. "We flew all the way here. We may as well go in."

Rory glanced at him, took a deep breath, and smiled weakly. "I guess so."

Bud didn't let go of her arm as they tramped across the wet, greet grass, making their way towards the road that led into the fortress. Rory's hazel eyes were rivet to the well-maintained, gravel road as they approached from the car park.

"Oh, my God," she breathed. "The last time I saw this road… it was muddy and full of pot holes and big rocks. It was horrible to travel on."

Bud didn't say anything. He kept his focus on the two men ahead, both of whom were now shaking hands and smiling at each other. But Rory wasn't looking at them; she was still looking at the road.

"And over there," she pointed to what was now a big, grassy area that seemed to stretch the length of the great wall. It disappeared off to the east side of the fortress and was about fifty feet in length, bordered by a ridge of short, thick, wooden posts and a road that skirted the edge of down. "That grassy area was full of Medieval homes. And right about where that street runs was the main road that led into the town."

Bud still didn't say anything as they came to the dirt and gravel road, neatly kept, that lead into the great gatehouse of Southwell. The moment Rory's boots hit the gravel, she suddenly found her attention drawn up to the castle.

It was an odd moment filled with a mixture of angst and exhilaration. She looked up, seeing the modern walls, remembering the Medieval ones. She was transported back in her memories to what had been, what she remembered. It was a comforting reflection, the last place she ever saw her husband. She could feel him everywhere.

"The last time I saw these walls, there were soldiers on them with big torches in their hands," she could feel her excitement gaining, realizing she was very happy to be back. Though her sight beheld modern visions, she could only see the Medieval memories at the moment. "They had big dogs with them, too, big greyhounds. These walls were constantly manned."

Bud looked up because she was pointing. Now he had her by the hand, leading her up the road. In spite of their reason for being here, he still wasn't sure what to believe. He was a man of science, and science dictated that things like time travel and past lives could not be proven. There had to be a logical explanation for the ancient letter with her name on it. Or maybe there wasn't. His indecision had him edgy and torn.

"And this gatehouse," Rory pointed at it as they approached. "There were two big portcullises, these big, nasty-looking things. They had modeled them to look like fangs. It was really awesome and scary-looking."

Bud suddenly came to a stop and faced her. "Honey, please do me a favor," he kept his voice down. "Please don't say any of this in front of the lawyers or the Hage family. Saying it to me is one thing, but saying it to them might give them cause to think you're crazy. You do realize how you sound, right? Put yourself in their shoes. If some woman showed up talking about having lived during Medieval times, what would you think? You'd think she was nuts. So please, for your sake, don't talk about this stuff in front of people we don't know. Okay?"

All of the joy accumulated over the past few minutes was gone from Rory's face. She looked at Bud, her expression wrought with disappointment and resignation. She knew he was right but she was still upset by his words. She wasn't crazy because everything that happened was real. Still, she understood what he was driving at. She didn't want to sound like a nut. With a faint shrug, then a nod, she silently agreed. Bud patted her hand and pulled her towards the waiting lawyers.

"Joseph, this is Dr. Rory Osgrove," Marc made the introductions as Bud and Rory came upon them. "Rory, this is my colleague, Joseph Saladin. He represents the Hage family."

Rory shook the man's hand, getting a good look at him for the first time. He was young, handsome and had a hint of Middle Eastern decent to his features. The eyes looked strangely familiar and it took her a moment to realize that he looked vaguely like Yusef. *Isn't the name Yusef a version of Joseph*? She thought to herself. Startled by the coincidence, she forced herself to come across as polite and in control.

"Nice to meet you," she said.

Saladin nodded, a half-grin on his face as he inspected Rory carefully. There was something of vague remembrance in his expression, too, one of those feelings of familiarity that he couldn't put his finger on.

"Likewise," he lifted an eyebrow. "I have wanted to meet you for a while, Doctor. Maybe you can shed some light on this big mystery."

Rory's smile faded as she gazed at the man. She wasn't sure what to say so she simply lifted her shoulders. "Maybe," she replied vaguely, her gaze moving to the courtyard beyond the gatehouse. "Is the letter here?"

Joseph nodded and began to lead them into the courtyard beyond. "It is," he replied as they emerged into the bright green, mowed and manicured courtyard. "The document has never left these walls." He suddenly put up his hands apologetically. "Let me start from the beginning and see if I can explain this satisfactorily. This letter isn't a letter proper as much as it is a scroll of parchment, rolled up and sealed. It is…"

Rory cut him off gently. "Whose seal?"

Joseph looked at her. "Sir Kieran Hage," he replied softly. "But I'm told you already know that."

Rory was trying not to get ahead of herself and keep her anxious thoughts in check but she wasn't doing a very good job. "When was it written?"

Joseph inhaled thoughtfully. "I'm told by the Hage family that it's dated March of eleven hundred and ninety-three."

Rory fell silent as they waited for her to come back with more questions but she didn't. Joseph passed a glance at Bud, a more pronounced one at Marc, before continuing.

"Kieran Hage, as you probably already know, was the eldest son of Jeffrey Hage, the fifth Earl of Newark," he went on as they neared the massive keep that hardly looked anything like what Rory remembered. "The man was a crusader during Richard the Lionheart's quest in the Holy Land but returned prior to the fall of Acre. He was a powerful man by all accounts and held several titles himself, all of which were passed to his only son."

Rory's head came up. She was suddenly fighting off a flood of tears as the man brought her son in to the mix. But she didn't miss the gist of what he had said. Kieran had returned home from the Crusades early, confirming the fact that there was no record of him ever having been excavated in Nahariya.

Rory had found in the days after her return that the dig in Nahariya was still nothing more than the excavation of an ancient trash pile, as it had been in the days before Kieran had been discovered. It was like it never progressed beyond potsherds and bits of ancient baskets; it was still stuck in the pre-Kieran discovery days. She had refused to return to the dig, not strong enough mentally to face it, which is why David Peck was sent to shut it down. In this new world, the Nahariya dig was considered a failure.

But the odd thing was that anyone who was on that rocky outcropping of beach in Nahariya remembered Kieran. Bud and David both remembered him. Rory wondered if the others there remembered Kieran, too; Darlow, the British Embassy man, or the British Marines who had also been there. She'd never contacted them to find out what they remembered. In hindsight, it didn't matter too much. History had been changed so much that she could do nothing more than accept what had happened and deal with it.

She refocused on the barrister and his comment about Kieran Hage's only son. "Are you speaking of Tevin Hage?" she asked hoarsely.

Joseph nodded, oblivious to the longing inflection in her tone. "He was a remarkable man by all accounts, very involved in royal affairs and wrote what is largely considered the basis of the United States Constitution." His gaze moved to the enormous, Georgian-style structure in front of him. "Moreover, he is widely regarded as the one who held England together through some very rough times following the death of Matilda's son, Henry V. There was a real power struggle at that point in history, if you recall. Tevin Hage was hugely influential in his time and quite well regarded."

Rory's heart swelled with pride as she heard of her son's accomplishments. She knew that Kieran would have been deeply proud as well. "I'm not surprised to hear that," she murmured gratefully. "His father set a fine example."

"You would think so, but that wasn't the case." Joseph glanced at her. "Tevin was raised by Kieran's brother, Sean, because Kieran died in the summer of eleven hundred and ninety-three. In fact, he…"

So much for dealing with the status of history; those few words had Rory bursting into hysterical tears. She would have fallen had Bud not still had hold of her arm. They were loud, painful gasps, hysterical, as Bud held her to keep her from falling. Marc even went to see if he could help, grasping her by the torso as Bud put his hands on her face and begged her to calm down. Joseph took a few steps towards the group, his brow furrowed with concern and curiosity.

"I'm sorry," he wasn't quite sure what to say. "Is… is there a problem? Why don't we go inside and sit down? Maybe Dr. Osgrove will feel better if we sit."

Bud had his hands full but he acknowledged the lawyer. "Good idea." He grabbed Rory around the waist, practically carrying her towards the massive Georgian building before them. "It's been a long flight and too much travel. Dr. Osgrove is… she's just exhausted."

Joseph bought the explanation, having no reason not to. With nothing more said, the group disappeared into the sixteenth century addition to Southwell's massive keep.

ꝏ

A HALF HOUR later, fortified by the two shots of brandy that Bud had forced her to down, Rory was seated in an enormous, Baroque-style parlor just off the main entrance to the building. Everything was lavish and over the top but not completely gaudy, decorated in shades of yellows and reds and golds. It was simply a testament to the wealth of the Hages, with pictures of Hage family members that Rory didn't recognize gracing the walls. One thing she did notice, however, was that all of the men had the Hage square jaw and many of the women seemed to have chestnut-colored hair. A coincidence? She wondered.

Marc and Joseph sat across from Bud and Rory, waiting patiently for Rory to pull herself together. Rory was coming to realize how foolish she had looked out in the courtyard and struggled not to be too embarrassed. Trouble was that she couldn't guarantee it wouldn't happen again. But she had reached the point now where she had to know everything. She'd stayed away from anything Hage or Medieval for six months. And now, she had to know everything no matter what. She took another shot of brandy before she dared continue.

"I'm sorry about that." She took a deep breath and faced the lawyers. "I guess I take my history too seriously."

Joseph watched her closely. "Not to worry, Doctor," he assured her. "Sometimes I do the same thing when I've lost a case."

Rory smiled weakly. As she prepared to reply, a man entered the hall and Joseph rose swiftly to greet him. Rory stood as well, followed by Bud and Marc. She studied the man who was amiably greeting Joseph. He was broad and fairly tall, with short blond hair that was graying at the temples. He looked like he might have played rugby at some point because of his muscular build. He had enormous hands. When he turned to Rory and extended a hand in greeting, Rory was struck by the square jaw and bright green eyes. She would have known those eyes anywhere. She had seen them, once, on a child she gave birth to. Shaken, she struggled not to come across like an idiot again.

Introductions went all around. Daniel Antony Christopher Hage, the eighteenth Earl of Newark, was a handsome man with an easygoing way about him. He insisted everyone call him Dan. Rory watched him, fascinated, because he seemed to be cut out of the same mold that Kieran and Sean had been. He was manly to a fault, intelligent and gracious. Rory sat back down in her chair, seated across from him, staring at the man because he seemed so familiar. She was so busy staring that she was caught off guard when Joseph drew her in to the conversation.

"Dr. Osgrove is the woman we have all been waiting to meet," he said to Dan. "I can't tell you how bizarre this all seems, but you wanted me to find Rory Osgrove, daughter of Lucas, so here she is. And what's even odder is that I'm told she knew the letter was from your ancestor, Kieran, before she was even told."

Dan looked at her with his bright green eyes, a faint smile playing off his lips. "Bizarre, indeed," he muttered, seeming to study her just as she was studying him. "How did you know it was from Kieran?"

Rory sighed faintly, averting her gaze as she thought of a believable answer. She had promised Bud she would be careful in what she said and she was trying to do so.

"I'm not sure," she lied. "I… I'm a Doctor of Medieval History and have done a lot of research, obviously, in the field, and I know a great deal about Kieran Hage. Can I please see the letter?"

Dan scratched his chin, snickering at her straight to the point request. "I think that can be arranged," he replied, glancing at Marc and the other men in the room as he stood up. "Would you gentlemen mind waiting here a moment? Dr. Osgrove and I will be right back."

Bud looked slightly panicked that Rory was leaving his presence but he sat tight. Rory's gaze lingered on him as she left the room, winking at him just before Dan took her into a small corridor off the main room. The corridor was narrow, opulently paneled, and led to a series of smaller rooms. When they entered the first red-wallpapered chamber, Dan shut the door behind them.

"Nosy lawyers," he muttered, grinning when Rory snickered. "Joseph will try to follow us just to spy."

She gave him a disbelieving look. "No," she drew the word out as if outraged. "Really?"

He snorted. "Really," he said. "He comes from generations of legal counsel to the Hages. He thinks he can snoop into all of my business."

Rory laughed as he led her through the red room and into another chamber, this one smaller and more cluttered. It smelled of pipe tobacco and tea. Rory came to a halt just inside the door, observing the books packed to the ceiling and taking a deep breath of the tobacco smell. Dan went to the desk that had to be three hundred years old; it was magnificent. Once she noticed the desk, she took a few steps towards it to get a better look.

"Wow," she murmured. "This desk is amazing. How old is it?"

Dan was digging in drawers, finally pulling out a key ring. He spoke as he turned to the shelf behind him, jiggled a book, and an entire shelf suddenly slid aside to reveal a wall safe.

"It was built in fourteen seventy," he replied.

Rory was amazed by both the desk and the hidden wall safe. "I'd have to say that this is seriously the coolest room in the house," she declared. "Ancient desks and hidden wall safes. It's so… so Sherlock Holmes. Are the Hounds of the Baskervilles in the next room?"

Dan laughed as the safe popped open and he pulled forth a long metal box. He set the box on the table and pulled up a chair for Rory. She ended up sitting next to him at the desk.

"No hounds," he assured her. "At least, not those types. I have a few dogs but they're house dogs. Anyway, I was hoping to get you alone. I have many questions."

She smiled faintly. "No doubt you do," she said quietly, looking to her lap.

Dan studied her a moment. She was undoubtedly beautiful, which had surprised him. He didn't know what he had expected, but a drop-dead gorgeous woman hadn't crossed his mind. His gaze lingered on her a moment before he moved to the box and, taking a small key from the same key ring that had opened the safe, used it on the box. The lid popped open and Rory looked up from her lap, seeing a yellowed scroll packed carefully in the box. She couldn't take her eyes off it, even when Dan set the keys down and looked at her.

"Now," he lowered his voice. "I sincerely cannot stress to you the importance of this document to my family, but as an archaeologist, I'm sure you can understand. This is one of the few family heirlooms we have that no one really talks about. It's sort of like the Shroud of Turin; only a select few have seen it and it drums up a great mystery for us. It's a mystery with your name on it and I would like to know what you know about it."

Rory stared at the parchment, her mind whirling with truths and deceptions. She didn't want to lie to the guy, but she wasn't too keen on telling him the truth. He might not believe her and slam the lid on the box, never to show it to her again. Still, it was worth a shot. She'd come this far so she decided to take a leap of faith. She fixed Dan in the eye.

"Your ancestor, Kieran Hage, wrote this document in the year eleven hundred and ninety-three, correct?"

"Correct."

"And he wrote my name and nationality on it, right?" Dan nodded. "It would seem so."

Rory took a deep breath and reached out, putting her soft hand on Dan's muscular, fuzzy forearm.

"Do you believe that there are things in this world that we can't explain?" When he cocked his head curiously, she explained. "Like ghosts and UFOs and stuff like that?"

He pursed his lips thoughtfully. "There's no proof of those things."

"There doesn't have to be. But do you have faith that things like that are possible?"

The twinkle was back in his bright green eyes. "Maybe."

She smiled. "Good," she whispered. "Because what I'm about to tell you is the God's honest truth. I swear I would never lie; I have no reason to. I'm not crazy and I don't do drugs. But before I say anything, I need to ask you a question."

"What's that?"

"Is there any record of Kieran having been married?"

Dan nodded. "He was, for about a year."

"What happened to his wife?"

Dan scratched his head thoughtfully again. "According to family records, she died sometime in the spring of eleven hundred and ninety-three, right about the time he wrote this letter." He cocked his head, confused. "Why? What's it all about?"

Rory smiled, understanding his confusion. "Do you know how she died?"

He nodded decisively. "Yes," he replied. "Executed by Prince John right before the prince's death, although we're not sure why she was killed. We don't have records that are that detailed."

"But Kieran had a journal. Surely he wrote about it in his journal."

Dan stared at her and Rory swore she could see the color drain from his face. His expression eventually twisted with great bewilderment. "How in the world would you know that?" he breathed.

"I know that and a lot more. Can I have my letter now, please?"

Dan shook his head, torn between extreme disbelief and, Rory thought, mounting anger. "No," he said firmly. "Not until you tell me what else you know."

"I know about the Crown of Thorns or, as Kieran called it, the diadem of Christ."

That bit of information caused Dan to bolt out of his seat with shock. It was as if he were suddenly repulsed by her but, more than that, he looked plainly ill. He ended up standing over by the wall safe, staring at Rory with his hands over his mouth. There was a huge amount of shock in his eyes. When he did speak, it came out sounding like a hiss.

"Tell me how you know about that," he demanded. "No one but the males in my family know about that. It's a family secret passed down from earl to earl, never to be revealed to outsiders. That is our treasure and ours alone. How do you know?"

Rory's gaze moved to the parchment. "If you let me read my letter, I'll tell you how I know."

Dan remained standing a moment longer before reclaiming his seat, somewhat shaken, and pulling the vellum from the steel, fireproof box. He handed it to Rory without another word.

Rory accepted the parchment, her hands quivering. She inspected the exterior, the seal, noting that it was Kieran's personal seal, and the tears began to come. She couldn't help it. Carefully, she ran her finger under the wax and popped the ancient seal. The wax remained surprisingly intact. Very carefully, she unrolled the parchment.

She struggled to blink away the tears because she couldn't read through all of the water in her eyes. But seeing the first three words at the top of the parchment had her weeping softly. She tried not to get salty tears on the ancient material as she absorbed Kieran's words, his writing, and the feel of his parchment in her hands. The more she read, the more evident her surprise became until she suddenly dropped the parchment onto the desk top, sobbing so hard that she could hardly breathe.

Dan watched her, concerned and baffled, as Rory suddenly reached out and yanked on his hand.

"Where is Kieran buried?" she wept.

Dan was both greatly disturbed and greatly confused. He instinctively grasped Rory's hand gently as if to give her comfort because the woman was seriously distressed.

"What?" his bafflement won over. "Why do you…?"

Rory was on her feet. But her feet wouldn't support her so she fell to her knees, her hands on Dan's thighs as if she were begging; begging him to understand her, begging him to do as she asked. Begging a man she had never met before. But nothing in this world had ever meant as much to her as this did.

"Please," she beseeched him. "Oh, God, please… where is he buried?"

Dan gazed down into her lovely face, finding himself swept up in her fervor whether or not he wanted to be. He just couldn't help it. Too much about this situation was bizarre and magical. There was some very small part of him that wanted to believe in the unbelievable, to solve a mystery that had been a part of his family's history for eight hundred years.

"He's at Southwell Minster," he said softly. "The entire family is buried there. Why? What in God's name does that parchment say?"

Rory was struggling to calm down; deep down, buried beneath the hysteria and tears, her level self told her that she'd never achieve her ends unless she was able to calmly and succinctly explain what needed to happen. And the only person in this world who could make things happen was seated in front of her. Still on her knees, she reached over to the table and handed him the parchment.

He took it hesitantly, eyeing her with some trepidation as he did so, but finally settled down and carefully read the secret that his family had guarded for eight hundred years. By the time he finished reading the parchment, his face was ashen.

"I… I don't understand." He looked at her, his bright green eyes wide with astonishment. "What does it all mean?"

Though there were tears still on Rory's face, she smiled. She couldn't help it. She suddenly began to laugh, looking up to the heavens as if to thank them for showing her this one final mercy. It was more than she could have ever hoped for but, given Kieran's intelligence, she wasn't surprised. He would stop at nothing to be reunited with her. She grasped one of Dan's hands tightly.

"It means that if you take me into town and open Sir Kieran's crypt,

I swear to God that you will witness a miracle," she murmured. "It means that right now, I need for you to trust me. I know this sounds absolutely crazy and I know that, if I were in your shoes, I would think that I was nuts, but I promise you that I'm not. I promise that everything will explain itself if you'll just take a very small chance and take me into town to Sir Kieran's crypt."

He stared at her, unnerved yet inherently curious. "You want me to open his crypt? I can't do that!"

Rory nodded patiently. "Yes, you can. You're the Earl of Newark and you can open your own family's crypt." She squeezed his hand, her hazel eyes moist and lovely and pleading. "I can't tell you how important this is or how this will change the way you view the world. All I can tell you is that I'm begging you to do this for a woman who had a letter written to her eight hundred years ago by your ancestor. Isn't that enough to convince you that I might be telling the truth?"

Dan just stared at her. He was, frankly, rather scared by all of this. But it wasn't enough to dampen the curiosity that was consuming him, the family mystery that was finally going to be solved. Too much about this circumstance was strange enough to cause him to think he might want to see what she was talking about. Odd clues from an eight hundred-year-old letter had him seriously considering it.

He let out a heavy sigh. "All right," he muttered, standing up and pulling her off the floor. "I'll take you there. But you tell me one thing and you be perfectly truthful. Who are you and why is this letter written to you?"

Rory wiped the moisture away from her eyes, facing Dan with a clear and level head for nearly the first time since their introduction.

"May I ask you a question first?" she ventured, speaking quickly before he could interrupt her. "Do you know the name of Sir Kieran's wife?"

His brow furrowed as he looked at her, an eyebrow lifting thoughtfully. He let go of her hand and made his way over to one of the innumerable bookshelves in the room and began thumbing through several huge, leather-bound volumes. He finally came to the one he was looking for, pulled it out, and began to thumb through it. Rory stood on pins and needles, watching him as he slowed in his perusing and came to rest on a particular page. About halfway down the sheet, he found what he was looking for. He read it back to her.

"Sir Kieran was married to an Irish heiress." He held the book out so he could read it better; he didn't have his glasses handy. Suddenly his eyes widened and his head came up, his accusing gaze locking with hers. "Roisin-Elizabeth."

Rory's lips creased with a smile. "Not Roisin," she said softly. "Rory Elizabeth. Your chroniclers didn't get it right. He called me Libby because he didn't like Rory. He thought it was a man's name."

Dan's eyes threatened to pop from his skull as he glanced back at the book. He just didn't know what to say. He finally closed the book and set it to the nearest table, all the while looking bewildered and lost. Rory went over to him.

"Please," she begged softly. "Take me to Southwell Minster and be a part of something that no one else in history has been a part of. Please?"

Dan stared at her, unsure what to think or believe any longer. Before he realized it, he had his car keys and they were headed out to the Land Rover. Rory jumped into the passenger side and Dan tore out of the bailey, kicking up the very carefully kept gravel drive. Since the castle and grounds were just to the northeast of the church and less than a half-mile distance, they would make it to their destination in a matter of minutes.

And the minutes were ticking.

CHAPTER TWENTY-FOUR

SOUTHWELL MINSTER WAS a large cathedral near the center of modern Southwell that had been built one hundred years before the Norman invasion. It was an enormous place with two beautiful spires that soared into the blue expanse of sky. Rory had seen it before, eight hundred years ago when it didn't look nearly as it did now. Several transformations had taken place. Dan made two sharp, left-hand turns and ended up in the driveway of Southwell Minster. But the big, iron gate was locked so he left the car in the driveway as he and Rory jumped out and ran down the long, dirt drive to the church.

Southwell Minster was surrounded by a well-manicured graveyard but the crypts of the nobles were, as in most other cathedrals, situated inside the church. Rory rushed into the sanctuary on Dan's heels, noticing the beautifully kept church and soaring Gothic ceiling. They had never put permanent pews in and folding chairs, in neat rows, lined the floor.

Rory bolted after Dan as he raced to the front of the church, leapt right up on the pulpit, and continued back down the aisle that divided the choir loft. In the very back of the church was a room, separated from the rest of the church by an ornately carved Gothic stone wall called a pulpitum.

Dan disappeared into the room and Rory immediately after him. But as soon as Rory charged in, she came face to face with several crypts, all of them with beautifully carved effigies. She slowed her pace. There was something respectful and holy about a place where the dead maintained their eternal rest. Dan was reading the names on the crypts until he came to one near the south side of the room.

"Here," he motioned Rory over. "Here he is."

Rory's heart was pounding in her ears as she moved to the crypt, noting the spectacular effigy on the top of it. She drew close, feeling more reverence and emotion than she ever thought possible as she gazed at Kieran's effigy. She could see his profile, the sightless stone eyes, and the helm still on his head exactly like the one he had worn during Richard's Crusade. She had seen that helm on him many a time.

With tears in her eyes again, she reached out a delicate hand, running gentle fingers on the bridge of the nose. Gazing into the stone face, she was unaware when her tears fell and created small, dark spots on the porous rock. The moment was spiritual, emotional, and powerful. She couldn't even put it into words. She was so close to Kieran that she could almost taste him.

As she reverently touched the effigy, Dan walked around the entire crypt, inspecting the beautiful stone box with scenes from the Third Crusade carved into it, looking for a way in. He finally stopped, put his hands on his hips, and shook his head.

"I've seen this thing many times but never paid much attention to it," he said. "It's really remarkable."

Rory sniffled faintly, not looking up from the effigy that had all of her attention. "More remarkable than you know," she murmured. "How can we open it?"

Dan scratched his head. "You know that they really cemented these things down. I'm not sure there's an easy way to get into it."

As he stood there and speculated, a small man in ecclesiastical garb entered the room. His pale blue eyes were curious until he recognized Dan. Then he held out his hand affably.

"My lord," he greeted, shaking the earl's hand happily. "Very nice to see you today. To what do we owe the pleasure of your visit?"

"Reverend Hogan," Dan greeted, suddenly wondering what sort of idiot he was about to come off looking like. He was the earl, after all, and had a reputation to uphold. But to hell with it. "I need to get into this crypt. Do you have any suggestions as to how we can open it?"

Reverend Hogan tried not to look too shocked. "Get into it?" he repeated. "Why on earth do you need to get into it?"

Dan could see that the reverend thought he was mad. He wasn't sure he could adequately explain the need.

"I've recently discovered that there is something of extreme value to my family buried with this knight." He hoped that God wouldn't punish him for lying to a man of the cloth. "I need to get in here. Is there any possibility you can help me?"

Hogan's white eyebrows lifted. "But… my lord, I'm sure you understand that this crypt is of great historical significance. The age alone is…"

"I understand all of that and I will pay to replace it," Dan cut the man off. "I will also pay to re-roof the pepperpot spires on the cathedral. I know you have been trying to raise money for that cause. I will pay for whatever the donations don't cover if you'll help me get into this crypt."

Hogan stared at him. His gaze inevitably moved to the lovely woman standing by the crypt, gazing so lovingly at the effigy. He sensed that she had something to do with the earl's request and to say that he was confused was to put it mildly. He finally shook his head.

"The Very Reverend Loring will be very thankful for your generosity, of course," he said. "But we should probably discuss with him the possibility of opening this crypt."

Dan stood his ground. "It's my family's crypt and I want it open. There's no law that says I can't open it."

Hogan wasn't about to tangle with the earl. He'd known Dan Hage since he had been a young boy, following his career through Eton and Sandhurst, a career in the Royal Marines and even a couple of years with the Leicester Tigers Rugby Club. Dan was a fine, strong example of the current British aristocracy. But the man didn't hear the word "no" very often and Reverend Hogan didn't want to offend him. He was forming his careful reply when three more men suddenly appeared in the old room. Startled, he turned to see two men in suits and one very blue-eyed, crew-cut man in casual jeans. The man with the ice blue eyes moved directly to the woman, ignoring everyone else.

"Rory," Bud went to her, deeply concerned. "What happened? We saw the earl's car leave and thought we'd better follow. Why are you here?"

Rory grabbed Bud by the arms, her hazel eyes wide with delirium. "I can't explain it right now," she insisted quietly. "We need to get this crypt open. Dan is trying to convince the reverend."

Bud looked to the earl, confused, before turning back to Rory. "Why do we need to open it now?"

"Please, Bud," there was great urgency in her voice. "You're the resident genius. Do you see a way into this?"

Bud's face was contorted with confusion but he'd learned long ago not to argue or make demands of Rory. It was better just to do what she wanted and ask questions later. His focus turned to the crypt.

"Seriously?" he asked. "You want to open this? It's hundreds of years old, Rory. It's a priceless artifact."

"I know that," Rory nodded eagerly. "But we need to open it."

"Whose is it?"

"Kieran's." She met Bud's surprised gaze with calm reassurance. "Can you please figure out how to do it, Bud? Please?"

His gaze lingered on her a moment before returning it to the crypt. He put his hand on the slab that held the effigy, tried to move it, before bending over to examine it more closely.

"Are you okay with this, Lord Hage?" Bud asked as he practically stood on his head in order to gain a better look at how the slab lid fit atop the sarcophagus. "It doesn't look like it will be a problem to lift this top with some manpower and crowbars, but it's going to end up on the floor and damaged. We don't have a crane to support it. We'll have to let it drop."

Dan waved a hand. "I'll get it fixed."

Bud stood up and looked at him. "This effigy is eight hundred years old." He lifted an eyebrow. "We'll be damaging a pristine artifact."

"Bud!" Rory hissed through clenched teeth. "What are you doing?"

He looked at her. "Making sure Lord Hage understands what will happen if we pry this off without taking the time to properly support it. It's going to fall over and probably break."

Rory's expression was both serious and pleading. "What's inside is more important," she whispered. "As much as I hate to see the effigy of my husband damaged, I'm willing to take the risk. Please, Bud, you have to trust me."

Bud's gaze lingered on her a moment longer, knowing they had come this far. They couldn't turn back now. "All right," he sighed reluctantly, looking at the reverend. "If you have a couple of crowbars, we can probably slide this off."

Reverend Hogan looked stricken. "I've not given permission yet."

"I have," Dan said in a tone that suggested he not be disobeyed. He looked at Reverend Hogan. "Go get what he needs. I'll take full responsibility."

The reverend hesitated a moment before very quickly walking away. Once he left the room, Saladin went over to Dan to engage him in quiet conversation while Bud continued to silently examine the crypt. Rory just stood there, staring at the effigy, her mind already with Kieran deep inside the stone. Every fiber of her being was reaching out to touch him. Marc wandered up behind her, watching her as she stared at the crypt.

"Did the letter tell you anything?" he asked softly.

Snapped from her train of thought, Rory turned to him. "We're about to find out."

"Then it really *was* meant for you?"

She nodded and returned her attention to the crypt. As Marc remained behind her in confused silence, Rory's attention turned to Bud as he moved around the crypt and ran his fingers in the crevice between the lid and the sarcophagus. Nobody said a word while Bud examined, Rory stood, and Dan observed. The lawyers seemed to be the only ones out of the loop, truly clueless as to what was about to take place. But that ignorance was about to end.

Reverend Hogan returned a short time later with a crowbar, a metal shovel, and two teenage boys. The boys were carrying the implements.

"This is all we had in the gardener's shed," he told Dan. "Will these work?"

Bud reached over and took the crowbar from a red-haired, freckle-faced kid of about fifteen. He tested the weight; it was a solid, heavy bar. He slung it over one shoulder and took the metal shovel; it, too, was heavy and well made. He inspected the rounded end of it and shrugged.

"We can give it a shot," he said, handing the shovel over to a surprised-looking Marc. "I'll use the crowbar to lift and you use the shovel to shove it forward. Lord Hage, why don't you, Saladin and the boys shove from this end? Let's get the momentum working in the same direction."

Rory stood back as Bud positioned everyone around the crypt. Hands folded before her lips as if praying, she watched anxiously as Bud took charge, positioned the crowbar, and began to pry the lid off. After three grunting heaves, there was a cracking sound and the lid shifted. Dust and pebbles rained down on the floor as Bud heaved again and, this time, the lid slid forward.

Everyone took deep breaths and wiped their hands off; the red-headed teenager had managed to pinch a finger and was nursing a bloody cuticle. But Dan had no patience for the weary or wounded. He wanted to see what was inside almost more than Rory did.

"Come on, now," Dan boomed. "Put your backs into it."

He sounded like he was hollering to his rugby buddies and not like a dignified earl with a family over one thousand years old. Rory saw more and more of Kieran in the man. Bud heaved with the crowbar again, Marc shoved with all his might, and the lid suddenly slid about a foot off its base. It was balanced precariously on the edge of the sarcophagus, but the coffin was now wide open and the contents easily viewed. Before Bud could stop her, Rory rushed up to take a look.

"Watch out," he cautioned. "The lid is just balancing. It could go crashing down and I don't want you to get hurt."

Rory couldn't even answer him as she gazed down into the dusty, ancient crypt that hadn't seen the light of day in over eight hundred years. Around her, everyone else was doing the same thing, including Reverend Hogan. Faces that had been previous filled with doubt or curiosity were now glazed with awe, for laying supine at the bottom of the well-made crypt was an enormous knight in nearly pristine twelfth century battle armor. A thin layer of sheer, white fabric covered him; some kind of linen. It was his burial shroud. Before Bud could grab her, Rory climbed in.

"Rory," Bud positioned himself next to the lid so he could at least try to hold it back should it shift and come crashing back down. "Honey, get out of there. Let us move the lid off completely."

Rory heard his words but ignored him. She was straddled over the massive body, her heart in her throat, her breathing coming in harsh pants. Flashes of the first time she had excavated him lit in her mind, an odd sense of déjà vu sweeping her. Once, she had stood in this exact same position over Kieran, inspecting the crusader she had just discovered in the dusty ruins of Nahariya. It was that moment all over again, only now in an ancient English cathedral.

The recurrence, the emotions, were too much to take. Rory went down on her knees, straddling Kieran's pelvis in much the same fashion as she had when they had made love eight hundred years ago. She could feel him hard and firm beneath her, but cold as the grave. With shaking hands, she carefully removed the thin veil of dusty fabric that covered his face.

It was a shock to see Kieran looking much the same as the effigy on the top of his crypt. His skin was colored by the dust that coated his skin, but the features were strong and handsome as if he were merely sleeping. She sat a moment, gazing at him, feeling the tears come yet again. Only this time, they were tears of joy and fairly short-lived. There was no more time for tears.

Without hesitation, Rory put her hands on either side of the man's face and leaned forward. Her short breaths were causing the dust on Kieran's face to flare up and cloud. Slowly and with great reverence,

Rory's soft and rosy lips gently touched his.

It was a tender kiss, one full of the love that had carried them across the span of time and ages. She suckled his bottom lip gently, his top lip, continuing to kiss his cheeks and nose, the only other flesh exposed beyond the mail and helm. *Like the first kiss she had ever given him, the one that had awakened him from his grave in Nahariya those years ago.*

"I'm here, baby," she murmured. "Wake up and look at me. I'm here."

She sat back, continuing to stroke his cheeks. Even though there were several faces watching the extremely odd and rather morbid exchange, for Rory, she and Kieran were the only two people in the entire world at the moment. She leaned down and kissed him again, trying to think back to the first time she had awoken him and wondering how long it took for him to awaken. She had been drunk at the time and had fallen asleep between the time she had kissed him and the time she had noticed he was becoming lucid. Therefore, there was no way of knowing. Only time would tell.

Minutes passed and he remained still. Rory tried not to feel rising despair as she remained straddled on him, gazing down at his face and looking for any signs of life. More minutes passed as she continued to watch and wait. Finally, someone reached down and put a hand on her shoulder.

"Rory." It was Bud. "What… what are you doing?"

Rory stroked Kieran's cheek. "Awaking him from his eternal sleep like I did the first time."

So much for her not sounding like an idiot in front of strangers, he thought. Bud didn't dare look at the people around him as he bent over the side of the crypt.

"Honey," he said softly. "He's dead. He's been dead for eight hundred years."

Rory's head snapped up, the hazel eyes intense and deadly serious. "No, he's not," she insisted strongly. "He had Kaleef put him into stasis again. He's waiting for me to awaken him again just like I did before.

Bud, somehow he knew that once I killed the prince, somehow, someway, Fates or God or whatever you believe in had transported me back to my time. I've been thinking about why that happened and the only thing I can come up with is either I did what I was supposed to do, thereby ending my need to be in Medieval times, or I changed history so much that everything, including my own life and timeline, was seriously altered. I just don't know which it is. But Kieran knew what had happened. He knew that I had come back to my time so he had Kaleef put him back to sleep with succotrine aloes, zedoary gentian, saffron, rhubarb and agaric. It was the same stuff he used before. He had Kaleef do it again and wrote me a letter about it, knowing that I would know how to awaken him."

She sounded completely, utterly insane. Bud looked at her, feeling so very sorry for her and thinking that she had completely snapped. He reached down gently, trying to get a good grip on her.

"Come on," he whispered. "Let me help you out of there. It's not good for you."

Rory threw herself down on top of Kieran's body, her head against his mailed chest and her arms gripping him tightly.

"No!" she cried. "Just give him a few minutes, Bud. You'll see what I mean. I'm not leaving."

Bud looked up then, glancing at Dan, the lawyers. They all gazed back at Bud with varied degrees of concern. The reverend even closed his eyes and began praying. Bud figured he'd better get her out of there before she started foaming at the mouth so he reached both hands inside the crypt and prepared to drag her out by the arms. But two words from Rory stopped him in his tracks.

"It's beating!" she suddenly screamed. "I can hear his heart. It's beating!"

Concerned expressions suddenly turned to those of shock and disbelief. Rory sat bolt upright, such joy on her face that all of the poets in the entire world could not have adequately described her expression. She was positively radiant. She grabbed Bud, pulling him down into the crypt as she struggled to make room for him.

"Listen!" she begged. "Listen for yourself!"

Bud nearly fell into the crypt as Rory pulled, trying not to make an ass of himself in the process. He truly thought she was losing her mind. But there was something so electric in her manner and expression that he couldn't resist doing as she asked. Rory practically shoved his head down against the dusty, ancient tunic, and Bud was feeling really stupid as he let her do it. But he laid his head down against the chest of the corpse, knowing he wasn't going to hear anything and genuinely shocked when he, too, thought he heard faint heartbeats. Startled, he remained with his ear pressed against the corpse for several long, painful moments.

"Well?" Dan finally couldn't stand it any longer. "What do you hear?"

Bud didn't move and he didn't respond. He lay there, listening intently, closing his eyes as if that would amplify his hearing. After several long moments, he finally opened his eyes and sat bolt upright, staring down at the body beneath him.

"I'll be damned," he breathed. "It… it sounds like heartbeats."

He looked at Rory, stricken. The truth was that Bud had never believed Kieran was who he said he was; he hadn't been there when Rory had resurrected him in the morgue at Middlesex Hospital and he'd never been able to accept that the massive, good-looking man had been Sir Kieran Hage in the flesh, the crusader he had excavated in Nahariya. But now here he was, at the beginning of what was looking like, for all the world, a miracle. He simply couldn't explain it. But his ears didn't lie.

"Do you hear it?" Rory asked softly.

He nodded, tearing his eyes away from her and looking back at the man beneath him. "I hear it," he muttered with some disbelief.

Bud leaned down to take a closer look at Kieran's face, the mucosa membrane, the texture of the flesh. He put his fingers on his carotid artery, feeling an extremely faint yet fairly regular pulse.

"I don't believe it," he whispered. "I don't goddamn believe it. He's got a pulse."

Rory was so excited that she was shaking. "I told you," she crowed, looking around to the faces staring back at her. She came to rest on Dan and her smile broadened. "You wanted to know who I am? My name is the Lady Rory Elizabeth Osgrove Hage. My husband is Kieran Hage and my son is Tevin Hage. I met my husband when Dr. Dietrich and I excavated a crusader's grave in the Syrian city of Nahariya. Based on ancient texts from a story passed down for centuries, we were looking for the reputed Crown of Thorns that Jesus Christ had worn on Mount Calvary but ended up finding a knight from the Third Crusade instead. What we didn't realize at the time is that the crusader was linked to the Crown of Thorns."

No one immediately responded. Dan wanted so badly to believe. In fact, he realized that he already did. It was the craziest, wildest story he'd ever heard, but he couldn't dispute the man coming to life before him. He almost felt as if he were living a dream; he was sure at some point he was going to wake up. But right now, he had to admit, it was pretty fascinating. Eight hundred years of a Hage mystery was finally coming to a conclusion.

"Dr. Dietrich?" He looked from Rory's smiling fact to the back of Bud's head as the man remained hunched over the supine knight. "Is this true?"

Bud was almost dull with shock and realization, but managed to nod his head. "It is," he grunted, turning to look at the stunned people around him. "Every word of it."

Dan swallowed hard, his gaze returning to Rory. "But I still don't understand," he murmured. "What's all this about an eternal sleep?"

Rory's gaze returned to Kieran, watching Bud as the man continued to feel his neck for a pulse. "Your ancestor, Kieran Hage, was entrusted with a peace mission while at the siege of Acre," she explained quietly. "The Muslims met with him in secret, asking him to take an offering of peace to King Richard. This offering was the Crown of Thorns worn by

Jesus Christ. However, some of the men in Kieran's peace party didn't want to see the war end. They turned against Kieran and tried to kill him. Mortally wounded, Kieran went to a man he thought was a physic but it turned out that the old guy was really an alchemist. He gave Kieran a potion that put him into a type of suspended animation so he wouldn't bleed to death. Eight hundred years in a grave sealed up his wound and that's when Bud and I discovered him."

Dan was listening with amazement and wonder. "But there has to be more," he insisted. "He's here, in this crypt, and not in a grave in Nahariya. More than that, I have the Crown of Thorns that he brought back from the Crusades in my possession. Nobody knows about it; or, at least, I thought nobody knew about it outside of immediate family but you knew about it. How did you know?"

Rory smiled faintly. "That's the other half of the story," she muttered, opening her mouth to explain but Bud abruptly cut her off.

"He's breathing," he announced. "It's faint and slow, but he's definitely breathing."

Everyone seemed to crowd around even closer, trying to gain a look at a dead man coming back to life. There was something mystical and magical happening in that ancient cathedral, none of which could be readily explained. Reverend Hogan had collected a Bible and now stood next to the crypt, repeating the book of John, chapter eleven verse twenty-five; *I am the resurrection and the life.*

"We should probably get the helm and the hauberk off him," Rory said. "Those things are heavy and uncomfortable."

Bud shook his head, feeling Kieran's pulse again and noting that it was stronger. "Let's not move him around," he replied. "Everything will come off in good time."

"Should we call a doctor?" Reverend Hogan blurted, genuinely concerned and fearful about the entire circumstance. He had no idea how he was going to explain this to his superior. "Perhaps the man needs a doctor."

"And tell him what?" Dan wanted to know. "That he has an eight hundred-year-old patient? I don't think that..."

A sound abruptly cut him off. It was low, mournful, growling. It was as if the Gates of Hell had just opened up and the Devil was issuing a beckoning call. Everyone looked at each other with wide-eyes, startled by the frightening sound, slowly turning to the source. They knew where it had come from; the knight lying supine in the crypt had emitted the noise. Rory was back on her knees beside him, trying to gain a better look as Bud nearly crowded her out of the way. Standing at the side of the crypt, the reverend suddenly shoved one of the teenage boys sideways.

"Go!" he cried. "Go and get the man some water! Hurry!"

The boy fled. Everyone else remained rooted to the spot, waiting and watching. Like something out of a low-budget horror movie, Kieran's mouth began to work very slowly and his eyes, closed for eight hundred years, began to twitch. The redheaded teenager standing next to the crypt started to bolt with fear but the reverend held him fast; he didn't want the lad running from the church, screaming. It would attract too much attention to what was going on inside and he didn't want any attention on this very mystical, very historic moment. Truth be told, he was swept up in the wonder of it like everyone else was.

"Kieran?" Bud gently tapped the man on the cheek. "Can you hear me? It's Dr. Dietrich. If you can hear me, lift your hand."

Bud scooted back so they could all have a good look at Kieran's arms. Rory was in the crypt, wedged in next to his right hand, when it suddenly twitched. After a few seconds of pause, it moved again and began to lift. Dan smiled, the lawyers gawked, and the reverend began to pray in earnest. Rory, however, saw the hand moving towards her and she clasped it tightly.

"I'm here, baby," she said, leaning over him, kissing him on the cheek again. "I'm right here. Everything is going to be fine."

It took her a moment to realize that his eyes were half-open, the dry eyeballs beginning to glimmer with a slight amount of moisture now that his heart was pumping and his lungs were working. She knew he could see her and she smiled at him, tenderly kissing his dry lips.

"Good morning, sunshine," she whispered. "It's good to have you back."

Kieran's mouth worked and very slowly, very laboriously, he licked his lips with his dry tongue. But the raised hand was moving to Rory's head and, as the group watched, an enormous, mailed glove grasped her gently behind the skull and pulled her down to him. But he didn't try to kiss her, not yet; he was attempting to speak.

"Bu…Bud," he breathed.

Rory looked at Bud just as the man moved up beside her, planting his face right next to hers. But that apparently wasn't what Kieran wanted. He managed to lift his left hand and, putting his dusty gloved palm on Bud's face, weakly shoved the man backwards. That brought laughter from Rory and Dan.

"So you don't want to see Bud?" Rory was leaning down, trying to make heads or tails of his halting speech. "What about Bud, then?"

Kieran struggled to take a deep breath, clearing his lungs of centuries of inactivity.

"I… I did not want Bud's face… to be the first one I saw," he whispered. "I wanted it… to be yours."

Rory smiled broadly, kissing him again and feeling him weakly respond. "Here I am," she murmured against his mouth. "I'll be here forever. I can't believe you had Kaleef put you to sleep again."

He grunted, coughing weakly as his lungs gained strength. "It was… the only way to be with you. And I would do… anything to see you again."

Tears stung her eyes. "So you voluntarily let him put you to sleep again, knowing I might not even figure out what you had done? God, Kieran, you took such a huge chance. What would have happened if your letter was destroyed over the centuries somehow? What would have happened if…?"

This time, Kieran pulled her down to his mouth for another kiss, cutting her off. "I had faith that you would receive my letter and come for me," he murmured. It was becoming easier to speak. "Whatever Fates have brought us together will not let us be separated. I have always had faith in the power between you and me, Lib. Always."

By this time, Dan had moved to the front of the crypt, watching with amazement as a man, his ancestor, believed dead for over eight hundred years gradually came to life. And the manner in which he was holding Dr. Osgrove told him everything he needed to know. He was watching a modern-day fairy tale; Sleeping Beauty as the tale had never been told or Lazarus in the most romantic sense. The man had put himself into some kind of suspended animation simply so he could be with the woman he loved. It was the most astounding thing he had ever witnessed.

Rory caught sight of Dan next to the head of the crypt and she looked up, smiling when their eyes met.

"Now do you understand everything?" she asked softly.

Dan's gaze moved between Rory and Kieran. After a moment, he shrugged. "Maybe I'm not supposed to understand everything." He gave her a wink. "I can take a few things on faith."

As he watched Bud and Rory very carefully remove Kieran's helm and eventually pull off the hauberk to make him more comfortable, Dan began to remember the words from the parchment that had been in his family for eight hundred years.

As he gazed down at the archaeologist and her crusader, the meaning of the words ran over and over in his head. He still didn't understand all of it.

But he believed.

My Dearest Libby;

We did wonder of our greater purpose in returning to my tyme. Though you were taken from me, I know our journey is not yet complete. The diadem will be kept with my family and perhaps its only purpose was to bring you and me together and nothing more. Perhaps the greater reason is our son, Tevin, as he grows and becomes a great man. Perhaps he will change history for the better and right wrongs that have been committed. Perhaps he will make my family stronger and perform great deeds. For now, I only know that I myss you with all my heart and soul. I will be with you again someday, I swear.

Kaleef came with us from The Levant for the greatest reason of all. He was meant to put me to sleep again as he did before so that you may once again awaken me with your kyss. I await you in my crypt, sleeping until such tyme as you will once again awaken me as you did before. Know this is true. We are meant to be together, you and I.

With my never ending love I await you.

Kieran

☙ THE END ❧

The Crusader Series includes the House of Hage, and includes the following novels:

The Crusader

Of note: The House of Hage has the distinction of being the only house with two characters – one hero and one popular secondary character – of the same name yet they are not the same man. It gets confusing, so let's explain:

Kieran Hage #1 is the hero from THE CRUSADER and KINGDOM COME. If you recall in KINGDOM COME, which is a time-travel novel dealing with Rory and Kieran being back in Medieval times, there's a big twist at the end of the book. I don't want to blow this twist for those of you who haven't read it (and you MUST read it because it's a killer twist), Kieran "disappears" from Medieval England at that point. He leaves behind his young son, Tevin, who was named after Tevin du Reims of WHILE ANGELS SLEPT, who was Kieran's mother's father (Kieran's grandfather). If you recall, Tevin from WHILE ANGELS SLEPT was the UNCLE of Christopher de Lohr because Tevin's sister, Val, married Myles de Lohr, a knight. These two became parents to Christopher and David de Lohr, making Christopher and David distantly related to both Kieran Hages.

Kieran Hage #1, having left Medieval England at the end of KINGDOM COME, left behind his son, Tevin, who his brother Sean raised as his own. Tevin Hage was a great man, a powerful knight, and he was told that his father, Kieran, had been killed, as had his mother. Both of his parents are gone. Therefore, he knew his father was Kieran #1 and that Sean, even though he raised him, was his uncle. Sean then had three sons of his own that were younger than his nephew, Tevin, and it was Sean's youngest son, Jeffrey (named for Kieran #1 and Sean's father) who had Kieran #2, named for Kieran #1. Kieran #2 is the Kieran who appears in The Wolfe and Serpent.

Therefore – Kieran #2 from THE WOLFE is Kieran #1's great-nephew.

Kevin Hage's father is Kieran Hage from The Wolfe.

The Wolfe

Kevin Hage also appears in Serpent.

Serpent

While Angels Slept

For more information on other series and family groups, as well as a list of all of Kathryn's novels, please visit her website at www.kathrynleveque.com.

About Kathryn Le Veque

Medieval Just Got Real.

KATHRYN LE VEQUE is a USA TODAY Bestselling author, an Amazon All-Star author, and a #1 bestselling, award-winning, multi-published author in Medieval Historical Romance and Historical Fiction. She has been featured in the NEW YORK TIMES and on USA TODAY's HEA blog. In March 2015, Kathryn was the featured cover story for the March issue of InD'Tale Magazine, the premier Indie author magazine. She was also a quadruple nominee (a record!) for the prestigious RONE awards for 2015.

Kathryn's Medieval Romance novels have been called 'detailed', 'highly romantic', and 'character-rich'. She crafts great adventures of love, battles, passion, and romance in the High Middle Ages. More than that, she writes for both women AND men – an unusual crossover for a romance author – and Kathryn has many male readers who enjoy her stories because of the male perspective, the action, and the adventure.

On October 29, 2015, Amazon launched Kathryn's Kindle Worlds Fan Fiction site WORLD OF DE WOLFE PACK. Please visit Kindle Worlds for Kathryn Le Veque's World of de Wolfe Pack and find many action-packed adventures written by some of the top authors in their genre using Kathryn's characters from the de Wolfe Pack series. As Kindle World's FIRST Historical Romance fan fiction world, Kathryn Le Veque's World of de Wolfe Pack will contain all of the great story-telling you have come to expect.

Kathryn loves to hear from her readers. Please find Kathryn on Facebook at Kathryn Le Veque, Author, or join her on Twitter @kathrynleveque, and don't forget to visit her website and sign up for her blog at www.kathrynleveque.com.

CPSIA information can be obtained
at www.ICGtesting.com
Printed in the USA
BVHW041728030521
606361BV00006B/83

9 781495 307997